PRAISE FOR *COUNT*

Ibrahim Moustafa is doing what many comic creators can only dream of. Writing, drawing, and creating a personal vision that no one can duplicate. In Count *he pulls a real Edmond Dantés, disappearing for a while, only to emerge as a master of the craft.*
—**Nick Dragotta** (storyteller, *East of West*)

An inspiring mix of swashbuckling action and technopunk ideas, this fantasy-etched retelling of The Count of Monte Cristo *will entertain young readers endlessly... and delight the rest of us yearning for a good ol' fashioned sci-romp.*
—**Eric Wallace** (Executive Producer & writer of TV's *The Flash*, *Teen Wolf*, and *Eureka*)

Count *is great! I was really impressed with the action; I wish I could draw sword fighting scenes like the ones Ibrahim drew in this book.*
—**Sophie Campbell** (writer/artist, *Wet Moon*, *TMNT*, *Shadoweyes*)

Come for the sweeping, beautifully-drawn tale of vengeance and rebellion, stay for the really cool robot.
—**Jody Houser** (writer, *Star Wars*, *Doctor Who*)

Count *is an impressive book, instantly immersive with great design and sharp storytelling. Ibrahim brings a special life to this story with skilled gestures and fantastic expressions, a combination that is not seen often enough in comics.* Count *is Ibrahim's best work to date, and that's saying something as a longtime fan."*
—**Justin Greenwood** (artist, *Stumptown*, *The Fuse*)

Even when people are quietly talking, there's a breathless quality to Count *that pulls you along the whole way through and never runs out of steam. From bloodied fists to impossible swords, Moustafa pulls from countless genres and ideas and somehow frankensteins them all together into a swashbuckling adventure that evokes the best of what made you love comics in the first place.*
—**Christopher Sebela** (writer, *Crowded*, *High Crimes*)

An all-star team to bring us an all-star adventure in this sprawling, futuristic retelling of The Count of Monte Cristo. *They've managed to take Alexandre Dumas' classic and craft it into something exciting and new. The art is simply gorgeous and the stunning designs are brimming with swashbuckling wonder. In Redxan Samud, we have a worthy hero–his plight for justice forming the gripping, emotional center of Moustafa's script.* Count *is a screen-worthy tale, putting a Hollywood blockbuster right in the reader's hands.*
—**Sydney Duncan** (writer, *Kill Whitey Donovan*)

Ibrahim Moustafa's Count *is an absolutely stunning OGN, establishing him as a high-caliber writer/artist well worthy of Humanoids' rich pedigree. I cannot wait to see where he goes from here.*
—**Joseph Keatinge** (writer, *Ringside*, *Shutter*)

Count *makes it extremely clear that Moustafa is one of the brightest talents in comics today.*
—**Nick Barber** (artist, *Ringside*, Sony Animation)

Revenge can only be found on the road to self-destruction.
—Wayne Gerard Trotman

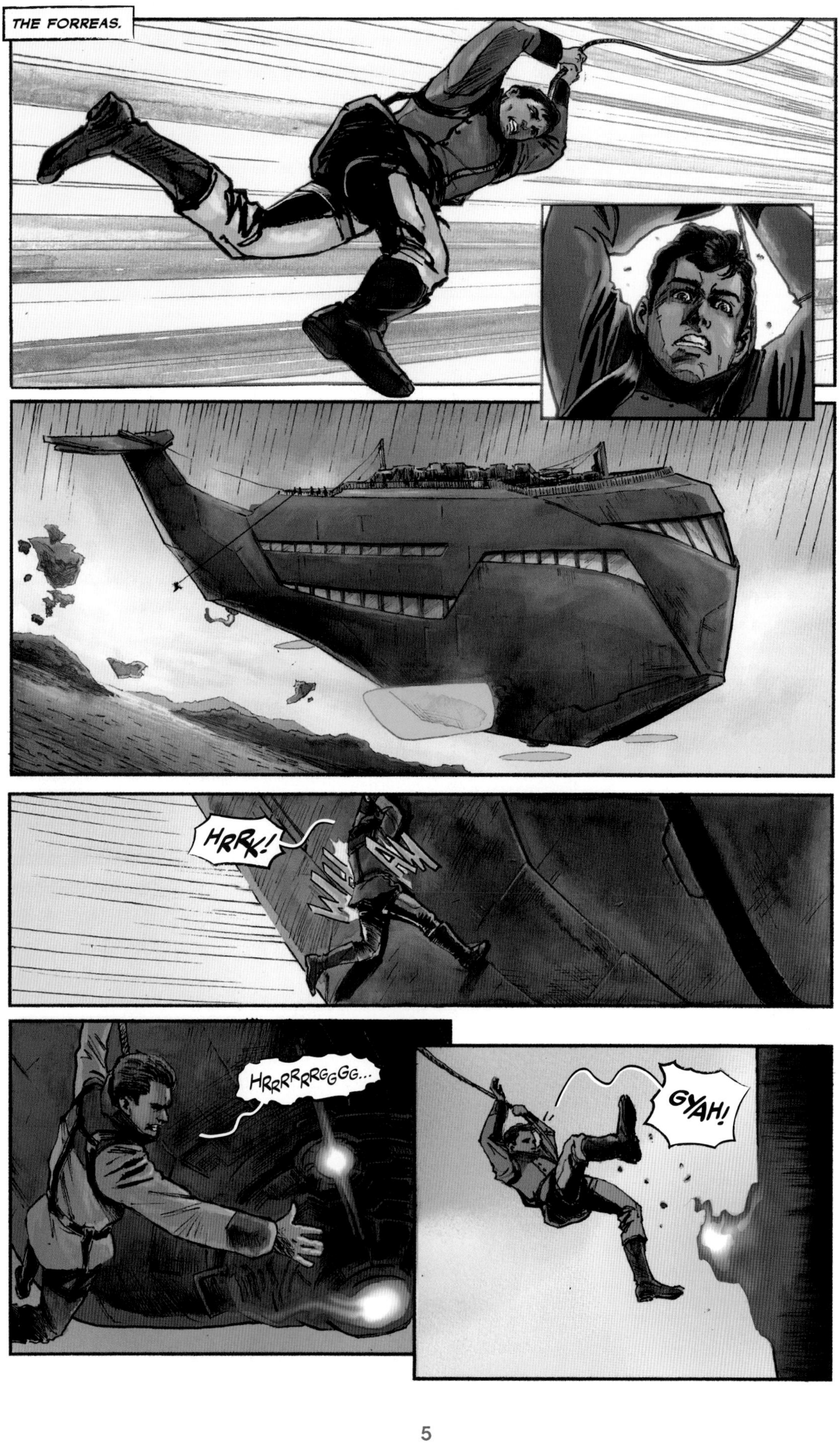
THE FORREAS.
HRRK!
WHAM
HRRRRRRGGGG...
GYAH!

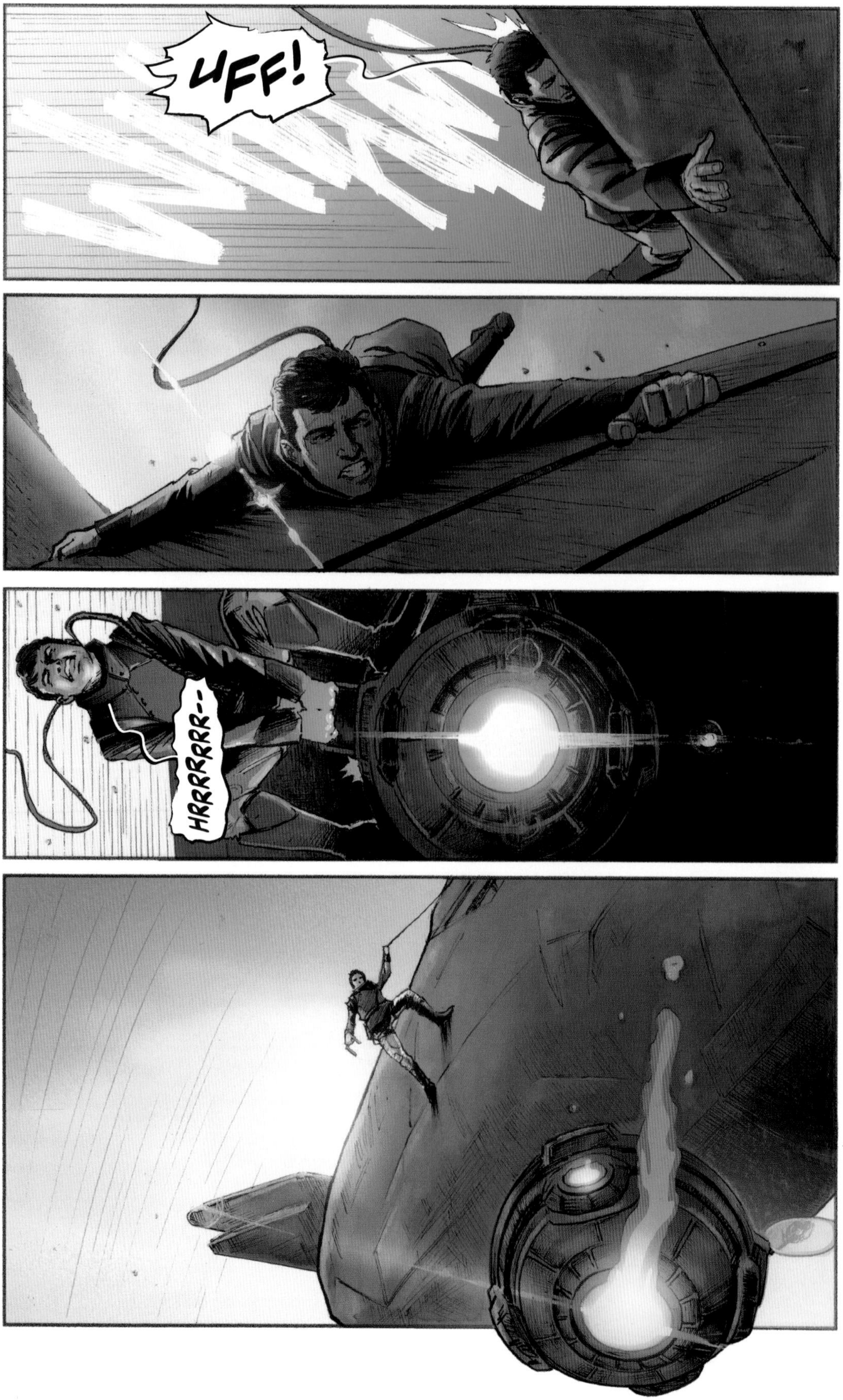
UFF!
HRRRRRRR--

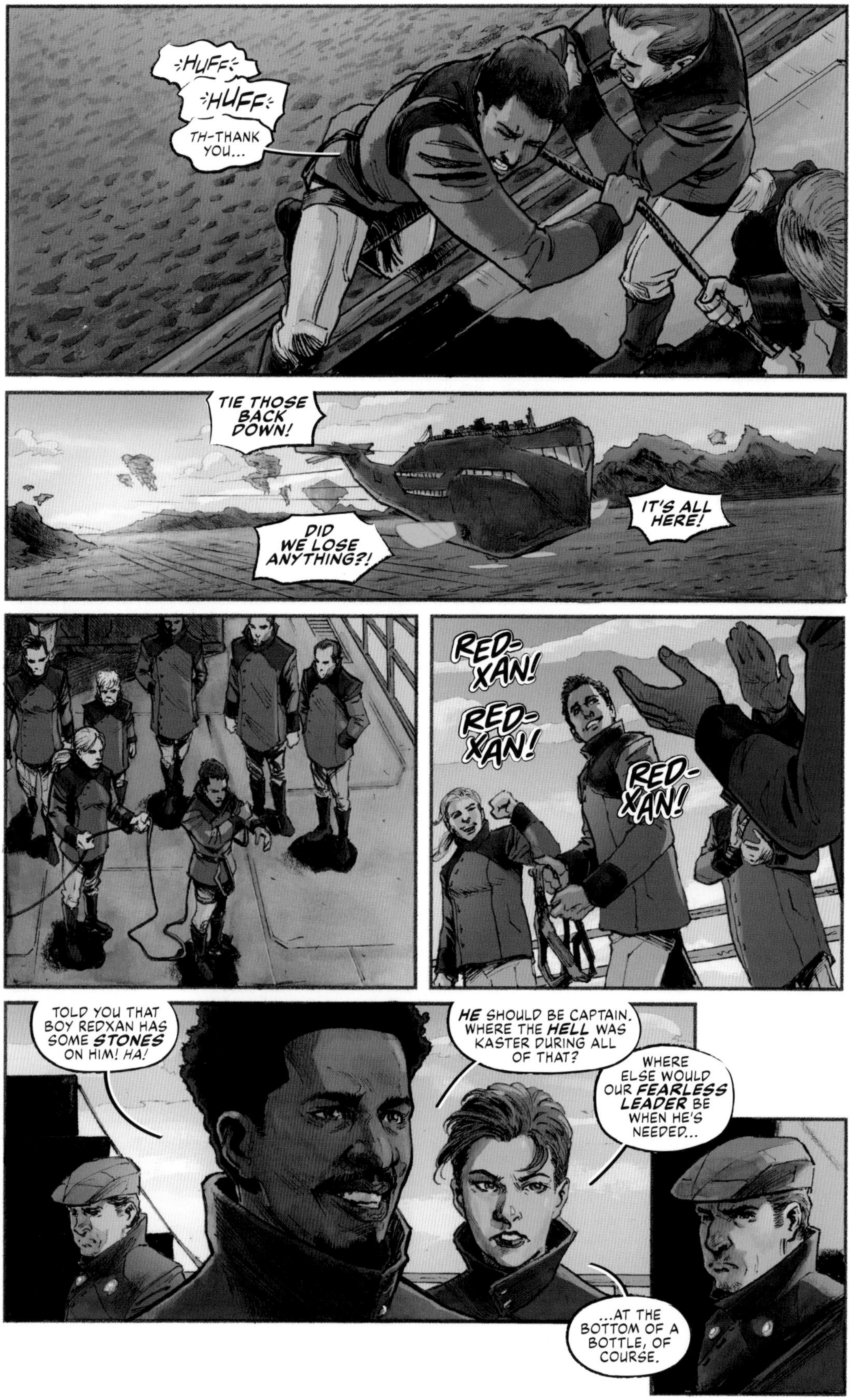
HUFF
HUFF
TH-THANK YOU...
TIE THOSE BACK DOWN!
DID WE LOSE ANYTHING?!
IT'S ALL HERE!
RED-XAN!
RED-XAN!
RED-XAN!
TOLD YOU THAT BOY REDXAN HAS SOME STONES ON HIM! HA!
HE SHOULD BE CAPTAIN. WHERE THE HELL WAS KASTER DURING ALL OF THAT?
WHERE ELSE WOULD OUR FEARLESS LEADER BE WHEN HE'S NEEDED...
...AT THE BOTTOM OF A BOTTLE, OF COURSE.

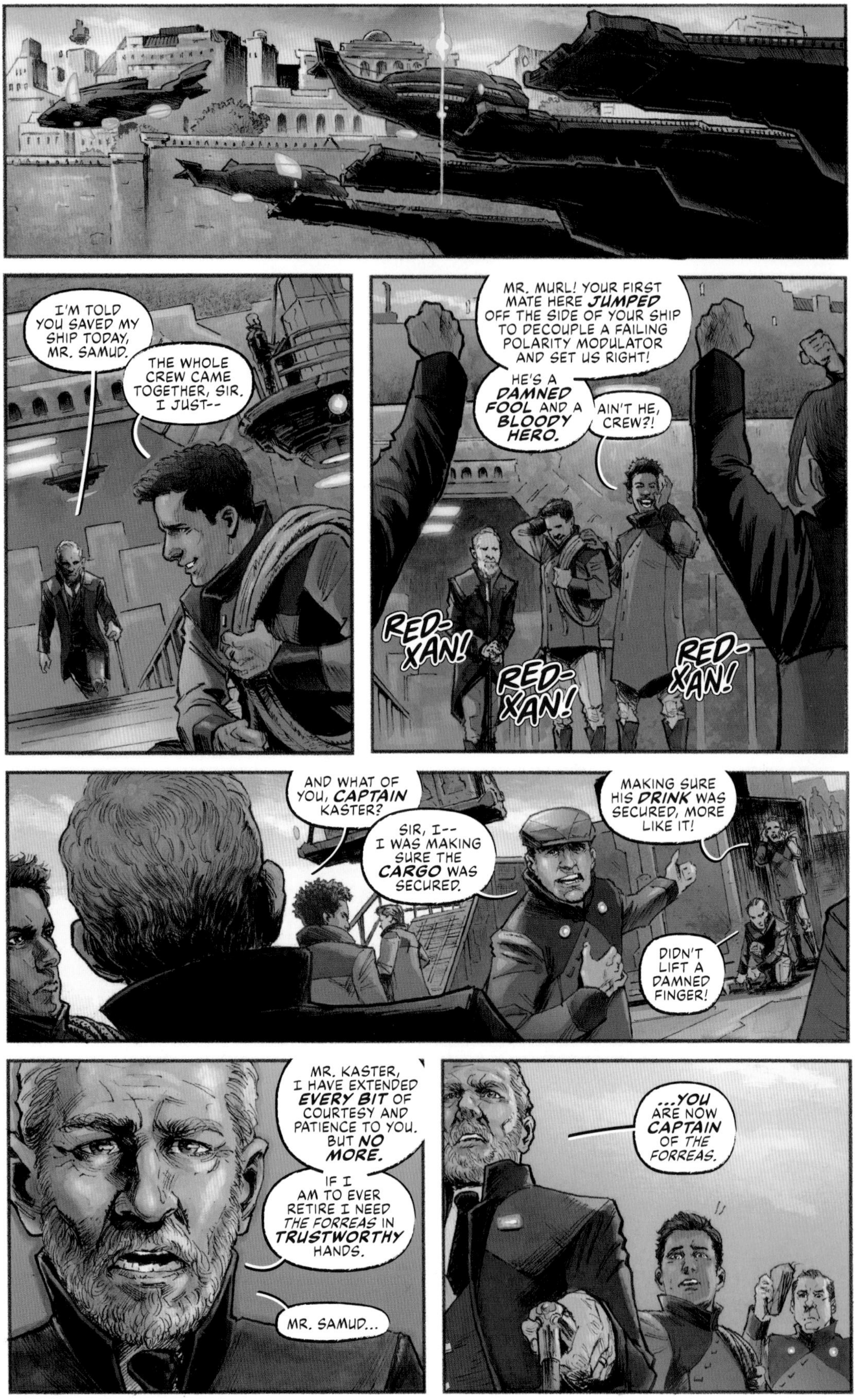
I'M TOLD YOU SAVED MY SHIP TODAY, MR. SAMUD.
THE WHOLE CREW CAME TOGETHER, SIR. I JUST--
MR. MURL! YOUR FIRST MATE HERE JUMPED OFF THE SIDE OF YOUR SHIP TO DECOUPLE A FAILING POLARITY MODULATOR AND SET US RIGHT!
HE'S A DAMNED FOOL AND A BLOODY HERO.
AIN'T HE, CREW?!
RED-XAN!
RED-XAN!
RED-XAN!
AND WHAT OF YOU, CAPTAIN KASTER?
SIR, I-- I WAS MAKING SURE THE CARGO WAS SECURED.
MAKING SURE HIS DRINK WAS SECURED, MORE LIKE IT!
DIDN'T LIFT A DAMNED FINGER!
MR. KASTER, I HAVE EXTENDED EVERY BIT OF COURTESY AND PATIENCE TO YOU. BUT NO MORE.
IF I AM TO EVER RETIRE I NEED THE FORREAS IN TRUSTWORTHY HANDS.
MR. SAMUD...
...YOU ARE NOW CAPTAIN OF THE FORREAS.

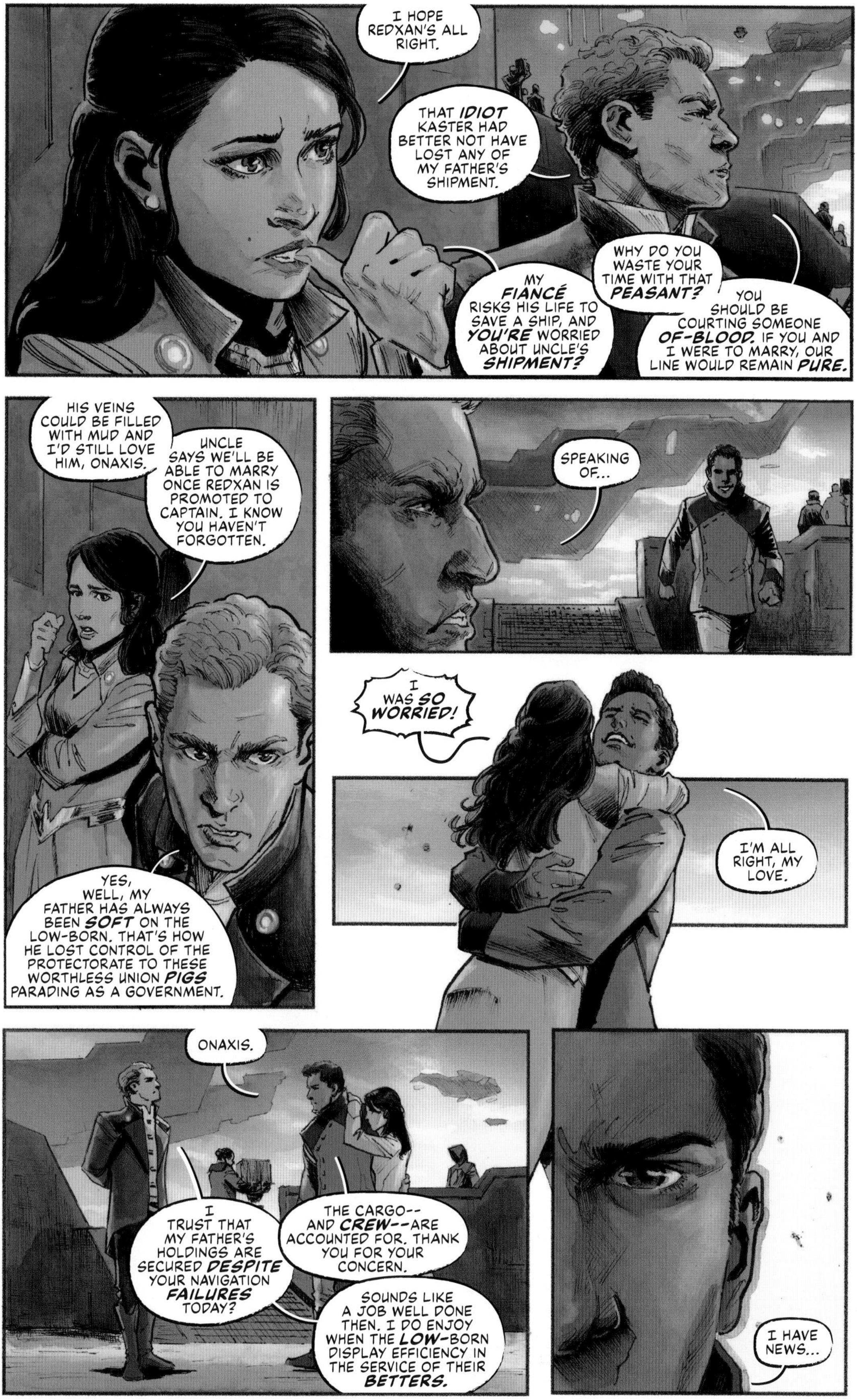
I HOPE REDXAN'S ALL RIGHT.
THAT IDIOT KASTER HAD BETTER NOT HAVE LOST ANY OF MY FATHER'S SHIPMENT.
MY FIANCÉ RISKS HIS LIFE TO SAVE A SHIP, AND YOU'RE WORRIED ABOUT UNCLE'S SHIPMENT?
WHY DO YOU WASTE YOUR TIME WITH THAT PEASANT?
YOU SHOULD BE COURTING SOMEONE OF-BLOOD. IF YOU AND I WERE TO MARRY, OUR LINE WOULD REMAIN PURE.
HIS VEINS COULD BE FILLED WITH MUD AND I'D STILL LOVE HIM, ONAXIS.
UNCLE SAYS WE'LL BE ABLE TO MARRY ONCE REDXAN IS PROMOTED TO CAPTAIN. I KNOW YOU HAVEN'T FORGOTTEN.
YES, WELL, MY FATHER HAS ALWAYS BEEN SOFT ON THE LOW-BORN. THAT'S HOW HE LOST CONTROL OF THE PROTECTORATE TO THESE WORTHLESS UNION PIGS PARADING AS A GOVERNMENT.
SPEAKING OF...
I WAS SO WORRIED!
I'M ALL RIGHT, MY LOVE.
ONAXIS.
I TRUST THAT MY FATHER'S HOLDINGS ARE SECURED DESPITE YOUR NAVIGATION FAILURES TODAY?
THE CARGO-- AND CREW--ARE ACCOUNTED FOR. THANK YOU FOR YOUR CONCERN.
SOUNDS LIKE A JOB WELL DONE THEN. I DO ENJOY WHEN THE LOW-BORN DISPLAY EFFICIENCY IN THE SERVICE OF THEIR BETTERS.
I HAVE NEWS...

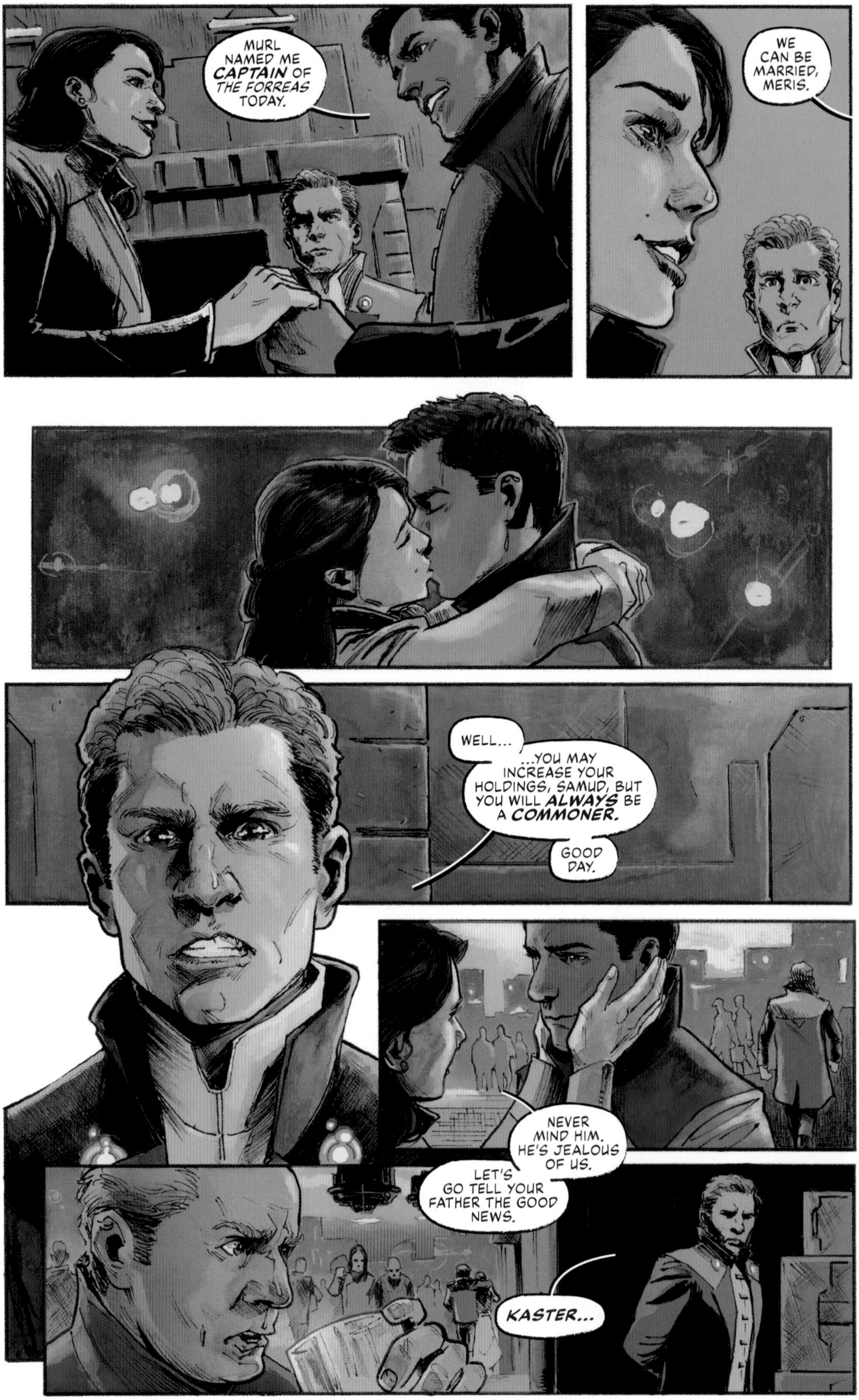
MURL NAMED ME CAPTAIN OF THE FORREAS TODAY.
WE CAN BE MARRIED, MERIS.
WELL...
...YOU MAY INCREASE YOUR HOLDINGS, SAMUD, BUT YOU WILL ALWAYS BE A COMMONER.
GOOD DAY.
NEVER MIND HIM. HE'S JEALOUS OF US.
LET'S GO TELL YOUR FATHER THE GOOD NEWS.
KASTER...

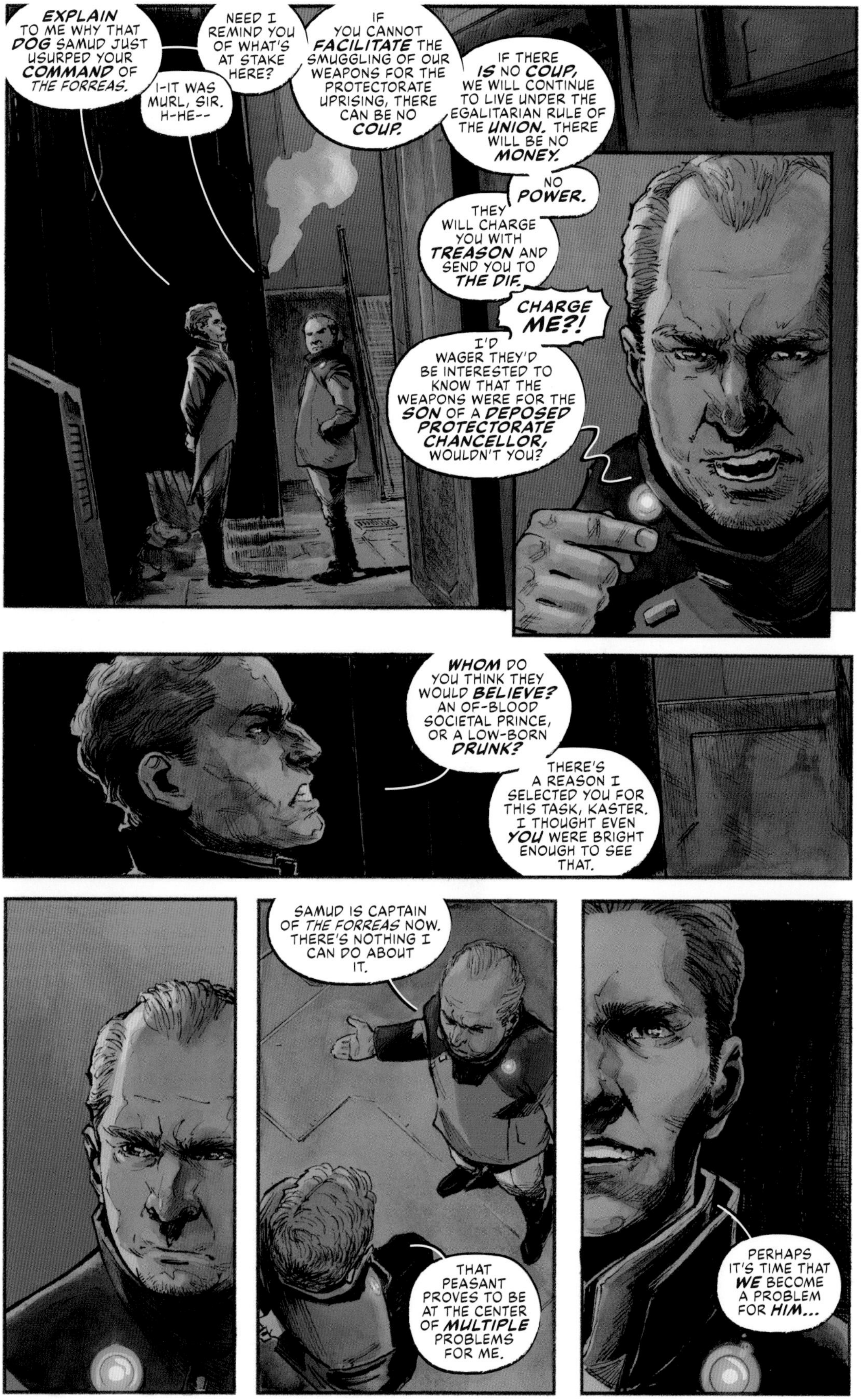
EXPLAIN TO ME WHY THAT DOG SAMUD JUST USURPED YOUR COMMAND OF THE FORREAS.
I-IT WAS MURL, SIR. H-HE--
NEED I REMIND YOU OF WHAT'S AT STAKE HERE?
IF YOU CANNOT FACILITATE THE SMUGGLING OF OUR WEAPONS FOR THE PROTECTORATE UPRISING, THERE CAN BE NO COUP.
IF THERE IS NO COUP, WE WILL CONTINUE TO LIVE UNDER THE EGALITARIAN RULE OF THE UNION. THERE WILL BE NO MONEY.
NO POWER.
THEY WILL CHARGE YOU WITH TREASON AND SEND YOU TO THE DIF.
CHARGE ME?!
I'D WAGER THEY'D BE INTERESTED TO KNOW THAT THE WEAPONS WERE FOR THE SON OF A DEPOSED PROTECTORATE CHANCELLOR, WOULDN'T YOU?
WHOM DO YOU THINK THEY WOULD BELIEVE? AN OF-BLOOD SOCIETAL PRINCE, OR A LOW-BORN DRUNK?
THERE'S A REASON I SELECTED YOU FOR THIS TASK, KASTER. I THOUGHT EVEN YOU WERE BRIGHT ENOUGH TO SEE THAT.
SAMUD IS CAPTAIN OF THE FORREAS NOW. THERE'S NOTHING I CAN DO ABOUT IT.
THAT PEASANT PROVES TO BE AT THE CENTER OF MULTIPLE PROBLEMS FOR ME.
PERHAPS IT'S TIME THAT WE BECOME A PROBLEM FOR HIM...

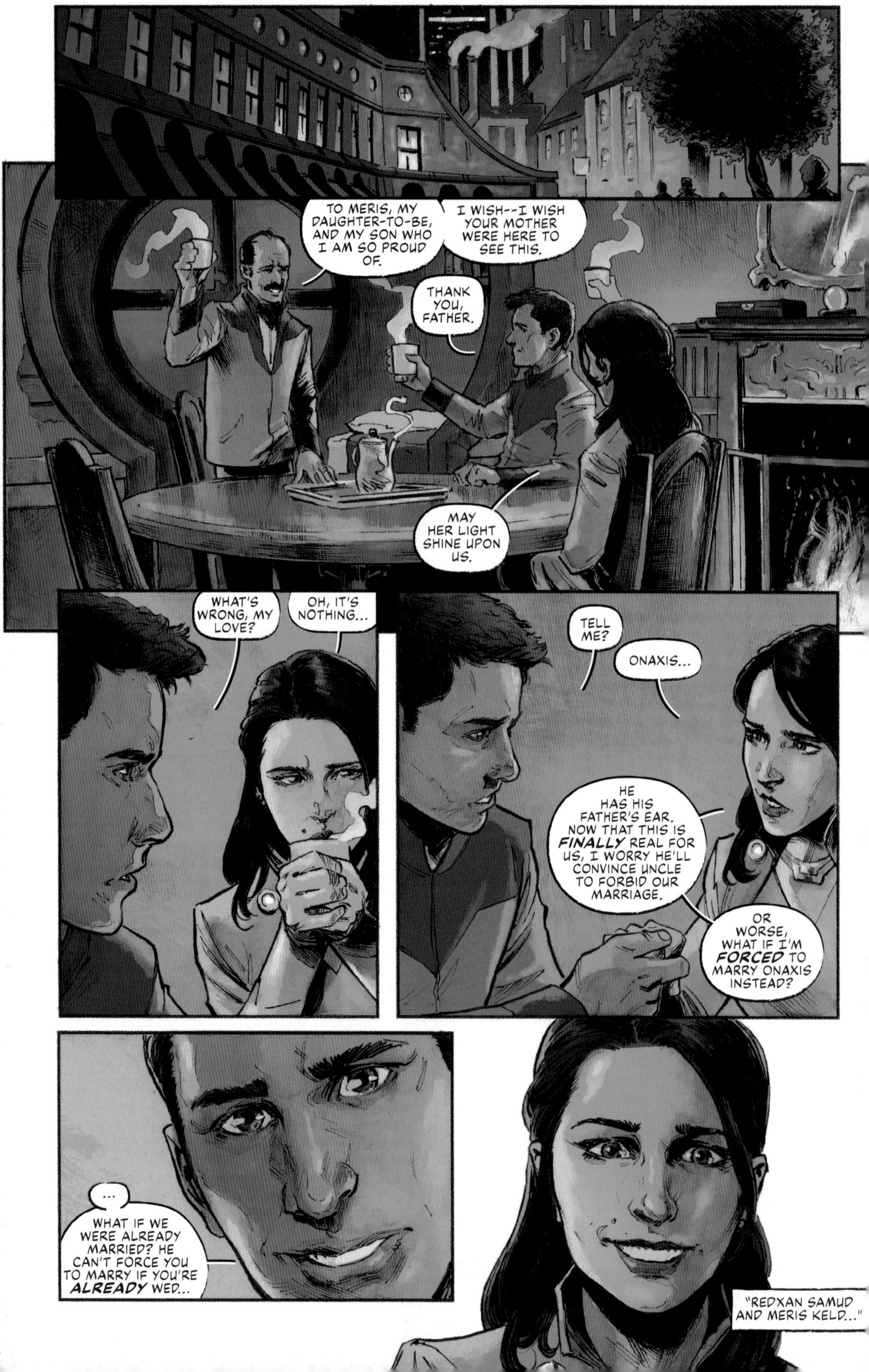
TO MERIS, MY DAUGHTER-TO-BE, AND MY SON WHO I AM SO PROUD OF.
I WISH--I WISH YOUR MOTHER WERE HERE TO SEE THIS.
THANK YOU, FATHER.
MAY HER LIGHT SHINE UPON US.
WHAT'S WRONG, MY LOVE?
OH, IT'S NOTHING...
TELL ME?
ONAXIS...
HE HAS HIS FATHER'S EAR. NOW THAT THIS IS FINALLY REAL FOR US, I WORRY HE'LL CONVINCE UNCLE TO FORBID OUR MARRIAGE.
OR WORSE, WHAT IF I'M FORCED TO MARRY ONAXIS INSTEAD?
...
WHAT IF WE WERE ALREADY MARRIED? HE CAN'T FORCE YOU TO MARRY IF YOU'RE ALREADY WED...
"REDXAN SAMUD AND MERIS KELD..."

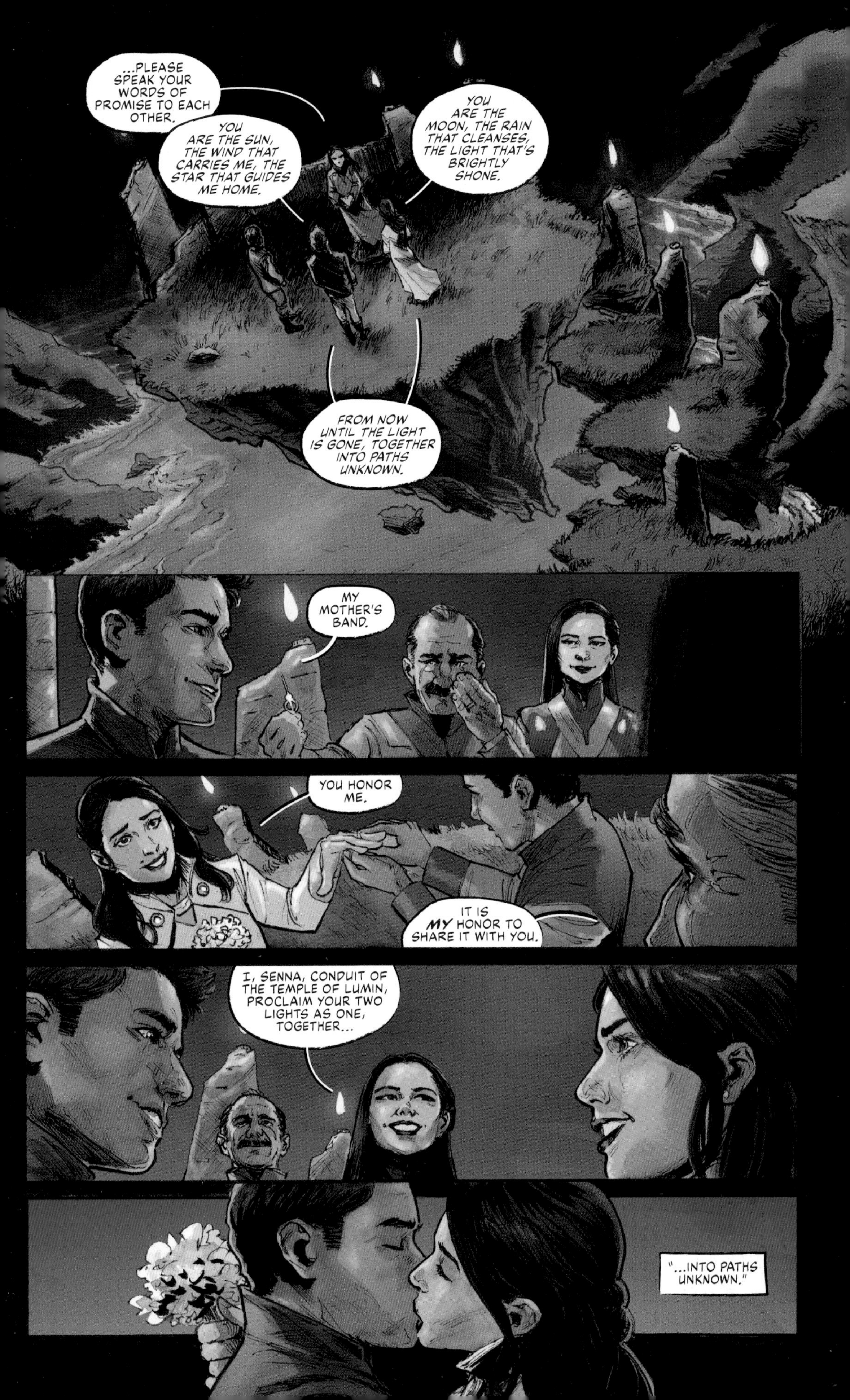
...PLEASE SPEAK YOUR WORDS OF PROMISE TO EACH OTHER.
YOU ARE THE SUN, THE WIND THAT CARRIES ME, THE STAR THAT GUIDES ME HOME.
YOU ARE THE MOON, THE RAIN THAT CLEANSES, THE LIGHT THAT'S BRIGHTLY SHONE.
FROM NOW UNTIL THE LIGHT IS GONE, TOGETHER INTO PATHS UNKNOWN.
MY MOTHER'S BAND.
YOU HONOR ME.
IT IS MY HONOR TO SHARE IT WITH YOU.
I, SENNA, CONDUIT OF THE TEMPLE OF LUMIN, PROCLAIM YOUR TWO LIGHTS AS ONE, TOGETHER...
"...INTO PATHS UNKNOWN."

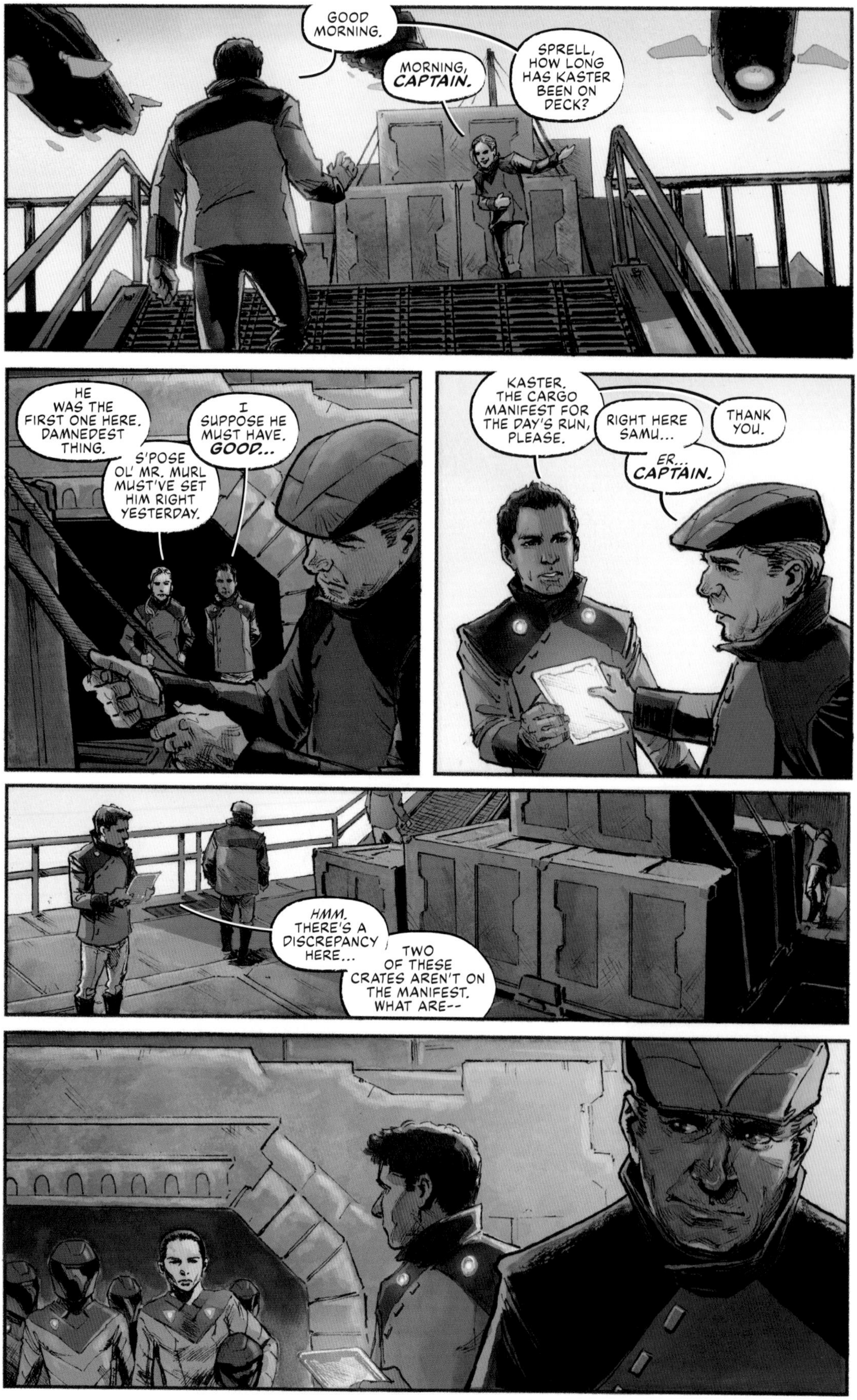
GOOD MORNING.
MORNING, *CAPTAIN.*
SPRELL, HOW LONG HAS KASTER BEEN ON DECK?
HE WAS THE FIRST ONE HERE. DAMNEDEST THING.
S'POSE OL' MR. MURL MUST'VE SET HIM RIGHT YESTERDAY.
I SUPPOSE HE MUST HAVE. *GOOD...*
KASTER. THE CARGO MANIFEST FOR THE DAY'S RUN, PLEASE.
RIGHT HERE SAMU...
ER... CAPTAIN.
THANK YOU.
HMM. THERE'S A DISCREPANCY HERE...
TWO OF THESE CRATES AREN'T ON THE MANIFEST. WHAT ARE--

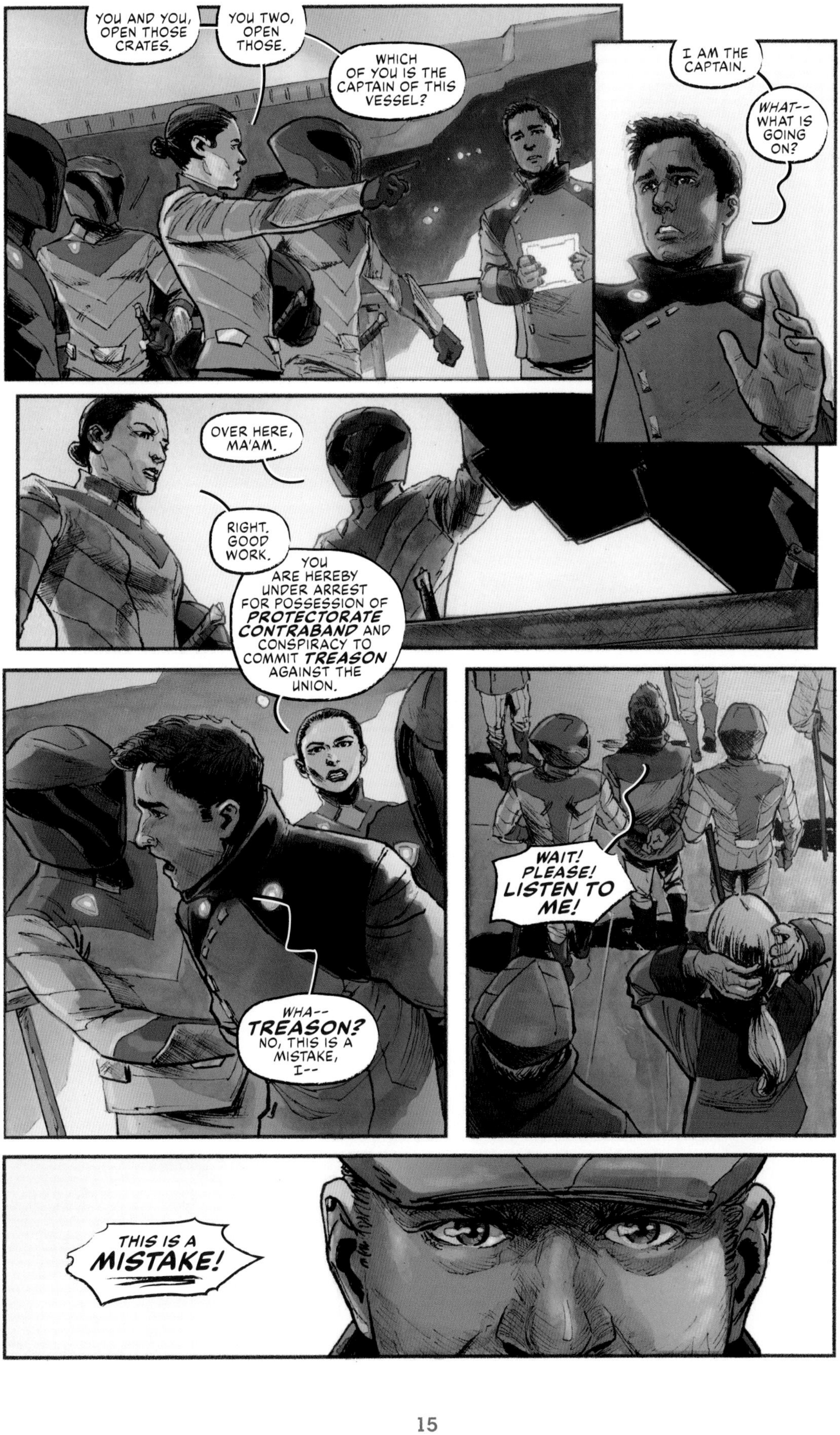
YOU AND YOU, OPEN THOSE CRATES.
YOU TWO, OPEN THOSE.
WHICH OF YOU IS THE CAPTAIN OF THIS VESSEL?
I AM THE CAPTAIN.
WHAT--WHAT IS GOING ON?
OVER HERE, MA'AM.
RIGHT. GOOD WORK.
YOU ARE HEREBY UNDER ARREST FOR POSSESSION OF PROTECTORATE CONTRABAND AND CONSPIRACY TO COMMIT TREASON AGAINST THE UNION.
WHA--TREASON? NO, THIS IS A MISTAKE, I--
WAIT! PLEASE! LISTEN TO ME!
THIS IS A MISTAKE!

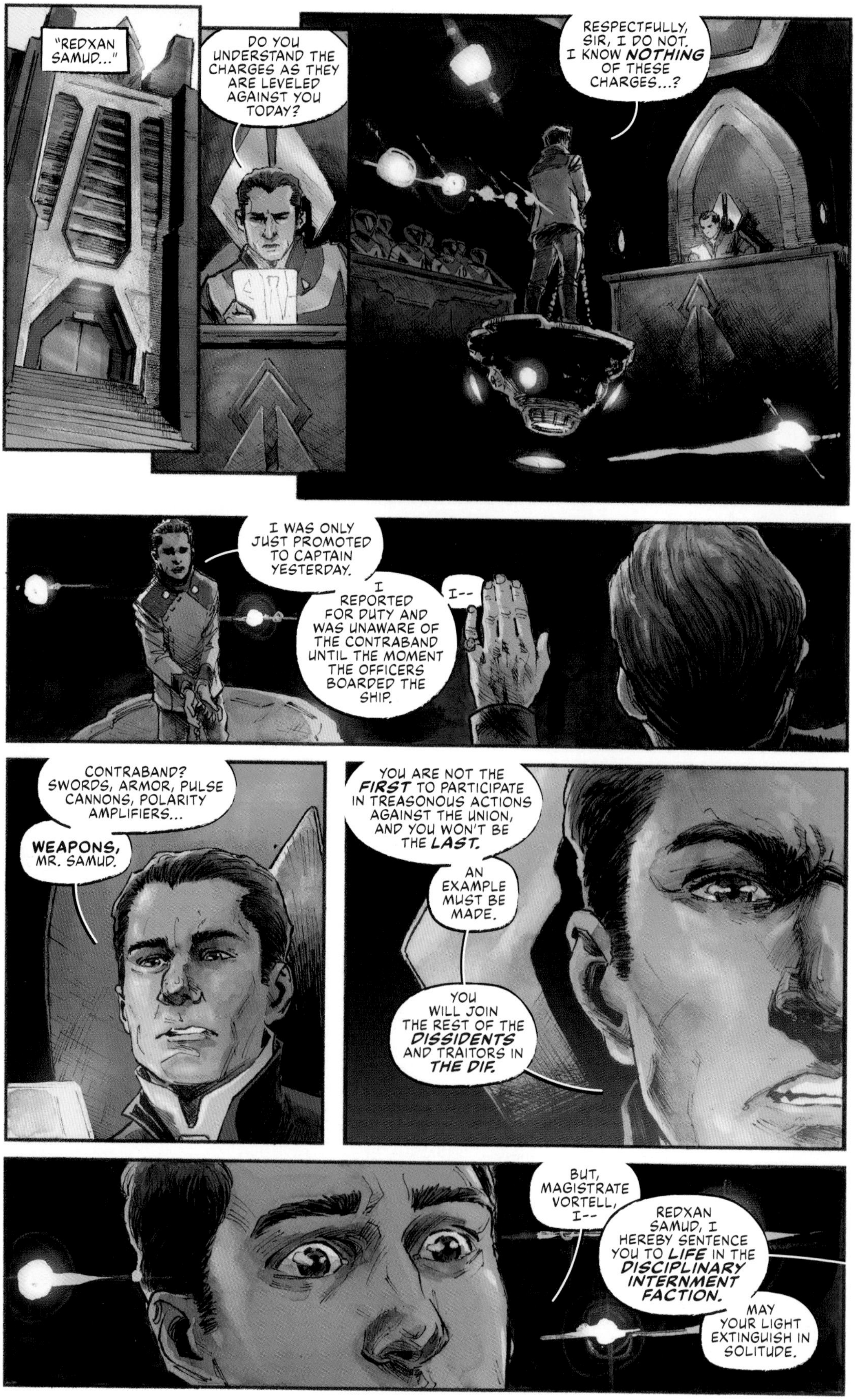
"REDXAN SAMUD..."
DO YOU UNDERSTAND THE CHARGES AS THEY ARE LEVELED AGAINST YOU TODAY?
RESPECTFULLY, SIR, I DO NOT. I KNOW NOTHING OF THESE CHARGES...?
I WAS ONLY JUST PROMOTED TO CAPTAIN YESTERDAY.
I REPORTED FOR DUTY AND WAS UNAWARE OF THE CONTRABAND UNTIL THE MOMENT THE OFFICERS BOARDED THE SHIP.
I--
CONTRABAND? SWORDS, ARMOR, PULSE CANNONS, POLARITY AMPLIFIERS...
WEAPONS, MR. SAMUD.
YOU ARE NOT THE FIRST TO PARTICIPATE IN TREASONOUS ACTIONS AGAINST THE UNION, AND YOU WON'T BE THE LAST.
AN EXAMPLE MUST BE MADE.
YOU WILL JOIN THE REST OF THE DISSIDENTS AND TRAITORS IN THE DIF.
BUT, MAGISTRATE VORTELL, I--
REDXAN SAMUD, I HEREBY SENTENCE YOU TO LIFE IN THE DISCIPLINARY INTERNMENT FACTION.
MAY YOUR LIGHT EXTINGUISH IN SOLITUDE.

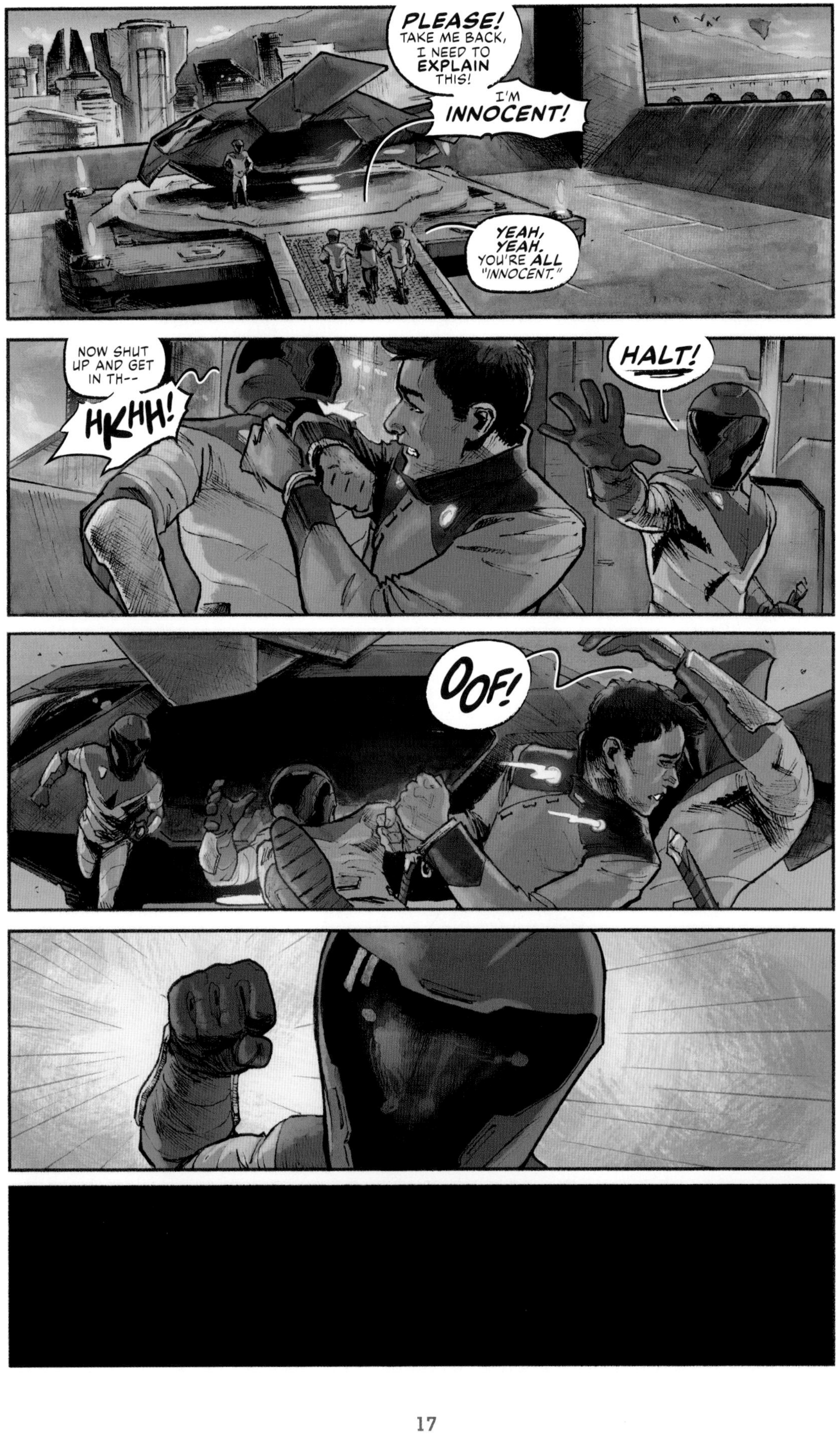
PLEASE! TAKE ME BACK, I NEED TO EXPLAIN THIS!
I'M INNOCENT!
YEAH, YEAH. YOU'RE ALL "INNOCENT."
NOW SHUT UP AND GET IN TH--
HKHH!
HALT!
OOF!

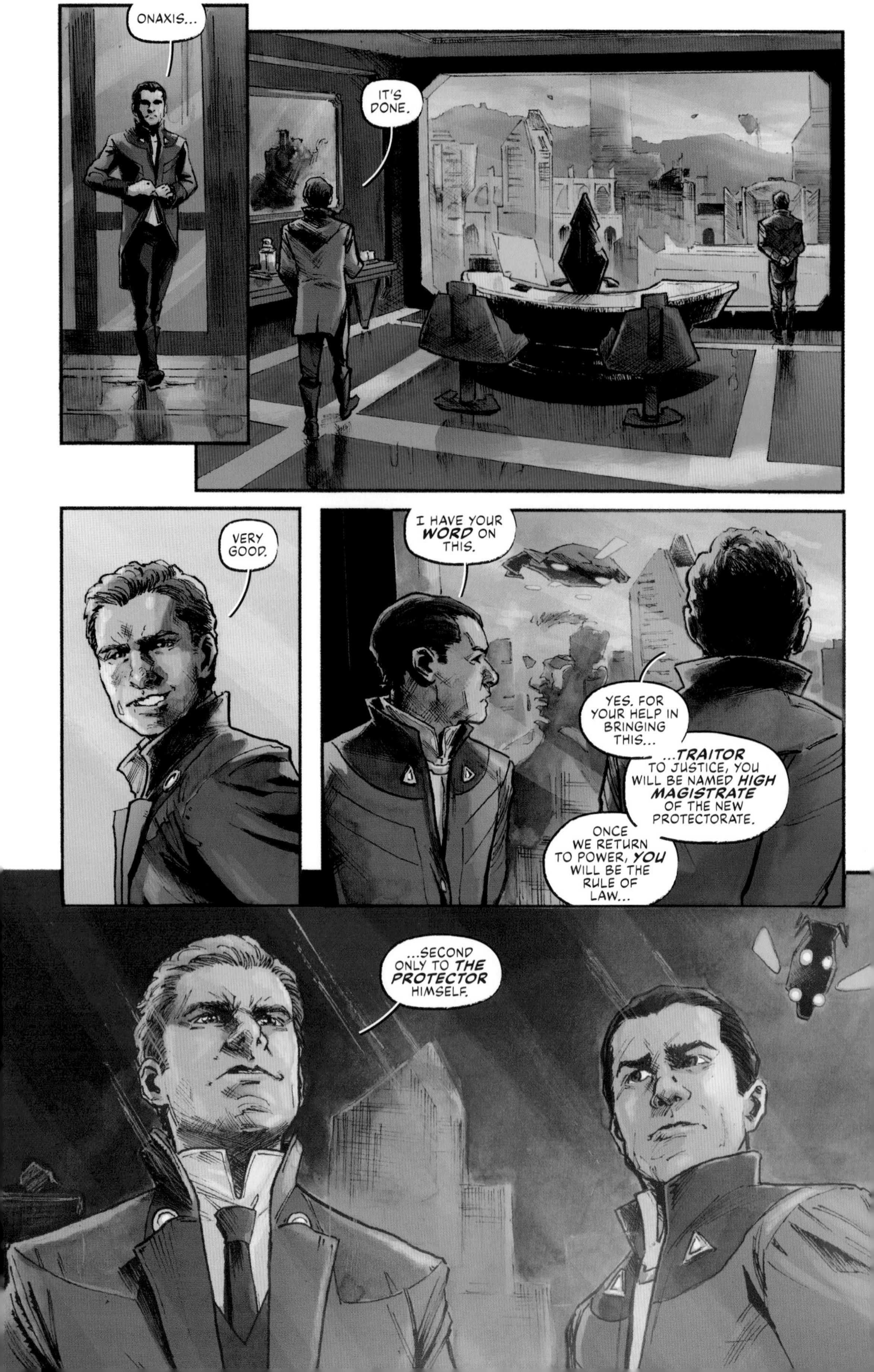
ONAXIS...
IT'S DONE.
VERY GOOD.
I HAVE YOUR WORD ON THIS.
YES. FOR YOUR HELP IN BRINGING THIS...
...TRAITOR TO JUSTICE, YOU WILL BE NAMED HIGH MAGISTRATE OF THE NEW PROTECTORATE.
ONCE WE RETURN TO POWER, YOU WILL BE THE RULE OF LAW...
...SECOND ONLY TO THE PROTECTOR HIMSELF.

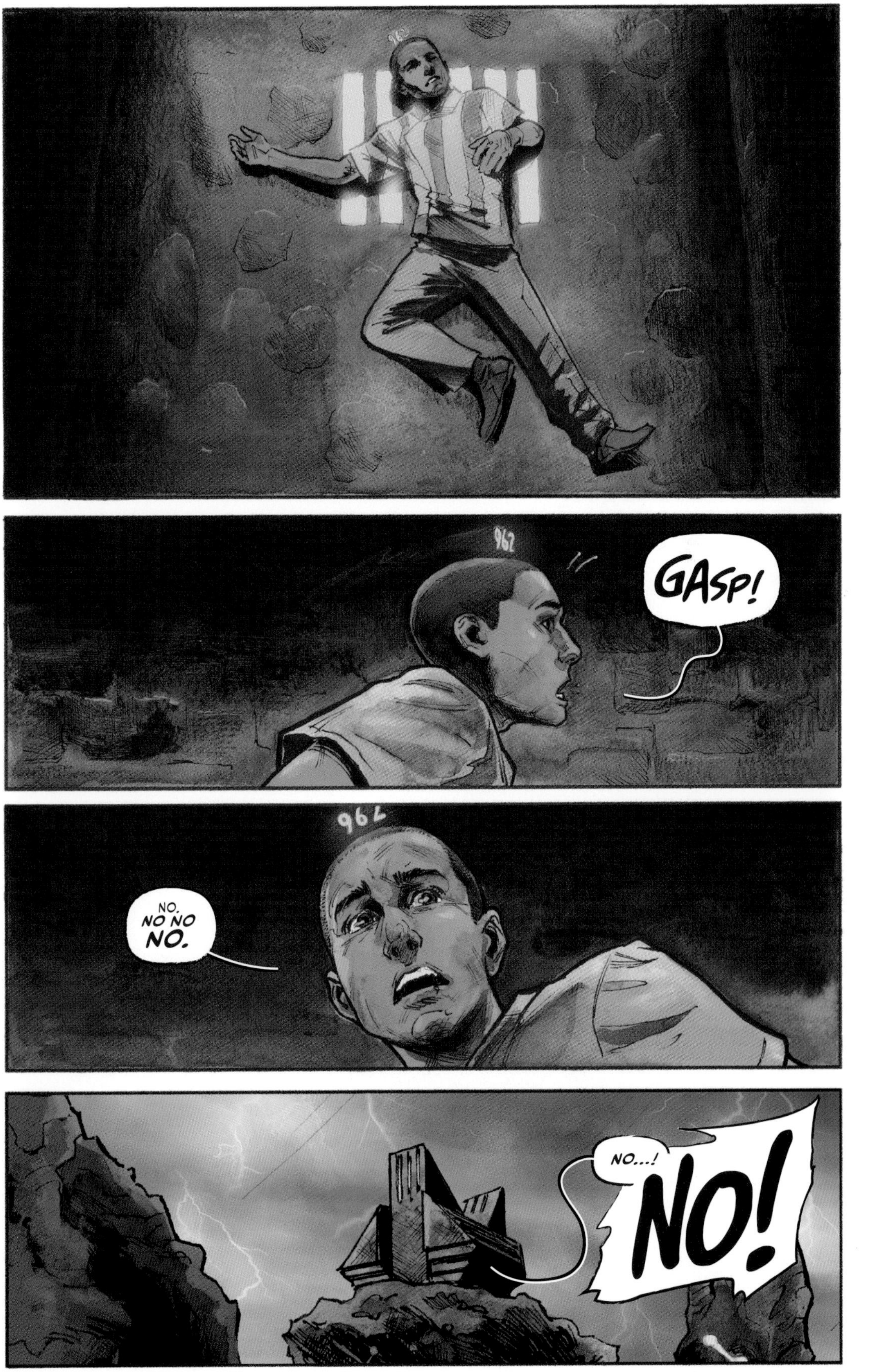
962
962
GASP!
962
NO, NO NO NO.
NO...!
NO!

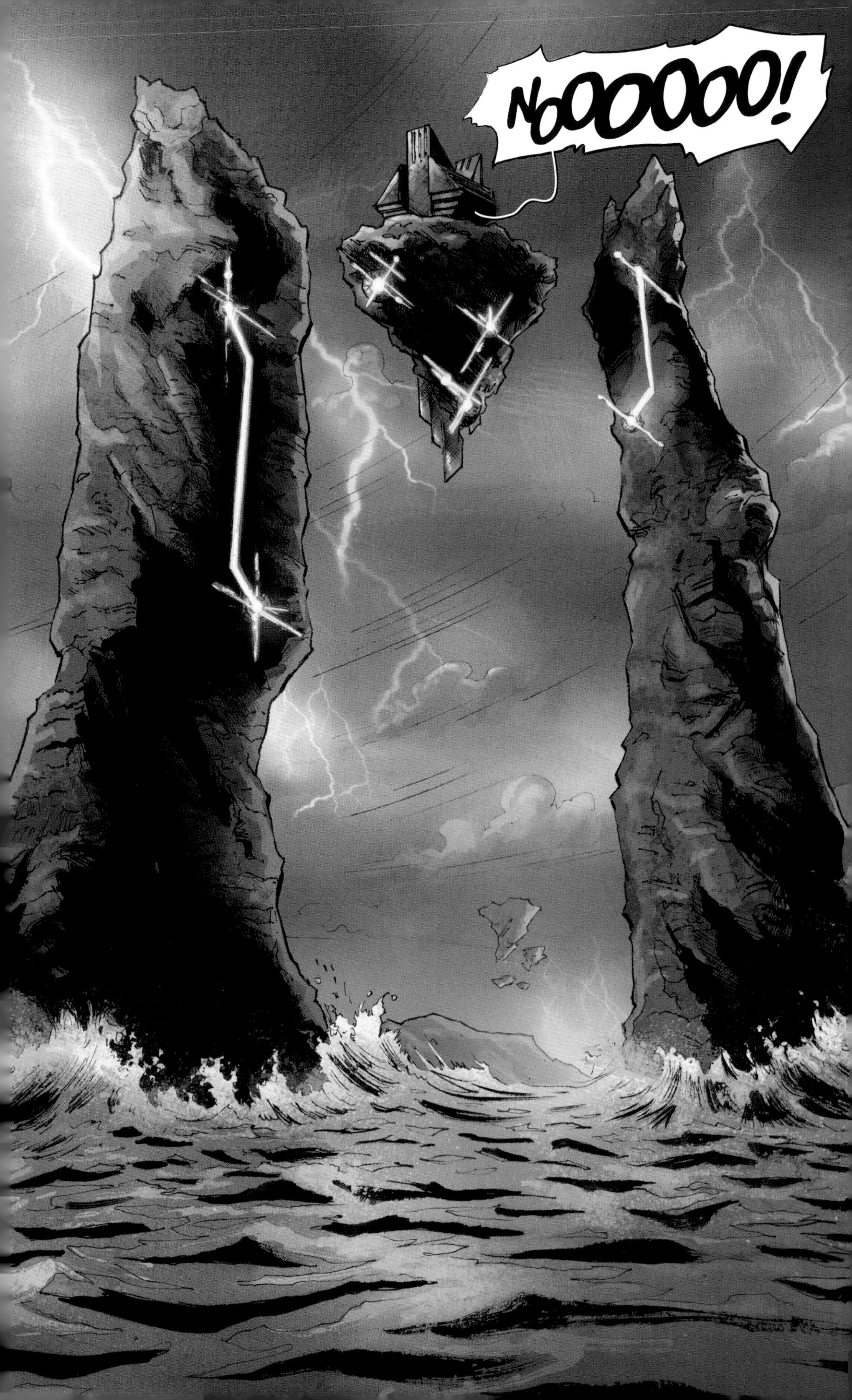
NOOOOOO!

Revenge proves its own executioner.
—John Ford

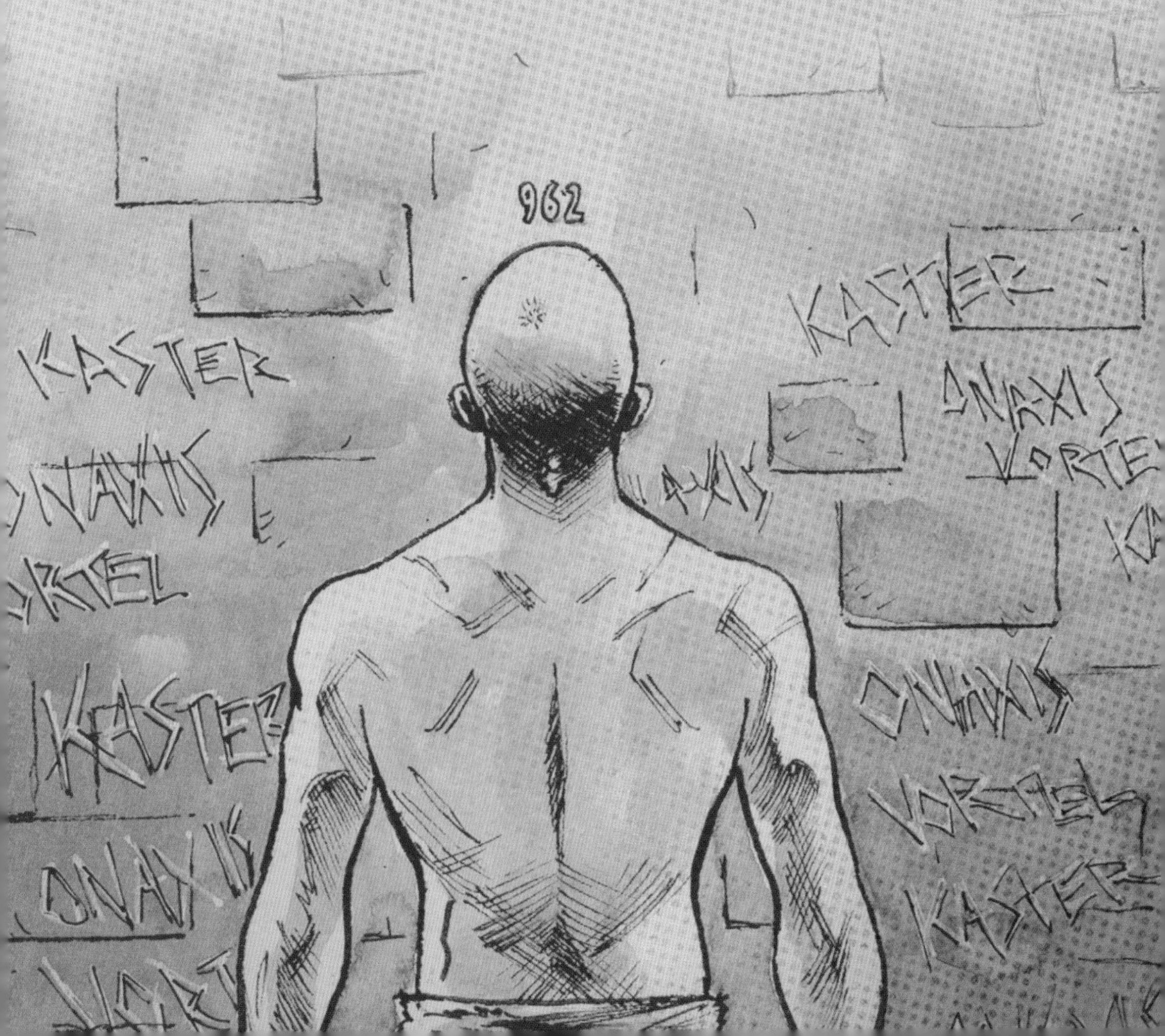
962
KASTER
KASTER
ONAXIS
KASTER

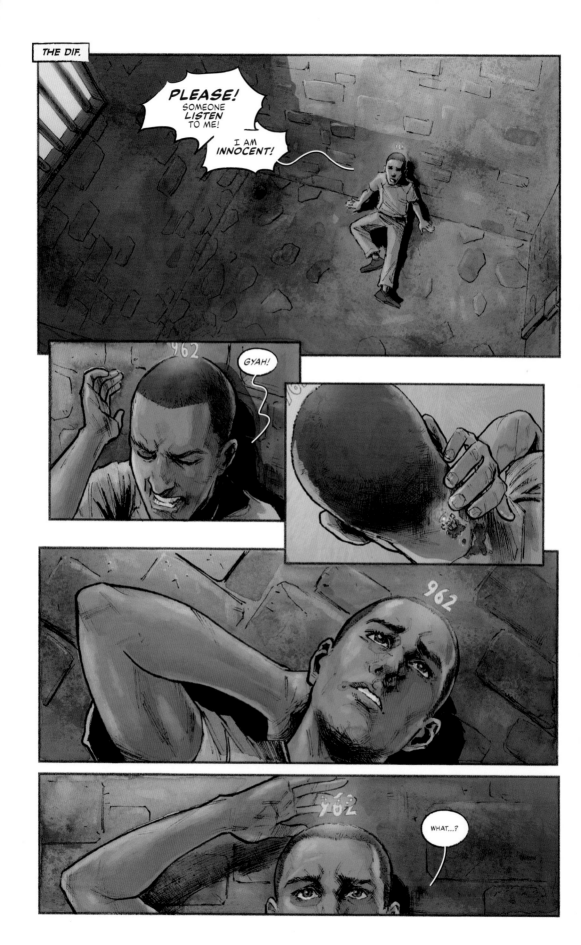

THE DIF.

PLEASE! SOMEONE LISTEN TO ME!

I AM INNOCENT!

GYAH!

WHAT...?

22

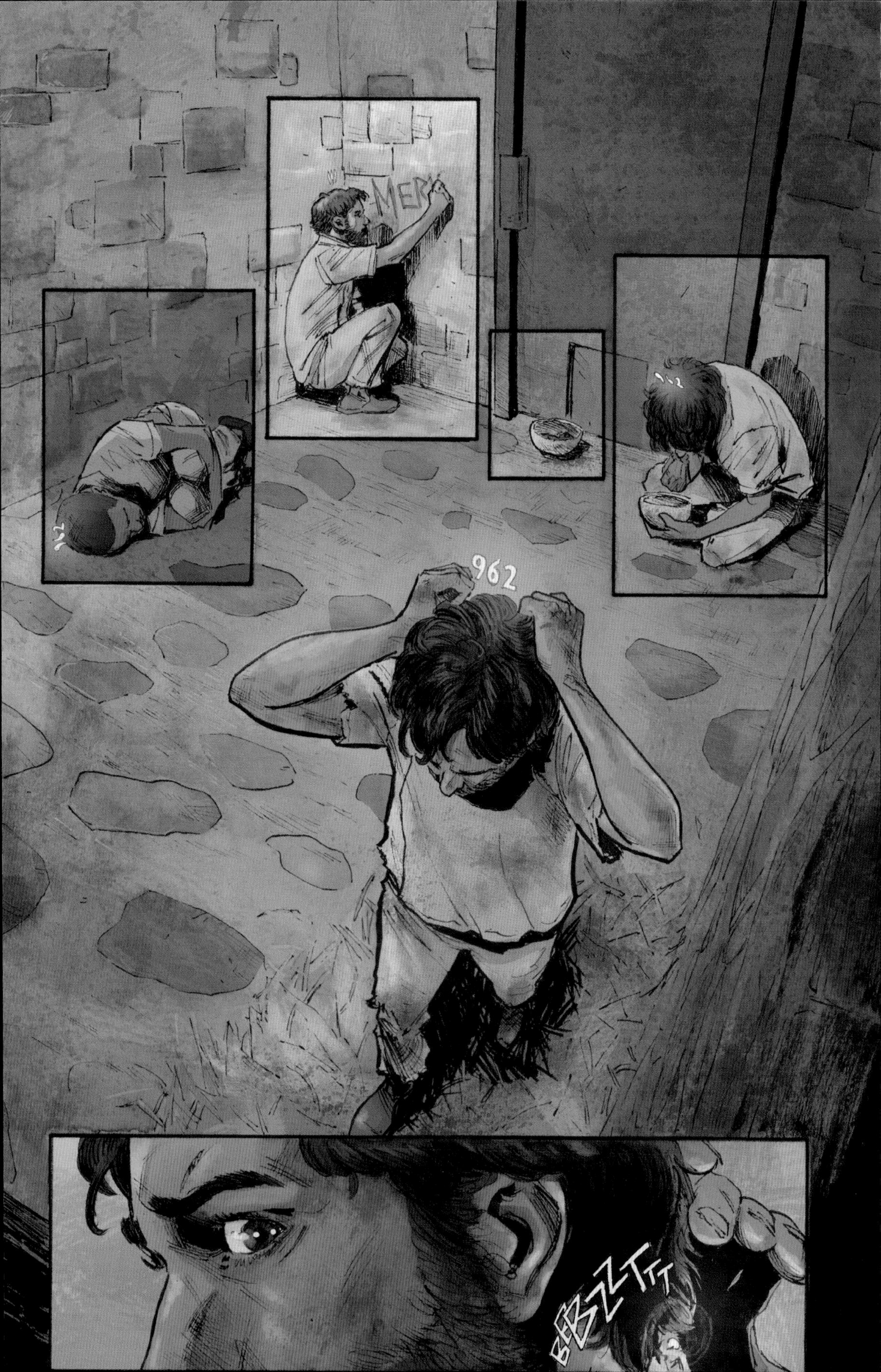
MER
962
BEBZZTTT

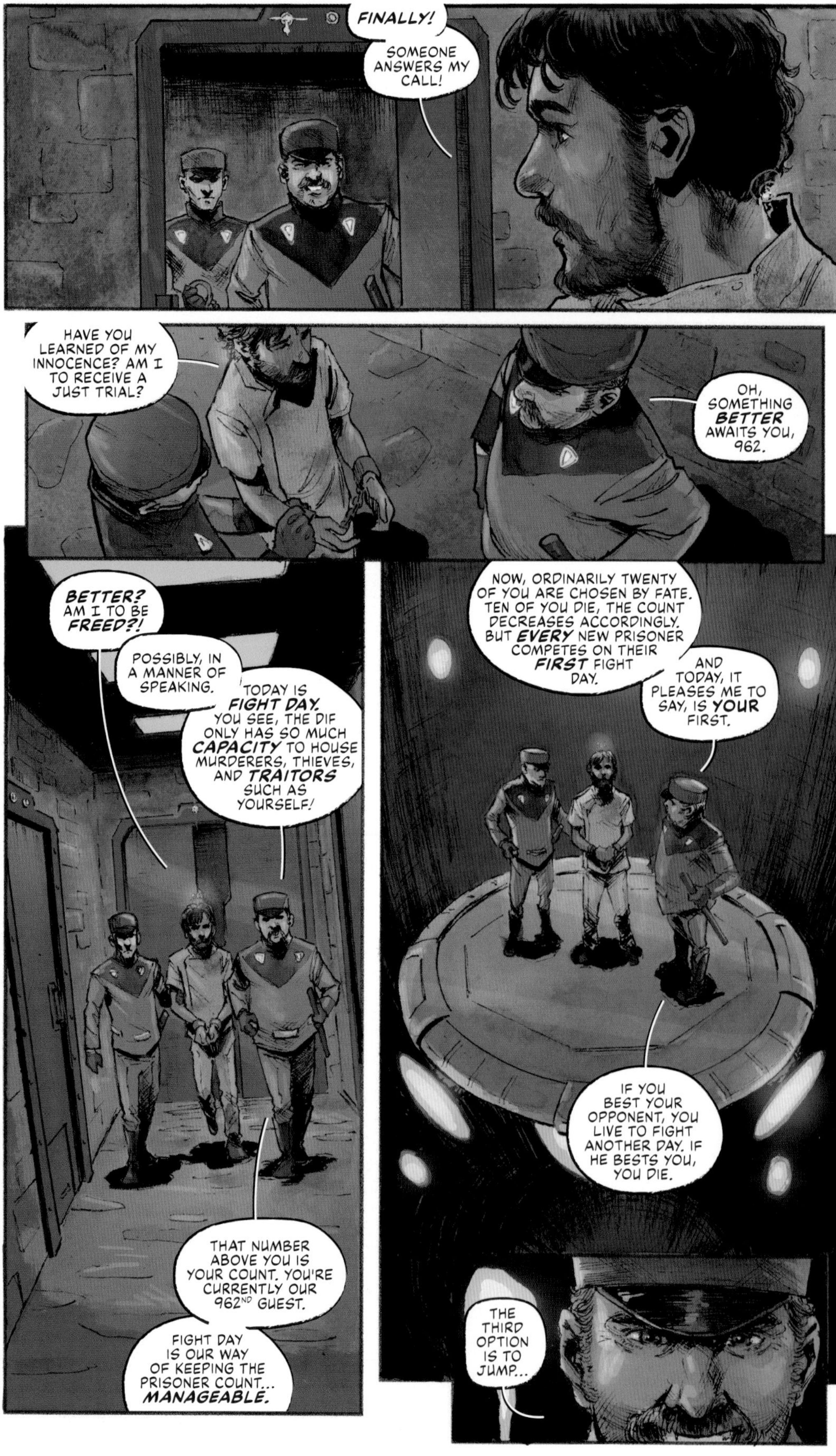
FINALLY!
SOMEONE ANSWERS MY CALL!
HAVE YOU LEARNED OF MY INNOCENCE? AM I TO RECEIVE A JUST TRIAL?
OH, SOMETHING BETTER AWAITS YOU, 962.
BETTER? AM I TO BE FREED?!
POSSIBLY, IN A MANNER OF SPEAKING.
TODAY IS FIGHT DAY. YOU SEE, THE DIF ONLY HAS SO MUCH CAPACITY TO HOUSE MURDERERS, THIEVES, AND TRAITORS SUCH AS YOURSELF!
THAT NUMBER ABOVE YOU IS YOUR COUNT. YOU'RE CURRENTLY OUR 962ND GUEST.
FIGHT DAY IS OUR WAY OF KEEPING THE PRISONER COUNT... MANAGEABLE.
NOW, ORDINARILY TWENTY OF YOU ARE CHOSEN BY FATE. TEN OF YOU DIE, THE COUNT DECREASES ACCORDINGLY. BUT EVERY NEW PRISONER COMPETES ON THEIR FIRST FIGHT DAY.
AND TODAY, IT PLEASES ME TO SAY, IS YOUR FIRST.
IF YOU BEST YOUR OPPONENT, YOU LIVE TO FIGHT ANOTHER DAY. IF HE BESTS YOU, YOU DIE.
THE THIRD OPTION IS TO JUMP...

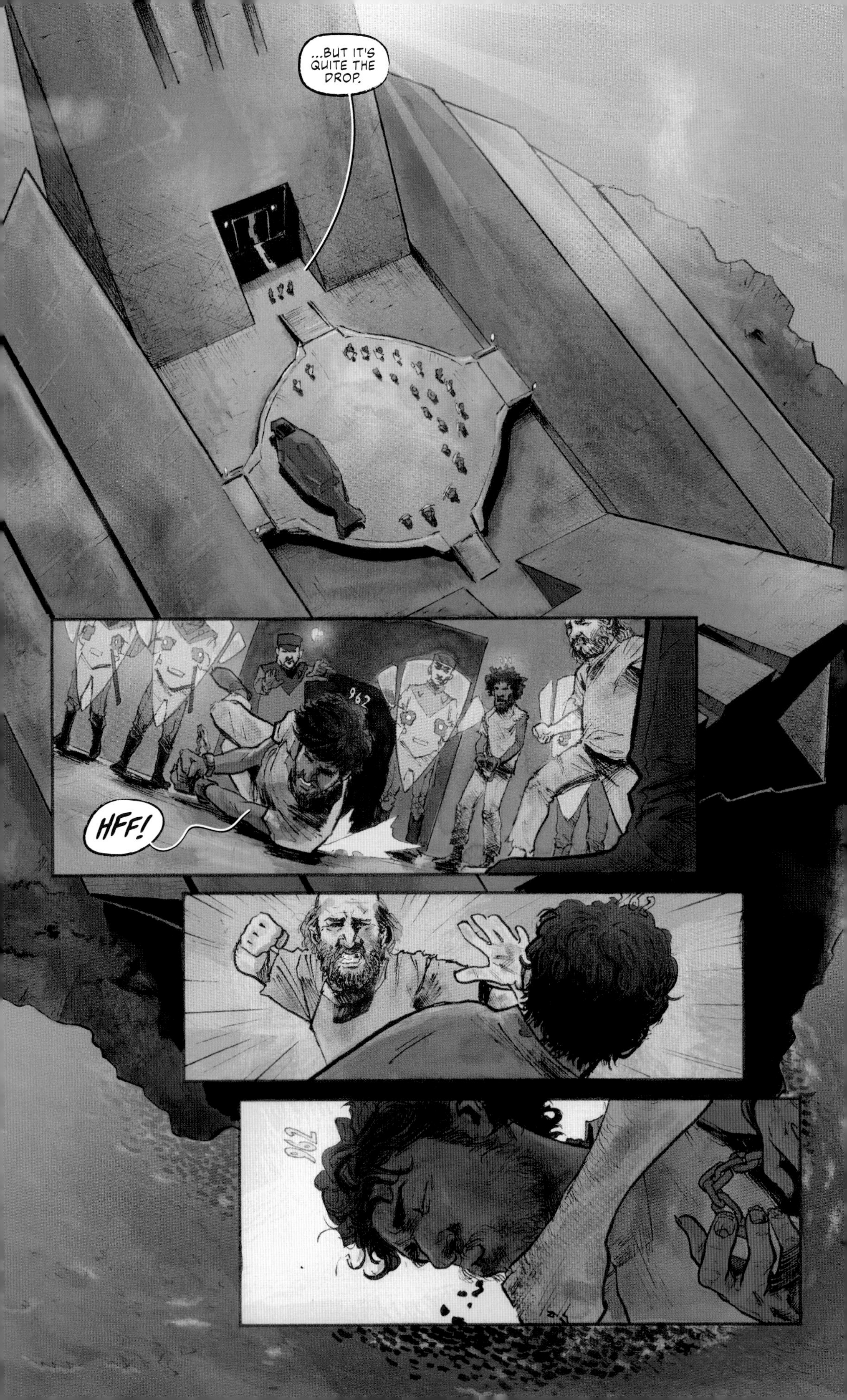
...BUT IT'S QUITE THE DROP.
HFF!
962

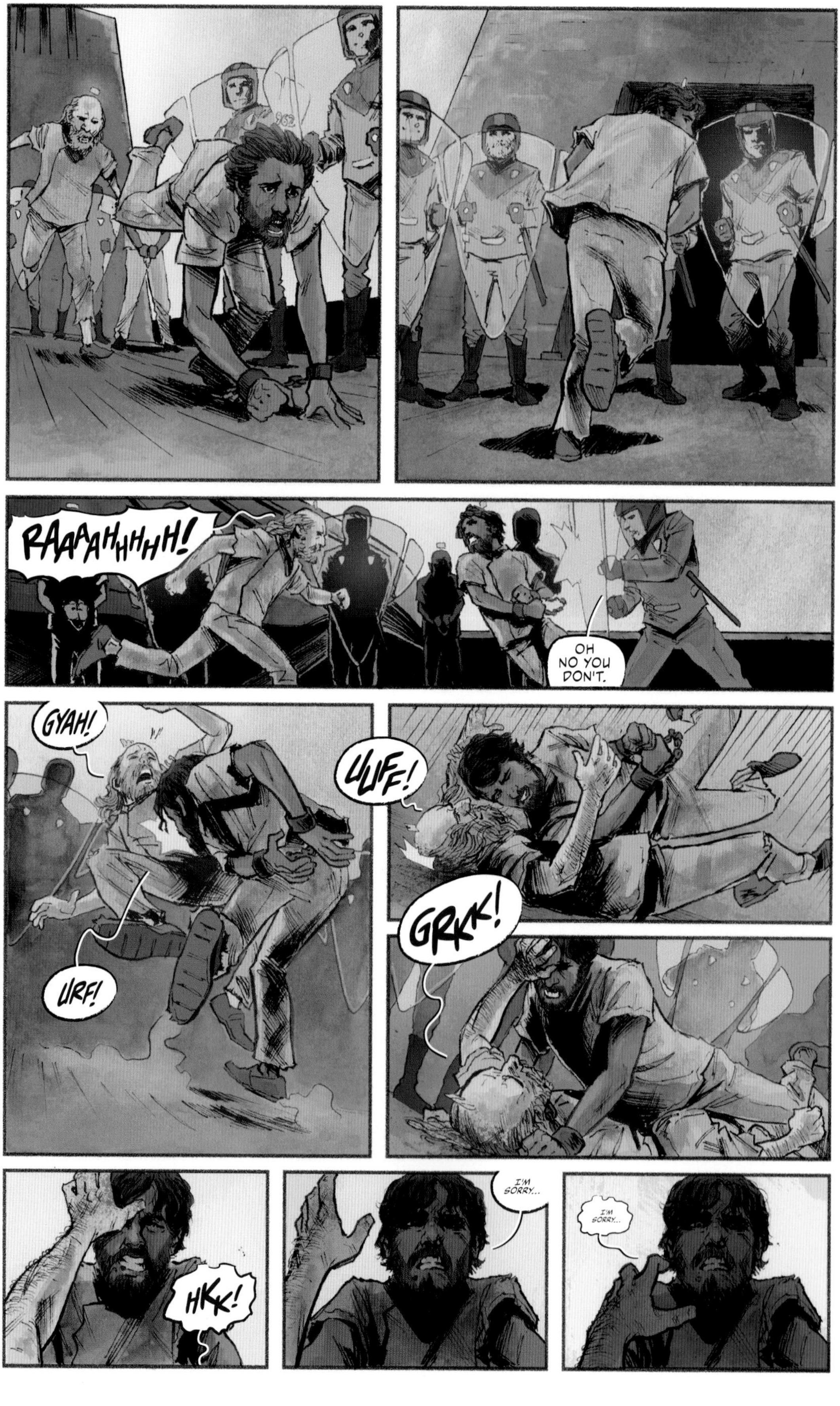
RAAAAHHHHH!
OH NO YOU DON'T.
GYAH!
URF!
UUFF!
GRKK!
HKK!
I'M SORRY...
I'M SORRY...

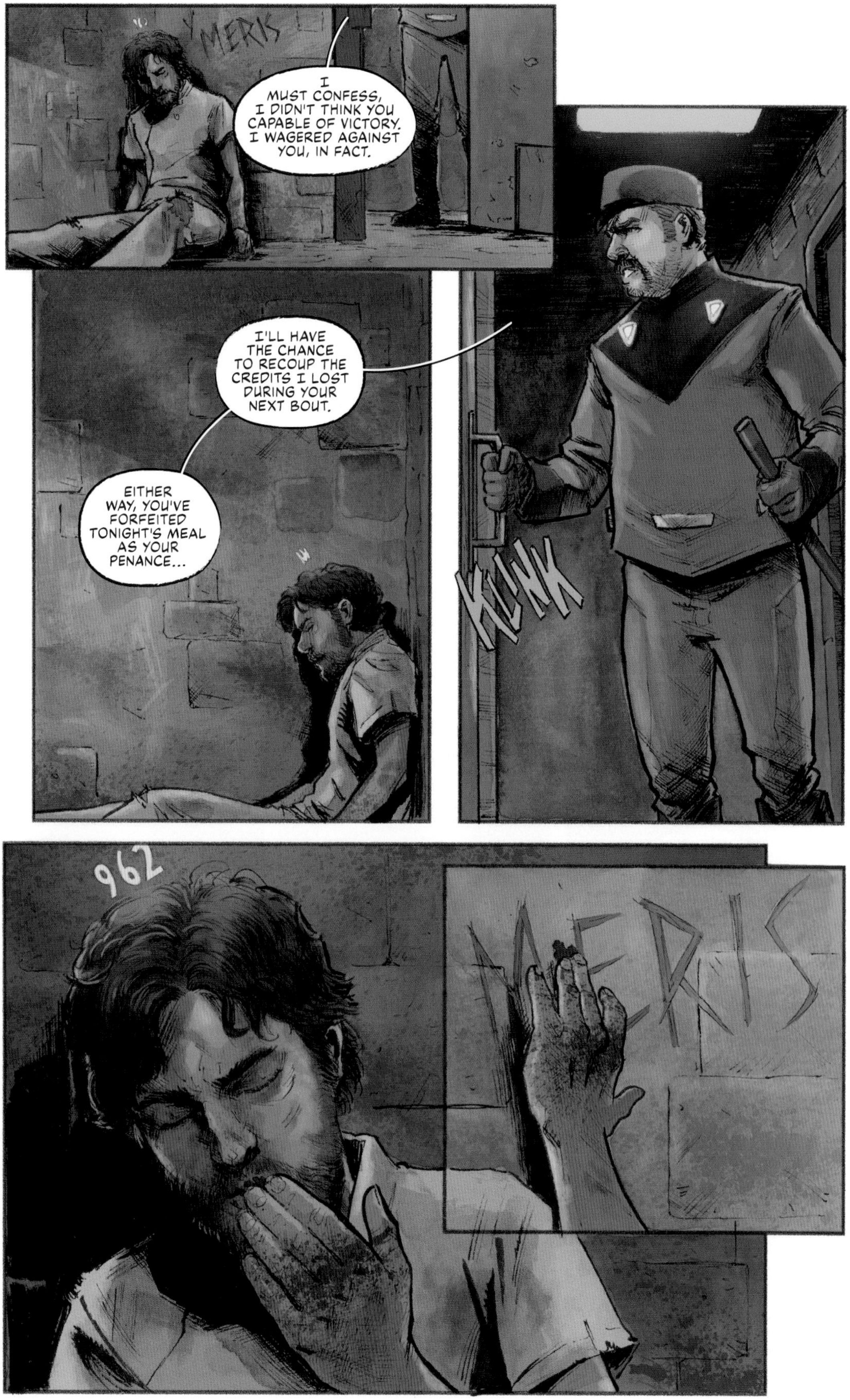
MERIS
I MUST CONFESS, I DIDN'T THINK YOU CAPABLE OF VICTORY. I WAGERED AGAINST YOU, IN FACT.
I'LL HAVE THE CHANCE TO RECOUP THE CREDITS I LOST DURING YOUR NEXT BOUT.
EITHER WAY, YOU'VE FORFEITED TONIGHT'S MEAL AS YOUR PENANCE...
KLUNK
962
MERIS

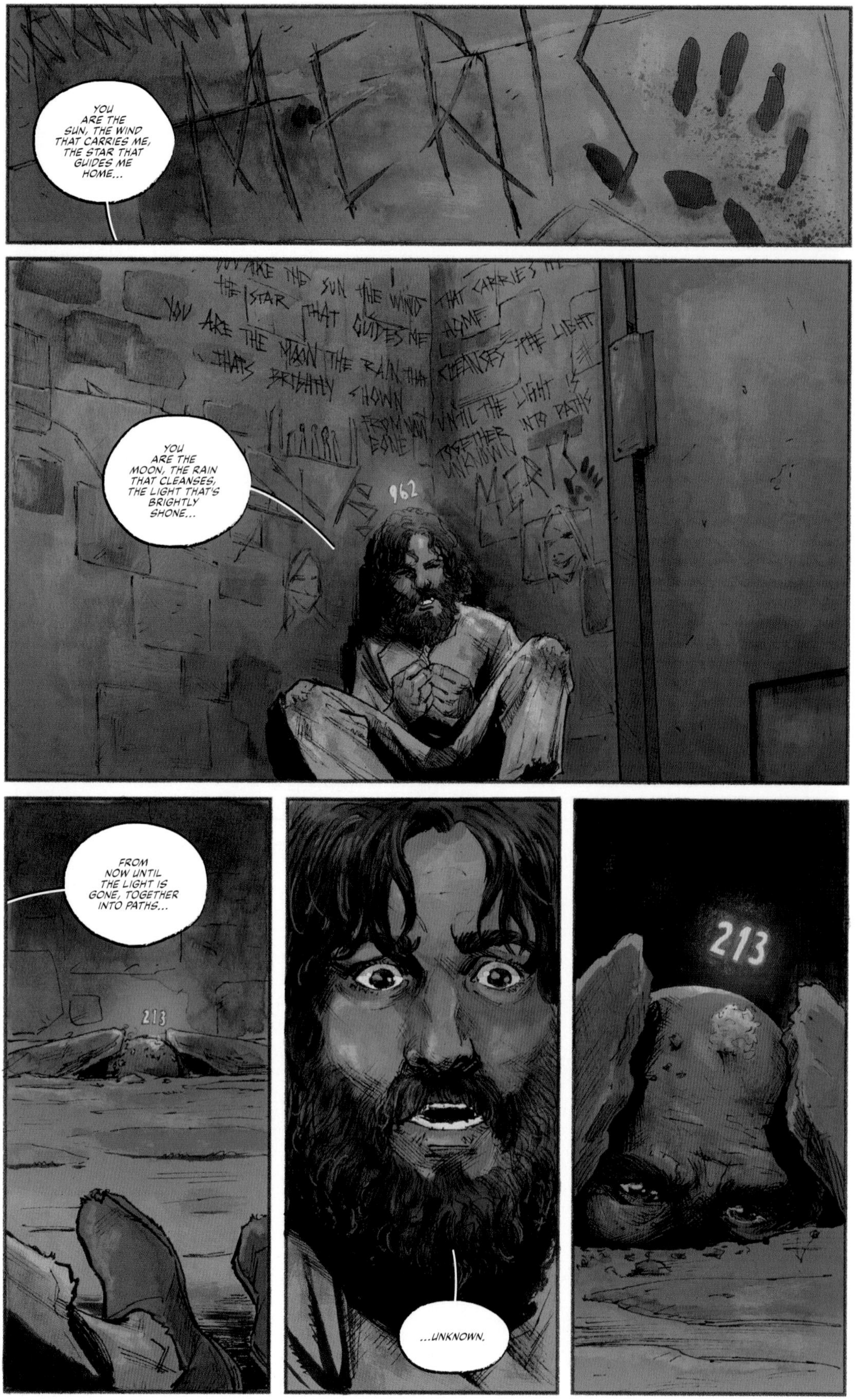
YOU ARE THE SUN, THE WIND THAT CARRIES ME, THE STAR THAT GUIDES ME HOME...
YOU ARE THE MOON, THE RAIN THAT CLEANSES, THE LIGHT THAT'S BRIGHTLY SHONE...
962
FROM NOW UNTIL THE LIGHT IS GONE, TOGETHER INTO PATHS...
213
...UNKNOWN.
213

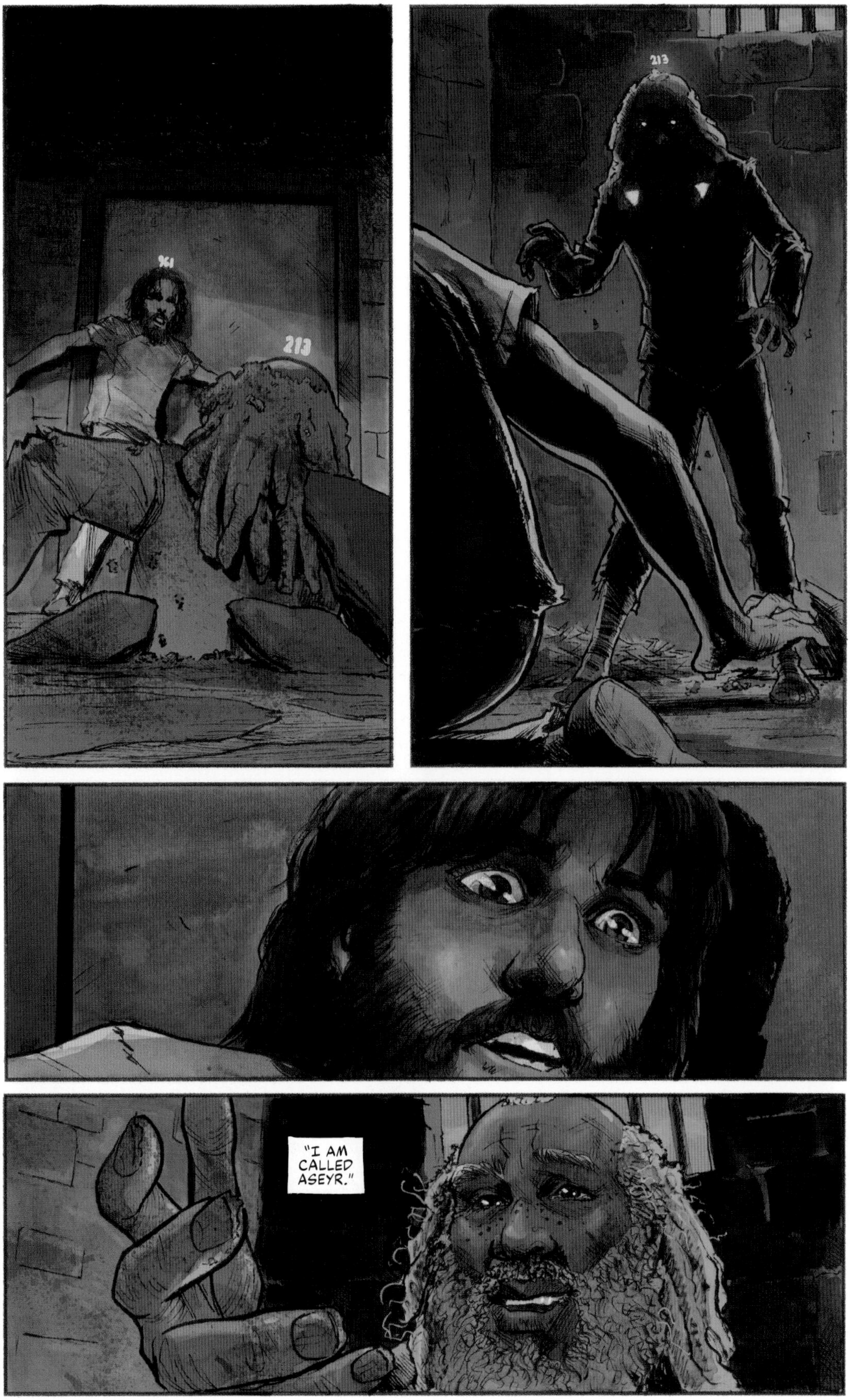
961
213
213
"I AM CALLED ASEYR."

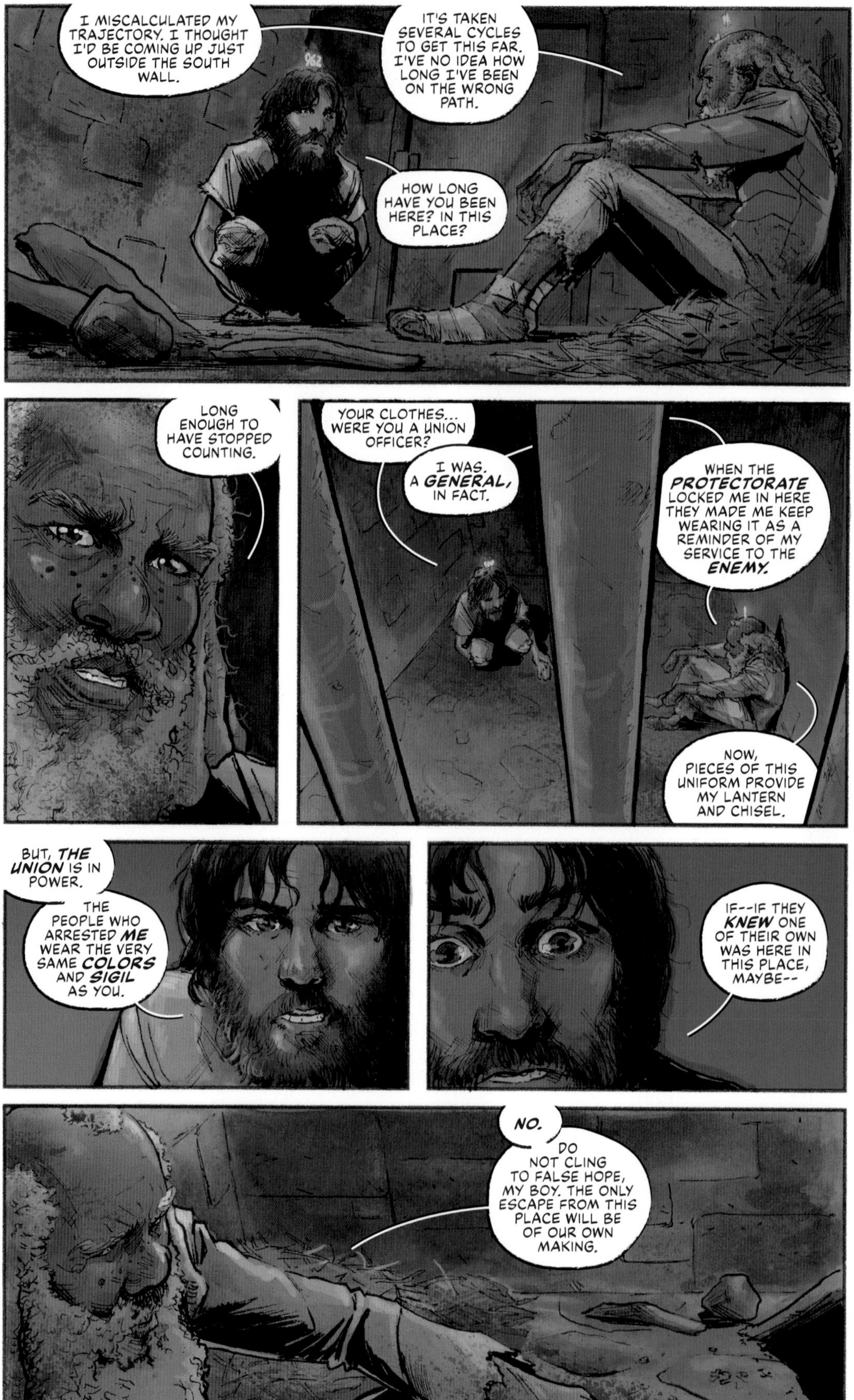
I MISCALCULATED MY TRAJECTORY. I THOUGHT I'D BE COMING UP JUST OUTSIDE THE SOUTH WALL.
IT'S TAKEN SEVERAL CYCLES TO GET THIS FAR. I'VE NO IDEA HOW LONG I'VE BEEN ON THE WRONG PATH.
HOW LONG HAVE YOU BEEN HERE? IN THIS PLACE?
LONG ENOUGH TO HAVE STOPPED COUNTING.
YOUR CLOTHES... WERE YOU A UNION OFFICER?
I WAS. A **GENERAL,** IN FACT.
WHEN THE **PROTECTORATE** LOCKED ME IN HERE THEY MADE ME KEEP WEARING IT AS A REMINDER OF MY SERVICE TO THE **ENEMY.**
NOW, PIECES OF THIS UNIFORM PROVIDE MY LANTERN AND CHISEL.
BUT, **THE UNION** IS IN POWER.
THE PEOPLE WHO ARRESTED **ME** WEAR THE VERY SAME **COLORS** AND **SIGIL** AS YOU.
IF--IF THEY **KNEW** ONE OF THEIR OWN WAS HERE IN THIS PLACE, MAYBE--
NO.
DO NOT CLING TO FALSE HOPE, MY BOY. THE ONLY ESCAPE FROM THIS PLACE WILL BE OF OUR OWN MAKING.

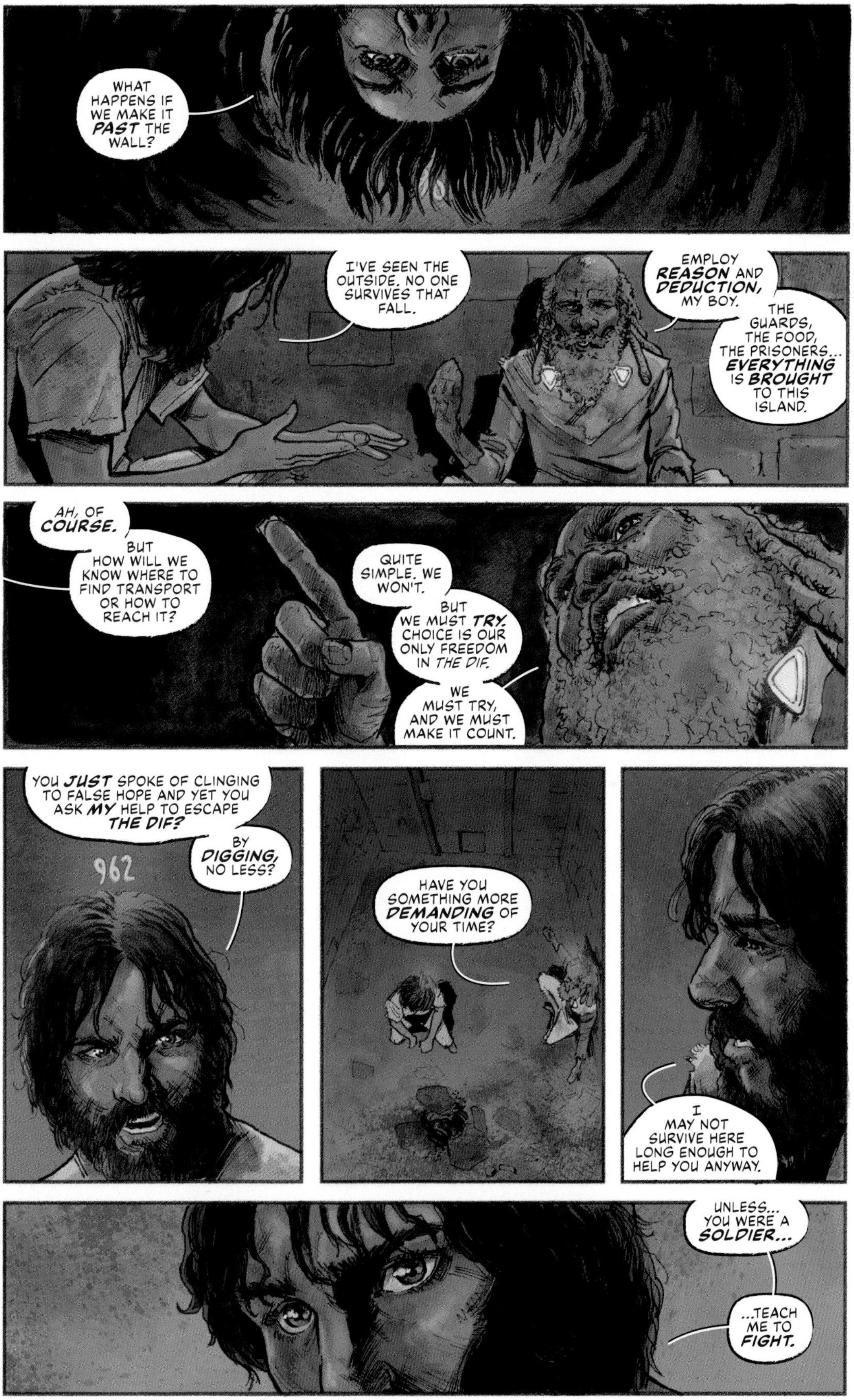
WHAT HAPPENS IF WE MAKE IT PAST THE WALL?
I'VE SEEN THE OUTSIDE. NO ONE SURVIVES THAT FALL.
EMPLOY REASON AND DEDUCTION, MY BOY.
THE GUARDS, THE FOOD, THE PRISONERS... EVERYTHING IS BROUGHT TO THIS ISLAND.
AH, OF COURSE.
BUT HOW WILL WE KNOW WHERE TO FIND TRANSPORT OR HOW TO REACH IT?
QUITE SIMPLE. WE WON'T.
BUT WE MUST TRY. CHOICE IS OUR ONLY FREEDOM IN THE DIF.
WE MUST TRY, AND WE MUST MAKE IT COUNT.
YOU JUST SPOKE OF CLINGING TO FALSE HOPE AND YET YOU ASK MY HELP TO ESCAPE THE DIF?
BY DIGGING, NO LESS?
962
HAVE YOU SOMETHING MORE DEMANDING OF YOUR TIME?
I MAY NOT SURVIVE HERE LONG ENOUGH TO HELP YOU ANYWAY.
UNLESS... YOU WERE A SOLDIER...
...TEACH ME TO FIGHT.

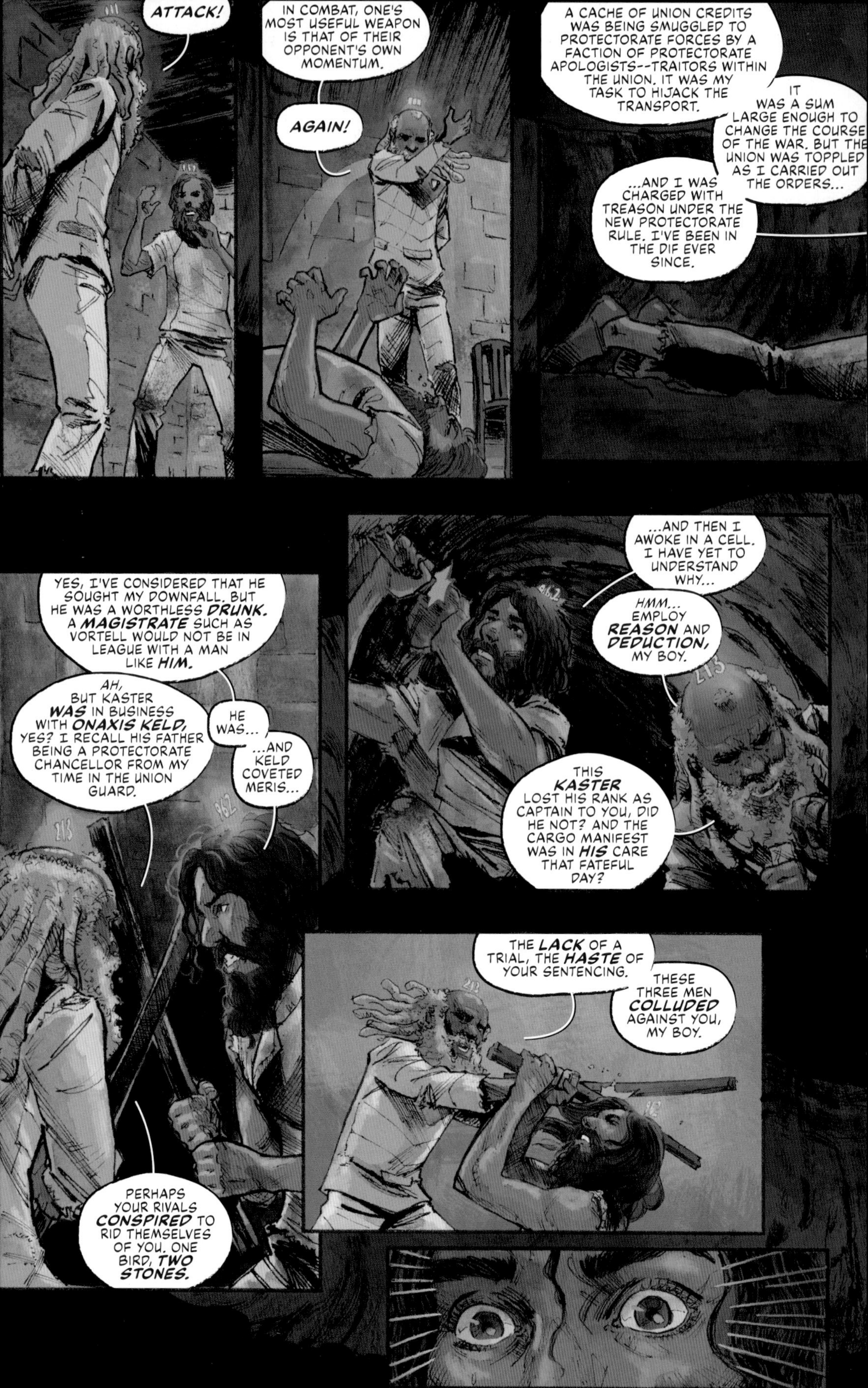

ATTACK!
IN COMBAT, ONE'S MOST USEFUL WEAPON IS THAT OF THEIR OPPONENT'S OWN MOMENTUM.
AGAIN!
A CACHE OF UNION CREDITS WAS BEING SMUGGLED TO PROTECTORATE FORCES BY A FACTION OF PROTECTORATE APOLOGISTS--TRAITORS WITHIN THE UNION. IT WAS MY TASK TO HIJACK THE TRANSPORT.
IT WAS A SUM LARGE ENOUGH TO CHANGE THE COURSE OF THE WAR. BUT THE UNION WAS TOPPLED AS I CARRIED OUT THE ORDERS...
...AND I WAS CHARGED WITH TREASON UNDER THE NEW PROTECTORATE RULE. I'VE BEEN IN THE DIF EVER SINCE.
...AND THEN I AWOKE IN A CELL. I HAVE YET TO UNDERSTAND WHY...
HMM... EMPLOY REASON AND DEDUCTION, MY BOY.
THIS KASTER LOST HIS RANK AS CAPTAIN TO YOU, DID HE NOT? AND THE CARGO MANIFEST WAS IN HIS CARE THAT FATEFUL DAY?
YES, I'VE CONSIDERED THAT HE SOUGHT MY DOWNFALL. BUT HE WAS A WORTHLESS DRUNK. A MAGISTRATE SUCH AS VORTELL WOULD NOT BE IN LEAGUE WITH A MAN LIKE HIM.
AH, BUT KASTER WAS IN BUSINESS WITH ONAXIS KELD, YES? I RECALL HIS FATHER BEING A PROTECTORATE CHANCELLOR FROM MY TIME IN THE UNION GUARD.
HE WAS...
...AND KELD COVETED MERIS...
PERHAPS YOUR RIVALS CONSPIRED TO RID THEMSELVES OF YOU. ONE BIRD, TWO STONES.
THE LACK OF A TRIAL, THE HASTE OF YOUR SENTENCING.
THESE THREE MEN COLLUDED AGAINST YOU, MY BOY.

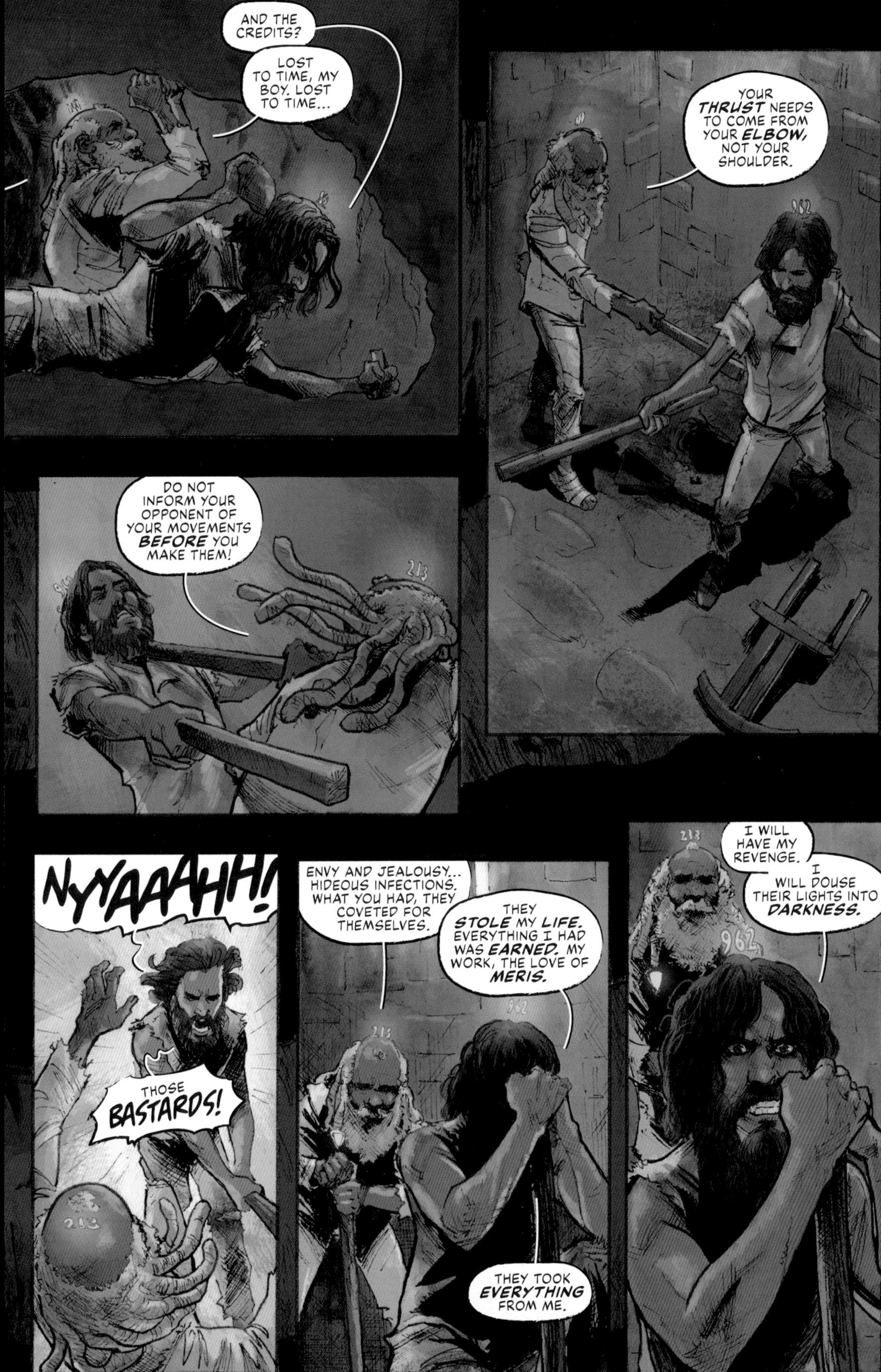
AND THE CREDITS?
LOST TO TIME, MY BOY. LOST TO TIME...
YOUR THRUST NEEDS TO COME FROM YOUR ELBOW, NOT YOUR SHOULDER.
DO NOT INFORM YOUR OPPONENT OF YOUR MOVEMENTS BEFORE YOU MAKE THEM!
213
962
NYYAAAHH!
THOSE BASTARDS!
ENVY AND JEALOUSY... HIDEOUS INFECTIONS. WHAT YOU HAD, THEY COVETED FOR THEMSELVES.
THEY STOLE MY LIFE. EVERYTHING I HAD WAS EARNED. MY WORK, THE LOVE OF MERIS.
THEY TOOK EVERYTHING FROM ME.
I WILL HAVE MY REVENGE.
I WILL DOUSE THEIR LIGHTS INTO DARKNESS.

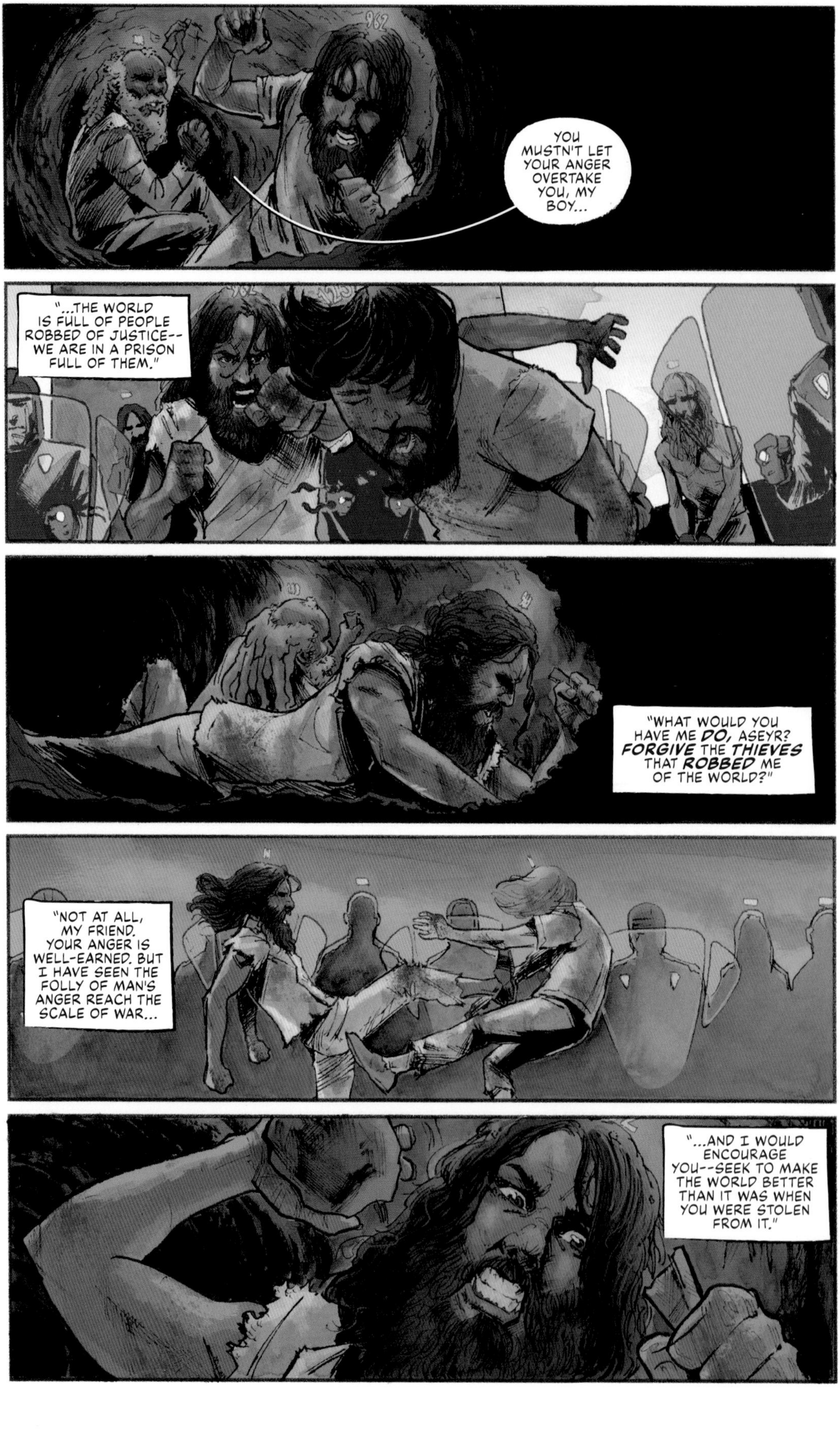
YOU MUSTN'T LET YOUR ANGER OVERTAKE YOU, MY BOY...
"...THE WORLD IS FULL OF PEOPLE ROBBED OF JUSTICE--WE ARE IN A PRISON FULL OF THEM."
"WHAT WOULD YOU HAVE ME DO, ASEYR? FORGIVE THE THIEVES THAT ROBBED ME OF THE WORLD?"
"NOT AT ALL, MY FRIEND. YOUR ANGER IS WELL-EARNED. BUT I HAVE SEEN THE FOLLY OF MAN'S ANGER REACH THE SCALE OF WAR...
"...AND I WOULD ENCOURAGE YOU--SEEK TO MAKE THE WORLD BETTER THAN IT WAS WHEN YOU WERE STOLEN FROM IT."

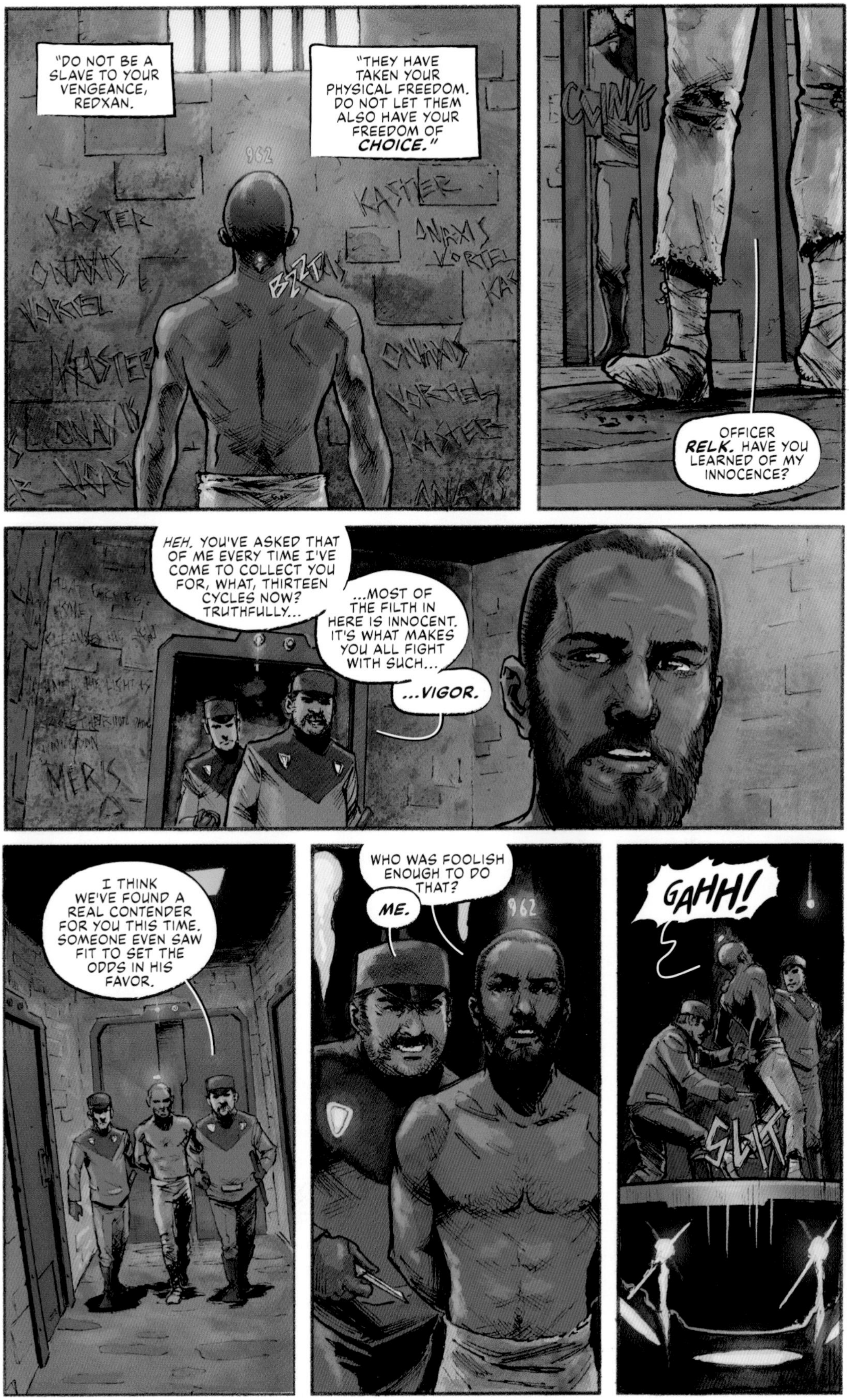

"DO NOT BE A SLAVE TO YOUR VENGEANCE, REDXAN.
"THEY HAVE TAKEN YOUR PHYSICAL FREEDOM. DO NOT LET THEM ALSO HAVE YOUR FREEDOM OF CHOICE."
962
CLINK
OFFICER RELK. HAVE YOU LEARNED OF MY INNOCENCE?
HEH. YOU'VE ASKED THAT OF ME EVERY TIME I'VE COME TO COLLECT YOU FOR, WHAT, THIRTEEN CYCLES NOW? TRUTHFULLY...
...MOST OF THE FILTH IN HERE IS INNOCENT. IT'S WHAT MAKES YOU ALL FIGHT WITH SUCH...
...VIGOR.
I THINK WE'VE FOUND A REAL CONTENDER FOR YOU THIS TIME. SOMEONE EVEN SAW FIT TO SET THE ODDS IN HIS FAVOR.
WHO WAS FOOLISH ENOUGH TO DO THAT?
ME.
962
GAHH!
SLIT

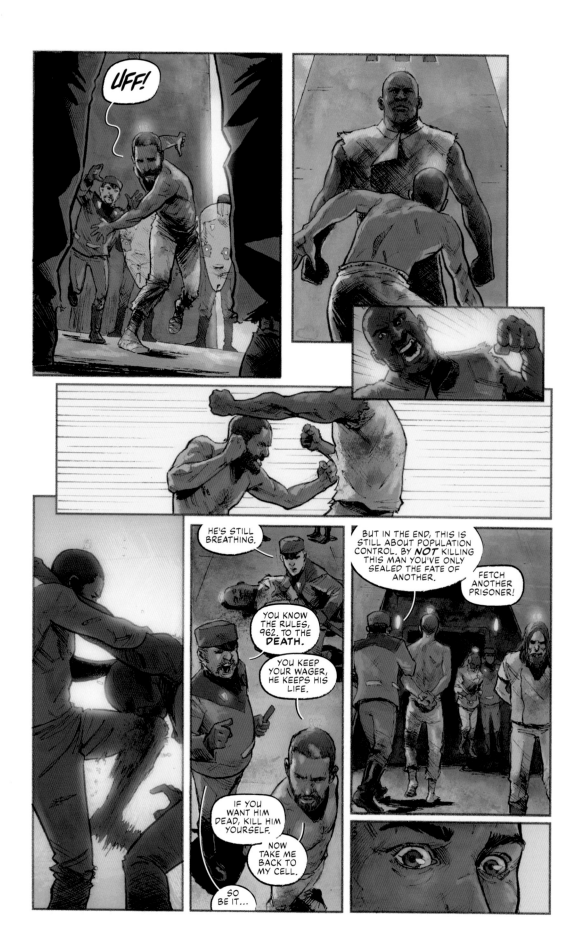

UFF!

HE'S STILL BREATHING.

YOU KNOW THE RULES, 962. TO THE **DEATH.**

YOU KEEP YOUR WAGER, HE KEEPS HIS LIFE.

IF YOU WANT HIM DEAD, KILL HIM YOURSELF.

NOW TAKE ME BACK TO MY CELL.

SO BE IT...

BUT IN THE END, THIS IS STILL ABOUT POPULATION CONTROL. BY **NOT** KILLING THIS MAN YOU'VE ONLY SEALED THE FATE OF ANOTHER.

FETCH ANOTHER PRISONER!

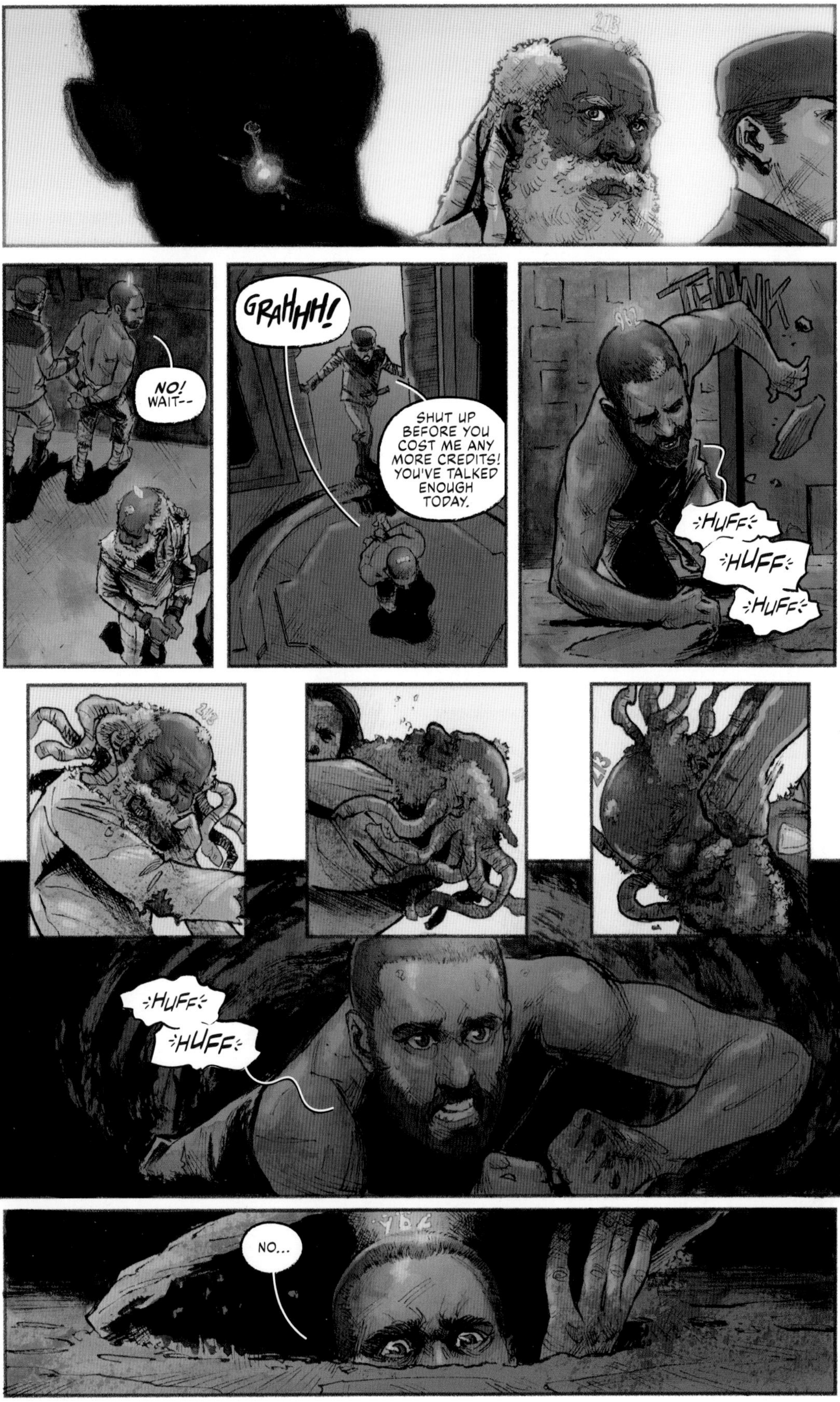
NO! WAIT--
GRAHHH!
SHUT UP BEFORE YOU COST ME ANY MORE CREDITS! YOU'VE TALKED ENOUGH TODAY.
THUNK
HUFF
HUFF
HUFF
HUFF
HUFF
NO...

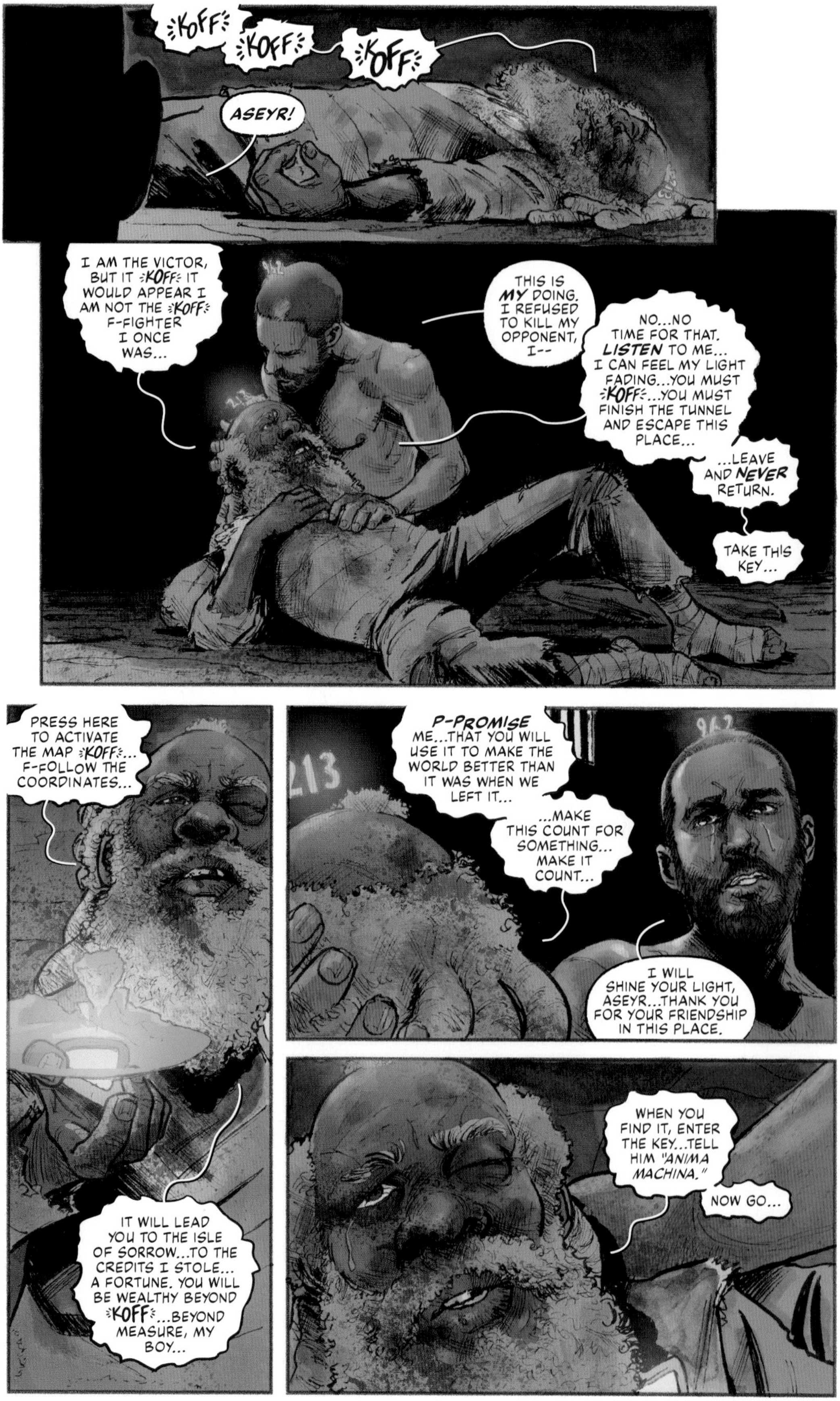
KOFF
KOFF
KOFF
ASEYR!
I AM THE VICTOR, BUT IT KOFF IT WOULD APPEAR I AM NOT THE KOFF F-FIGHTER I ONCE WAS...
THIS IS MY DOING. I REFUSED TO KILL MY OPPONENT, I--
NO...NO TIME FOR THAT. LISTEN TO ME... I CAN FEEL MY LIGHT FADING...YOU MUST KOFF...YOU MUST FINISH THE TUNNEL AND ESCAPE THIS PLACE...
...LEAVE AND NEVER RETURN.
TAKE THIS KEY...
PRESS HERE TO ACTIVATE THE MAP KOFF... F-FOLLOW THE COORDINATES...
IT WILL LEAD YOU TO THE ISLE OF SORROW...TO THE CREDITS I STOLE... A FORTUNE. YOU WILL BE WEALTHY BEYOND KOFF...BEYOND MEASURE, MY BOY...
P-PROMISE ME...THAT YOU WILL USE IT TO MAKE THE WORLD BETTER THAN IT WAS WHEN WE LEFT IT...
...MAKE THIS COUNT FOR SOMETHING... MAKE IT COUNT...
I WILL SHINE YOUR LIGHT, ASEYR...THANK YOU FOR YOUR FRIENDSHIP IN THIS PLACE.
WHEN YOU FIND IT, ENTER THE KEY...TELL HIM "ANIMA MACHINA."
NOW GO...

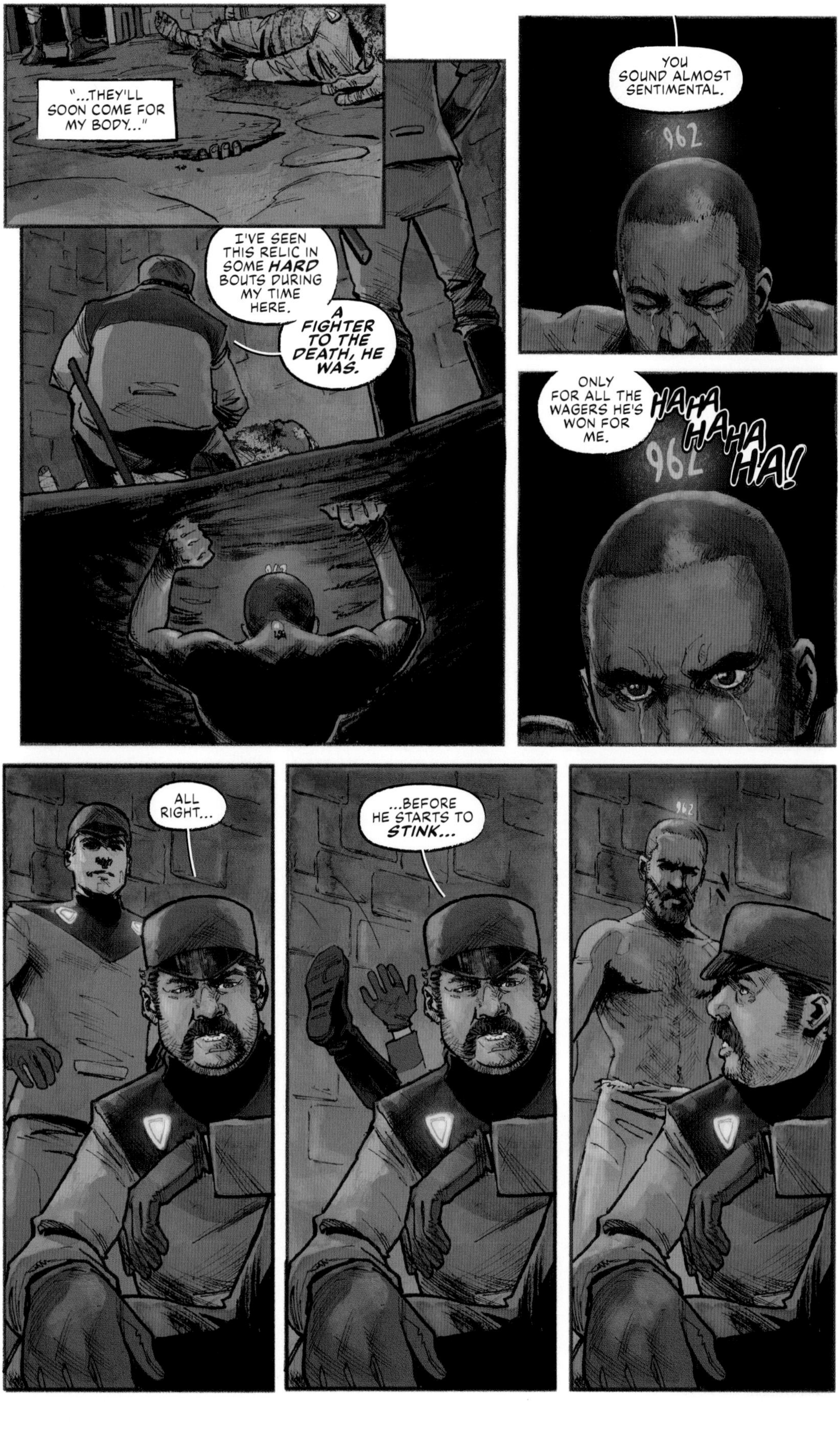
"...THEY'LL SOON COME FOR MY BODY..."
YOU SOUND ALMOST SENTIMENTAL.
962
I'VE SEEN THIS RELIC IN SOME HARD BOUTS DURING MY TIME HERE.
A FIGHTER TO THE DEATH, HE WAS.
ONLY FOR ALL THE WAGERS HE'S WON FOR ME.
HAHA HAHA HA!
962
ALL RIGHT...
...BEFORE HE STARTS TO STINK...
962

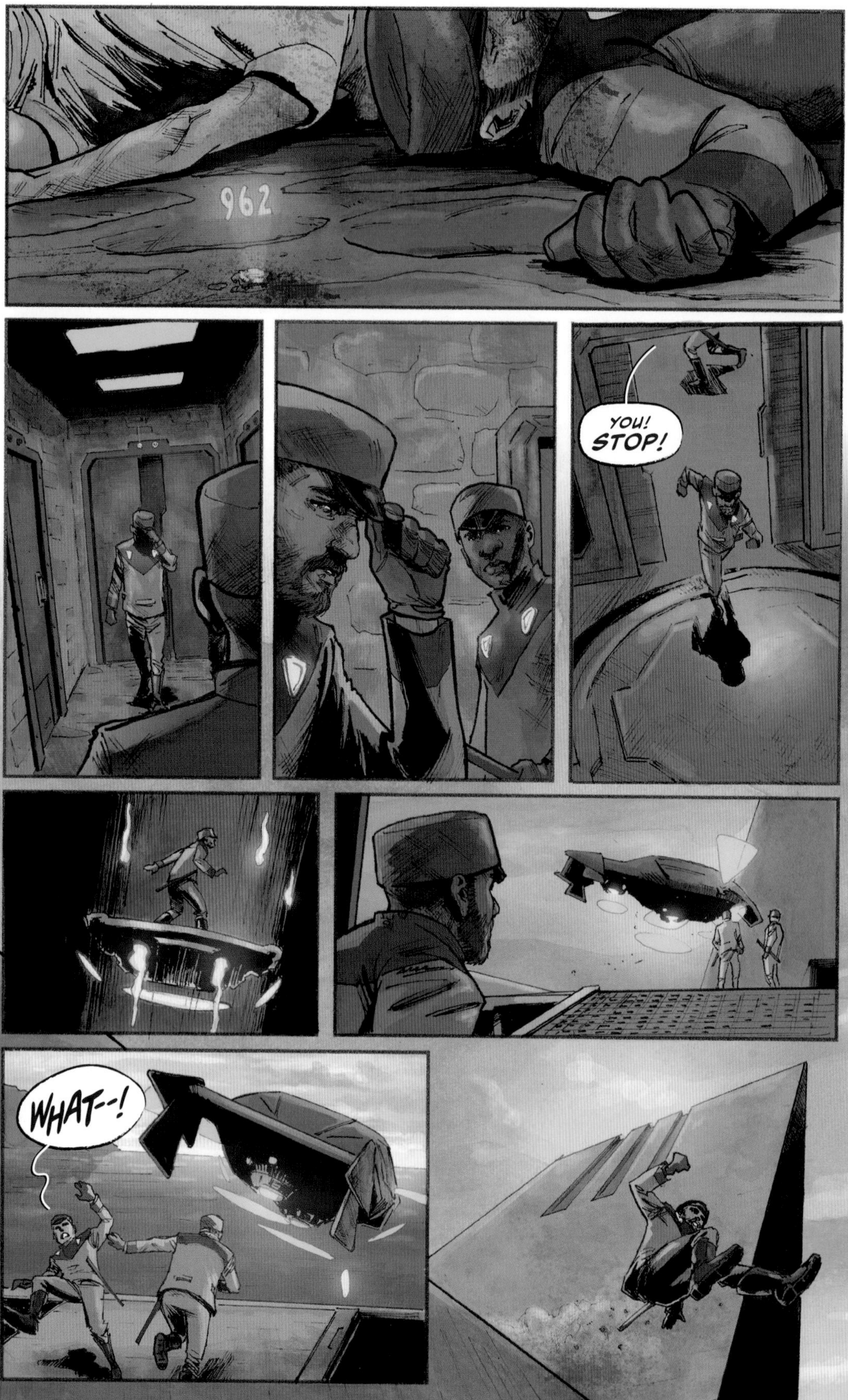
962
YOU! STOP!
WHAT--!

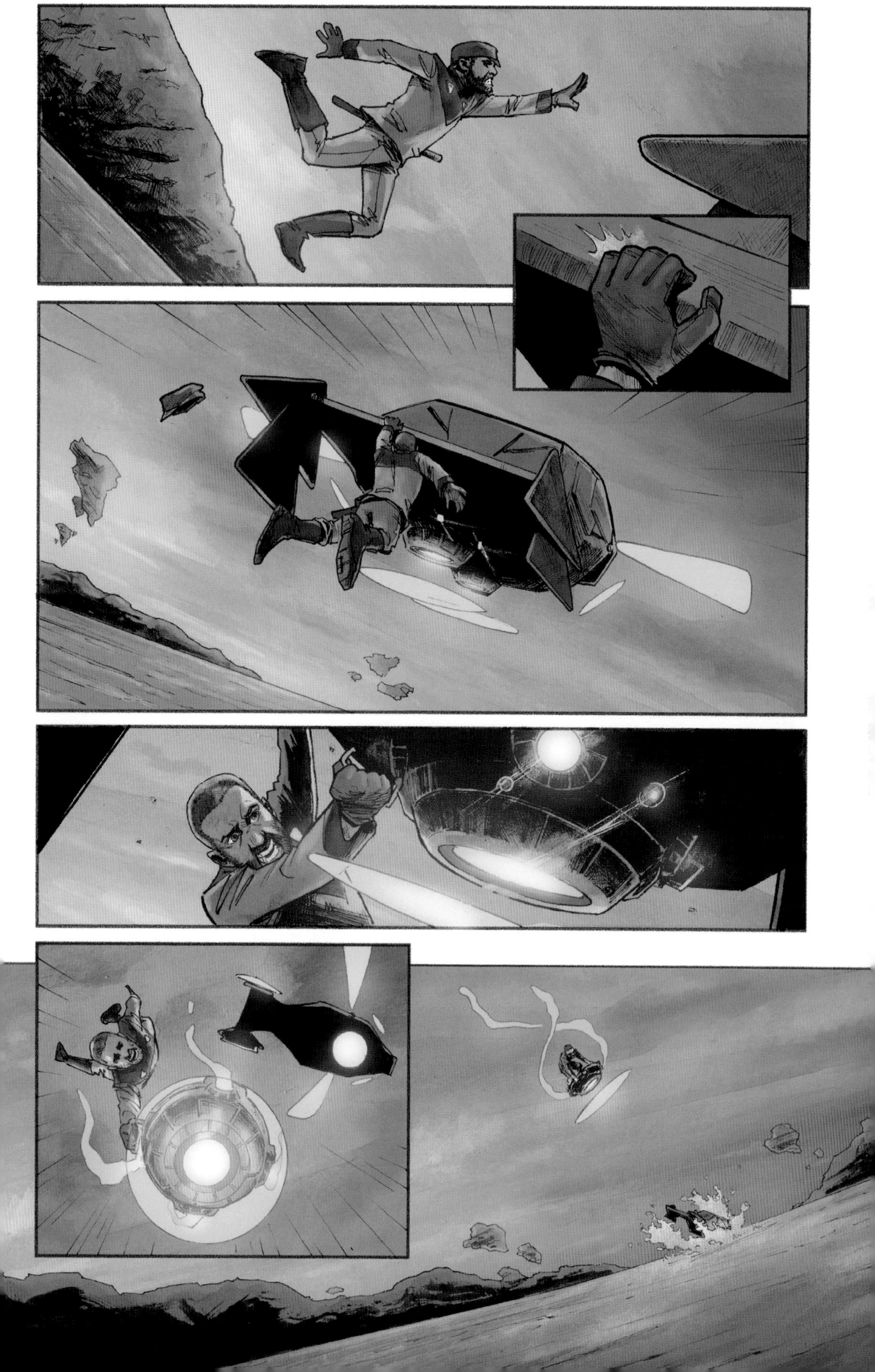

Revenge may be wicked, but it's natural.
—William Makepeace Thackeray

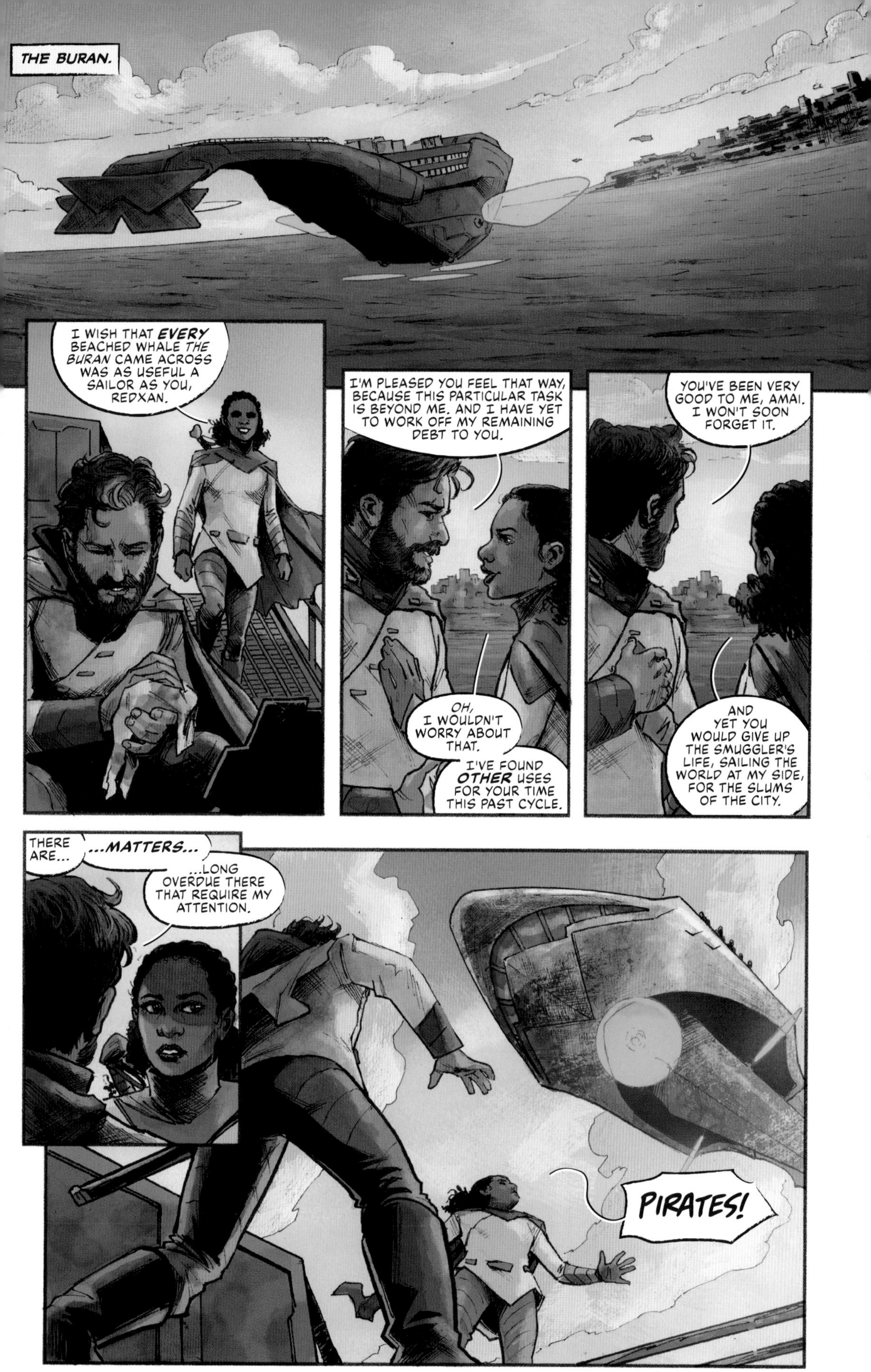

THE BURAN.
I WISH THAT EVERY BEACHED WHALE THE BURAN CAME ACROSS WAS AS USEFUL A SAILOR AS YOU, REDXAN.
I'M PLEASED YOU FEEL THAT WAY, BECAUSE THIS PARTICULAR TASK IS BEYOND ME. AND I HAVE YET TO WORK OFF MY REMAINING DEBT TO YOU.
OH, I WOULDN'T WORRY ABOUT THAT.
I'VE FOUND OTHER USES FOR YOUR TIME THIS PAST CYCLE.
YOU'VE BEEN VERY GOOD TO ME, AMAI. I WON'T SOON FORGET IT.
AND YET YOU WOULD GIVE UP THE SMUGGLER'S LIFE, SAILING THE WORLD AT MY SIDE, FOR THE SLUMS OF THE CITY.
THERE ARE...
...MATTERS...
...LONG OVERDUE THERE THAT REQUIRE MY ATTENTION.
PIRATES!

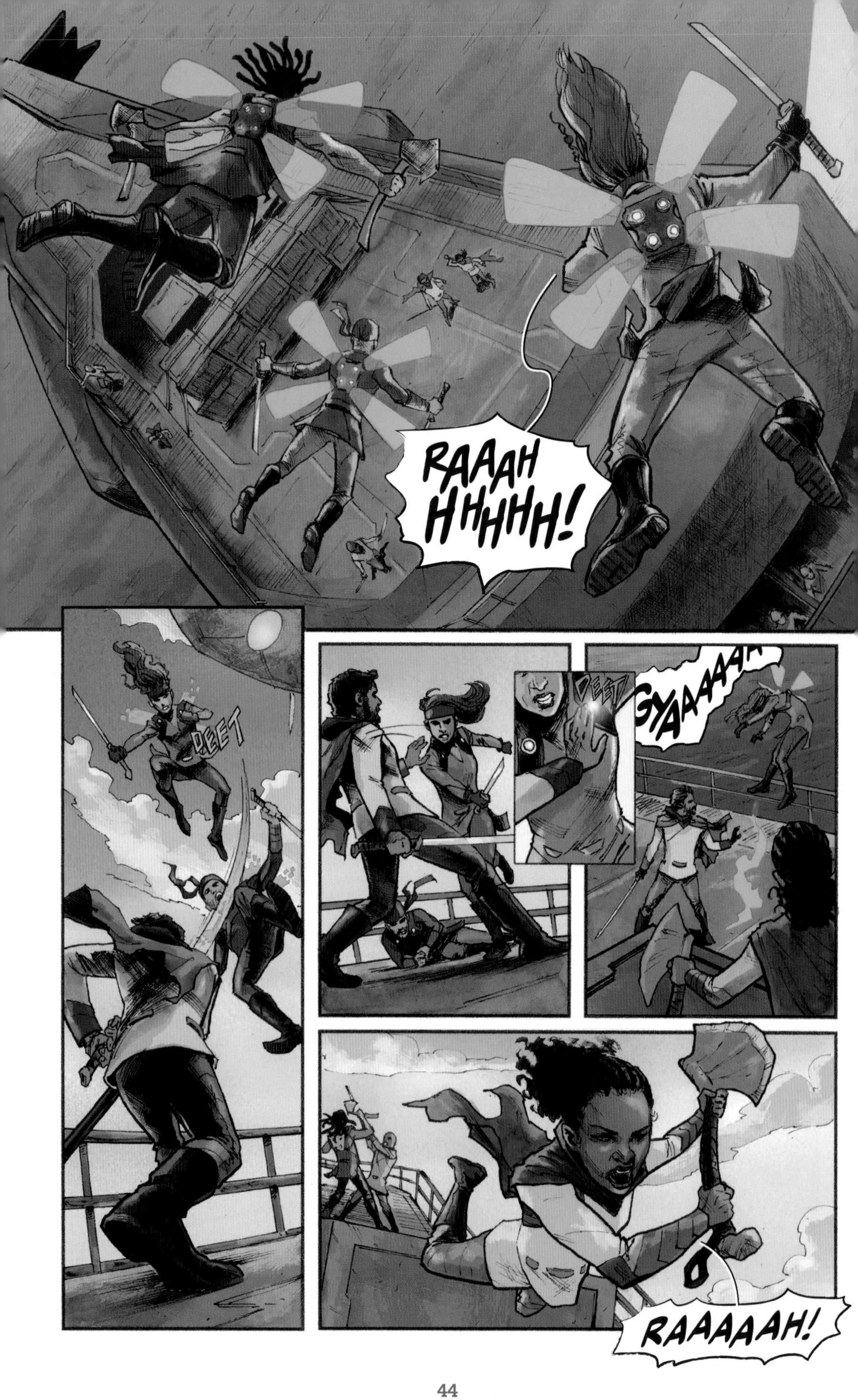
RAAAH HHHHH!
DEET
DEET
GYAAAAAA
RAAAAAH!

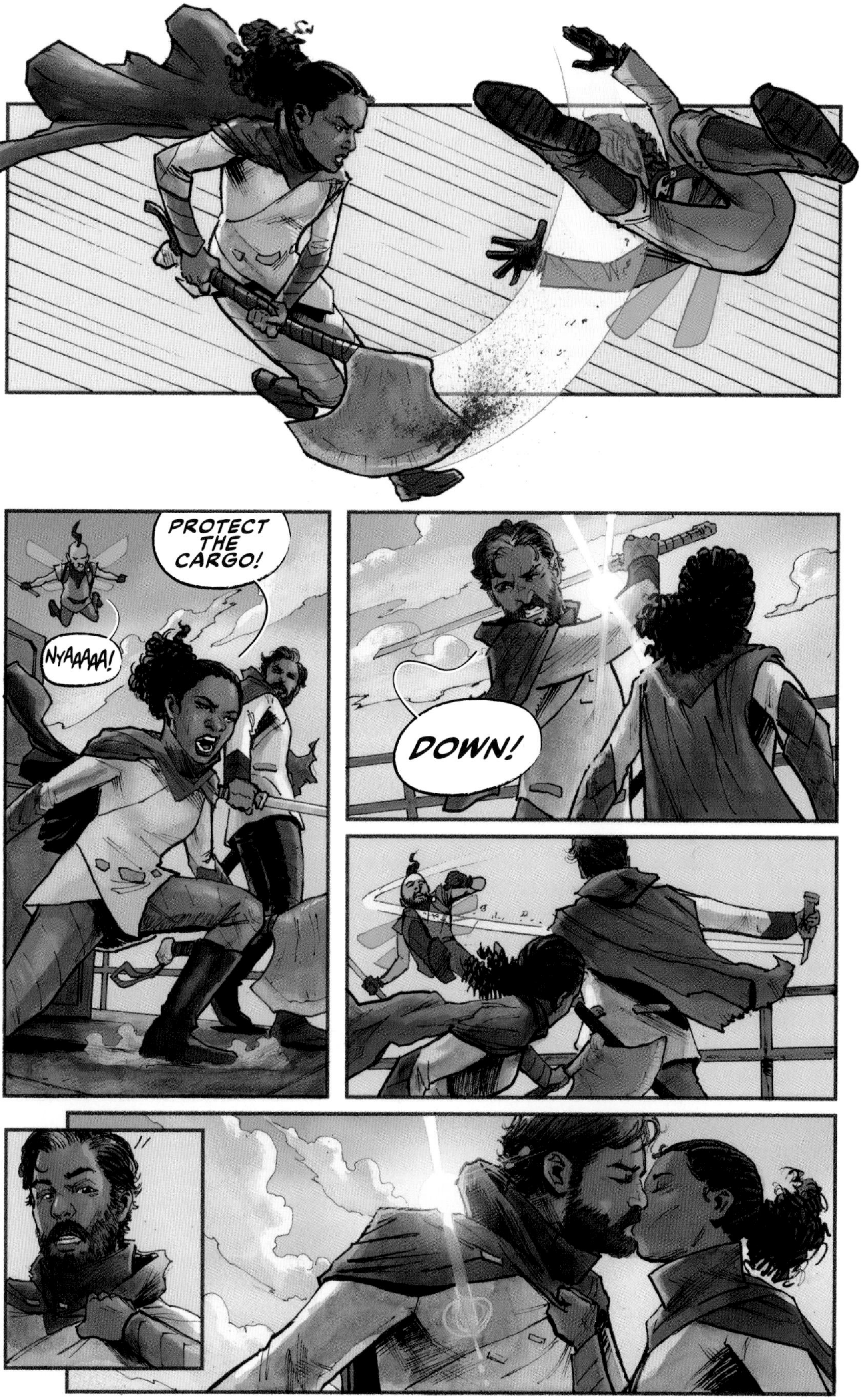
PROTECT THE CARGO!
NYAAAAA!
DOWN!

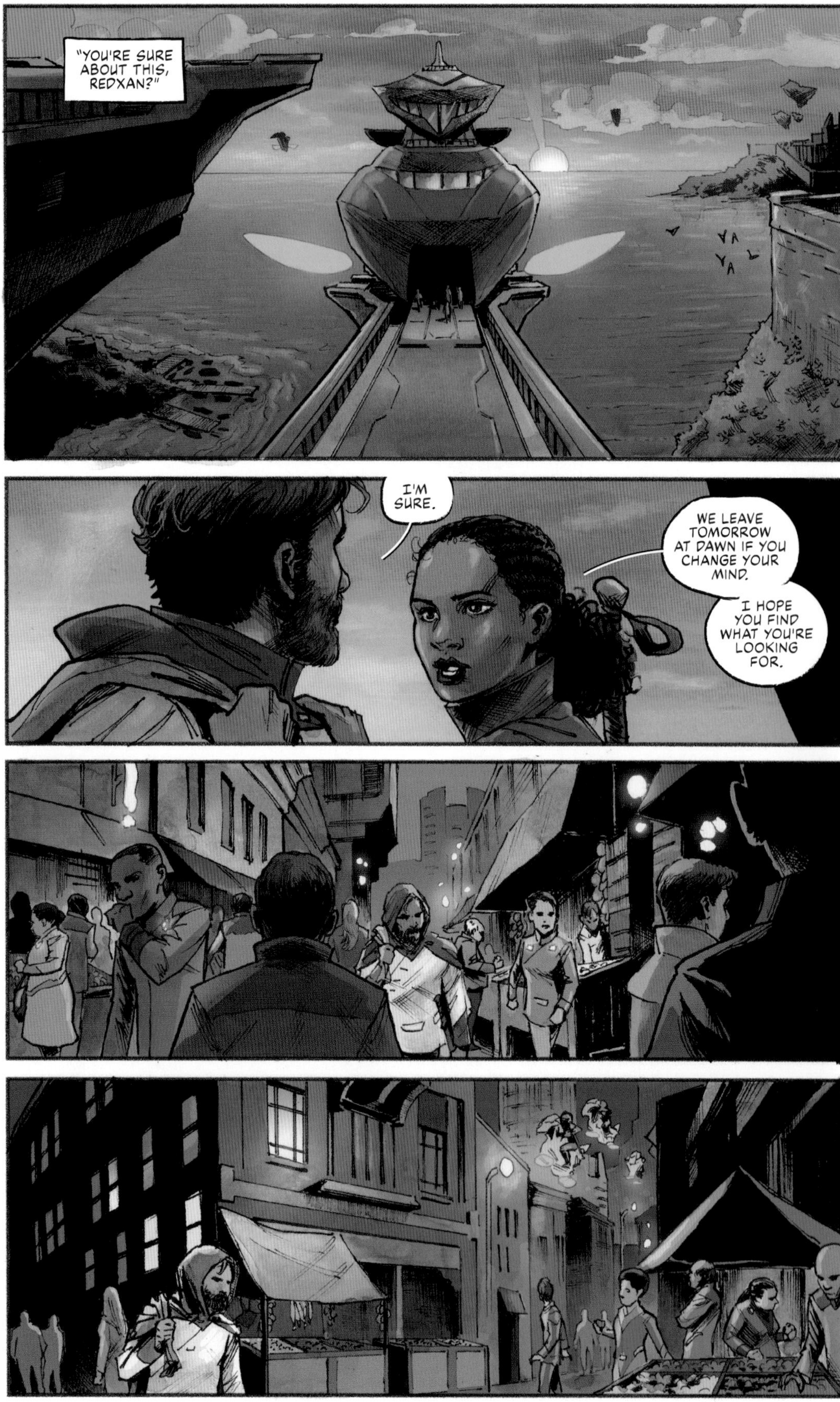
"YOU'RE SURE ABOUT THIS, REDXAN?"
I'M SURE.
WE LEAVE TOMORROW AT DAWN IF YOU CHANGE YOUR MIND.
I HOPE YOU FIND WHAT YOU'RE LOOKING FOR.

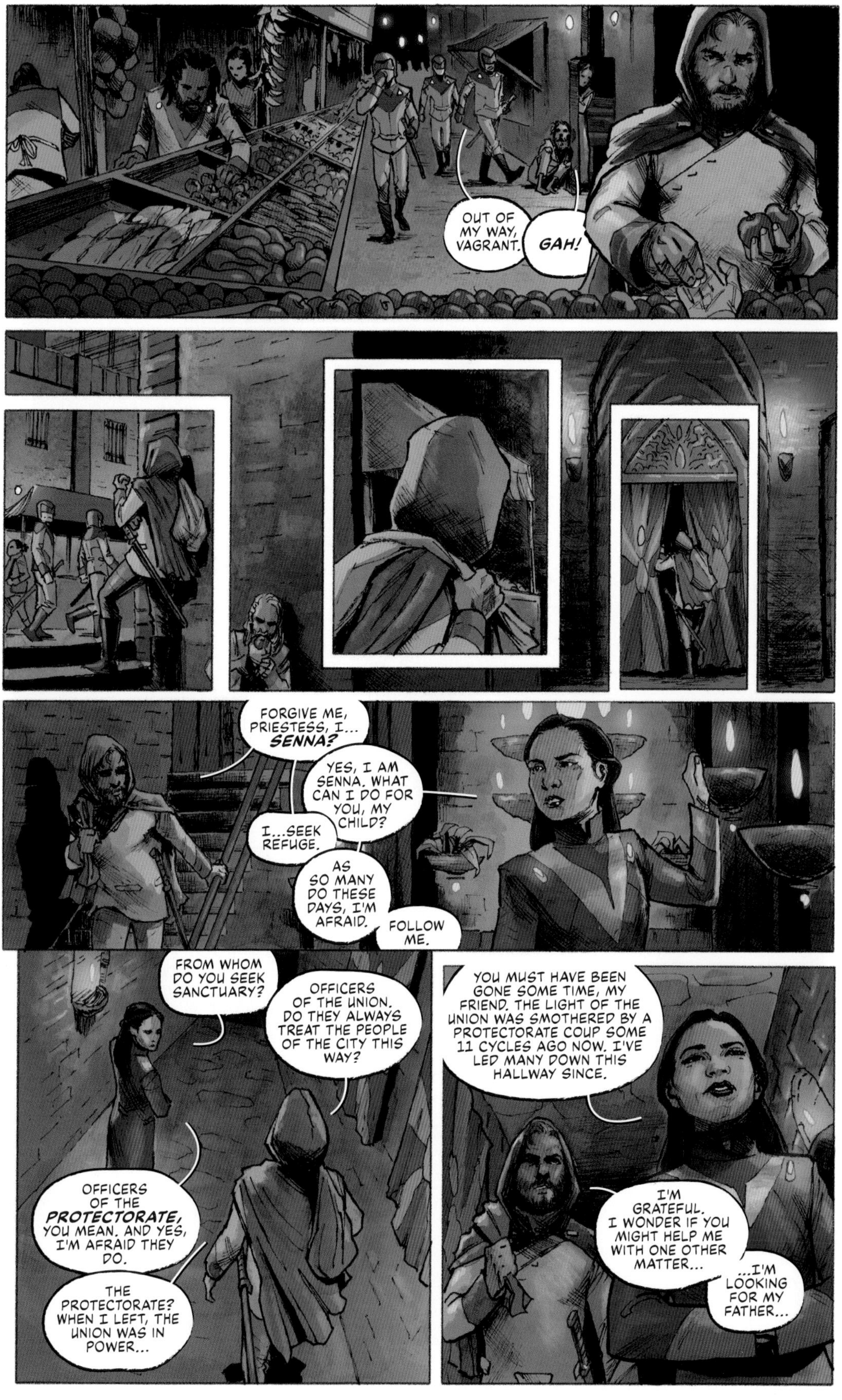
OUT OF MY WAY, VAGRANT.
GAH!
FORGIVE ME, PRIESTESS, I... SENNA?
YES, I AM SENNA. WHAT CAN I DO FOR YOU, MY CHILD?
I...SEEK REFUGE.
AS SO MANY DO THESE DAYS, I'M AFRAID.
FOLLOW ME.
FROM WHOM DO YOU SEEK SANCTUARY?
OFFICERS OF THE UNION. DO THEY ALWAYS TREAT THE PEOPLE OF THE CITY THIS WAY?
OFFICERS OF THE PROTECTORATE, YOU MEAN. AND YES, I'M AFRAID THEY DO.
THE PROTECTORATE? WHEN I LEFT, THE UNION WAS IN POWER...
YOU MUST HAVE BEEN GONE SOME TIME, MY FRIEND. THE LIGHT OF THE UNION WAS SMOTHERED BY A PROTECTORATE COUP SOME 11 CYCLES AGO NOW. I'VE LED MANY DOWN THIS HALLWAY SINCE.
I'M GRATEFUL. I WONDER IF YOU MIGHT HELP ME WITH ONE OTHER MATTER...
...I'M LOOKING FOR MY FATHER...

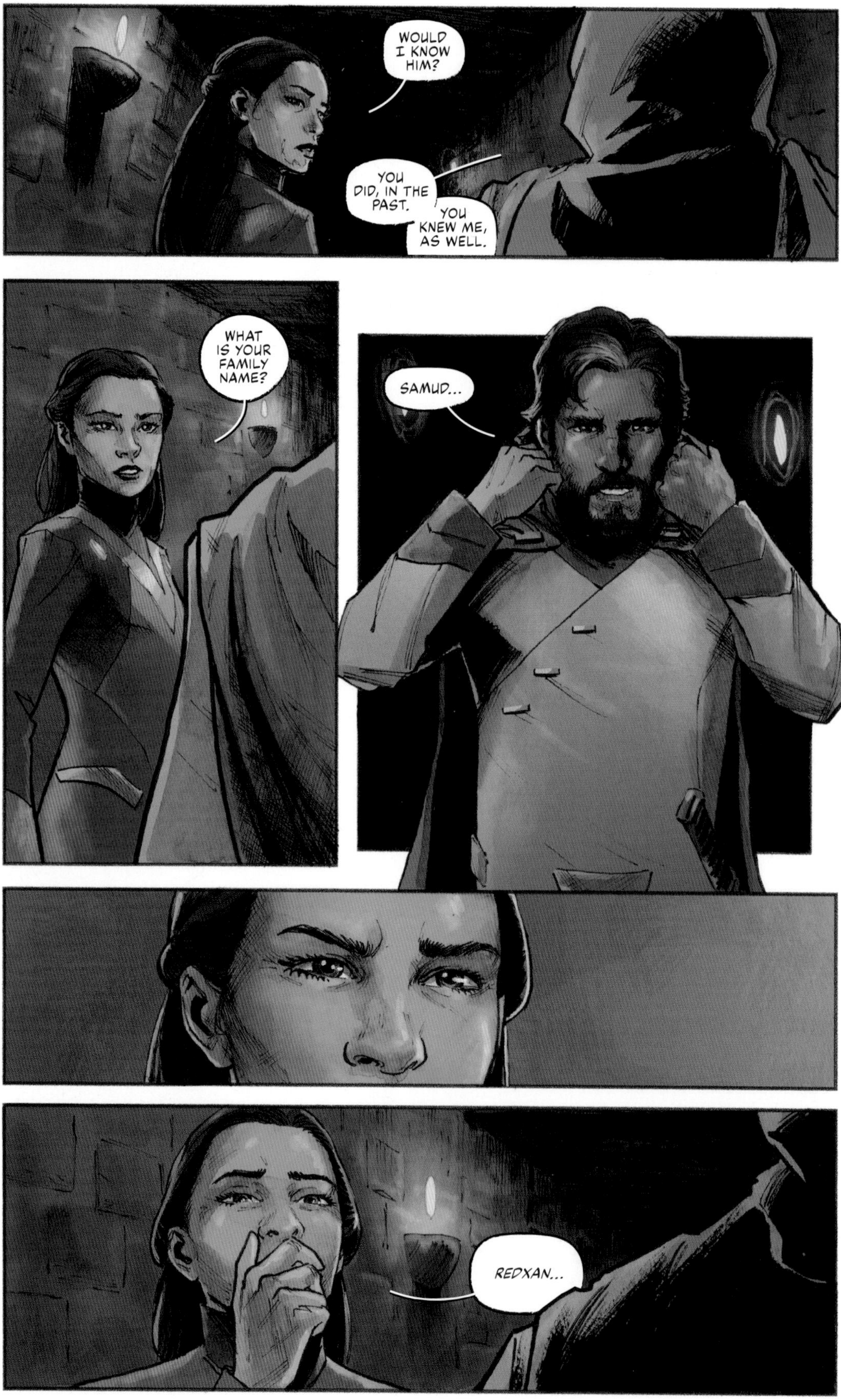
WOULD I KNOW HIM?
YOU DID, IN THE PAST.
YOU KNEW ME, AS WELL.
WHAT IS YOUR FAMILY NAME?
SAMUD...
REDXAN...

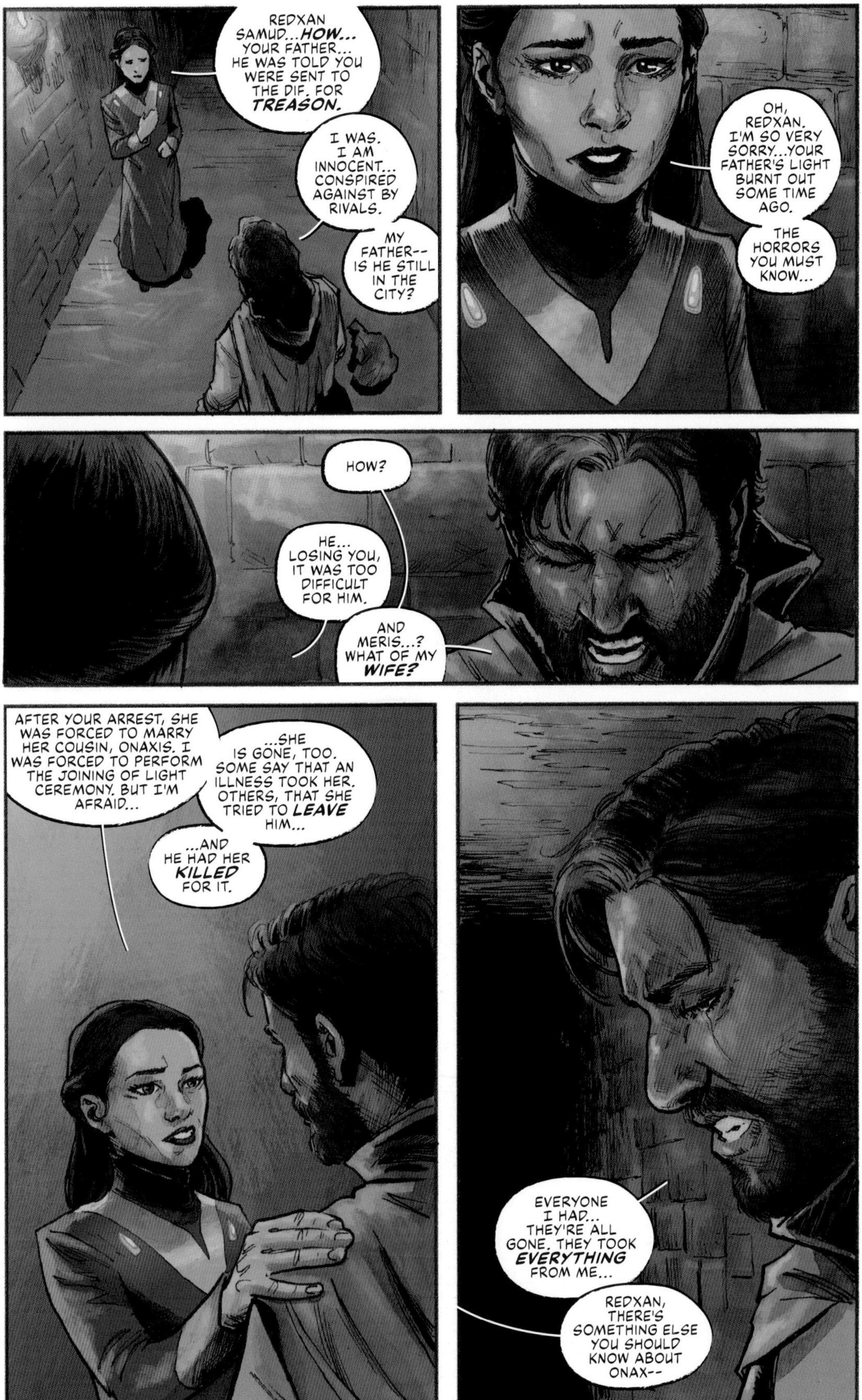
REDXAN SAMUD...HOW... YOUR FATHER... HE WAS TOLD YOU WERE SENT TO THE DIF. FOR TREASON.
I WAS. I AM INNOCENT... CONSPIRED AGAINST BY RIVALS.
MY FATHER-- IS HE STILL IN THE CITY?
OH, REDXAN. I'M SO VERY SORRY...YOUR FATHER'S LIGHT BURNT OUT SOME TIME AGO.
THE HORRORS YOU MUST KNOW...
HOW?
HE... LOSING YOU, IT WAS TOO DIFFICULT FOR HIM.
AND MERIS...? WHAT OF MY WIFE?
AFTER YOUR ARREST, SHE WAS FORCED TO MARRY HER COUSIN, ONAXIS. I WAS FORCED TO PERFORM THE JOINING OF LIGHT CEREMONY. BUT I'M AFRAID...
...SHE IS GONE, TOO. SOME SAY THAT AN ILLNESS TOOK HER. OTHERS, THAT SHE TRIED TO LEAVE HIM...
...AND HE HAD HER KILLED FOR IT.
EVERYONE I HAD... THEY'RE ALL GONE. THEY TOOK EVERYTHING FROM ME...
REDXAN, THERE'S SOMETHING ELSE YOU SHOULD KNOW ABOUT ONAX--

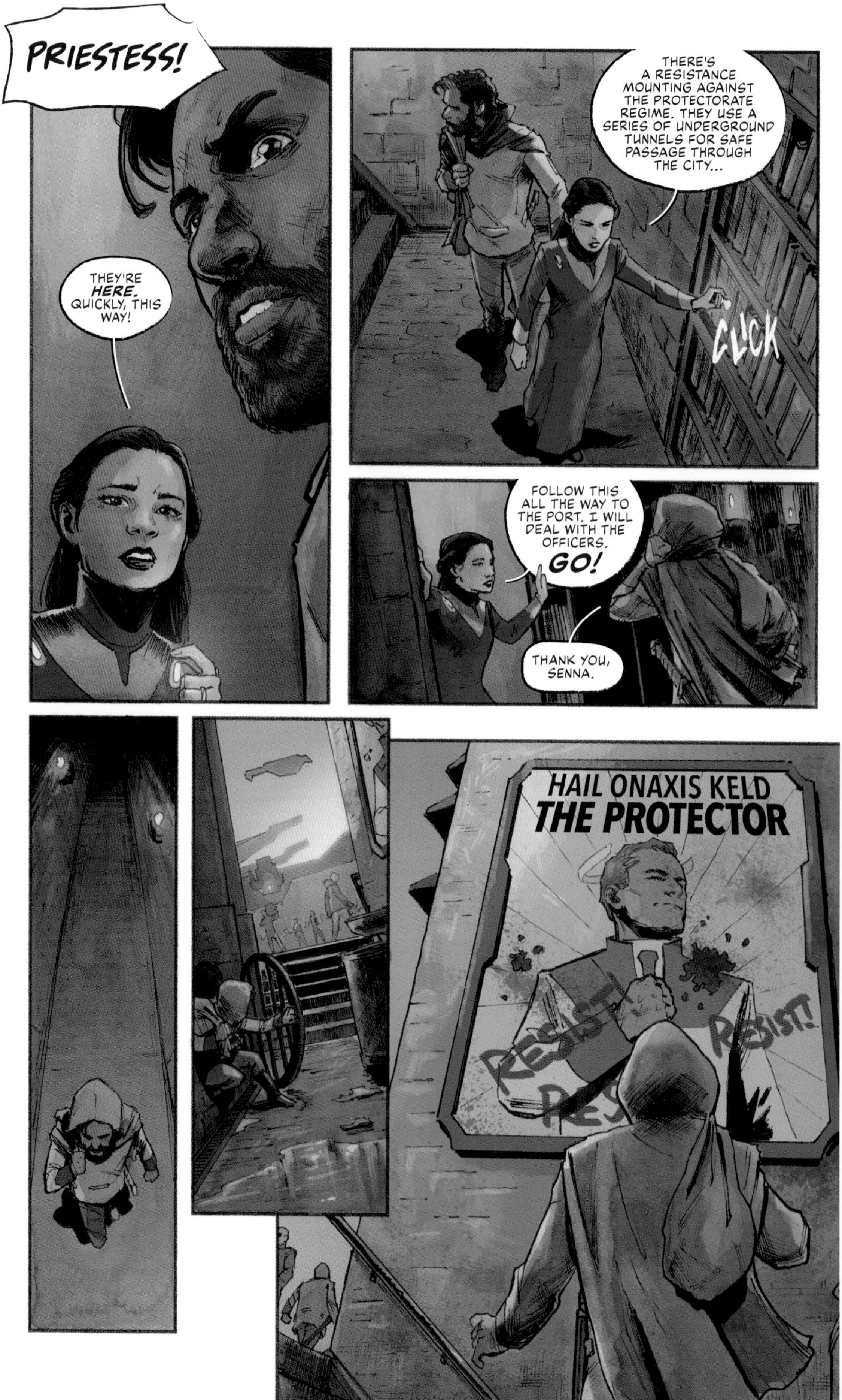
PRIESTESS!
THEY'RE HERE. QUICKLY, THIS WAY!
THERE'S A RESISTANCE MOUNTING AGAINST THE PROTECTORATE REGIME. THEY USE A SERIES OF UNDERGROUND TUNNELS FOR SAFE PASSAGE THROUGH THE CITY...
CLICK
FOLLOW THIS ALL THE WAY TO THE PORT. I WILL DEAL WITH THE OFFICERS. GO!
THANK YOU, SENNA.
HAIL ONAXIS KELD
THE PROTECTOR
RESIST!
RESIST!

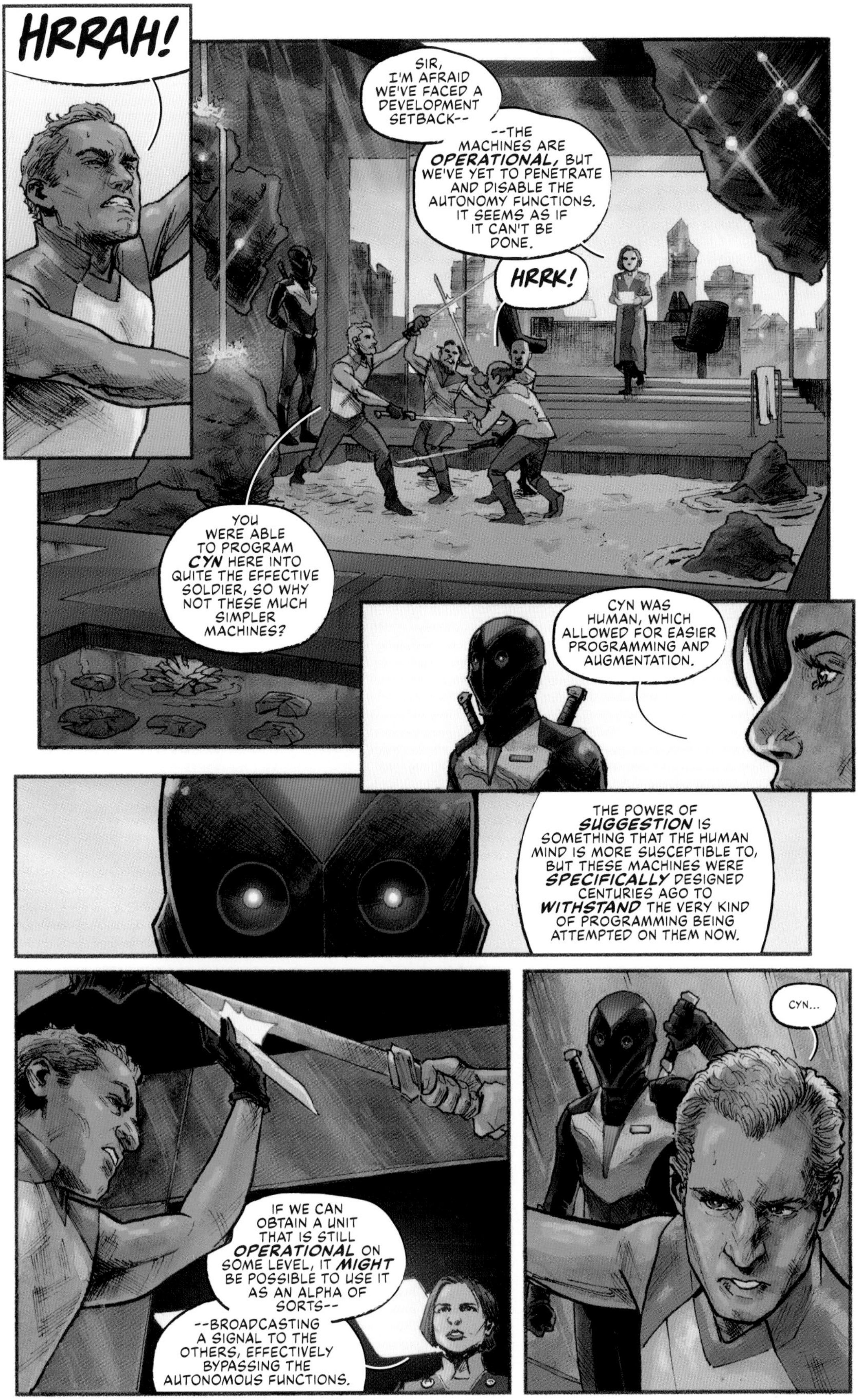
HRRAH!
SIR, I'M AFRAID WE'VE FACED A DEVELOPMENT SETBACK--
--THE MACHINES ARE OPERATIONAL, BUT WE'VE YET TO PENETRATE AND DISABLE THE AUTONOMY FUNCTIONS. IT SEEMS AS IF IT CAN'T BE DONE.
HRRK!
YOU WERE ABLE TO PROGRAM CYN HERE INTO QUITE THE EFFECTIVE SOLDIER, SO WHY NOT THESE MUCH SIMPLER MACHINES?
CYN WAS HUMAN, WHICH ALLOWED FOR EASIER PROGRAMMING AND AUGMENTATION.
THE POWER OF SUGGESTION IS SOMETHING THAT THE HUMAN MIND IS MORE SUSCEPTIBLE TO, BUT THESE MACHINES WERE SPECIFICALLY DESIGNED CENTURIES AGO TO WITHSTAND THE VERY KIND OF PROGRAMMING BEING ATTEMPTED ON THEM NOW.
IF WE CAN OBTAIN A UNIT THAT IS STILL OPERATIONAL ON SOME LEVEL, IT MIGHT BE POSSIBLE TO USE IT AS AN ALPHA OF SORTS--
--BROADCASTING A SIGNAL TO THE OTHERS, EFFECTIVELY BYPASSING THE AUTONOMOUS FUNCTIONS.
CYN...

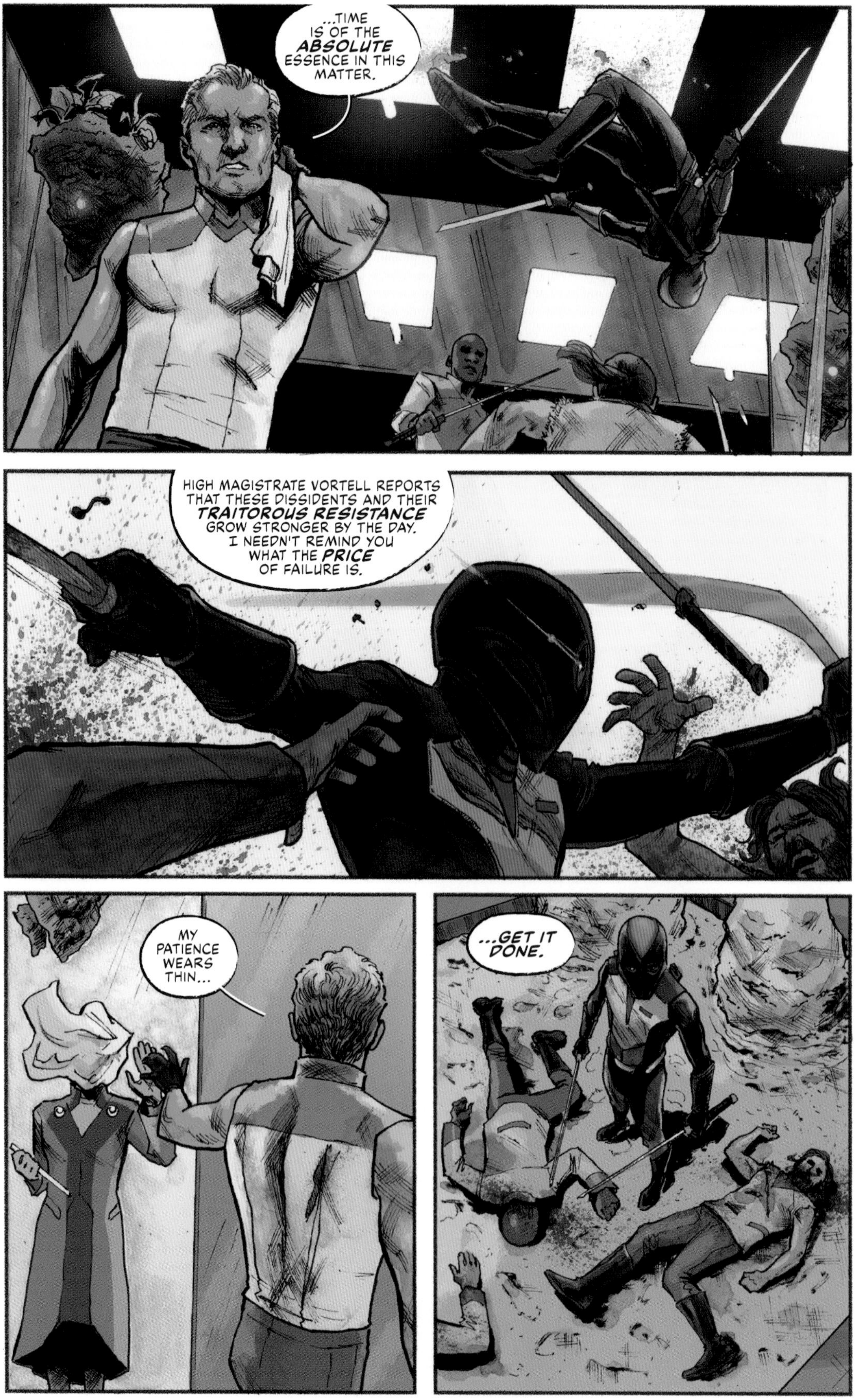
...TIME IS OF THE ABSOLUTE ESSENCE IN THIS MATTER.
HIGH MAGISTRATE VORTELL REPORTS THAT THESE DISSIDENTS AND THEIR TRAITOROUS RESISTANCE GROW STRONGER BY THE DAY. I NEEDN'T REMIND YOU WHAT THE PRICE OF FAILURE IS.
MY PATIENCE WEARS THIN...
...GET IT DONE.

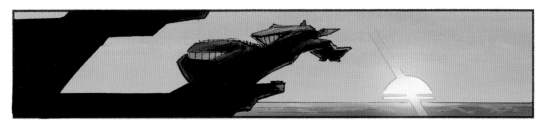

SHALL WE WAIT A LITTLE LONGER, CAPTAIN?

...

NO. ENGAGE THE THRUSTERS.

WE BRINGING THE PIRATE VESSEL AS WELL?

FOR NOW. SHOULD GET A FEW CREDITS FOR IT, ANYWAY.

DID YOU FIND WHAT YOU WERE LOOKING FOR?

THEY'RE GONE. MY FAMILY...

...DEAD.

THEN FORGET THIS PLACE. COME *WITH* US.

SAIL THE WORLD BY MY SIDE. THERE'S NOTHING *LEFT* FOR YOU *HERE*, REDXAN.

THERE *IS* ONE THING LEFT FOR ME...

...*MY REVENGE.*

53

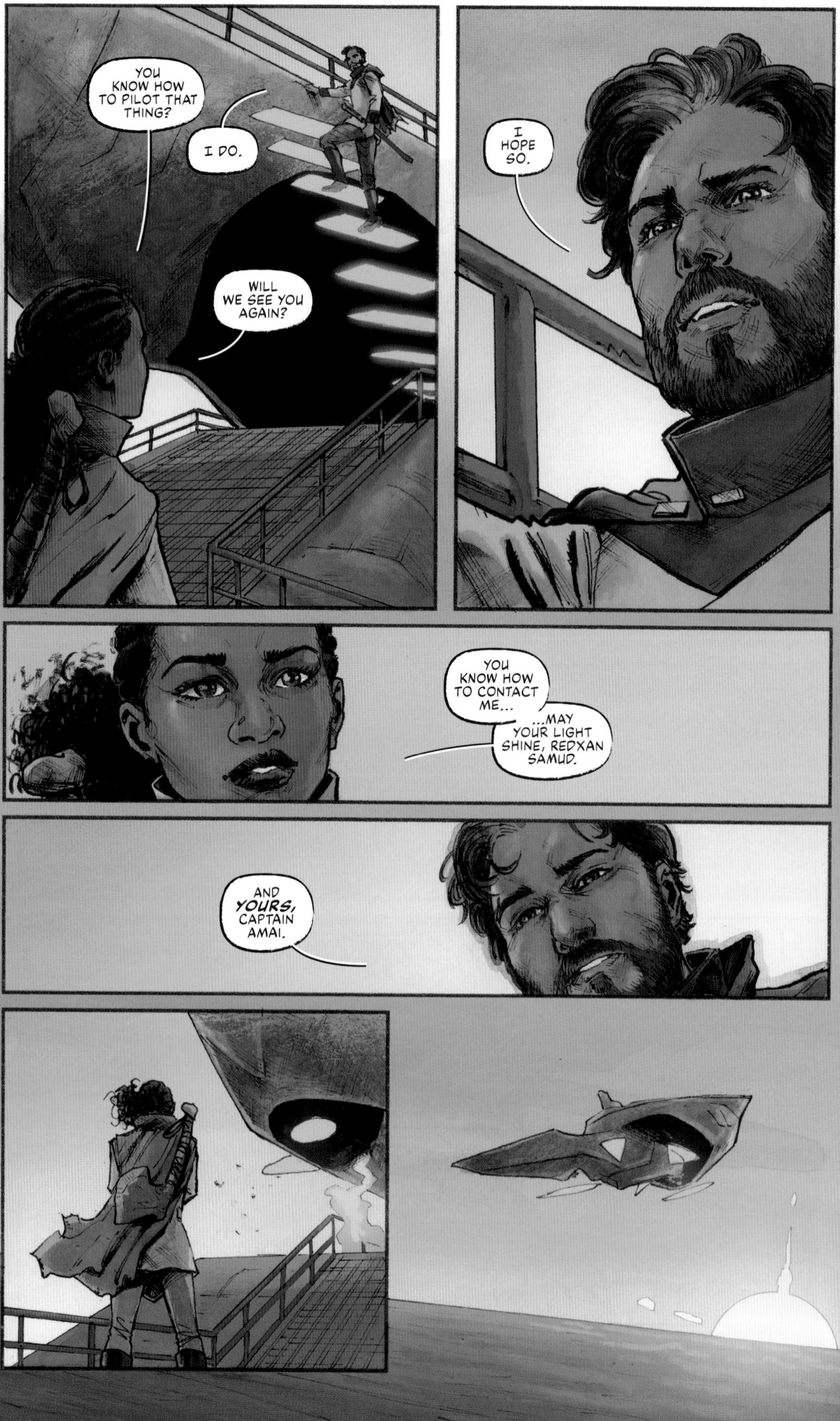
YOU KNOW HOW TO PILOT THAT THING?
I DO.
WILL WE SEE YOU AGAIN?
I HOPE SO.
YOU KNOW HOW TO CONTACT ME...
...MAY YOUR LIGHT SHINE, REDXAN SAMUD.
AND *YOURS*, CAPTAIN AMAI.

Revenge is a confession of pain.
—Latin Proverb

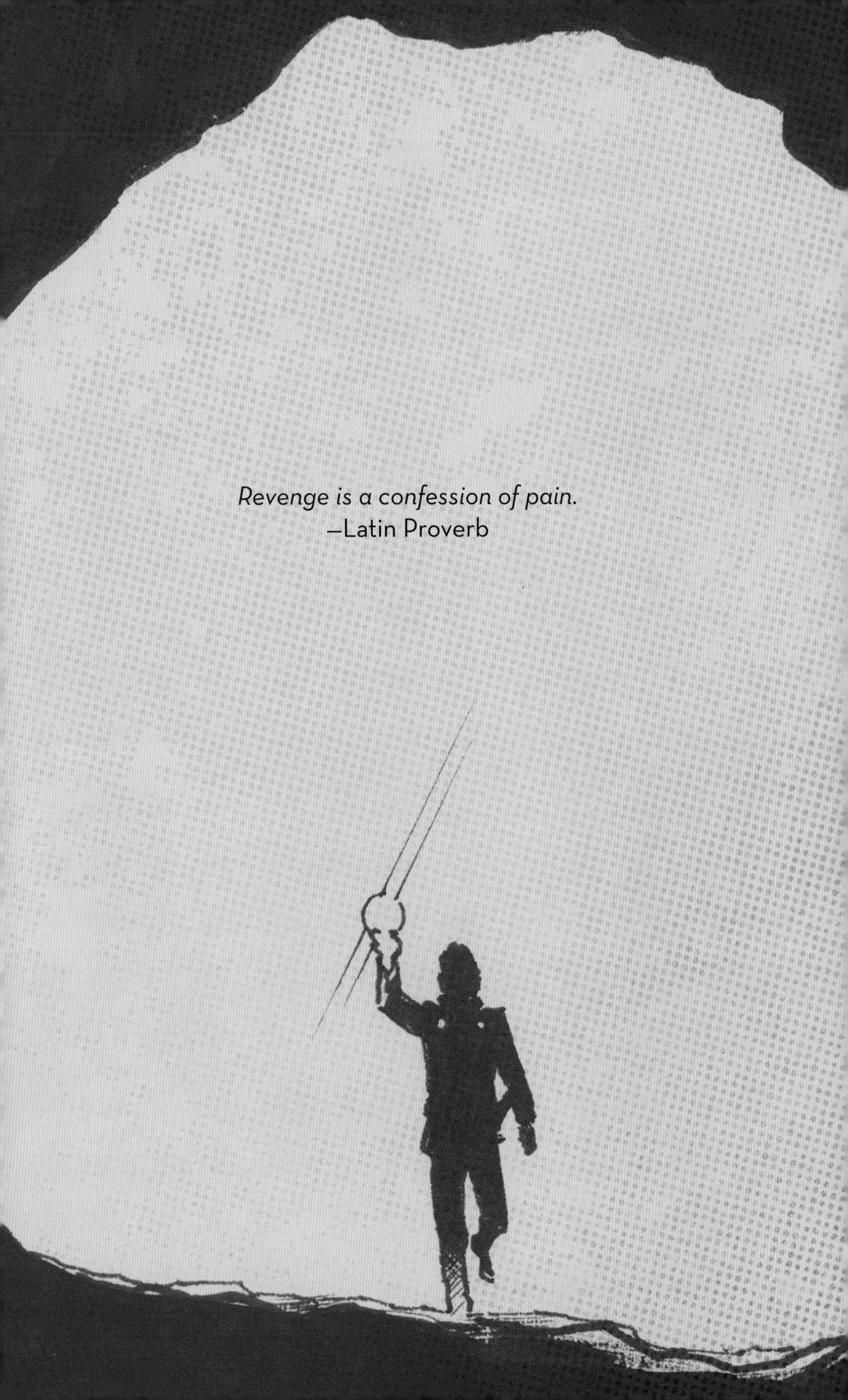

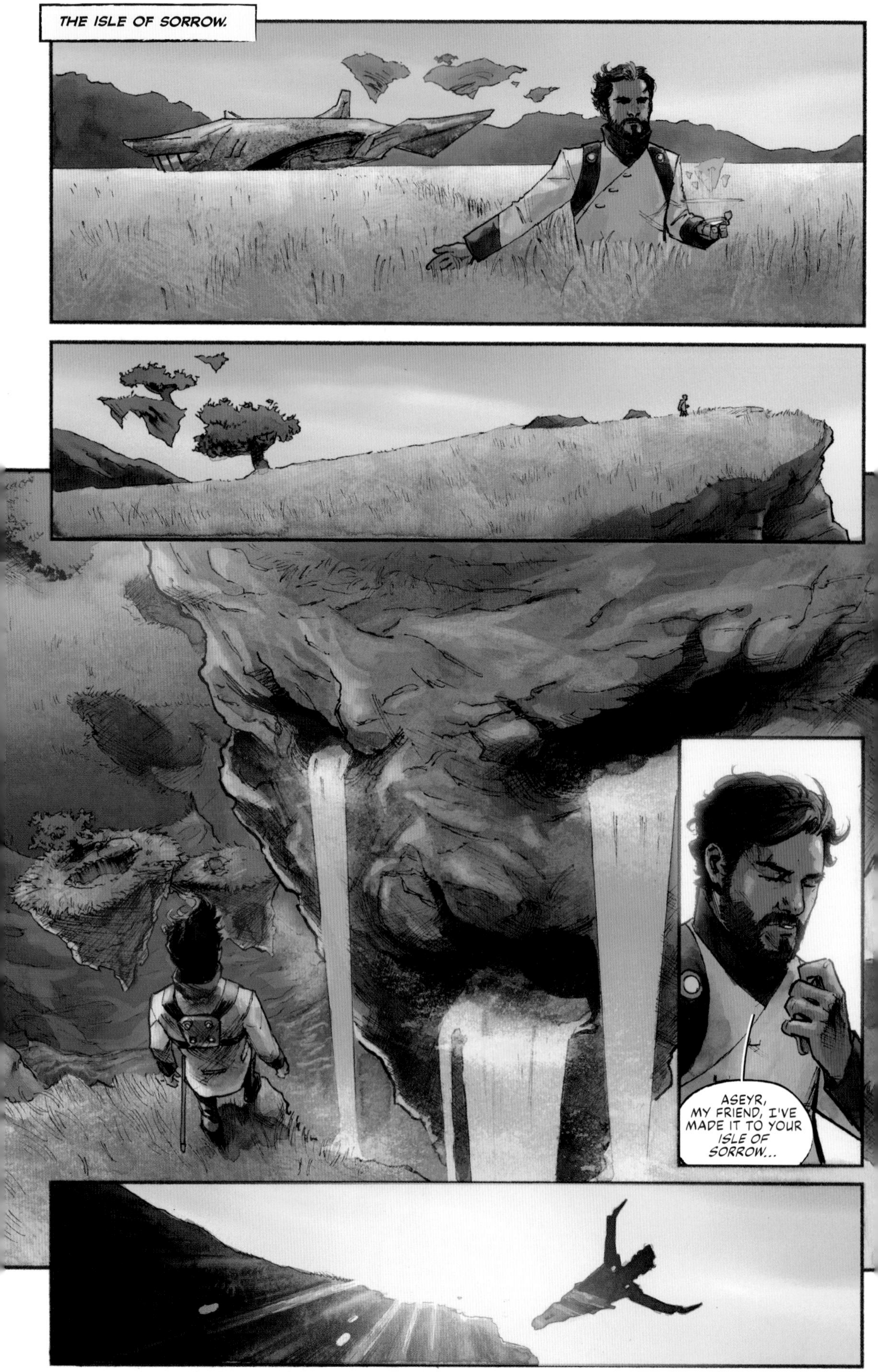
THE ISLE OF SORROW.
ASEYR, MY FRIEND, I'VE MADE IT TO YOUR ISLE OF SORROW...

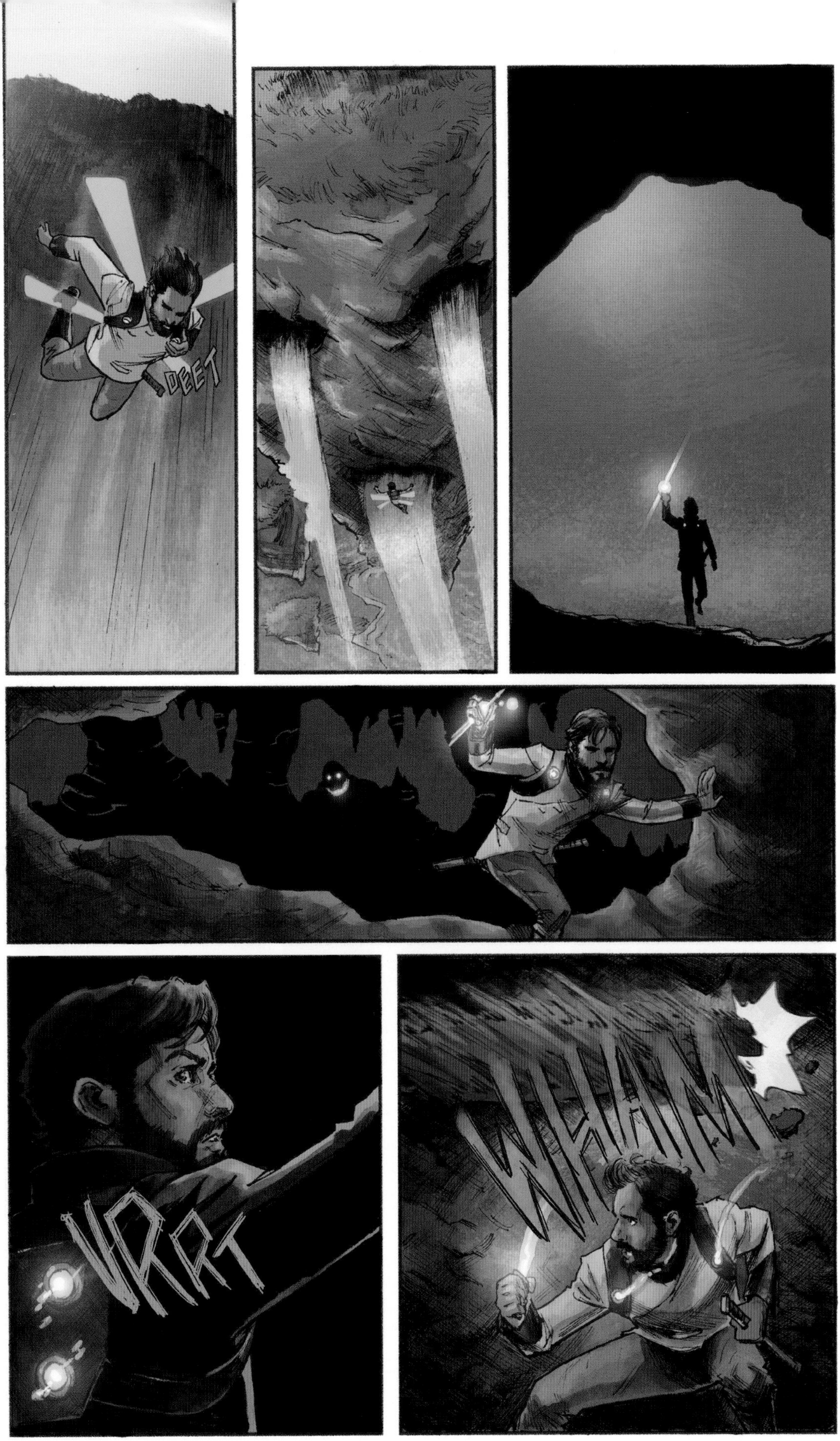
DEET
VRRT
WHAM

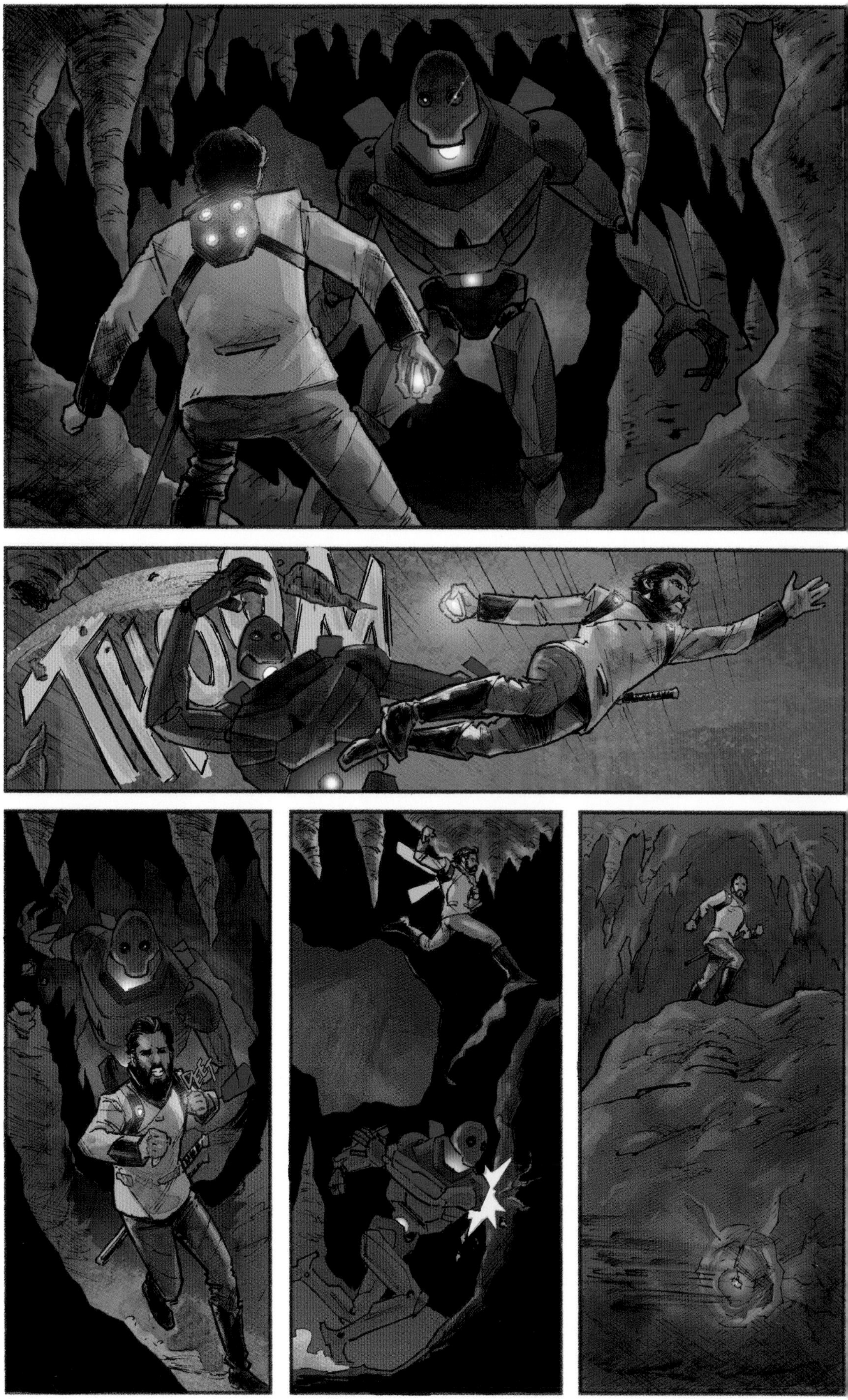
THOOM

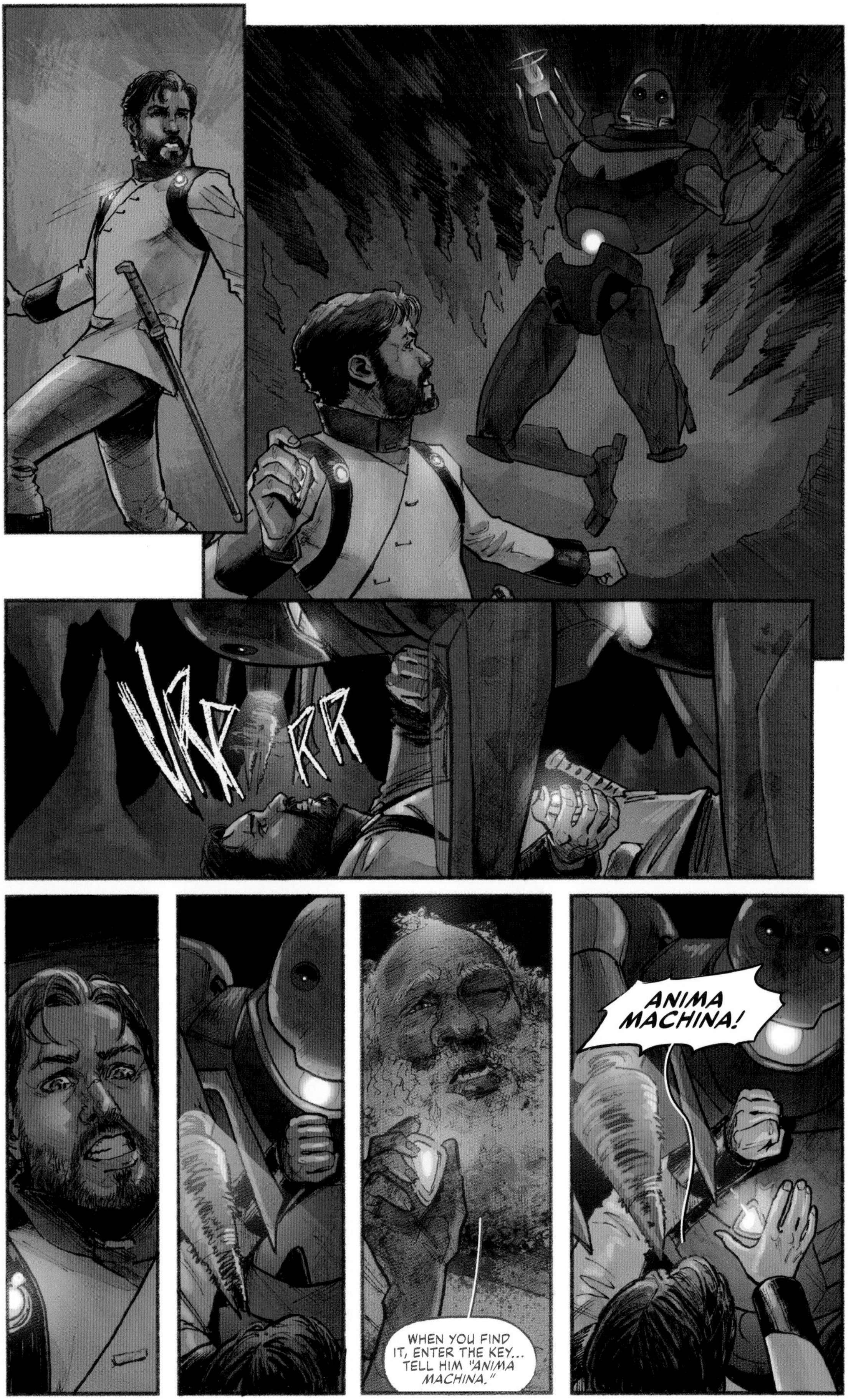
VRRRRR
WHEN YOU FIND IT, ENTER THE KEY... TELL HIM "ANIMA MACHINA."
ANIMA MACHINA!

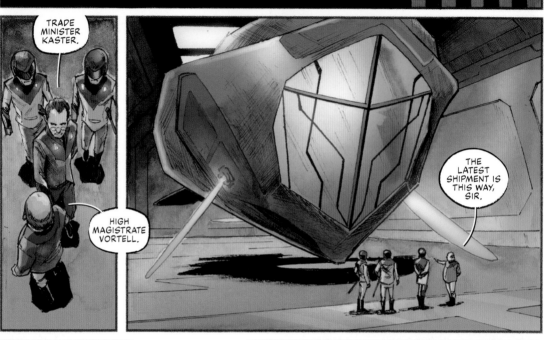

TRADE MINISTER KASTER.

HIGH MAGISTRATE VORTELL.

THE LATEST SHIPMENT IS THIS WAY, SIR.

I TRUST THERE WERE NO PROBLEMS GETTING THE *ITEMS* INTO PORT?

NO, SIR. YOUR MEN IN THE FIRST GUARD KNEW TO LOOK THE OTHER WAY AND DEAL WITH ANYONE WHO WAS OVERLY INQUISITIVE.

AND THE LABORERS?

BURIED IN THE VERY HOLES THEY DUG THESE MACHINES OUT OF, SIR.

AS ORDERED.

I DON'T REQUIRE THE GRIM DETAILS, MINISTER. JUST CONFIRMATION OF A JOB DONE, THANK YOU.

VERY GOOD, THEN. PROTECTOR KELD WILL BE *PLEASED...*

"...PERHAPS WE'VE FOUND THE RIGHT SPECIMEN THIS TIME."

HELLO.

...s-STAY BACK!

MY APOLOGIES. I WAS IN DEFENSE PROTOCOL. YOU HAVE SPOKEN THE PASSPHRASE AND ENGAGED MY DEFAULT MODE.

I AM AN **AUTOMATON RETAINER UNIT.** YOU MAY CALL ME ARU. I AM AT YOUR SERVICE.

W-WHAT **ARE YOU?**

THAT'S CORRECT: A-R-U. ARU. I BELIEVE I AM THE LAST OF MY KIND FROM A LONG-BYGONE ERA. I WAS RESURRECTED BY MY MASTER, ASEYR, FOR WHOM I SERVED AS RETAINER.

HE CHARGED ME WITH PROTECTING THIS CAVE AND ITS CONTENTS FOR THE LAST 25 CYCLES.

YOU'VE BEEN IN **HERE** FOR 25 CYCLES?

YES.

YOU POSSESS ASEYR'S KEY AND PASSPHRASE. THESE CIRCUMSTANCES, COUPLED WITH HIS ABSENCE AND THE MANY CYCLES PASSED, SEEM TO CONVERGE ON THE PROBABLE OUTCOME THAT MASTER ASEYR HAS PERISHED.

I'M AFRAID HE HAS...

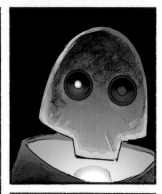

I SEE...

HE WAS YOUR FRIEND.

HE WAS. MY **ONLY** FRIEND, IN FACT. FOR A VERY LONG TIME. WE WERE MEANT TO COME HERE TOGETHER.

WHAT DOES IT **MEAN**, *ANIMA MACHINA?*

ITS APPROXIMATE TRANSLATION IS "SOUL OF THE MACHINE." MY KIND WAS ERADICATED 200 CYCLES AGO FOR FEAR OF WHAT WE MIGHT BECOME--WEAPONS FOR EVIL MEN. ASEYR BELIEVED ME CAPABLE OF MORE.

PROVIDING YOU WITH KNOWLEDGE OF THIS LOCATION AND MY PASSPHRASE WOULD INDICATE HIS BELIEF IN YOU, AS WELL.

SO YOU ARE TO BE **MY** RETAINER NOW?

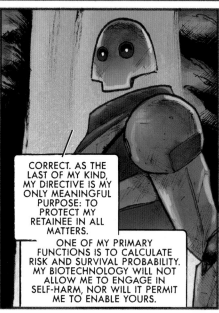

CORRECT. AS THE LAST OF MY KIND, MY DIRECTIVE IS MY ONLY MEANINGFUL PURPOSE: TO PROTECT MY RETAINEE IN ALL MATTERS.

ONE OF MY PRIMARY FUNCTIONS IS TO CALCULATE RISK AND SURVIVAL PROBABILITY. MY BIOTECHNOLOGY WILL NOT ALLOW ME TO ENGAGE IN SELF-HARM, NOR WILL IT PERMIT ME TO ENABLE YOURS.

VERY WELL, THEN.

ASEYR SENT ME HERE TO COLLECT A HIDDEN TREASURE-- A FORTUNE OF CREDITS HE STOLE FOR THE UNION...

YES. THE CREDITS ARE HERE, ON THIS CHIP. AS ASEYR SAID TO ME WHEN HE LEFT IT IN MY CHARGE: *"YOU NOW COMMAND AN UNIMAGINABLE AMOUNT OF WEALTH."*

...

WHAT'S THAT NEXT TO IT?

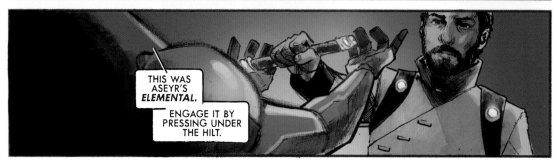

THIS WAS ASEYR'S *ELEMENTAL.*

ENGAGE IT BY PRESSING UNDER THE HILT.

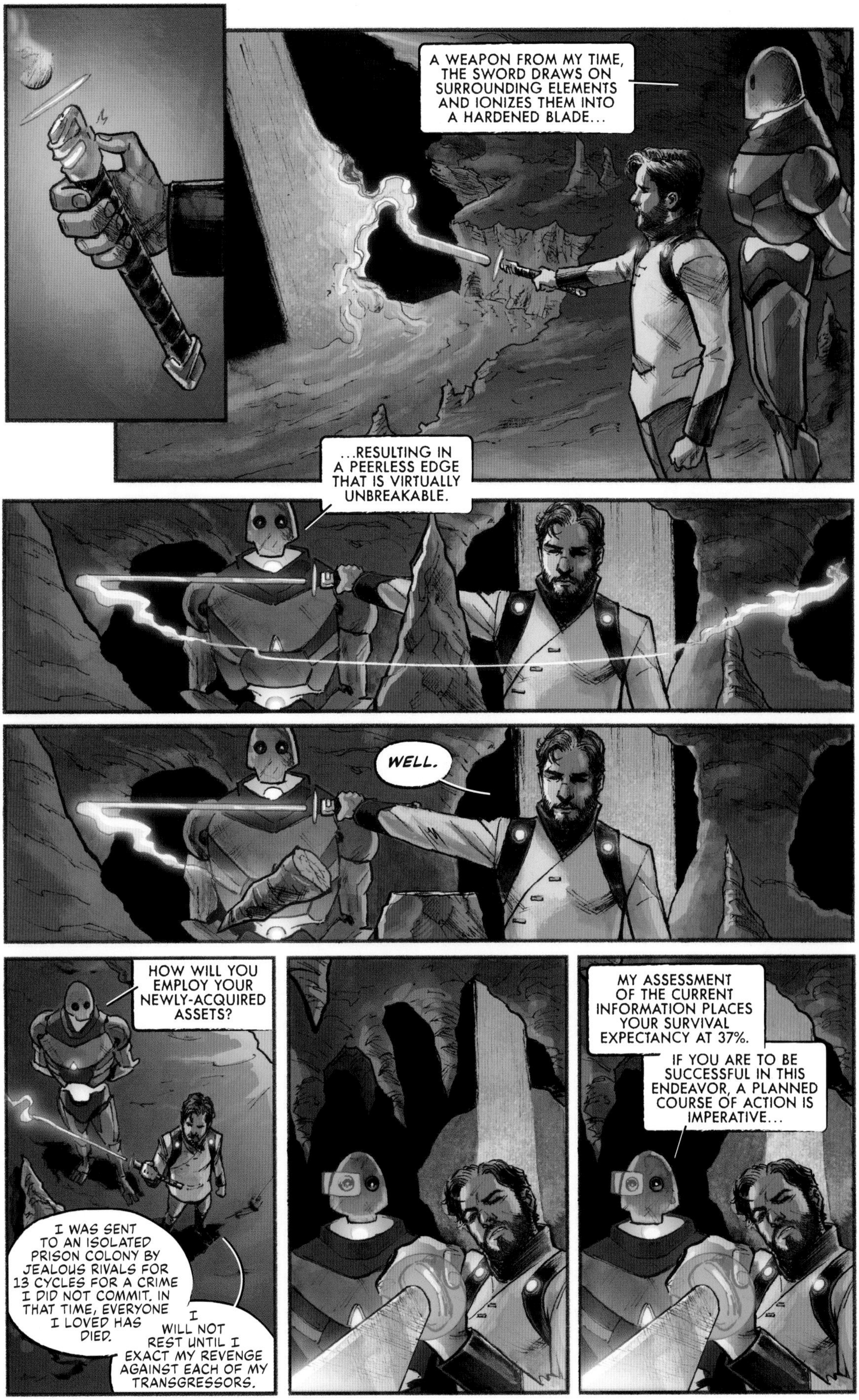
A WEAPON FROM MY TIME, THE SWORD DRAWS ON SURROUNDING ELEMENTS AND IONIZES THEM INTO A HARDENED BLADE...
...RESULTING IN A PEERLESS EDGE THAT IS VIRTUALLY UNBREAKABLE.
WELL.
HOW WILL YOU EMPLOY YOUR NEWLY-ACQUIRED ASSETS?
I WAS SENT TO AN ISOLATED PRISON COLONY BY JEALOUS RIVALS FOR 13 CYCLES FOR A CRIME I DID NOT COMMIT. IN THAT TIME, EVERYONE I LOVED HAS DIED.
I WILL NOT REST UNTIL I EXACT MY REVENGE AGAINST EACH OF MY TRANSGRESSORS.
MY ASSESSMENT OF THE CURRENT INFORMATION PLACES YOUR SURVIVAL EXPECTANCY AT 37%.
IF YOU ARE TO BE SUCCESSFUL IN THIS ENDEAVOR, A PLANNED COURSE OF ACTION IS IMPERATIVE...

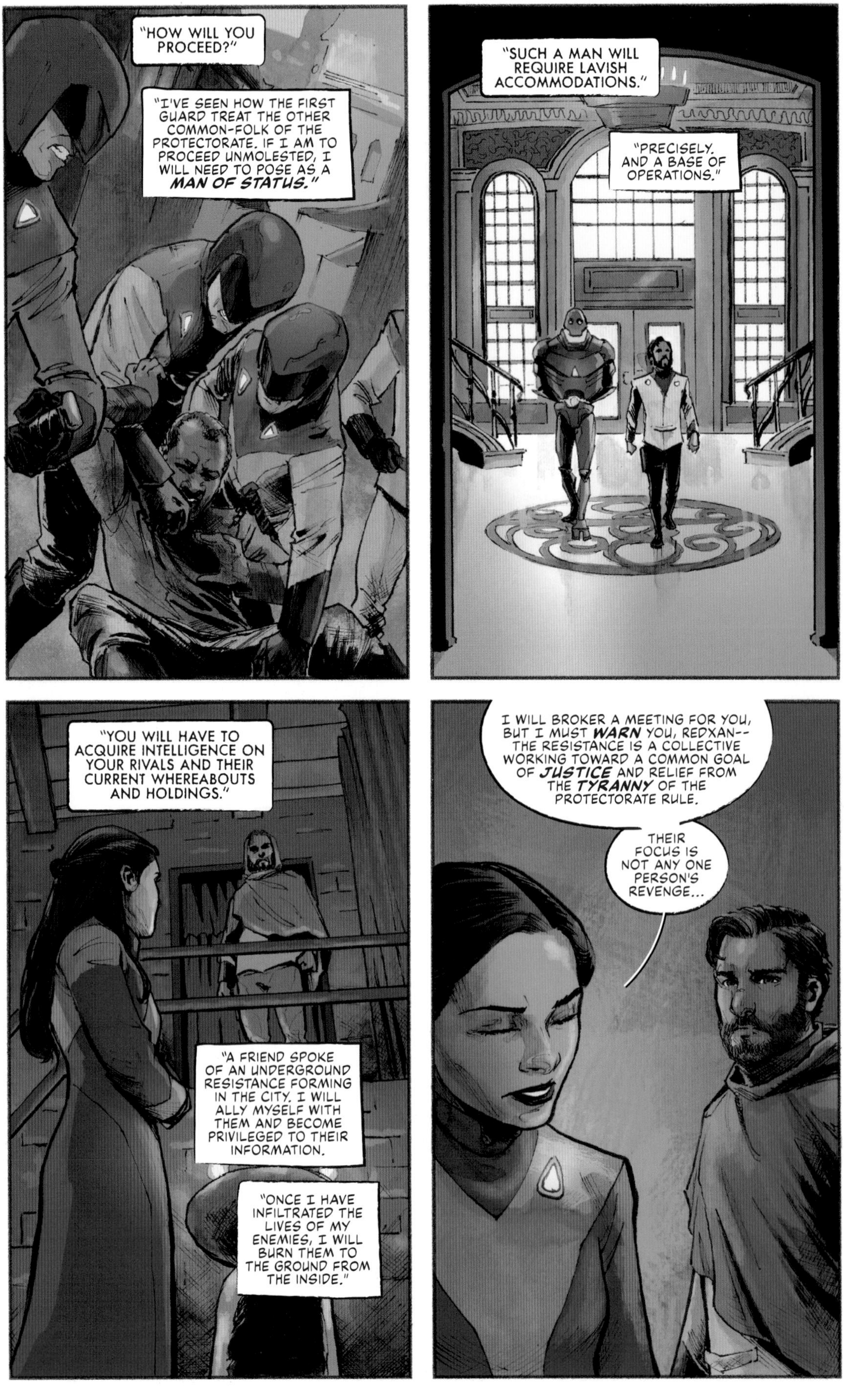
"HOW WILL YOU PROCEED?"
"I'VE SEEN HOW THE FIRST GUARD TREAT THE OTHER COMMON-FOLK OF THE PROTECTORATE. IF I AM TO PROCEED UNMOLESTED, I WILL NEED TO POSE AS A MAN OF STATUS."
"SUCH A MAN WILL REQUIRE LAVISH ACCOMMODATIONS."
"PRECISELY. AND A BASE OF OPERATIONS."
"YOU WILL HAVE TO ACQUIRE INTELLIGENCE ON YOUR RIVALS AND THEIR CURRENT WHEREABOUTS AND HOLDINGS."
"A FRIEND SPOKE OF AN UNDERGROUND RESISTANCE FORMING IN THE CITY. I WILL ALLY MYSELF WITH THEM AND BECOME PRIVILEGED TO THEIR INFORMATION.
"ONCE I HAVE INFILTRATED THE LIVES OF MY ENEMIES, I WILL BURN THEM TO THE GROUND FROM THE INSIDE."
I WILL BROKER A MEETING FOR YOU, BUT I MUST WARN YOU, REDXAN-- THE RESISTANCE IS A COLLECTIVE WORKING TOWARD A COMMON GOAL OF JUSTICE AND RELIEF FROM THE TYRANNY OF THE PROTECTORATE RULE.
THEIR FOCUS IS NOT ANY ONE PERSON'S REVENGE...

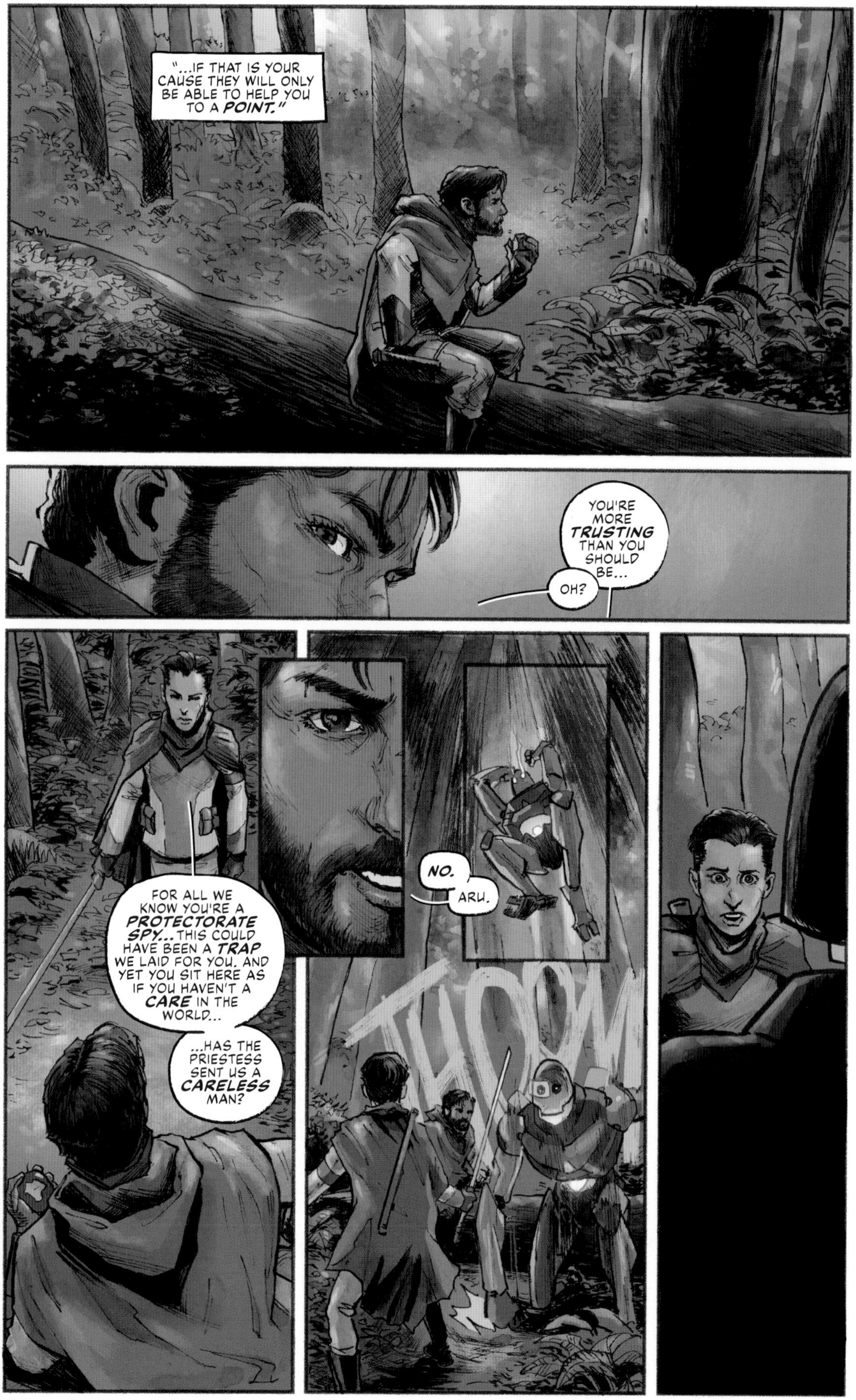

"...IF THAT IS YOUR CAUSE THEY WILL ONLY BE ABLE TO HELP YOU TO A POINT."
YOU'RE MORE TRUSTING THAN YOU SHOULD BE...
OH?
FOR ALL WE KNOW YOU'RE A PROTECTORATE SPY... THIS COULD HAVE BEEN A TRAP WE LAID FOR YOU. AND YET YOU SIT HERE AS IF YOU HAVEN'T A CARE IN THE WORLD...
...HAS THE PRIESTESS SENT US A CARELESS MAN?
NO.
ARU.
THOOM

UPHEAVE...

CLEARLY WE ALL CARE VERY MUCH. STAND DOWN, ARU.

HELLO. I AM AN AUTOMATON RETAIN--

I DON'T HAVE TIME FOR UNDERLINGS. WHERE IS YOUR LEADER?

BECAUSE YOU'RE HERE. WHAT IS YOUR NAME?

HOW DO YOU KNOW THAT *I'M* NOT THE LEADER?

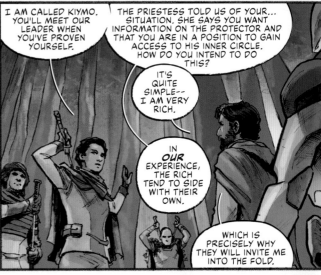

I AM CALLED KIYMO. YOU'LL MEET OUR LEADER WHEN YOU'VE PROVEN YOURSELF.

THE PRIESTESS TOLD US OF YOUR... SITUATION. SHE SAYS YOU WANT INFORMATION ON THE PROTECTOR AND THAT YOU ARE IN A POSITION TO GAIN ACCESS TO HIS INNER CIRCLE. HOW DO YOU INTEND TO DO THIS?

IT'S QUITE SIMPLE-- I AM VERY RICH.

IN *OUR* EXPERIENCE, THE RICH TEND TO SIDE WITH THEIR OWN.

WHICH IS PRECISELY WHY THEY WILL INVITE ME INTO THE FOLD.

VERY WELL...THE PROTECTOR IS PLANNING SOMETHING. *WHAT*, WE DON'T KNOW EXACTLY, BUT THE SCALE IS LARGE. OUR SPIES HAVE LEARNED THAT HIS TRADE MINISTER KASTER IS SMUGGLING IN SOME KIND OF SECRET WEAPON.

BUT EVERYONE THAT WE MANAGE TO SEND ON ONE OF HIS SMUGGLING RUNS DOESN'T COME BACK.

KASTER IS TRADE MINISTER?

YOU KNOW HIM?

...

I WILL FIND OUT WHAT THAT OLD DRUNK IS SMUGGLING AND REMOVE HIM FROM THE EQUATION. SEND SOME OF YOUR SPIES ALONG IF YOU LIKE...

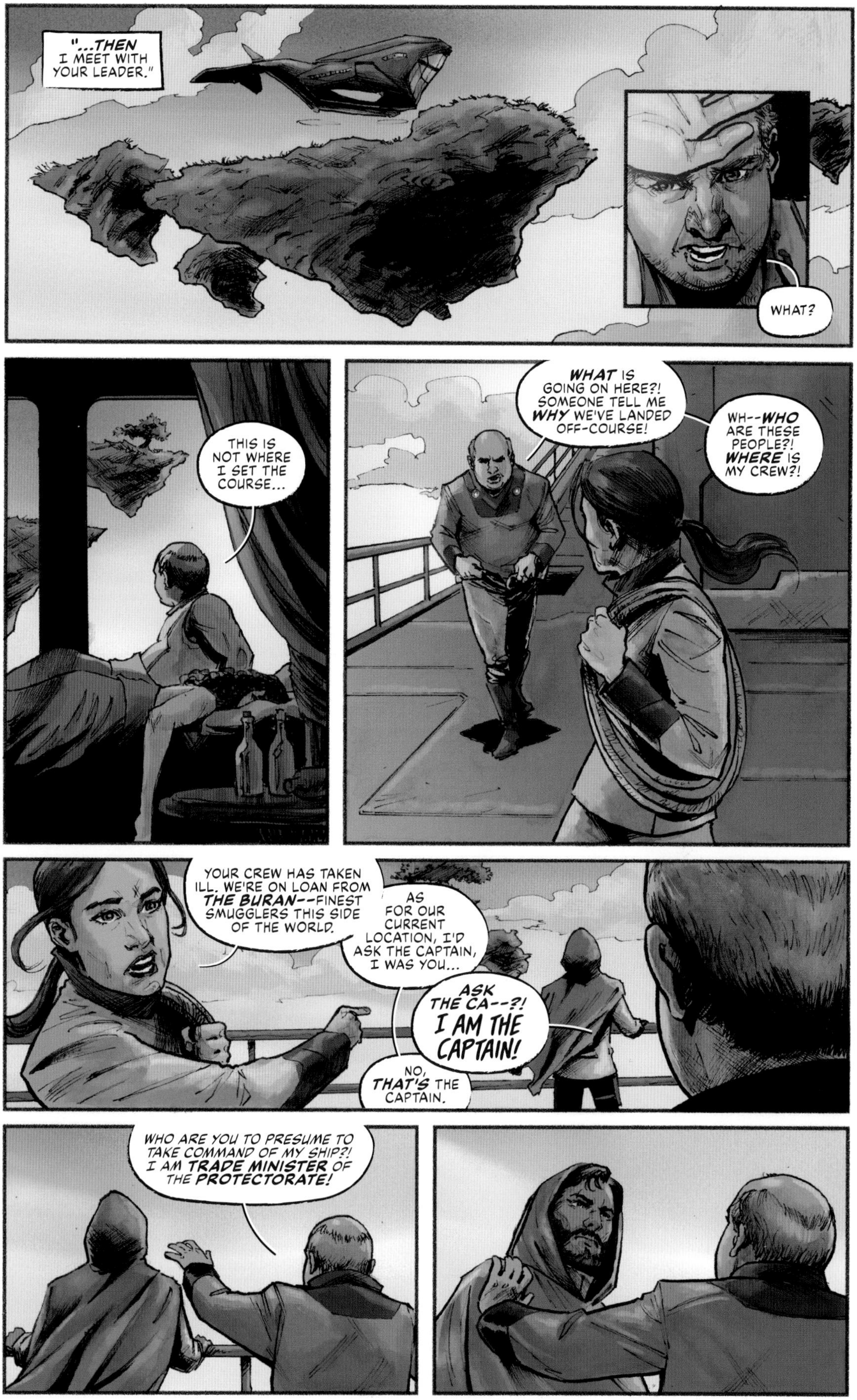
"...THEN I MEET WITH YOUR LEADER."
WHAT?
THIS IS NOT WHERE I SET THE COURSE...
WHAT IS GOING ON HERE?! SOMEONE TELL ME WHY WE'VE LANDED OFF-COURSE!
WH--WHO ARE THESE PEOPLE?! WHERE IS MY CREW?!
YOUR CREW HAS TAKEN ILL. WE'RE ON LOAN FROM THE BURAN--FINEST SMUGGLERS THIS SIDE OF THE WORLD.
AS FOR OUR CURRENT LOCATION, I'D ASK THE CAPTAIN, I WAS YOU...
ASK THE CA--?! I AM THE CAPTAIN!
NO, THAT'S THE CAPTAIN.
WHO ARE YOU TO PRESUME TO TAKE COMMAND OF MY SHIP?! I AM TRADE MINISTER OF THE PROTECTORATE!

P-PLEASE! *WHY* ARE YOU DOING THIS TO ME?!

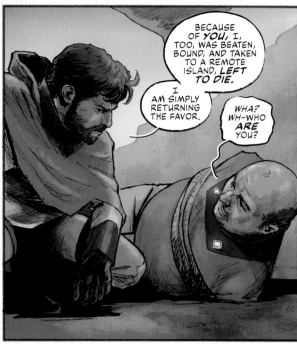

BECAUSE OF *YOU*, I, TOO, WAS BEATEN, BOUND, AND TAKEN TO A REMOTE ISLAND, *LEFT TO DIE.*

I AM SIMPLY RETURNING THE FAVOR.

WHA? WH–WHO *ARE* YOU?

REDXAN SAMUD.

THUNK

NNNNNN...

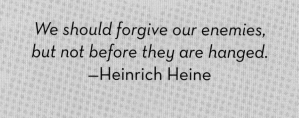

*We should forgive our enemies,
but not before they are hanged.*
—Heinrich Heine

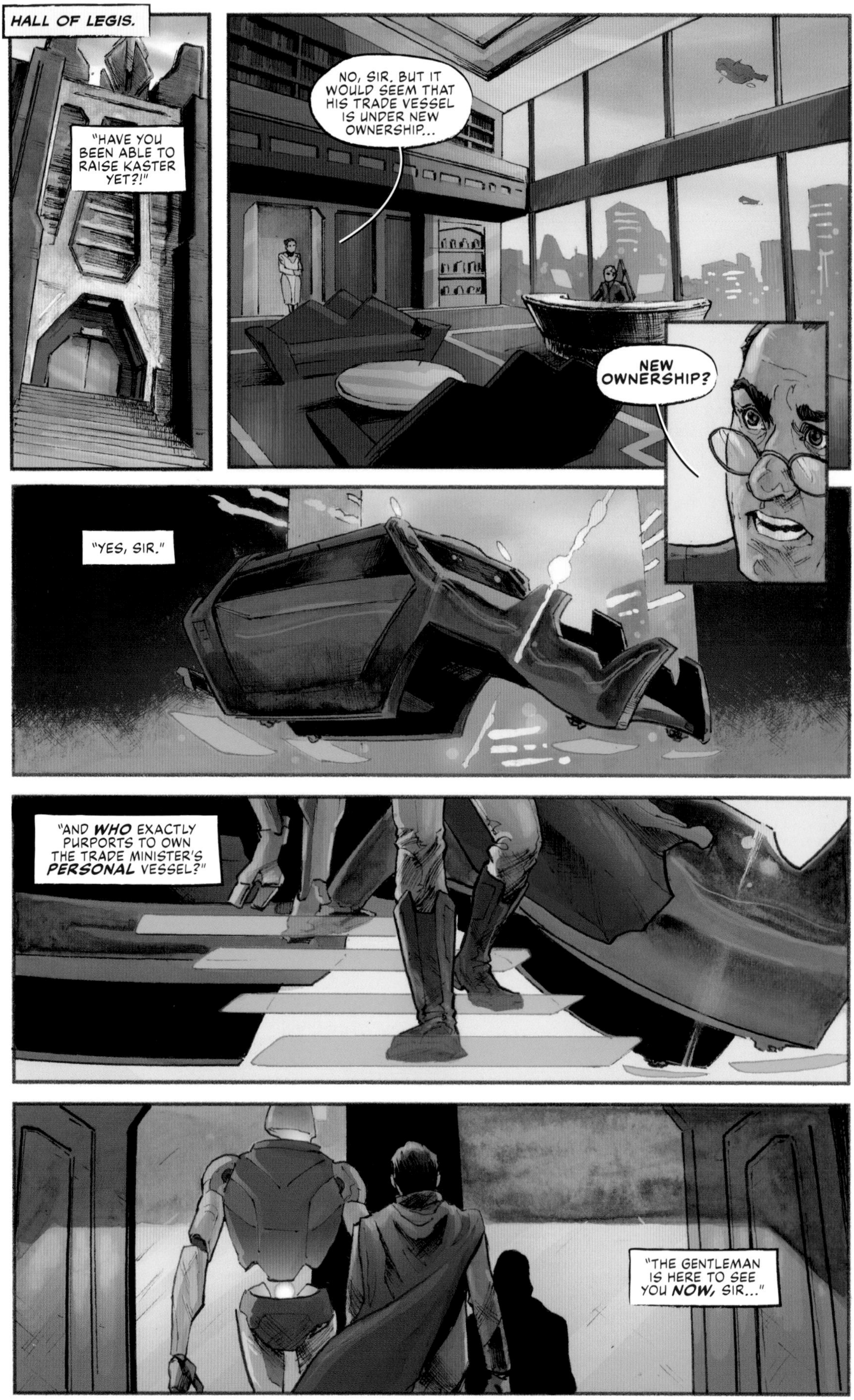
HALL OF LEGIS.
"HAVE YOU BEEN ABLE TO RAISE KASTER YET?!"
NO, SIR. BUT IT WOULD SEEM THAT HIS TRADE VESSEL IS UNDER NEW OWNERSHIP...
NEW OWNERSHIP?
"YES, SIR."
"AND WHO EXACTLY PURPORTS TO OWN THE TRADE MINISTER'S PERSONAL VESSEL?"
"THE GENTLEMAN IS HERE TO SEE YOU NOW, SIR..."

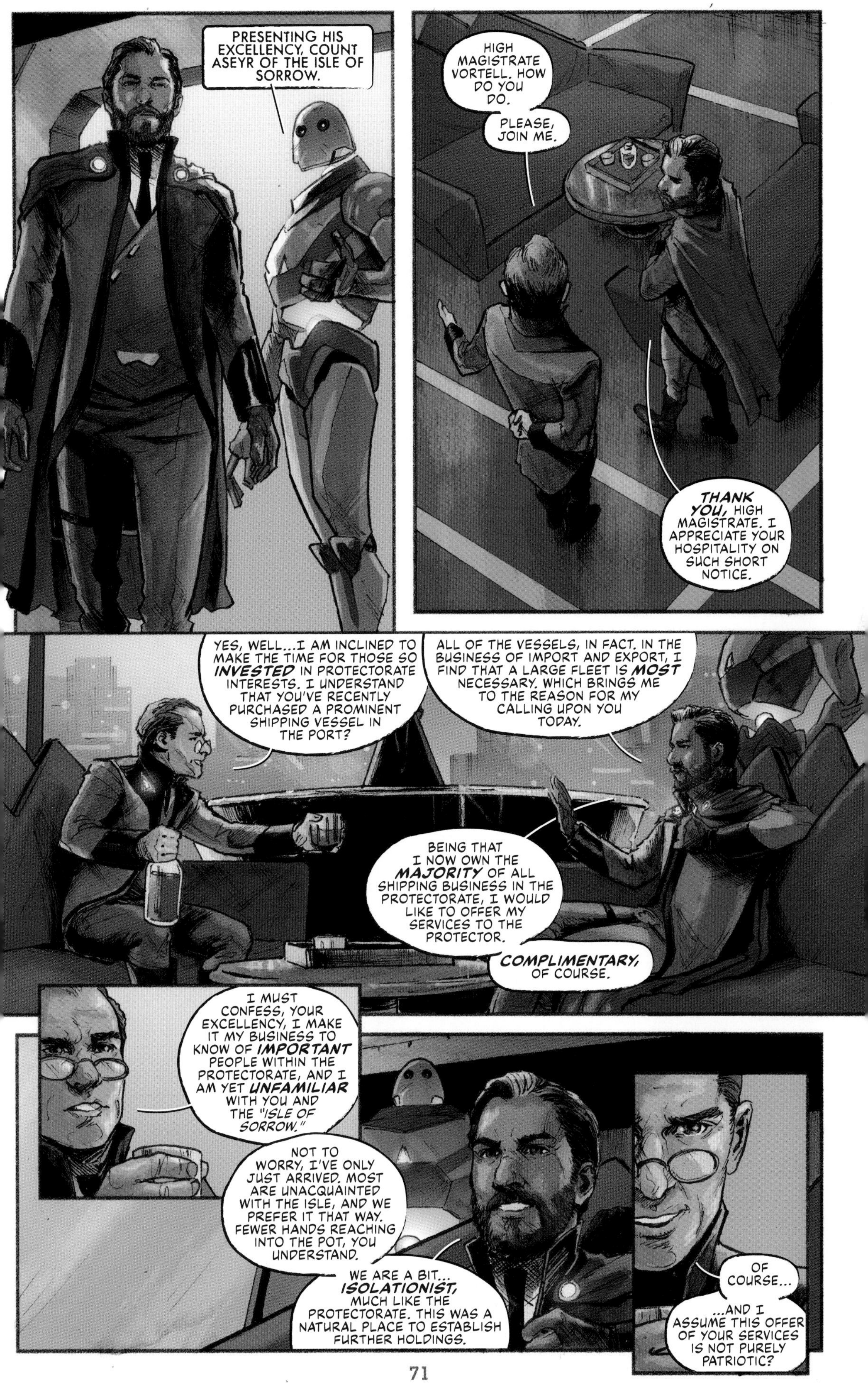
PRESENTING HIS EXCELLENCY, COUNT ASEYR OF THE ISLE OF SORROW.
HIGH MAGISTRATE VORTELL. HOW DO YOU DO.
PLEASE, JOIN ME.
THANK YOU, HIGH MAGISTRATE. I APPRECIATE YOUR HOSPITALITY ON SUCH SHORT NOTICE.
YES, WELL...I AM INCLINED TO MAKE THE TIME FOR THOSE SO INVESTED IN PROTECTORATE INTERESTS. I UNDERSTAND THAT YOU'VE RECENTLY PURCHASED A PROMINENT SHIPPING VESSEL IN THE PORT?
ALL OF THE VESSELS, IN FACT. IN THE BUSINESS OF IMPORT AND EXPORT, I FIND THAT A LARGE FLEET IS MOST NECESSARY. WHICH BRINGS ME TO THE REASON FOR MY CALLING UPON YOU TODAY.
BEING THAT I NOW OWN THE MAJORITY OF ALL SHIPPING BUSINESS IN THE PROTECTORATE, I WOULD LIKE TO OFFER MY SERVICES TO THE PROTECTOR.
COMPLIMENTARY, OF COURSE.
I MUST CONFESS, YOUR EXCELLENCY, I MAKE IT MY BUSINESS TO KNOW OF IMPORTANT PEOPLE WITHIN THE PROTECTORATE, AND I AM YET UNFAMILIAR WITH YOU AND THE "ISLE OF SORROW."
NOT TO WORRY, I'VE ONLY JUST ARRIVED. MOST ARE UNACQUAINTED WITH THE ISLE, AND WE PREFER IT THAT WAY. FEWER HANDS REACHING INTO THE POT, YOU UNDERSTAND.
WE ARE A BIT... ISOLATIONIST, MUCH LIKE THE PROTECTORATE. THIS WAS A NATURAL PLACE TO ESTABLISH FURTHER HOLDINGS.
OF COURSE...
...AND I ASSUME THIS OFFER OF YOUR SERVICES IS NOT PURELY PATRIOTIC?

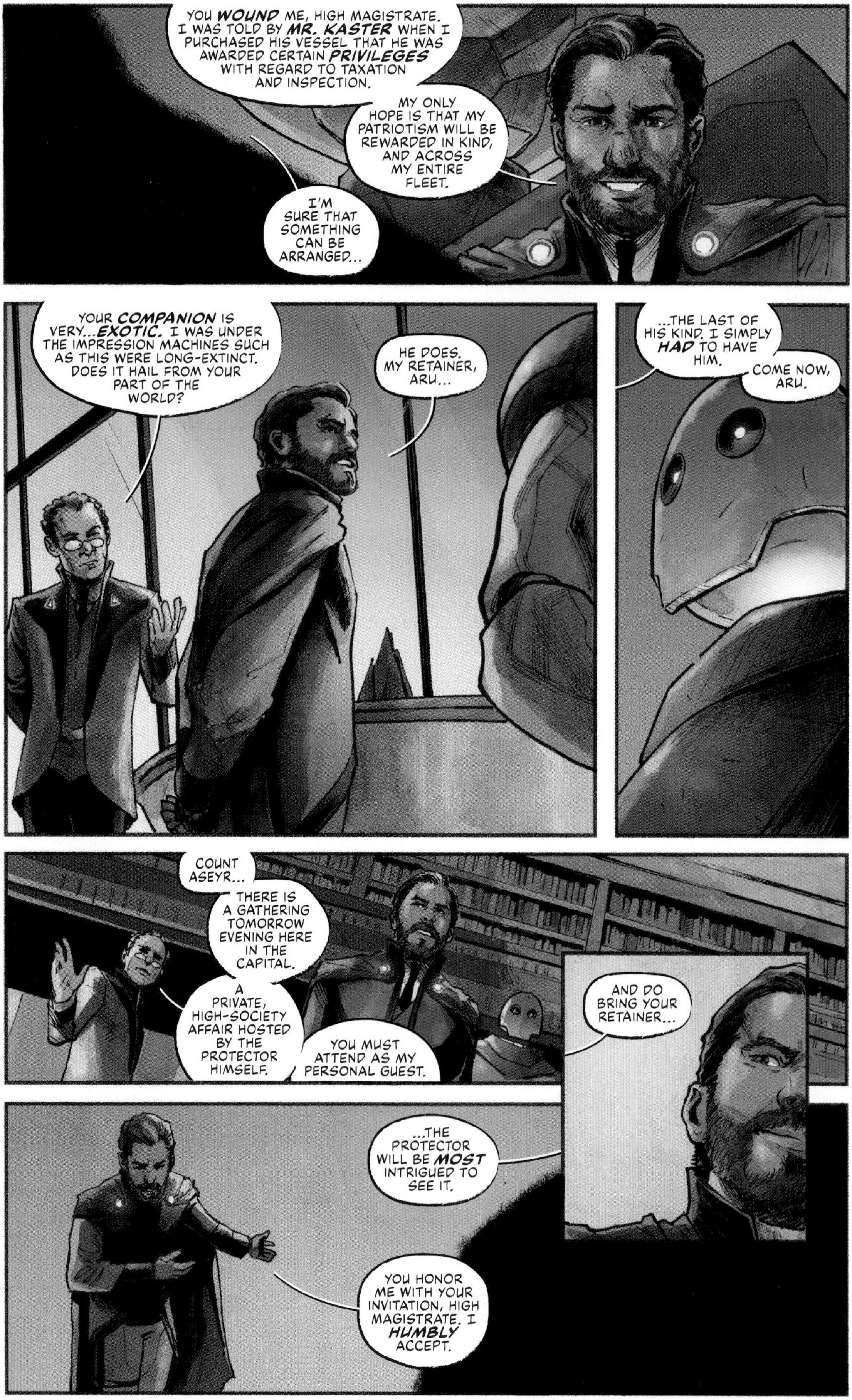
YOU WOUND ME, HIGH MAGISTRATE. I WAS TOLD BY MR. KASTER WHEN I PURCHASED HIS VESSEL THAT HE WAS AWARDED CERTAIN PRIVILEGES WITH REGARD TO TAXATION AND INSPECTION.
MY ONLY HOPE IS THAT MY PATRIOTISM WILL BE REWARDED IN KIND, AND ACROSS MY ENTIRE FLEET.
I'M SURE THAT SOMETHING CAN BE ARRANGED...
YOUR COMPANION IS VERY...EXOTIC. I WAS UNDER THE IMPRESSION MACHINES SUCH AS THIS WERE LONG-EXTINCT. DOES IT HAIL FROM YOUR PART OF THE WORLD?
HE DOES. MY RETAINER, ARU...
...THE LAST OF HIS KIND. I SIMPLY HAD TO HAVE HIM.
COME NOW, ARU.
COUNT ASEYR...
THERE IS A GATHERING TOMORROW EVENING HERE IN THE CAPITAL.
A PRIVATE, HIGH-SOCIETY AFFAIR HOSTED BY THE PROTECTOR HIMSELF.
YOU MUST ATTEND AS MY PERSONAL GUEST.
AND DO BRING YOUR RETAINER...
...THE PROTECTOR WILL BE MOST INTRIGUED TO SEE IT.
YOU HONOR ME WITH YOUR INVITATION, HIGH MAGISTRATE. I HUMBLY ACCEPT.

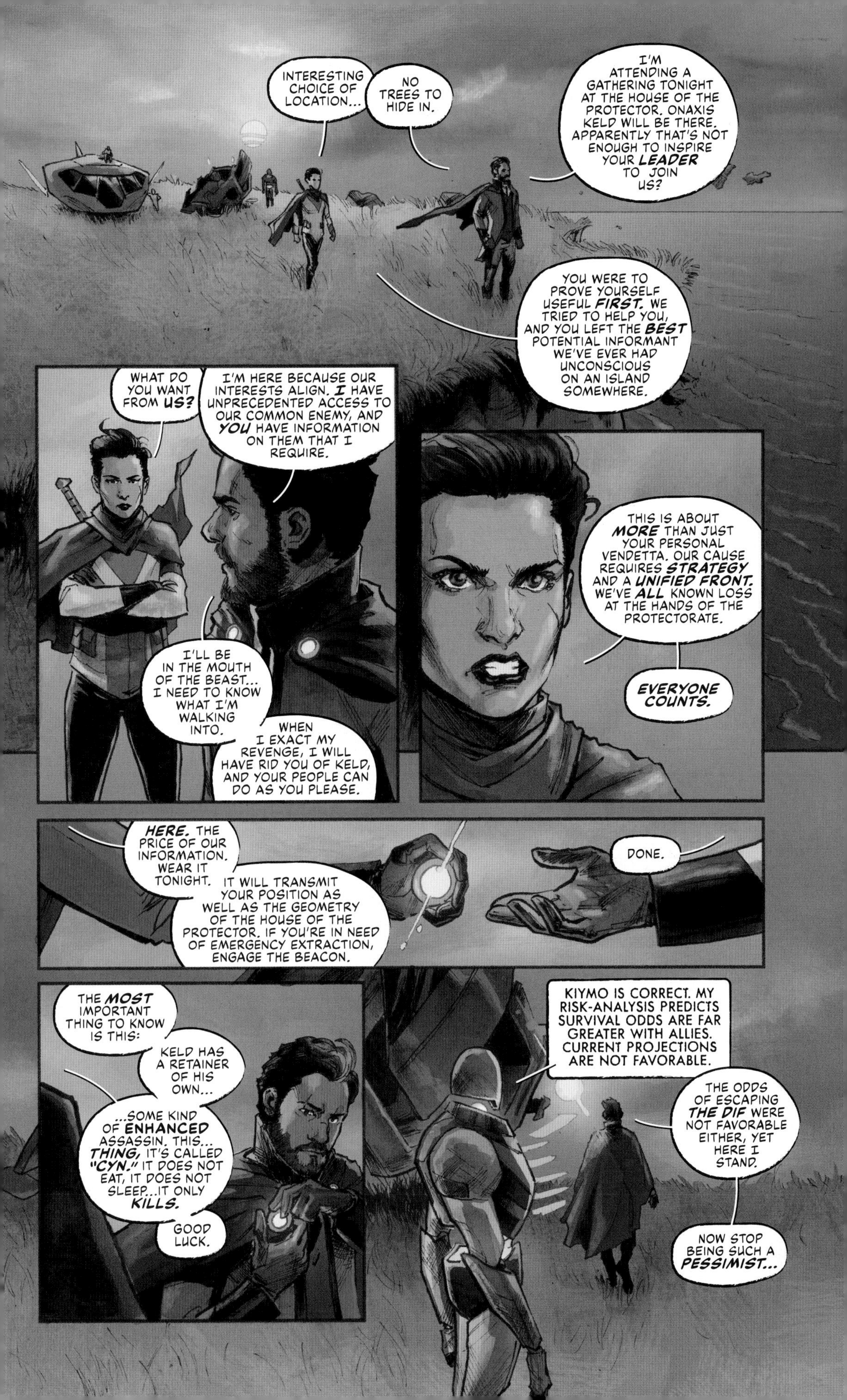

INTERESTING CHOICE OF LOCATION...
NO TREES TO HIDE IN.
I'M ATTENDING A GATHERING TONIGHT AT THE HOUSE OF THE PROTECTOR. ONAXIS KELD WILL BE THERE. APPARENTLY THAT'S NOT ENOUGH TO INSPIRE YOUR LEADER TO JOIN US?
YOU WERE TO PROVE YOURSELF USEFUL FIRST. WE TRIED TO HELP YOU, AND YOU LEFT THE BEST POTENTIAL INFORMANT WE'VE EVER HAD UNCONSCIOUS ON AN ISLAND SOMEWHERE.
WHAT DO YOU WANT FROM US?
I'M HERE BECAUSE OUR INTERESTS ALIGN. I HAVE UNPRECEDENTED ACCESS TO OUR COMMON ENEMY, AND YOU HAVE INFORMATION ON THEM THAT I REQUIRE.
I'LL BE IN THE MOUTH OF THE BEAST... I NEED TO KNOW WHAT I'M WALKING INTO.
WHEN I EXACT MY REVENGE, I WILL HAVE RID YOU OF KELD, AND YOUR PEOPLE CAN DO AS YOU PLEASE.
THIS IS ABOUT MORE THAN JUST YOUR PERSONAL VENDETTA. OUR CAUSE REQUIRES STRATEGY AND A UNIFIED FRONT. WE'VE ALL KNOWN LOSS AT THE HANDS OF THE PROTECTORATE.
EVERYONE COUNTS.
HERE. THE PRICE OF OUR INFORMATION. WEAR IT TONIGHT.
IT WILL TRANSMIT YOUR POSITION AS WELL AS THE GEOMETRY OF THE HOUSE OF THE PROTECTOR. IF YOU'RE IN NEED OF EMERGENCY EXTRACTION, ENGAGE THE BEACON.
DONE.
THE MOST IMPORTANT THING TO KNOW IS THIS:
KELD HAS A RETAINER OF HIS OWN...
...SOME KIND OF ENHANCED ASSASSIN. THIS... THING, IT'S CALLED "CYN." IT DOES NOT EAT, IT DOES NOT SLEEP...IT ONLY KILLS.
GOOD LUCK.
KIYMO IS CORRECT. MY RISK-ANALYSIS PREDICTS SURVIVAL ODDS ARE FAR GREATER WITH ALLIES. CURRENT PROJECTIONS ARE NOT FAVORABLE.
THE ODDS OF ESCAPING THE DIF WERE NOT FAVORABLE EITHER, YET HERE I STAND.
NOW STOP BEING SUCH A PESSIMIST...

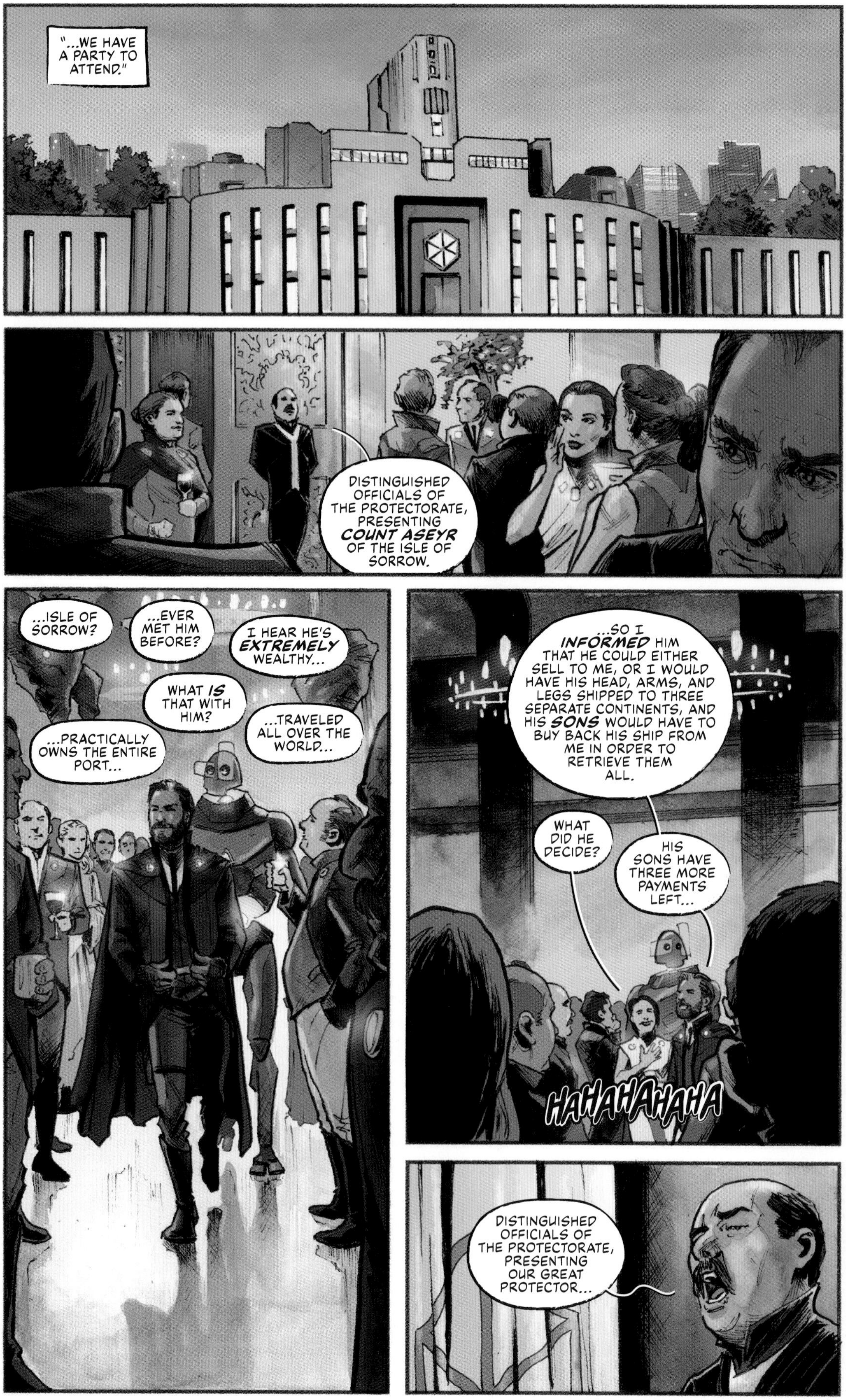
"...WE HAVE A PARTY TO ATTEND."
DISTINGUISHED OFFICIALS OF THE PROTECTORATE, PRESENTING COUNT ASEYR OF THE ISLE OF SORROW.
...ISLE OF SORROW?
...EVER MET HIM BEFORE?
I HEAR HE'S EXTREMELY WEALTHY...
WHAT IS THAT WITH HIM?
...TRAVELED ALL OVER THE WORLD...
...PRACTICALLY OWNS THE ENTIRE PORT...
...SO I INFORMED HIM THAT HE COULD EITHER SELL TO ME, OR I WOULD HAVE HIS HEAD, ARMS, AND LEGS SHIPPED TO THREE SEPARATE CONTINENTS, AND HIS SONS WOULD HAVE TO BUY BACK HIS SHIP FROM ME IN ORDER TO RETRIEVE THEM ALL.
WHAT DID HE DECIDE?
HIS SONS HAVE THREE MORE PAYMENTS LEFT...
HAHAHAHAHA
DISTINGUISHED OFFICIALS OF THE PROTECTORATE, PRESENTING OUR GREAT PROTECTOR...

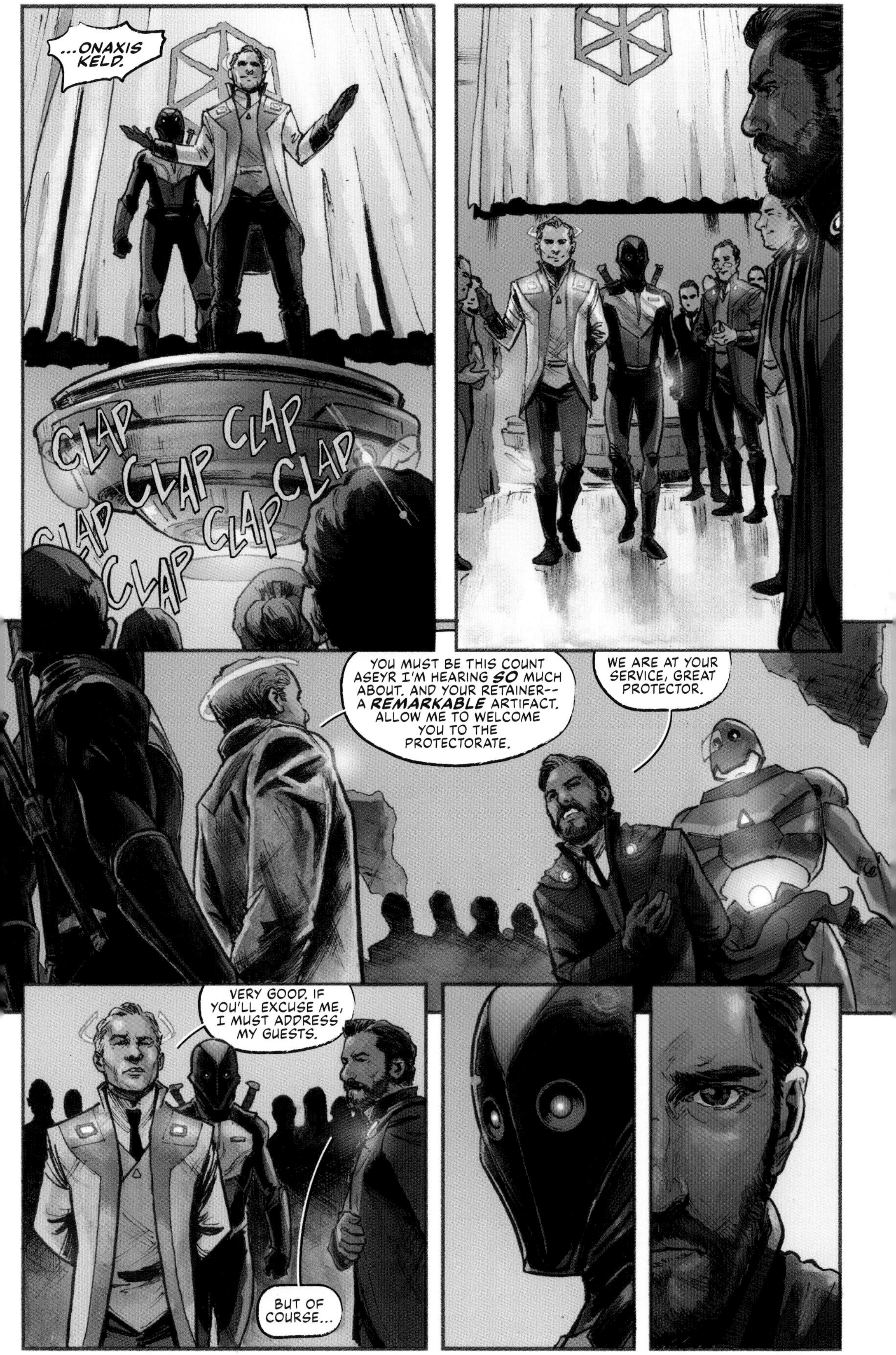
...ONAXIS KELD.
CLAP CLAP CLAP CLAP CLAP CLAP CLAP CLAP
YOU MUST BE THIS COUNT ASEYR I'M HEARING SO MUCH ABOUT. AND YOUR RETAINER-- A REMARKABLE ARTIFACT. ALLOW ME TO WELCOME YOU TO THE PROTECTORATE.
WE ARE AT YOUR SERVICE, GREAT PROTECTOR.
VERY GOOD. IF YOU'LL EXCUSE ME, I MUST ADDRESS MY GUESTS.
BUT OF COURSE...

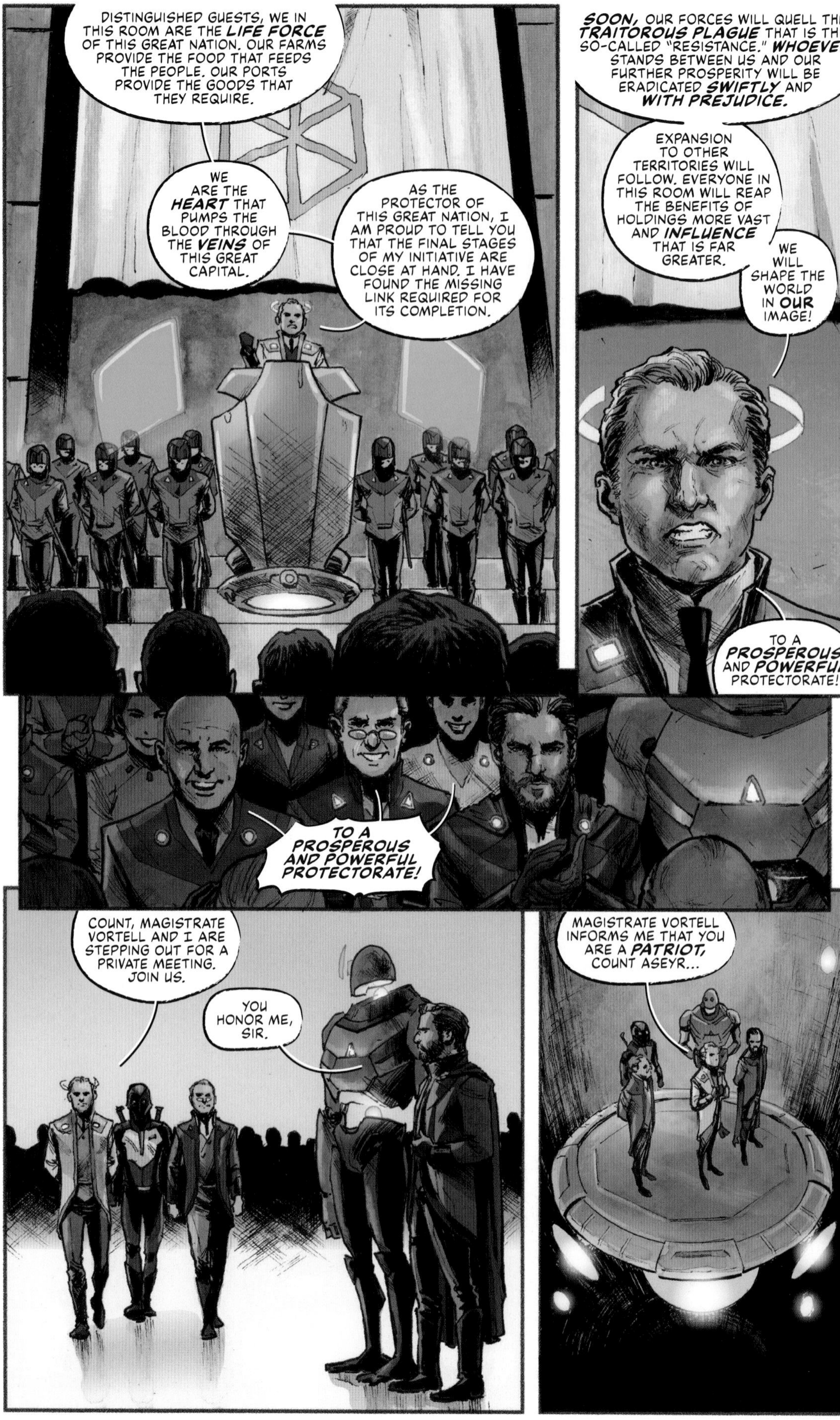
DISTINGUISHED GUESTS, WE IN THIS ROOM ARE THE LIFE FORCE OF THIS GREAT NATION. OUR FARMS PROVIDE THE FOOD THAT FEEDS THE PEOPLE. OUR PORTS PROVIDE THE GOODS THAT THEY REQUIRE.
WE ARE THE HEART THAT PUMPS THE BLOOD THROUGH THE VEINS OF THIS GREAT CAPITAL.
AS THE PROTECTOR OF THIS GREAT NATION, I AM PROUD TO TELL YOU THAT THE FINAL STAGES OF MY INITIATIVE ARE CLOSE AT HAND. I HAVE FOUND THE MISSING LINK REQUIRED FOR ITS COMPLETION.
SOON, OUR FORCES WILL QUELL THE TRAITOROUS PLAGUE THAT IS THIS SO-CALLED "RESISTANCE." WHOEVER STANDS BETWEEN US AND OUR FURTHER PROSPERITY WILL BE ERADICATED SWIFTLY AND WITH PREJUDICE.
EXPANSION TO OTHER TERRITORIES WILL FOLLOW. EVERYONE IN THIS ROOM WILL REAP THE BENEFITS OF HOLDINGS MORE VAST AND INFLUENCE THAT IS FAR GREATER.
WE WILL SHAPE THE WORLD IN OUR IMAGE!
TO A PROSPEROUS AND POWERFUL PROTECTORATE!
TO A PROSPEROUS AND POWERFUL PROTECTORATE!
COUNT, MAGISTRATE VORTELL AND I ARE STEPPING OUT FOR A PRIVATE MEETING. JOIN US.
YOU HONOR ME, SIR.
MAGISTRATE VORTELL INFORMS ME THAT YOU ARE A PATRIOT, COUNT ASEYR...

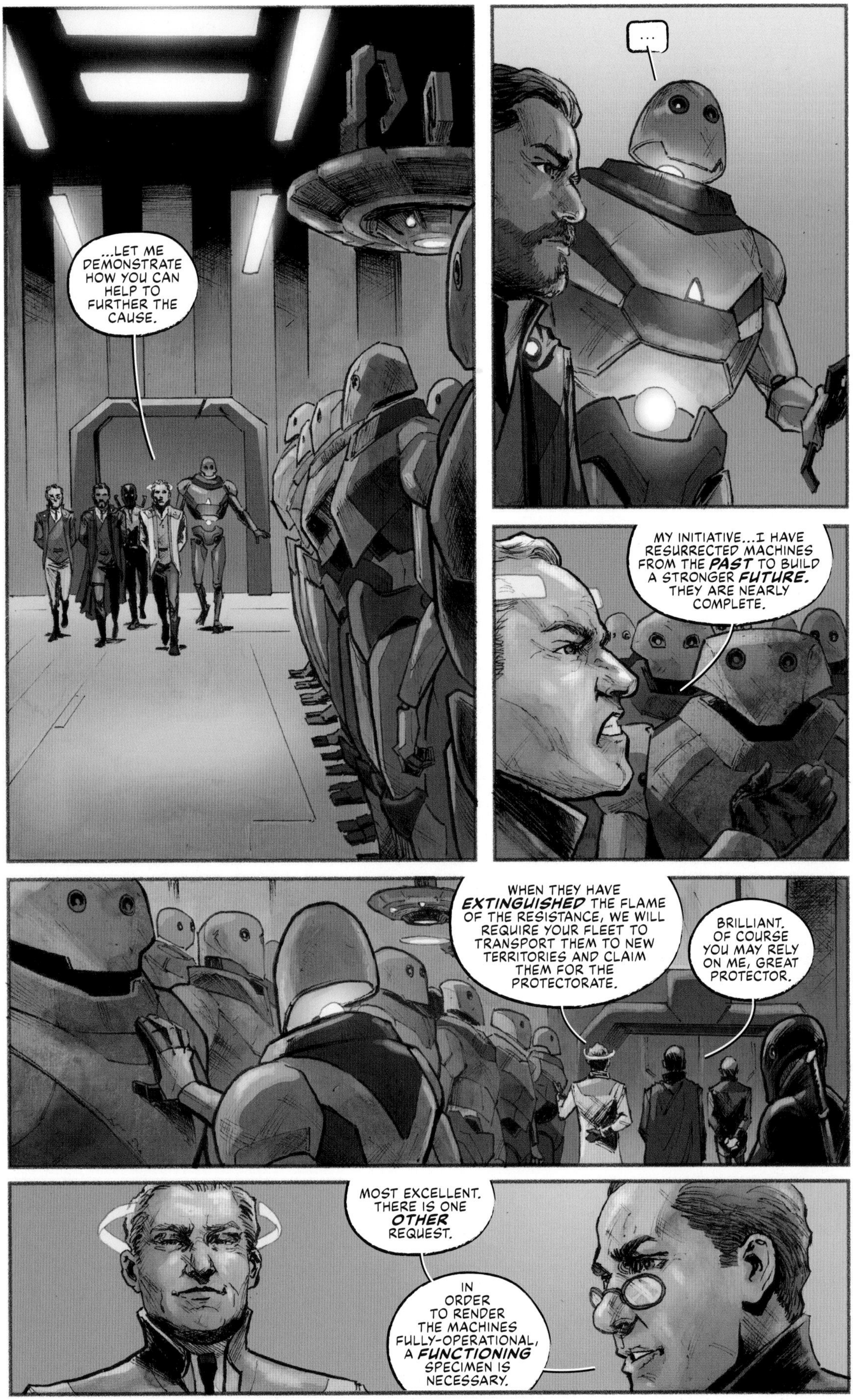

...LET ME DEMONSTRATE HOW YOU CAN HELP TO FURTHER THE CAUSE.
...
MY INITIATIVE...I HAVE RESURRECTED MACHINES FROM THE PAST TO BUILD A STRONGER FUTURE. THEY ARE NEARLY COMPLETE.
WHEN THEY HAVE EXTINGUISHED THE FLAME OF THE RESISTANCE, WE WILL REQUIRE YOUR FLEET TO TRANSPORT THEM TO NEW TERRITORIES AND CLAIM THEM FOR THE PROTECTORATE.
BRILLIANT. OF COURSE YOU MAY RELY ON ME, GREAT PROTECTOR.
MOST EXCELLENT. THERE IS ONE OTHER REQUEST.
IN ORDER TO RENDER THE MACHINES FULLY-OPERATIONAL, A FUNCTIONING SPECIMEN IS NECESSARY.

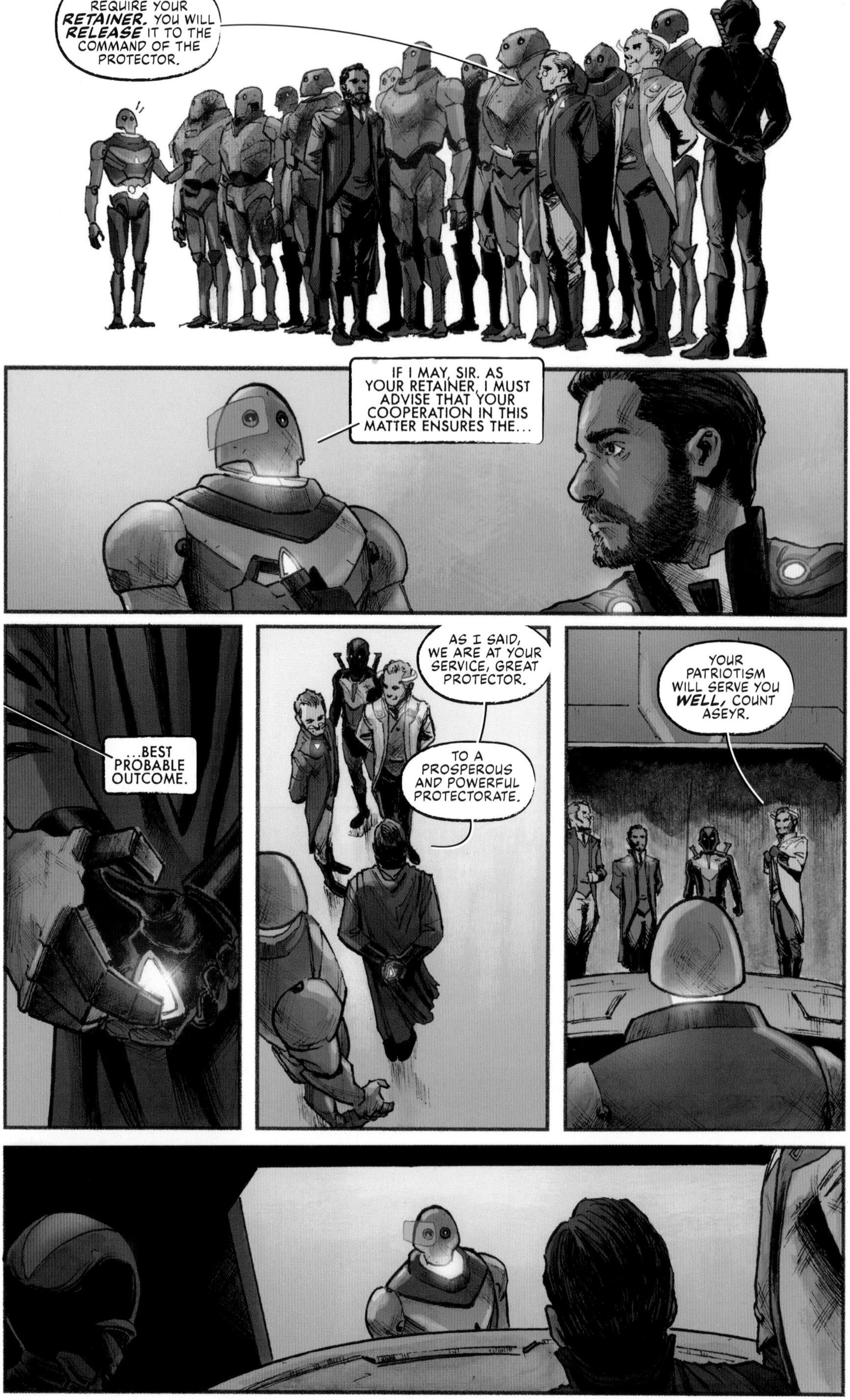
WE REQUIRE YOUR RETAINER. YOU WILL RELEASE IT TO THE COMMAND OF THE PROTECTOR.
IF I MAY, SIR. AS YOUR RETAINER, I MUST ADVISE THAT YOUR COOPERATION IN THIS MATTER ENSURES THE...
...BEST PROBABLE OUTCOME.
AS I SAID, WE ARE AT YOUR SERVICE, GREAT PROTECTOR.
TO A PROSPEROUS AND POWERFUL PROTECTORATE.
YOUR PATRIOTISM WILL SERVE YOU WELL, COUNT ASEYR.

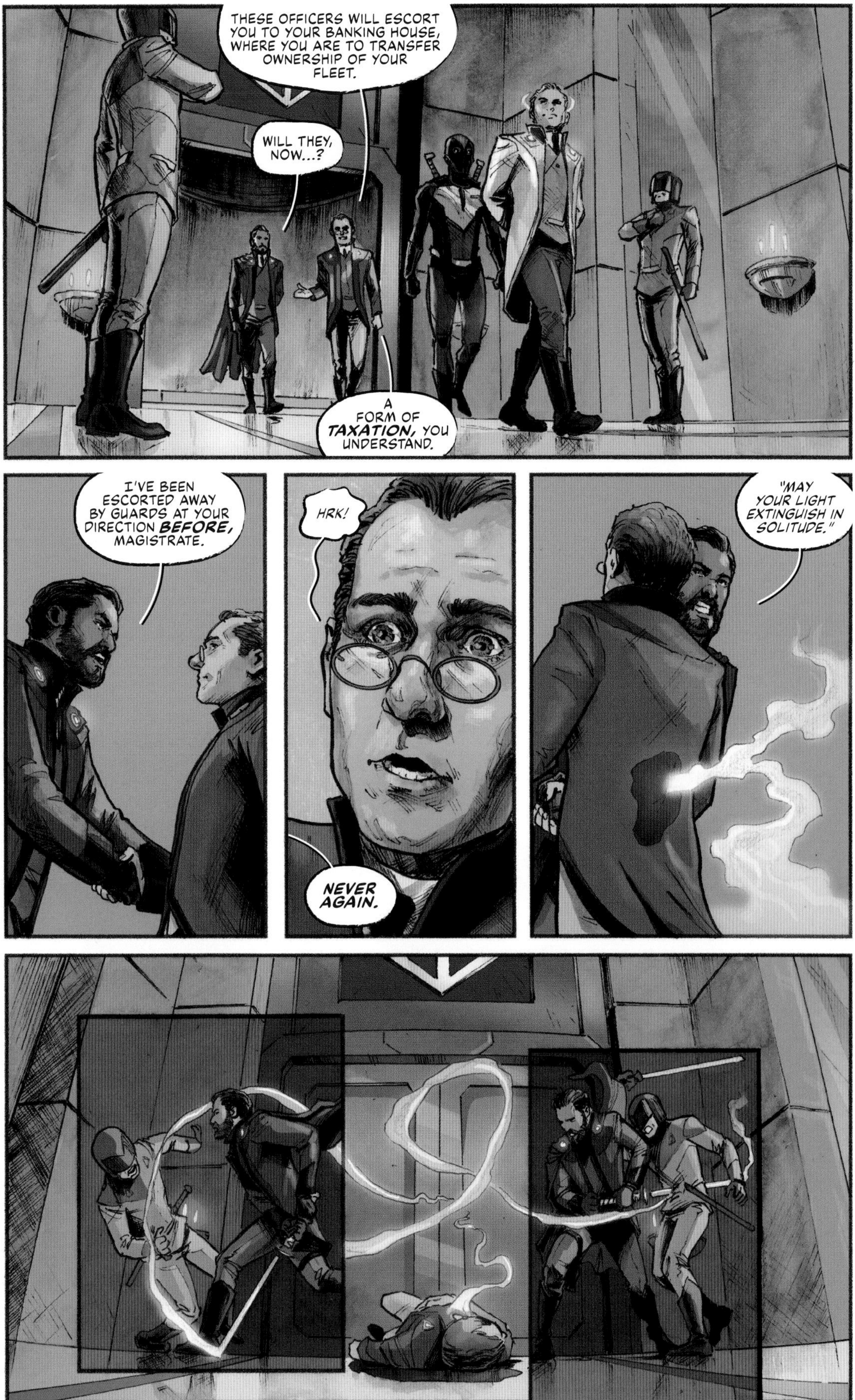
THESE OFFICERS WILL ESCORT YOU TO YOUR BANKING HOUSE, WHERE YOU ARE TO TRANSFER OWNERSHIP OF YOUR FLEET.
WILL THEY, NOW...?
A FORM OF TAXATION, YOU UNDERSTAND.
I'VE BEEN ESCORTED AWAY BY GUARDS AT YOUR DIRECTION BEFORE, MAGISTRATE.
HRK!
NEVER AGAIN.
"MAY YOUR LIGHT EXTINGUISH IN SOLITUDE."

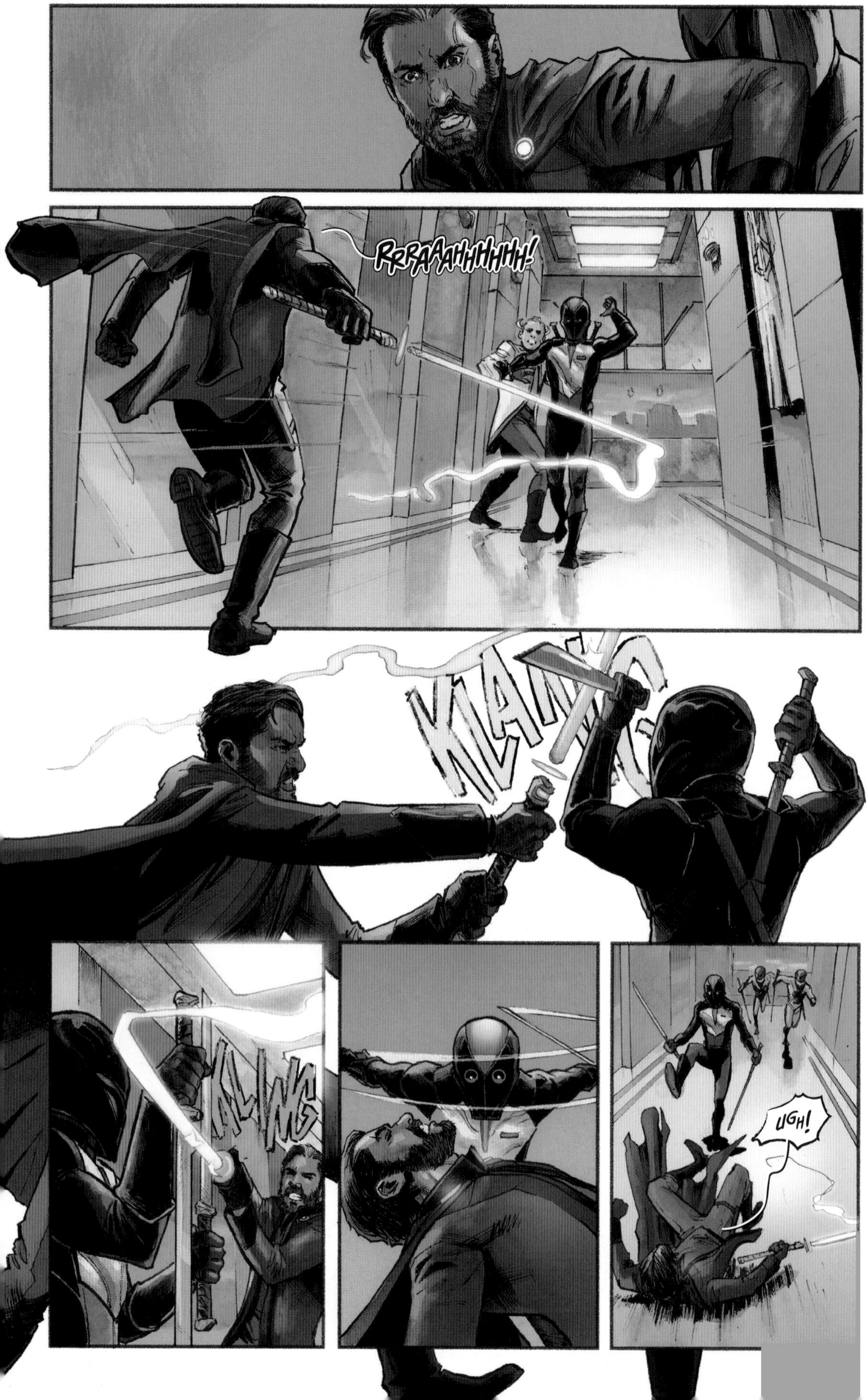
RRRAAAHHHHHH!
KLANG
KLING
UGH!

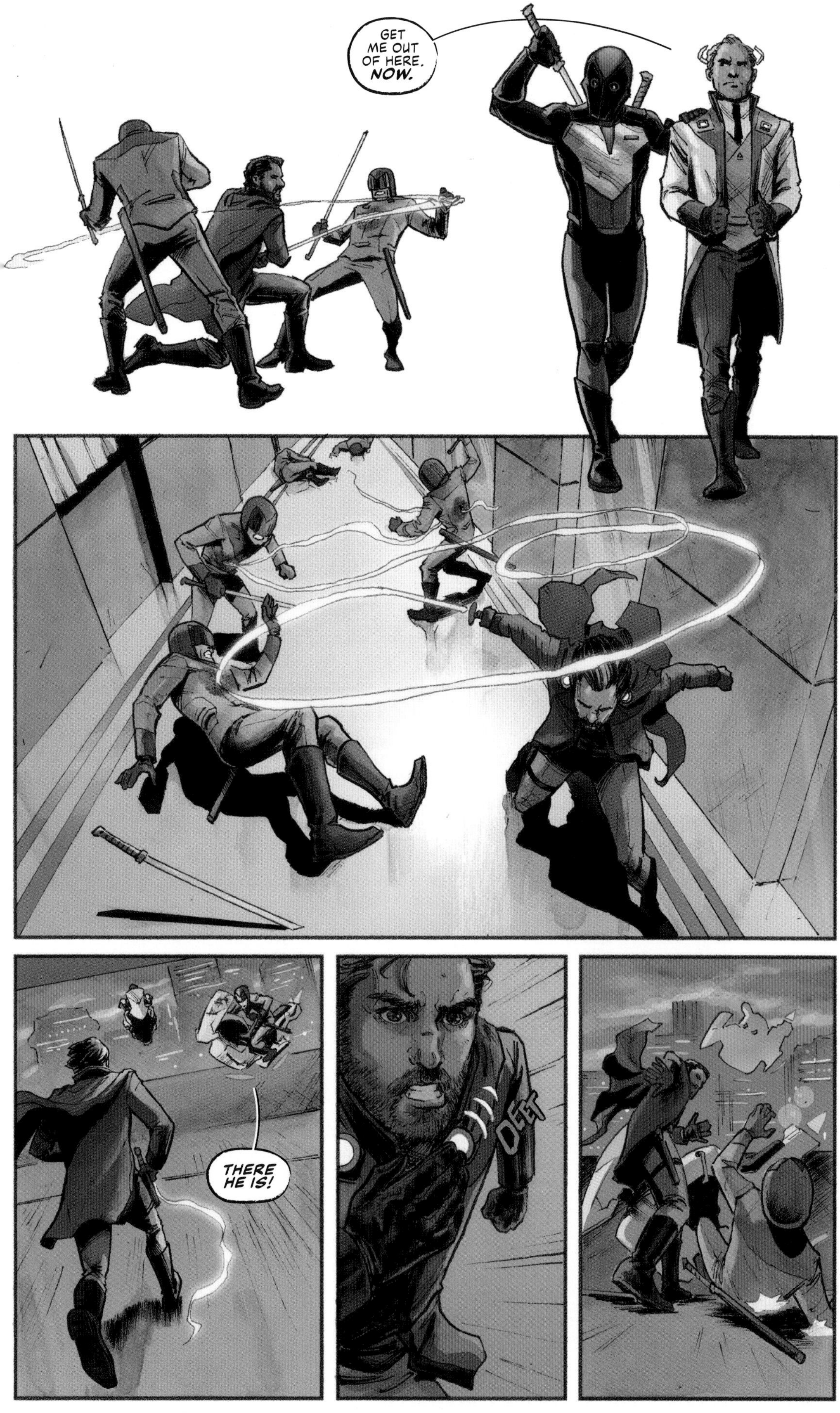
GET ME OUT OF HERE. NOW.
THERE HE IS!

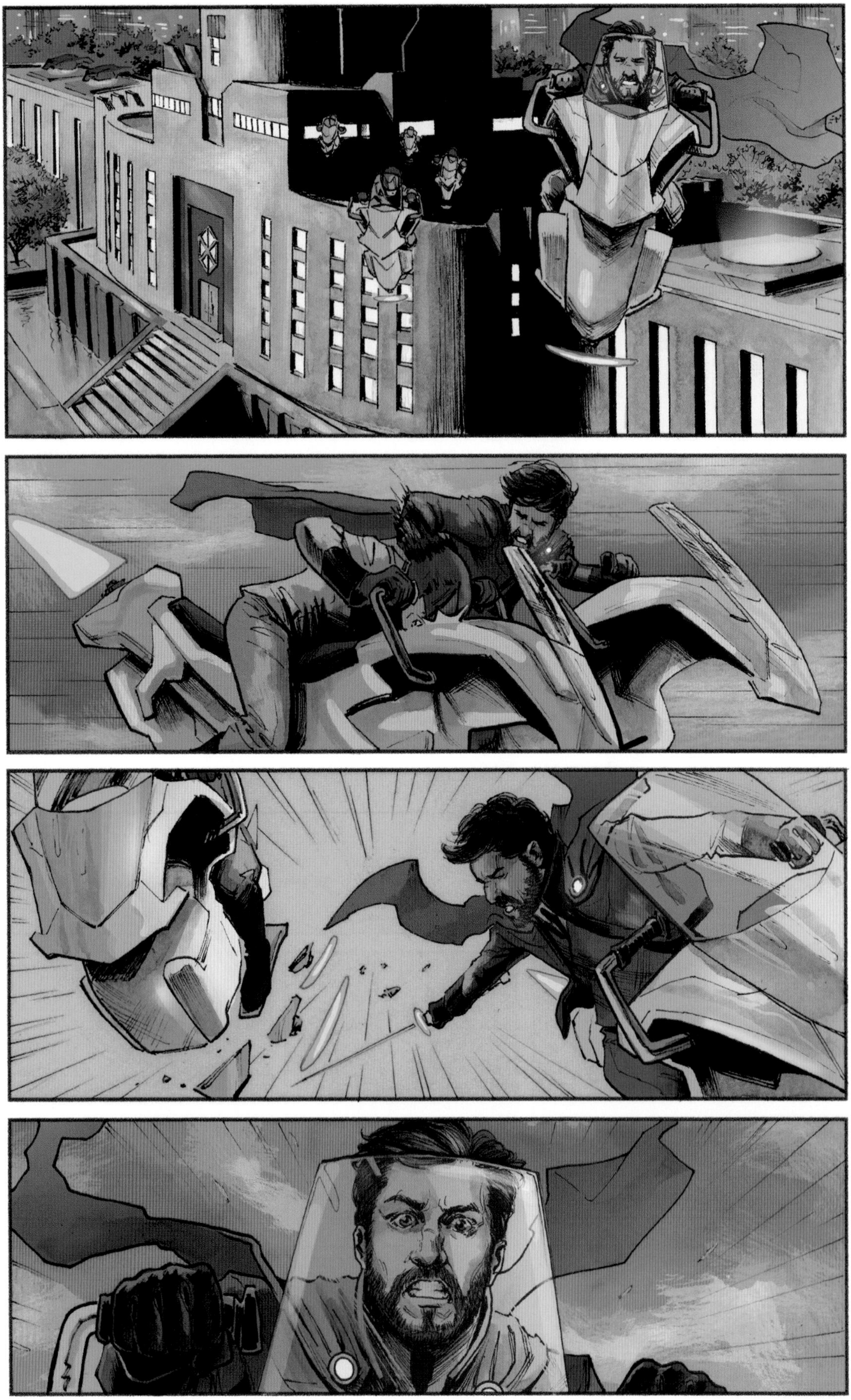

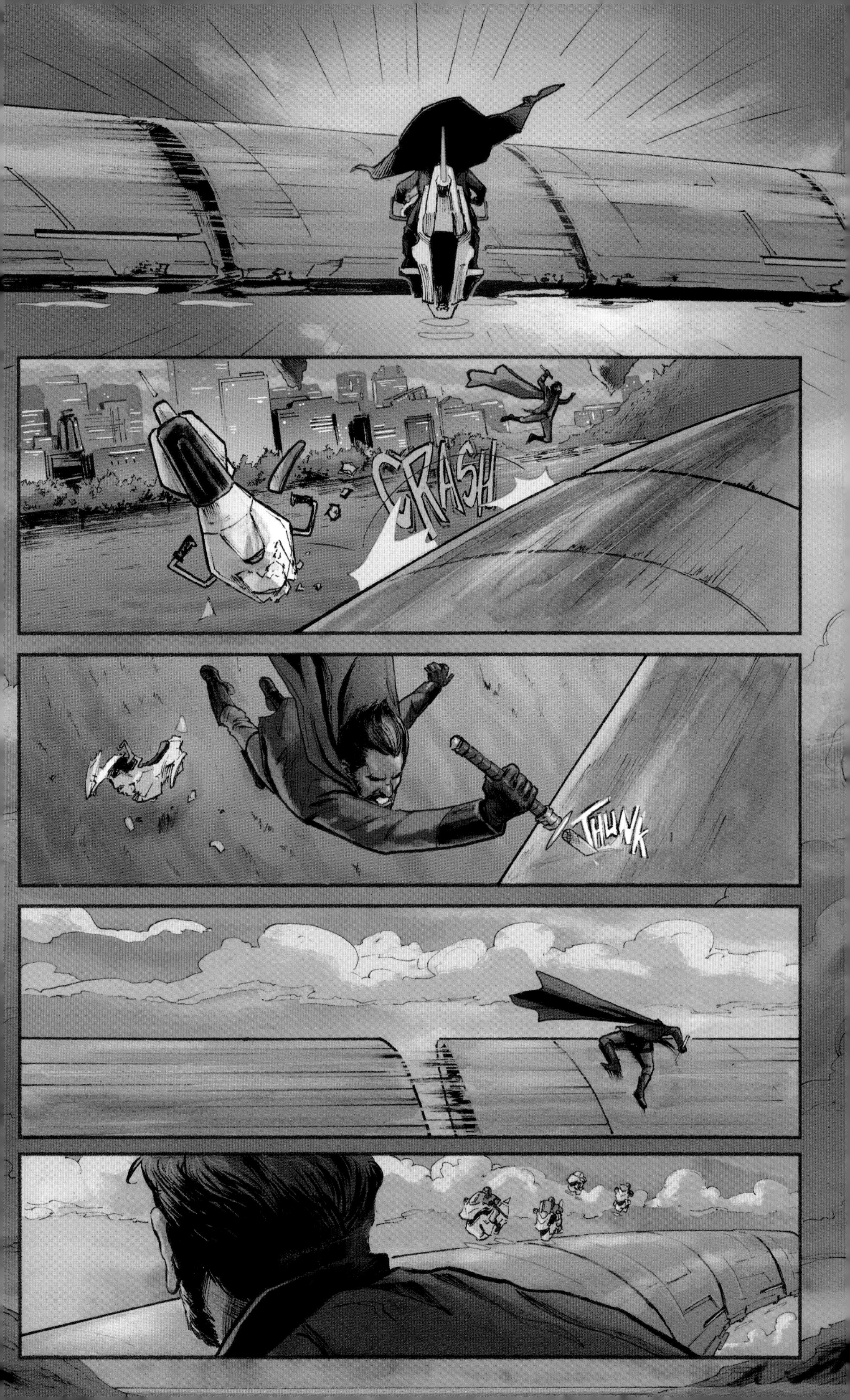
CRASH
THUNK

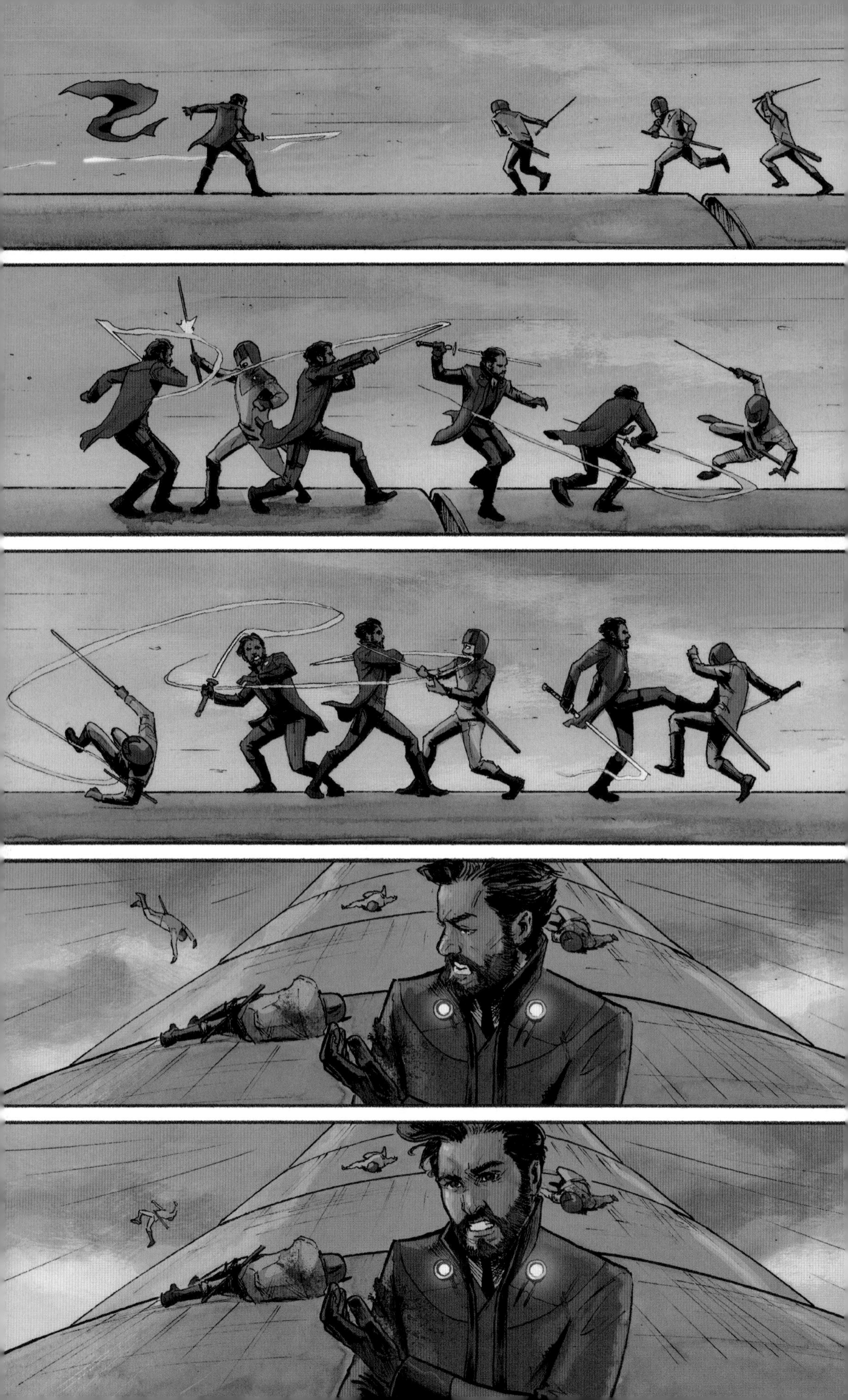

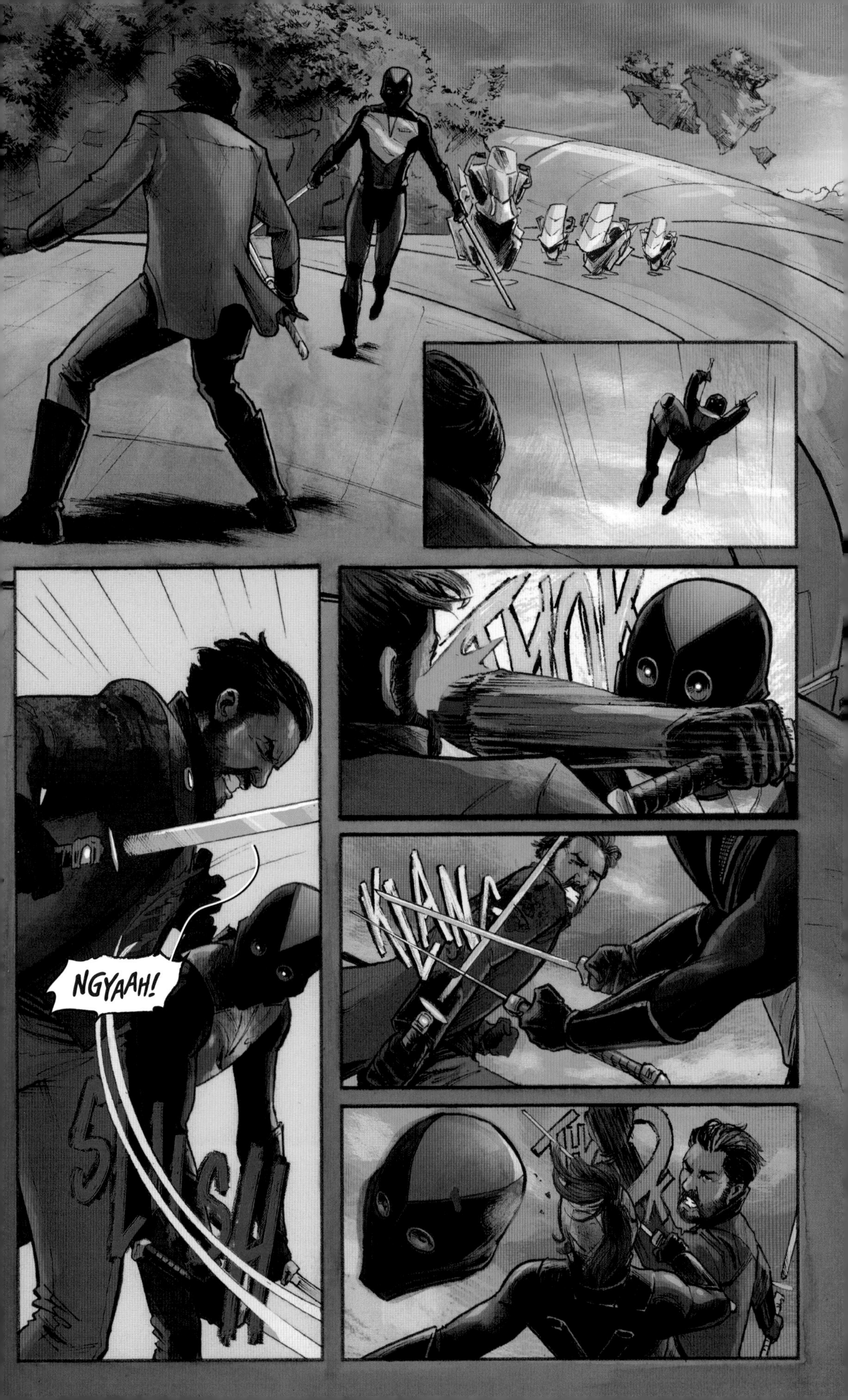
NGYAAH!
KLANG

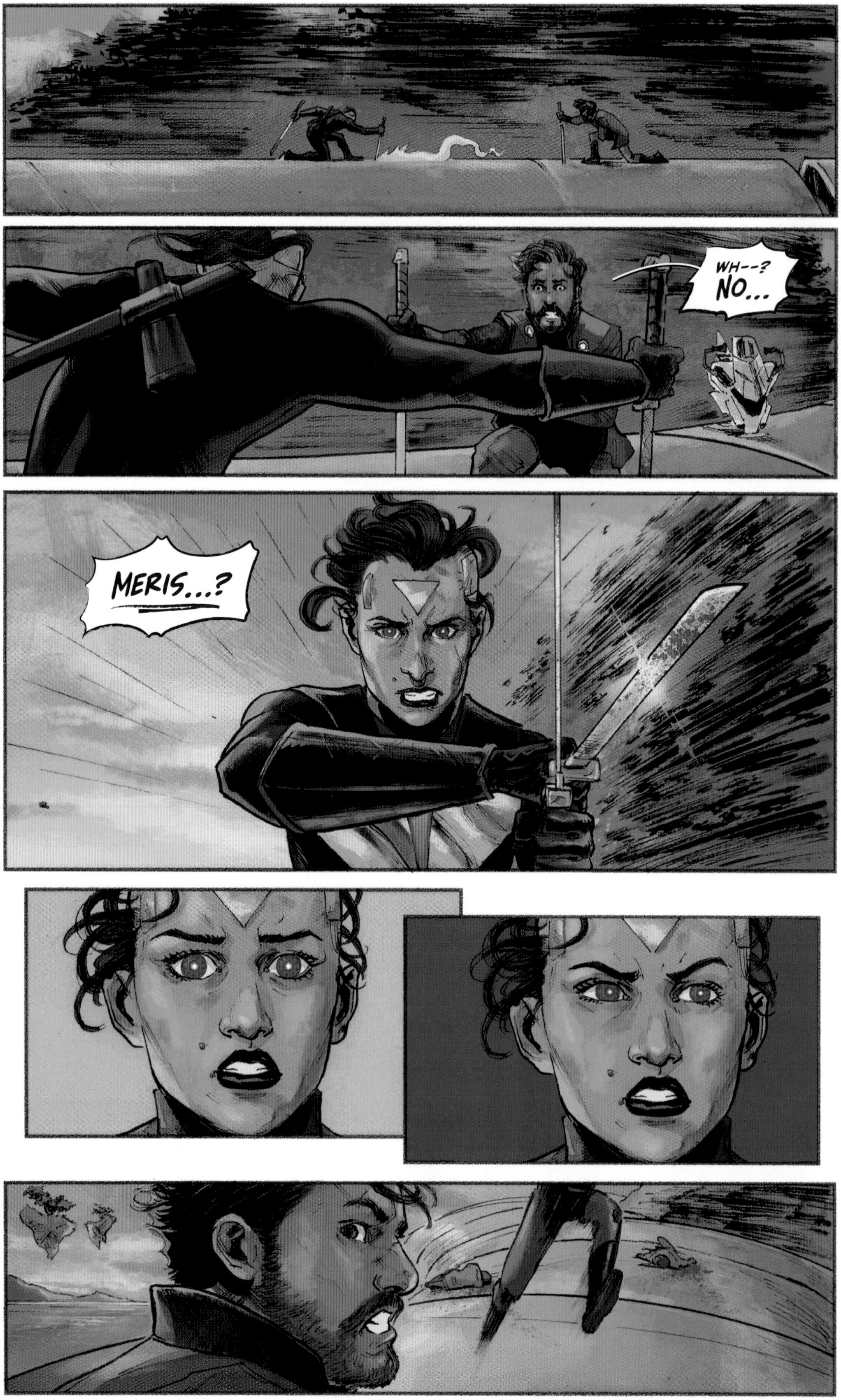
WH--? NO...
MERIS...?

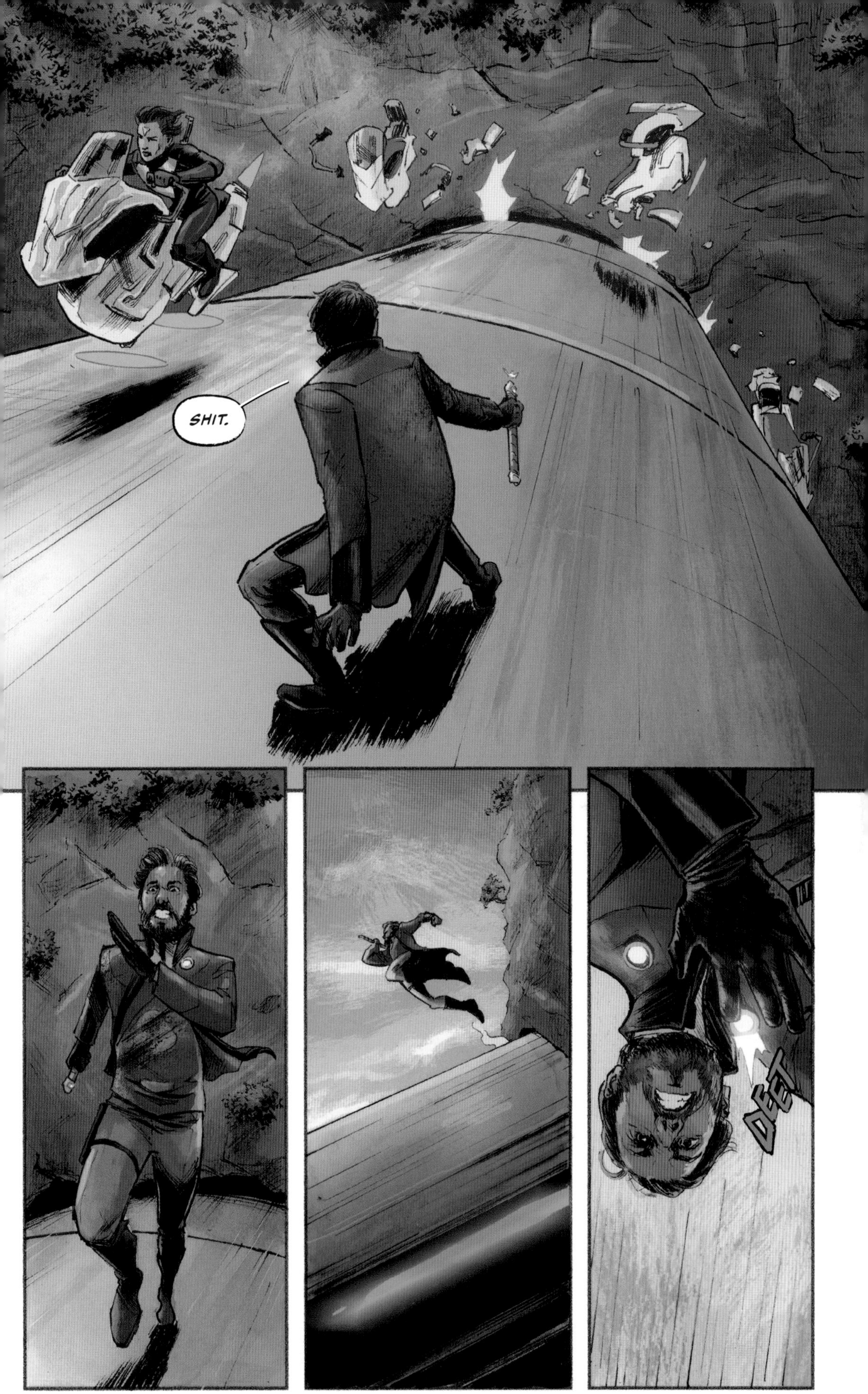
SHIT.
DEET

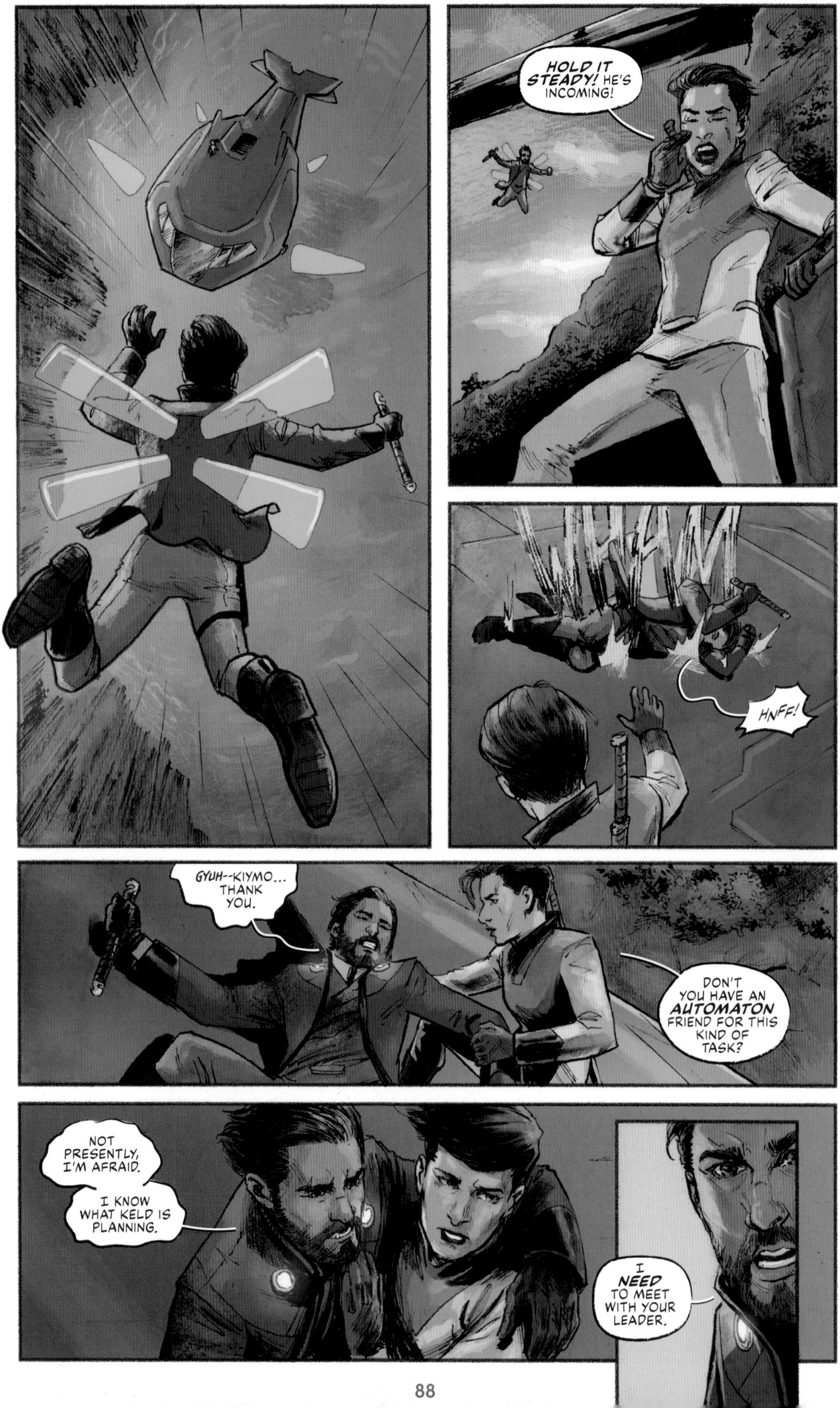
HOLD IT STEADY! HE'S INCOMING!
WHAM
HNFF!
GYUH--KIYMO... THANK YOU.
DON'T YOU HAVE AN AUTOMATON FRIEND FOR THIS KIND OF TASK?
NOT PRESENTLY, I'M AFRAID.
I KNOW WHAT KELD IS PLANNING.
I NEED TO MEET WITH YOUR LEADER.

The best revenge is to be unlike
him who performed the injury.
—Marcus Aurelius

THANK YOU.

KIYMO... YOUR LEADER?

SHE'S HERE...

SENNA. I SHOULD HAVE KNOWN...

YOU SHOULD NOT HAVE, AND SO YOU DID NOT. I'VE BEEN DOING THIS A LONG TIME.

I'M TOLD YOU HAVE NEWS OF KELD'S PLAN?

IT'S ON A LARGER SCALE THAN YOU IMAGINED. HE INTENDS TO EXTINGUISH THE RESISTANCE, THEN HE AIMS TO CONQUER OTHER LANDS, EXTENDING HIS RULE UNTIL HE CONTROLS ALL.

HOW? OTHER RULERS HAVE ARMIES TO DEFEND THEIR LANDS...

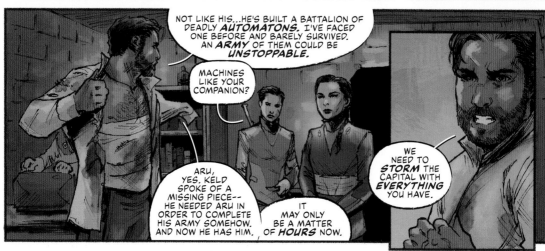

NOT LIKE HIS...HE'S BUILT A BATTALION OF DEADLY AUTOMATONS. I'VE FACED ONE BEFORE AND BARELY SURVIVED. AN ARMY OF THEM COULD BE UNSTOPPABLE.

MACHINES LIKE YOUR COMPANION?

ARU, YES. KELD SPOKE OF A MISSING PIECE-- HE NEEDED ARU IN ORDER TO COMPLETE HIS ARMY SOMEHOW. AND NOW HE HAS HIM.

IT MAY ONLY BE A MATTER OF HOURS NOW.

WE NEED TO STORM THE CAPITAL WITH EVERYTHING YOU HAVE.

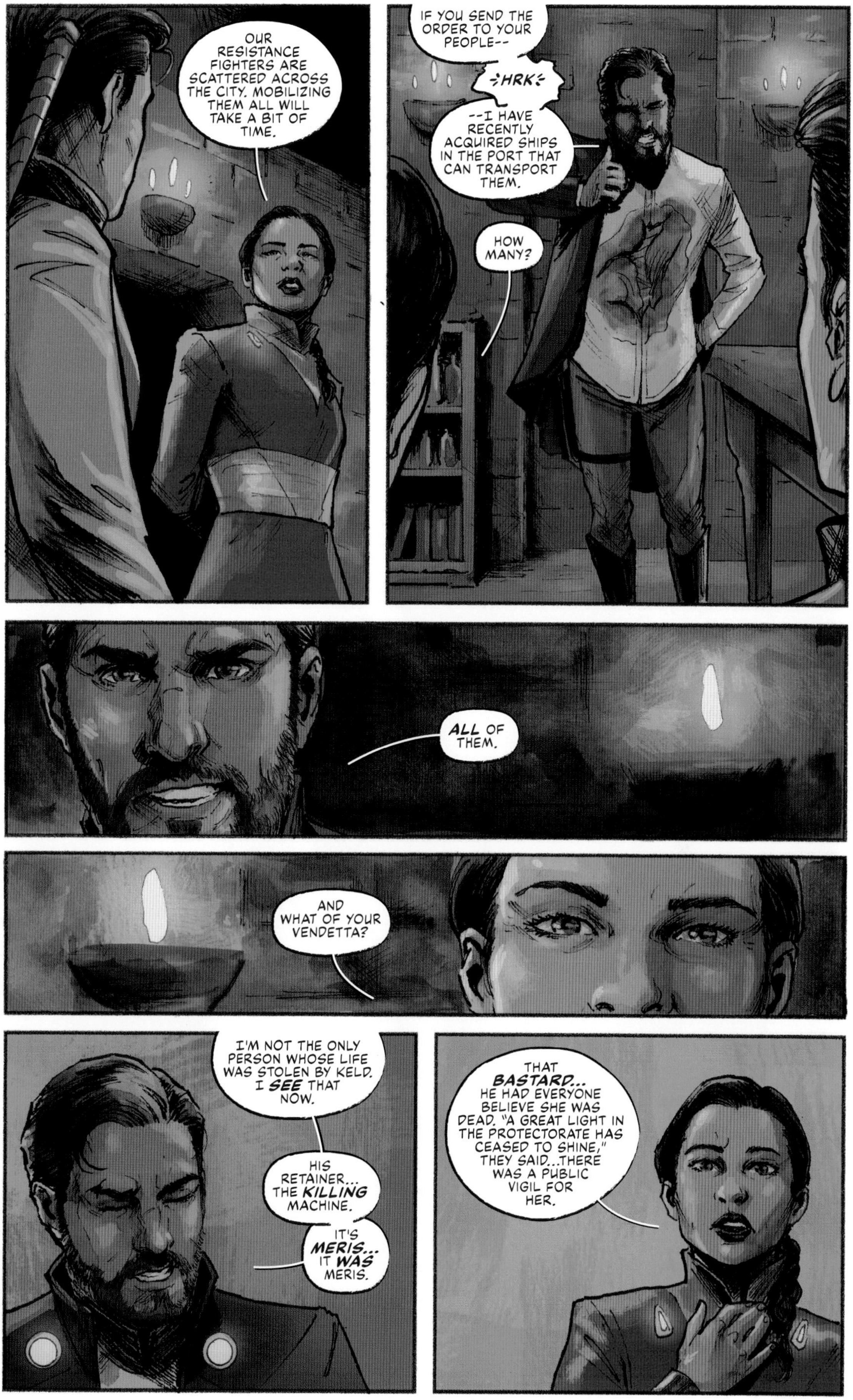
OUR RESISTANCE FIGHTERS ARE SCATTERED ACROSS THE CITY. MOBILIZING THEM ALL WILL TAKE A BIT OF TIME.
IF YOU SEND THE ORDER TO YOUR PEOPLE--
HRK
--I HAVE RECENTLY ACQUIRED SHIPS IN THE PORT THAT CAN TRANSPORT THEM.
HOW MANY?
ALL OF THEM.
AND WHAT OF YOUR VENDETTA?
I'M NOT THE ONLY PERSON WHOSE LIFE WAS STOLEN BY KELD. I SEE THAT NOW.
HIS RETAINER... THE KILLING MACHINE.
IT'S MERIS... IT WAS MERIS.
THAT BASTARD... HE HAD EVERYONE BELIEVE SHE WAS DEAD. "A GREAT LIGHT IN THE PROTECTORATE HAS CEASED TO SHINE," THEY SAID...THERE WAS A PUBLIC VIGIL FOR HER.

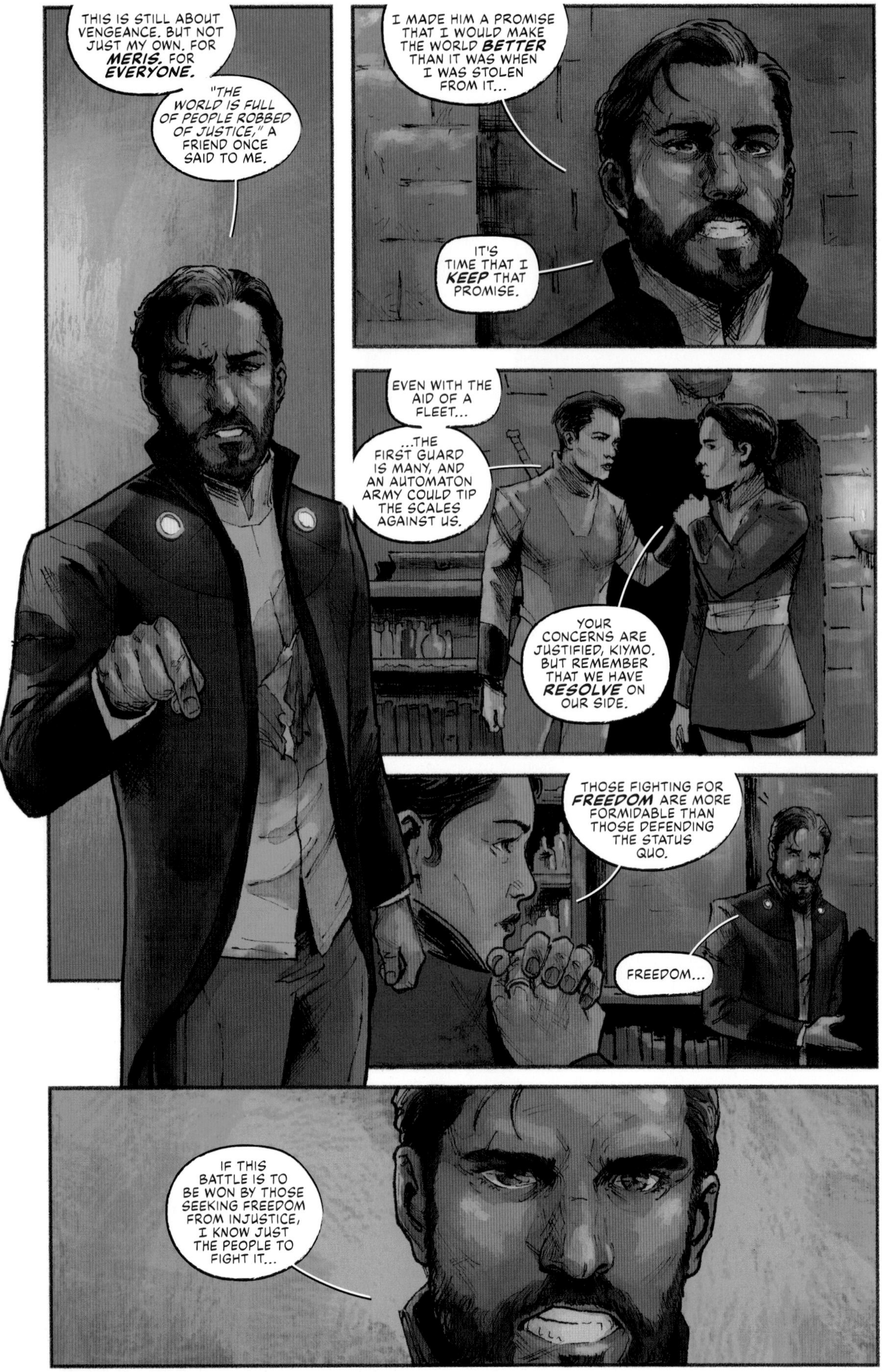
THIS IS STILL ABOUT VENGEANCE. BUT NOT JUST MY OWN. FOR MERIS. FOR EVERYONE.
"THE WORLD IS FULL OF PEOPLE ROBBED OF JUSTICE," A FRIEND ONCE SAID TO ME.
I MADE HIM A PROMISE THAT I WOULD MAKE THE WORLD BETTER THAN IT WAS WHEN I WAS STOLEN FROM IT...
IT'S TIME THAT I KEEP THAT PROMISE.
EVEN WITH THE AID OF A FLEET...
...THE FIRST GUARD IS MANY, AND AN AUTOMATON ARMY COULD TIP THE SCALES AGAINST US.
YOUR CONCERNS ARE JUSTIFIED, KIYMO. BUT REMEMBER THAT WE HAVE RESOLVE ON OUR SIDE.
THOSE FIGHTING FOR FREEDOM ARE MORE FORMIDABLE THAN THOSE DEFENDING THE STATUS QUO.
FREEDOM...
IF THIS BATTLE IS TO BE WON BY THOSE SEEKING FREEDOM FROM INJUSTICE, I KNOW JUST THE PEOPLE TO FIGHT IT...

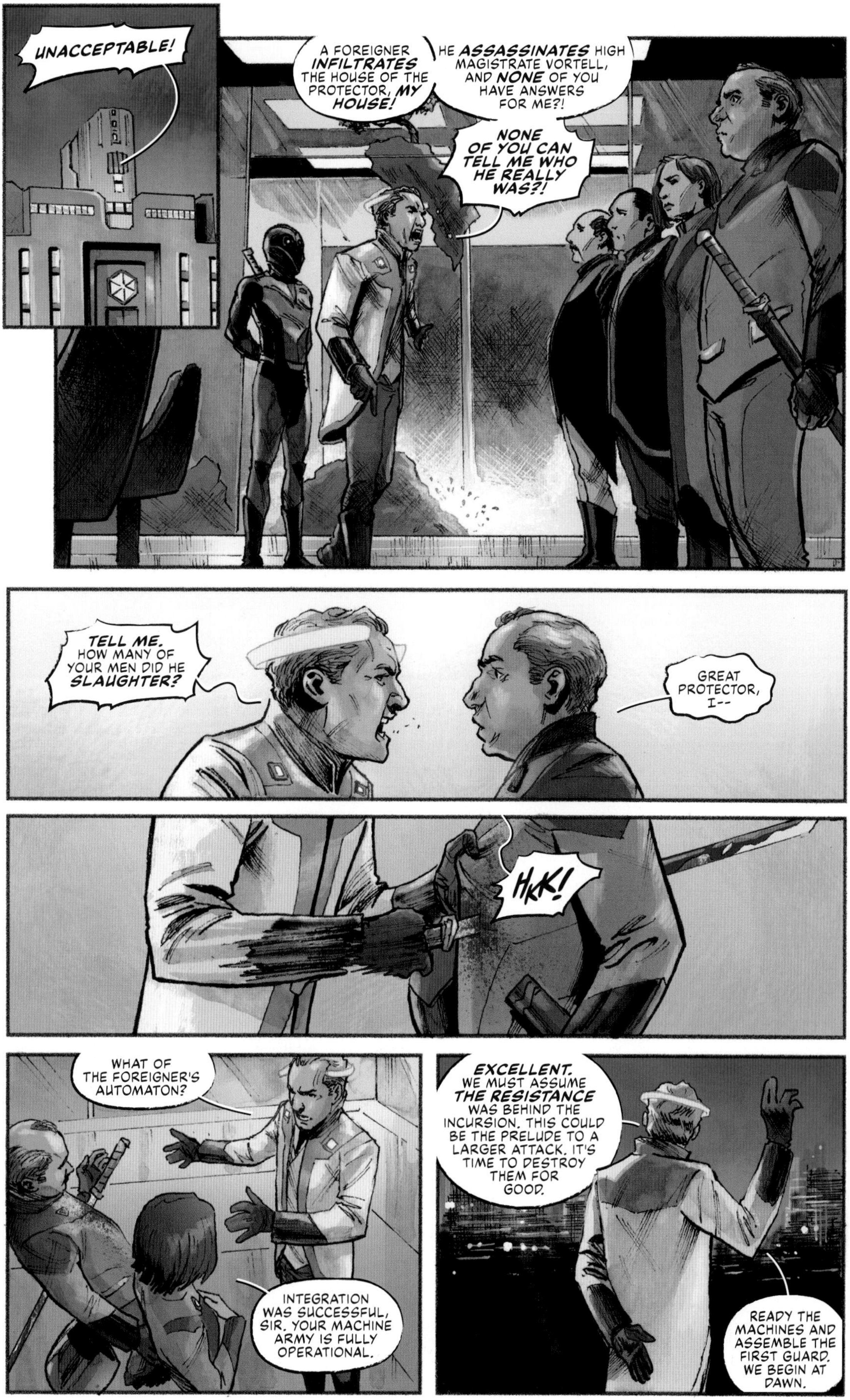
UNACCEPTABLE!
A FOREIGNER INFILTRATES THE HOUSE OF THE PROTECTOR, MY HOUSE!
HE ASSASSINATES HIGH MAGISTRATE VORTELL, AND NONE OF YOU HAVE ANSWERS FOR ME?!
NONE OF YOU CAN TELL ME WHO HE REALLY WAS?!
TELL ME. HOW MANY OF YOUR MEN DID HE SLAUGHTER?
GREAT PROTECTOR, I--
HKK!
WHAT OF THE FOREIGNER'S AUTOMATON?
INTEGRATION WAS SUCCESSFUL, SIR. YOUR MACHINE ARMY IS FULLY OPERATIONAL.
EXCELLENT. WE MUST ASSUME THE RESISTANCE WAS BEHIND THE INCURSION. THIS COULD BE THE PRELUDE TO A LARGER ATTACK. IT'S TIME TO DESTROY THEM FOR GOOD.
READY THE MACHINES AND ASSEMBLE THE FIRST GUARD. WE BEGIN AT DAWN.

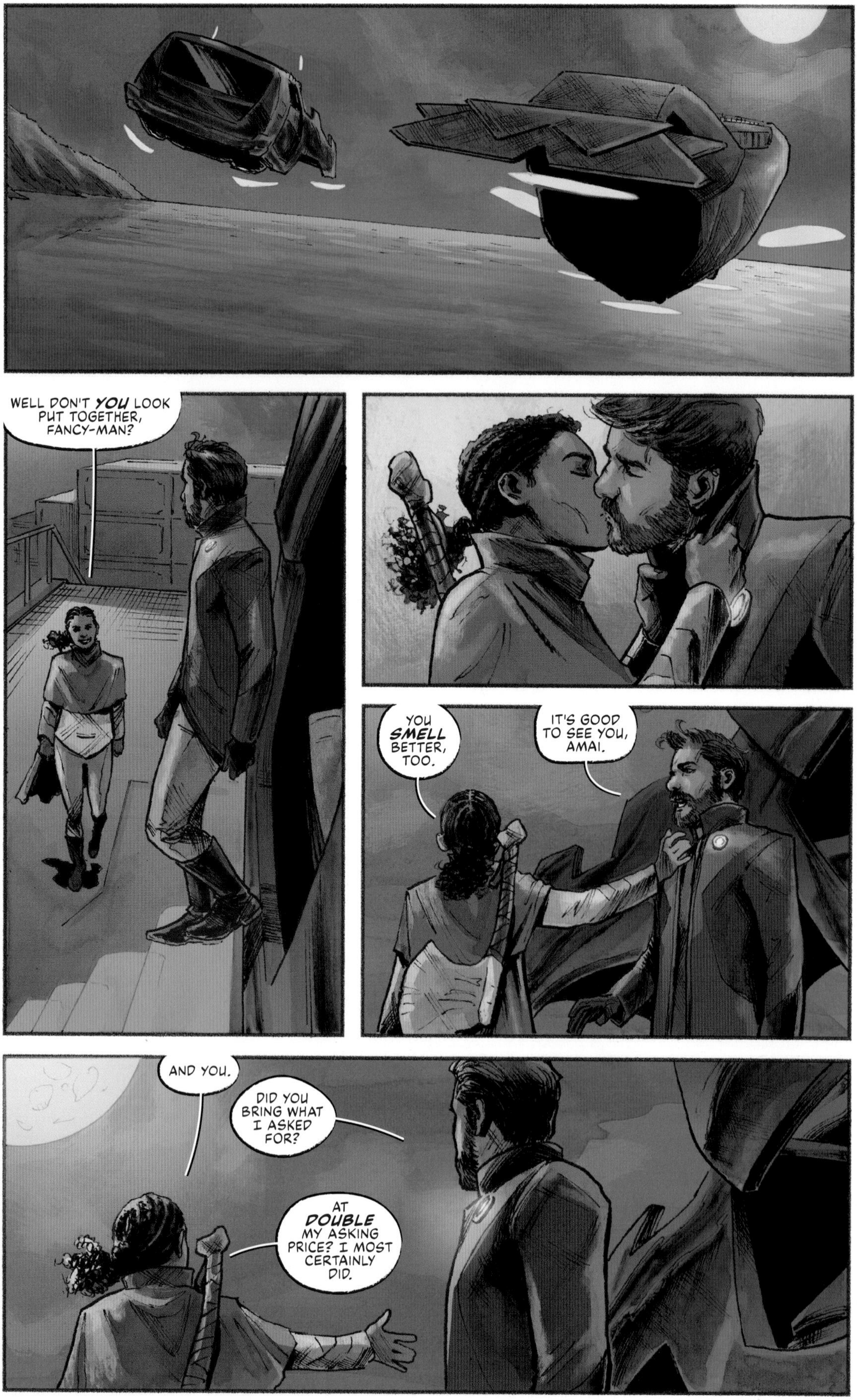
WELL DON'T YOU LOOK PUT TOGETHER, FANCY-MAN?
YOU SMELL BETTER, TOO.
IT'S GOOD TO SEE YOU, AMAI.
AND YOU.
DID YOU BRING WHAT I ASKED FOR?
AT DOUBLE MY ASKING PRICE? I MOST CERTAINLY DID.

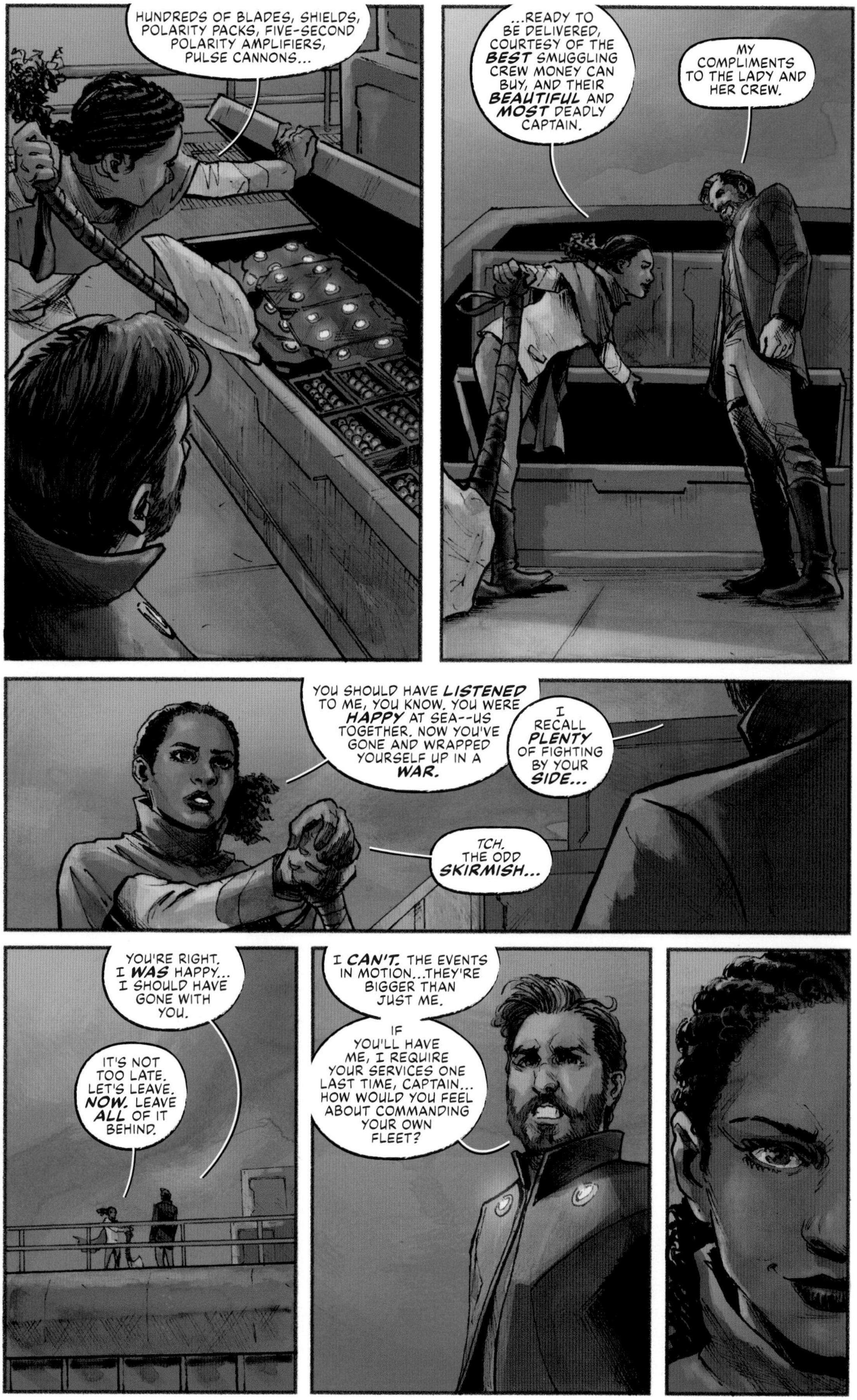
HUNDREDS OF BLADES, SHIELDS, POLARITY PACKS, FIVE-SECOND POLARITY AMPLIFIERS, PULSE CANNONS...
...READY TO BE DELIVERED, COURTESY OF THE BEST SMUGGLING CREW MONEY CAN BUY, AND THEIR BEAUTIFUL AND MOST DEADLY CAPTAIN.
MY COMPLIMENTS TO THE LADY AND HER CREW.
YOU SHOULD HAVE LISTENED TO ME, YOU KNOW. YOU WERE HAPPY AT SEA--US TOGETHER. NOW YOU'VE GONE AND WRAPPED YOURSELF UP IN A WAR.
I RECALL PLENTY OF FIGHTING BY YOUR SIDE...
TCH. THE ODD SKIRMISH...
YOU'RE RIGHT. I WAS HAPPY... I SHOULD HAVE GONE WITH YOU.
IT'S NOT TOO LATE. LET'S LEAVE. NOW. LEAVE ALL OF IT BEHIND.
I CAN'T. THE EVENTS IN MOTION...THEY'RE BIGGER THAN JUST ME.
IF YOU'LL HAVE ME, I REQUIRE YOUR SERVICES ONE LAST TIME, CAPTAIN... HOW WOULD YOU FEEL ABOUT COMMANDING YOUR OWN FLEET?

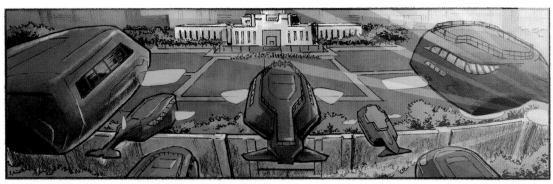

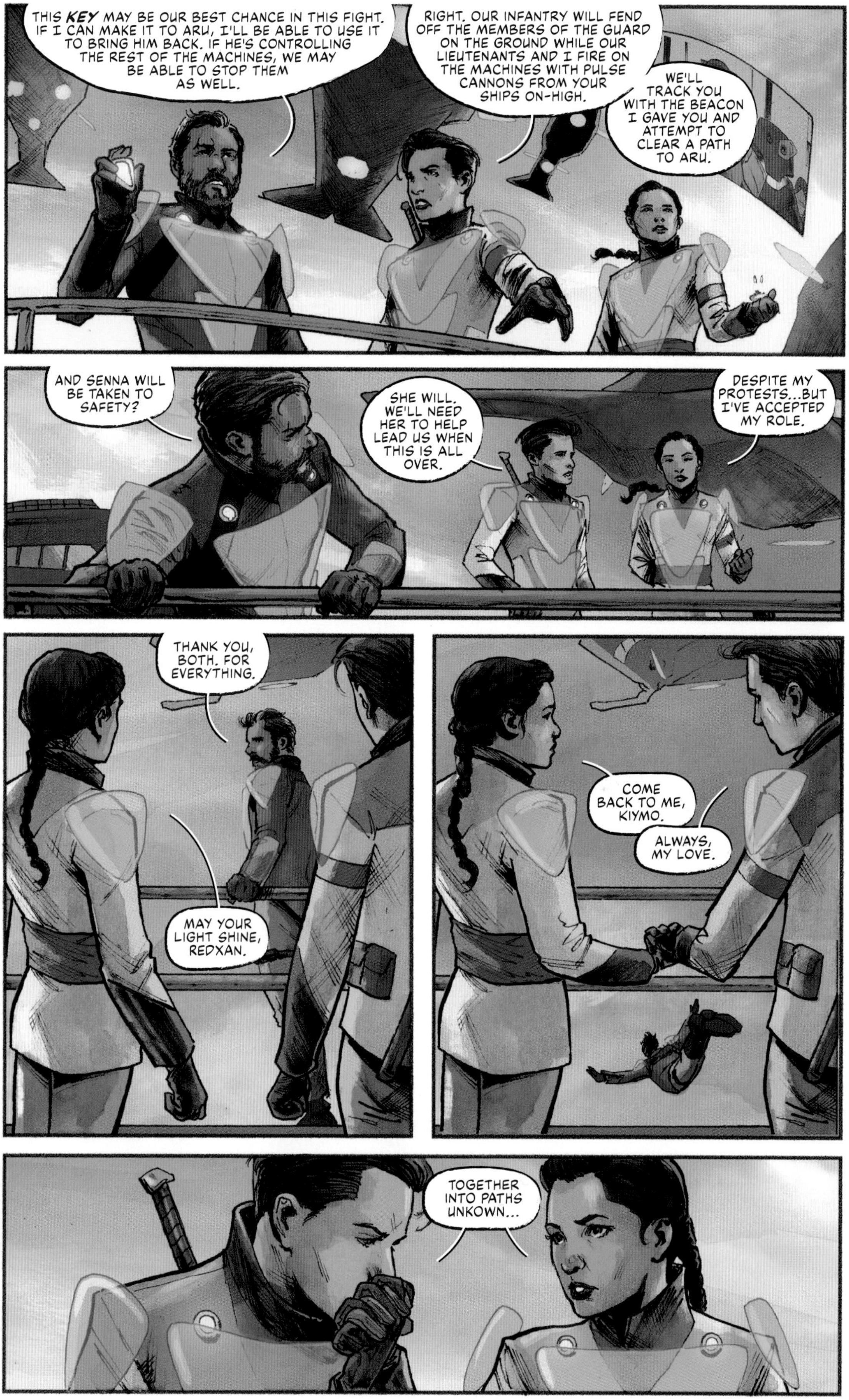
THIS KEY MAY BE OUR BEST CHANCE IN THIS FIGHT. IF I CAN MAKE IT TO ARU, I'LL BE ABLE TO USE IT TO BRING HIM BACK. IF HE'S CONTROLLING THE REST OF THE MACHINES, WE MAY BE ABLE TO STOP THEM AS WELL.
RIGHT. OUR INFANTRY WILL FEND OFF THE MEMBERS OF THE GUARD ON THE GROUND WHILE OUR LIEUTENANTS AND I FIRE ON THE MACHINES WITH PULSE CANNONS FROM YOUR SHIPS ON-HIGH.
WE'LL TRACK YOU WITH THE BEACON I GAVE YOU AND ATTEMPT TO CLEAR A PATH TO ARU.
AND SENNA WILL BE TAKEN TO SAFETY?
SHE WILL. WE'LL NEED HER TO HELP LEAD US WHEN THIS IS ALL OVER.
DESPITE MY PROTESTS...BUT I'VE ACCEPTED MY ROLE.
THANK YOU, BOTH. FOR EVERYTHING.
MAY YOUR LIGHT SHINE, REDXAN.
COME BACK TO ME, KIYMO.
ALWAYS, MY LOVE.
TOGETHER INTO PATHS UNKOWN...

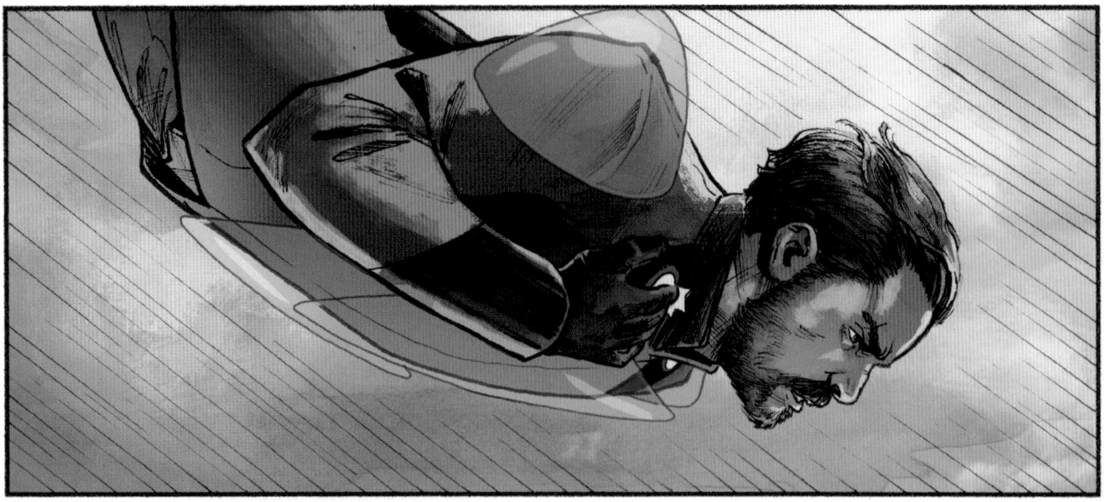

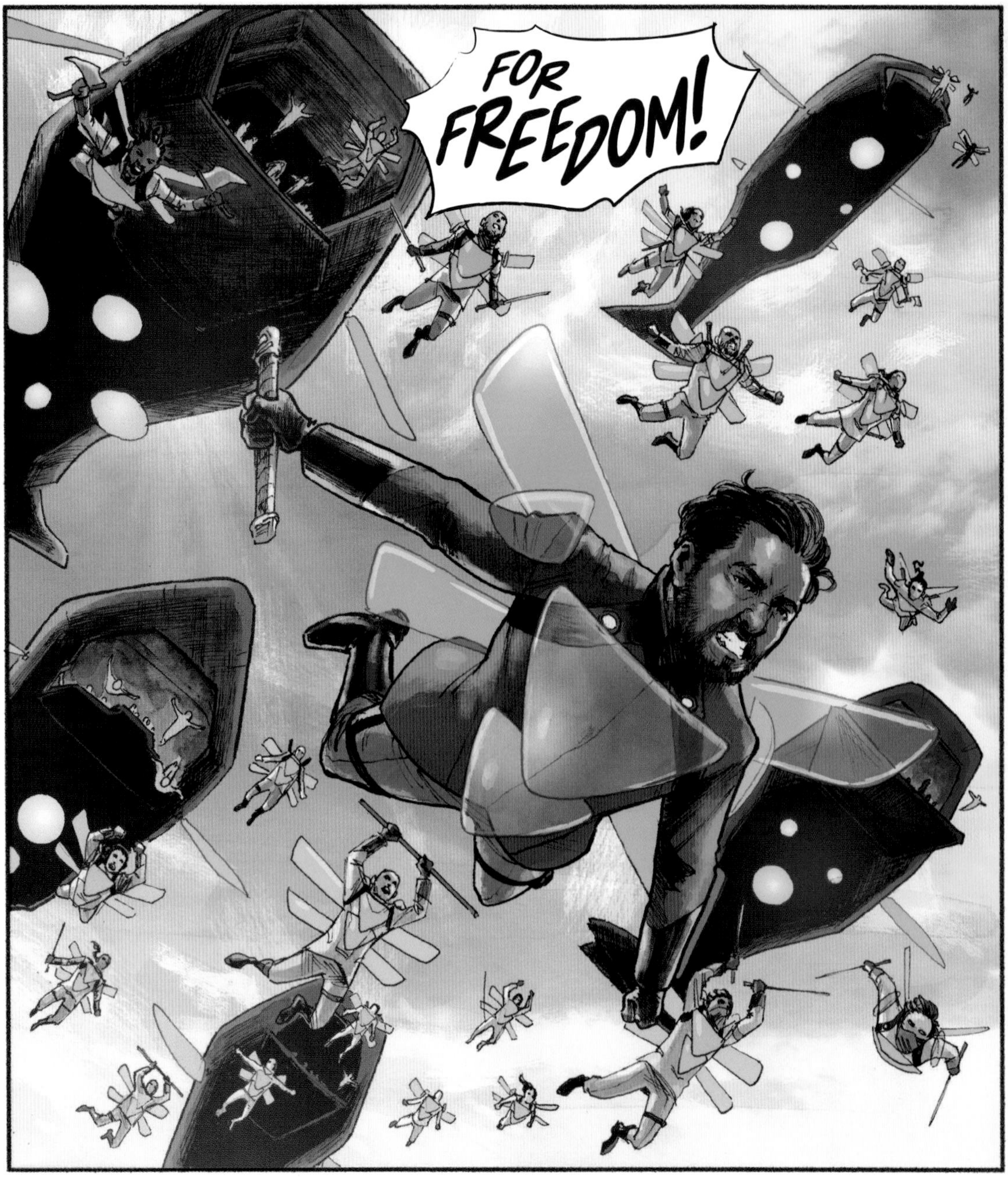
FOR FREEDOM!

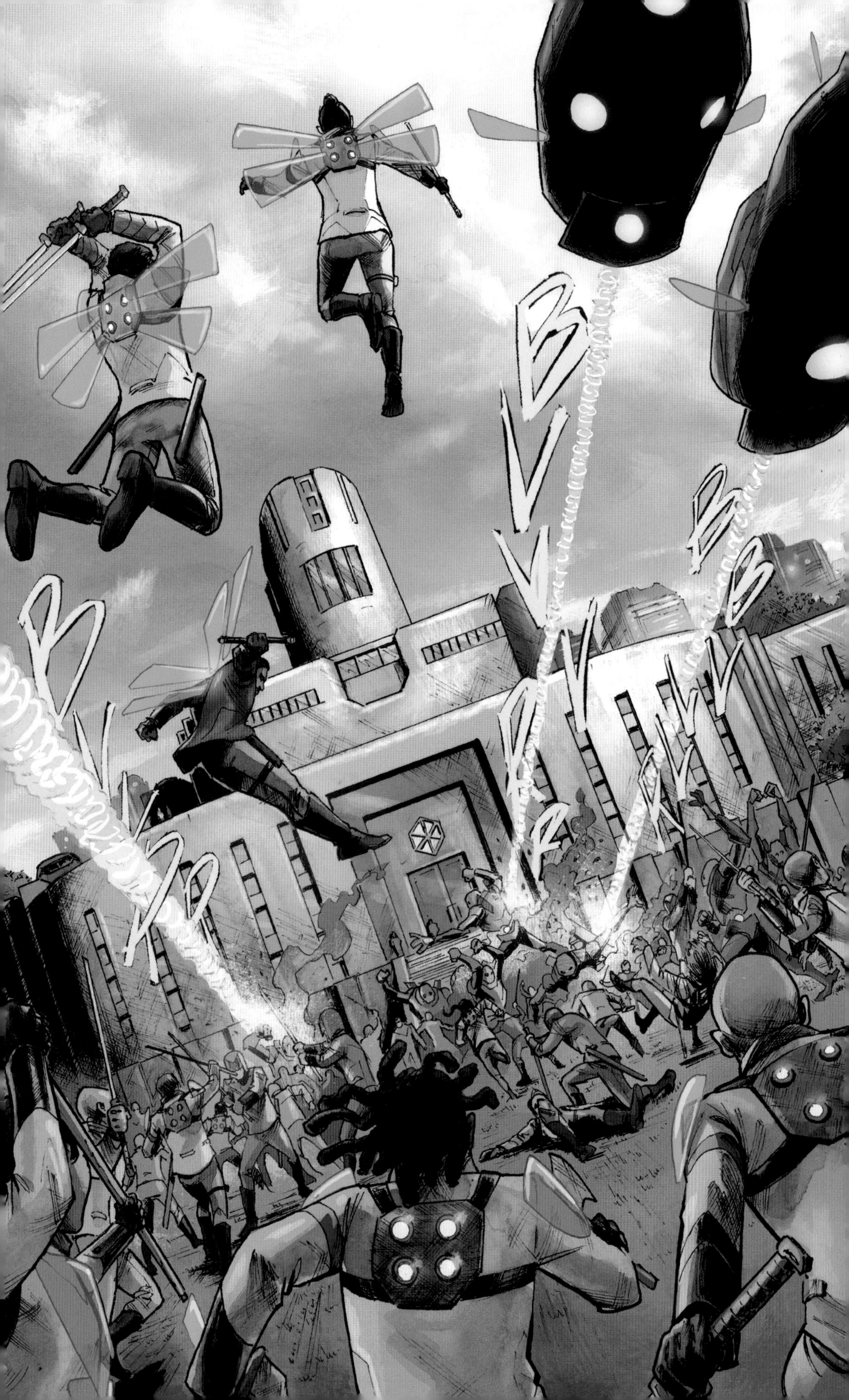

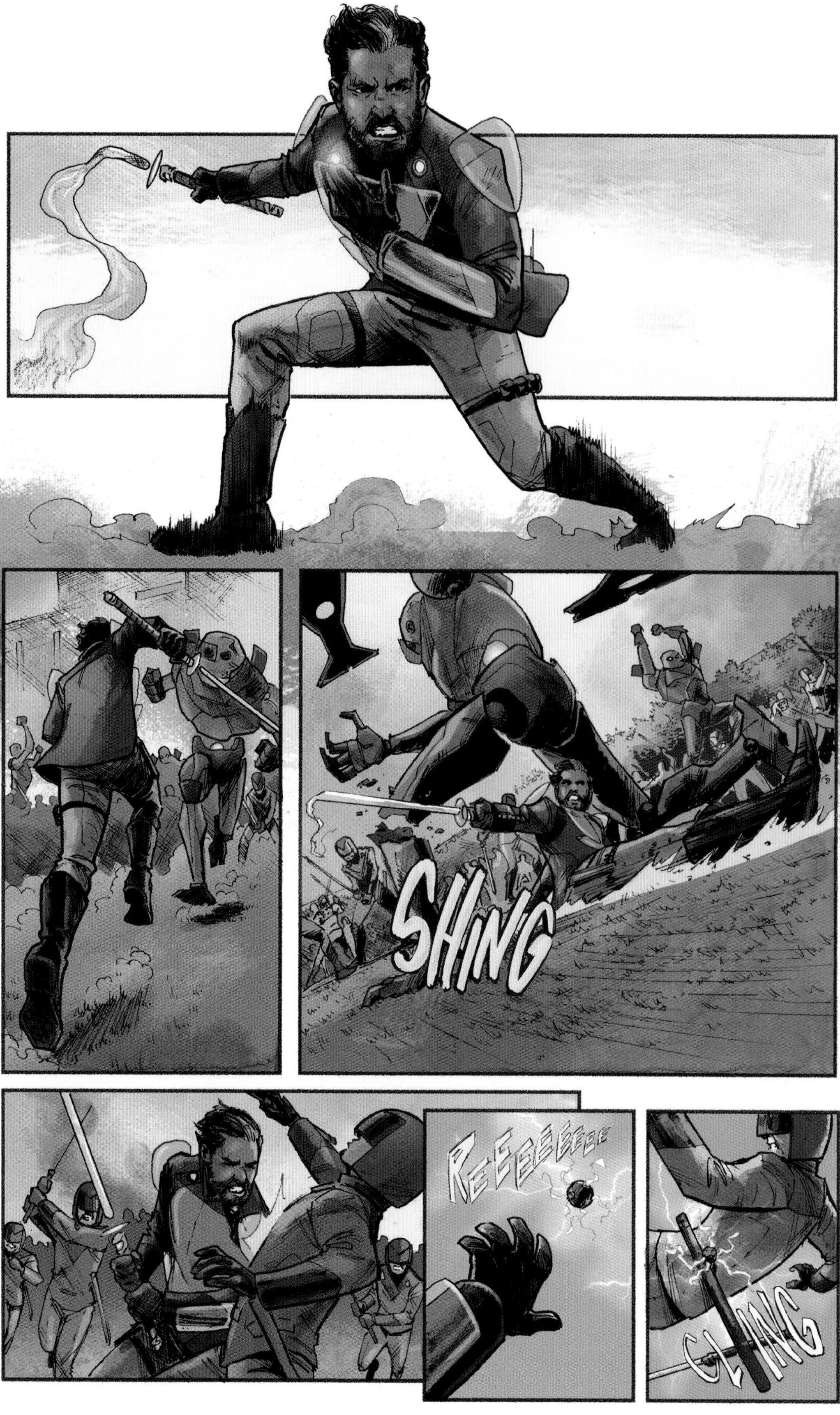
SHING
REEEEEEEE
CLING

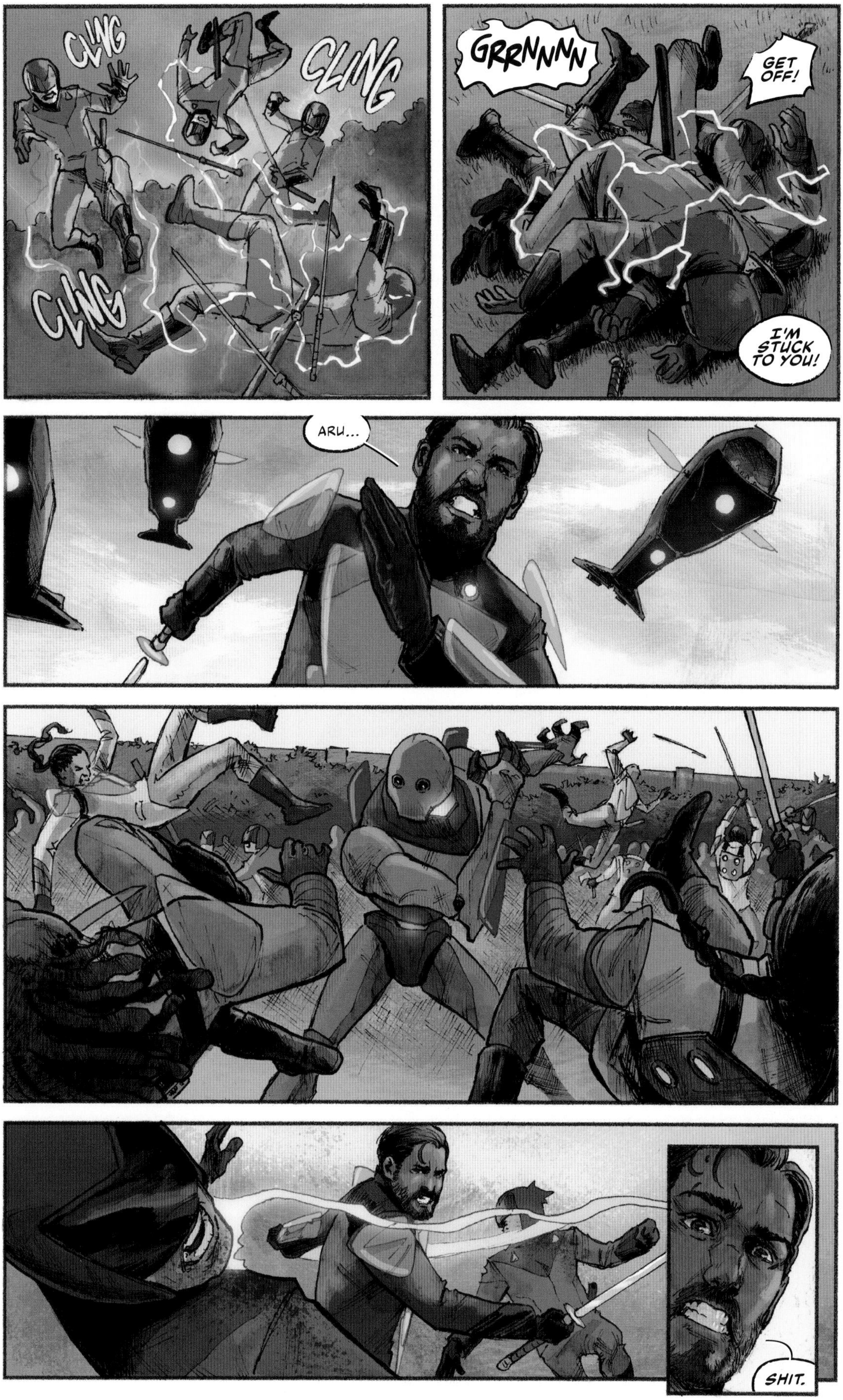
CLING
CLING
CLING
GRRNNNN
GET OFF!
I'M STUCK TO YOU!
ARU...
SHIT.

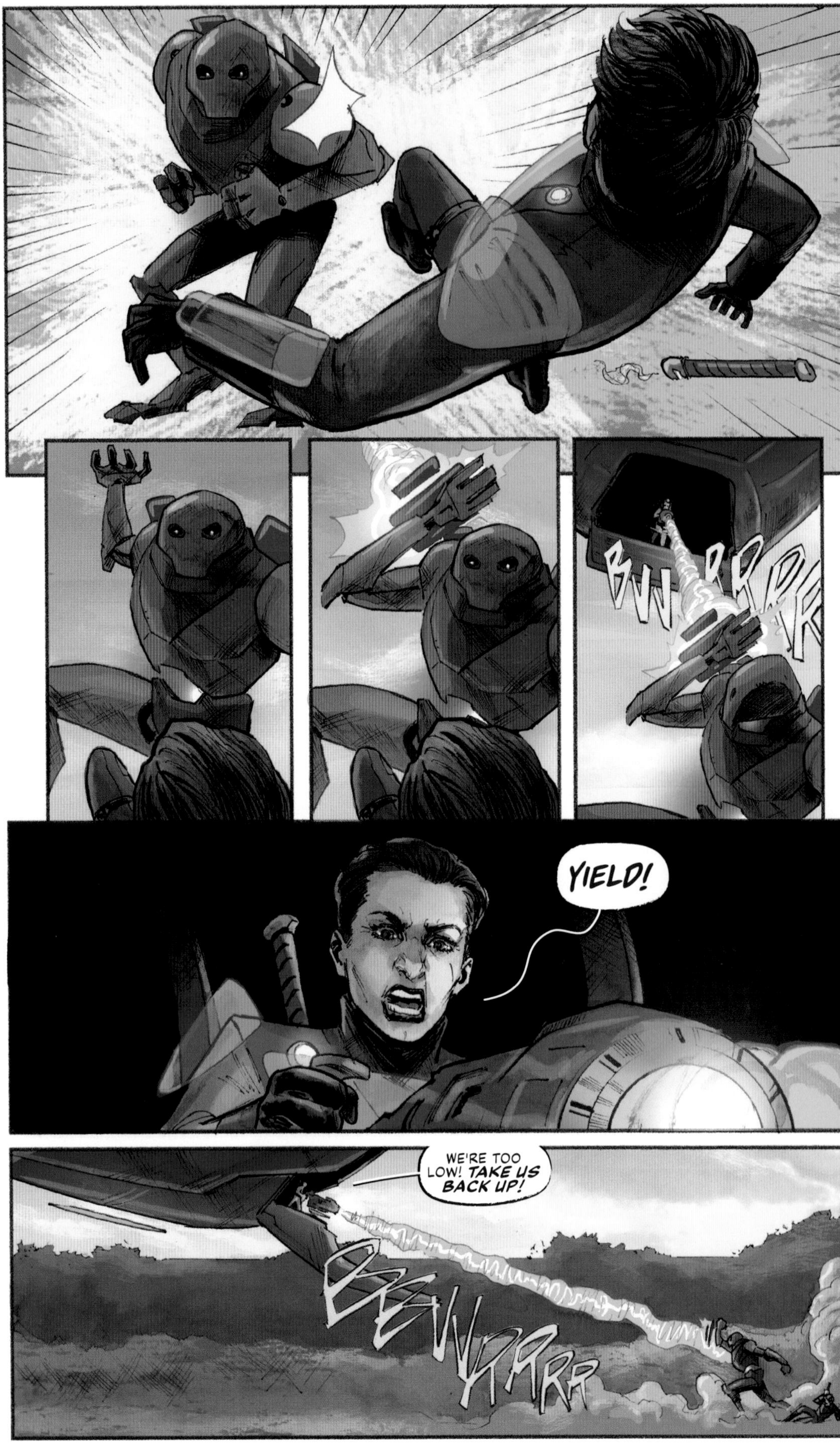
BVVRRRR
YIELD!
WE'RE TOO LOW! TAKE US BACK UP!
BEEVVRRRR

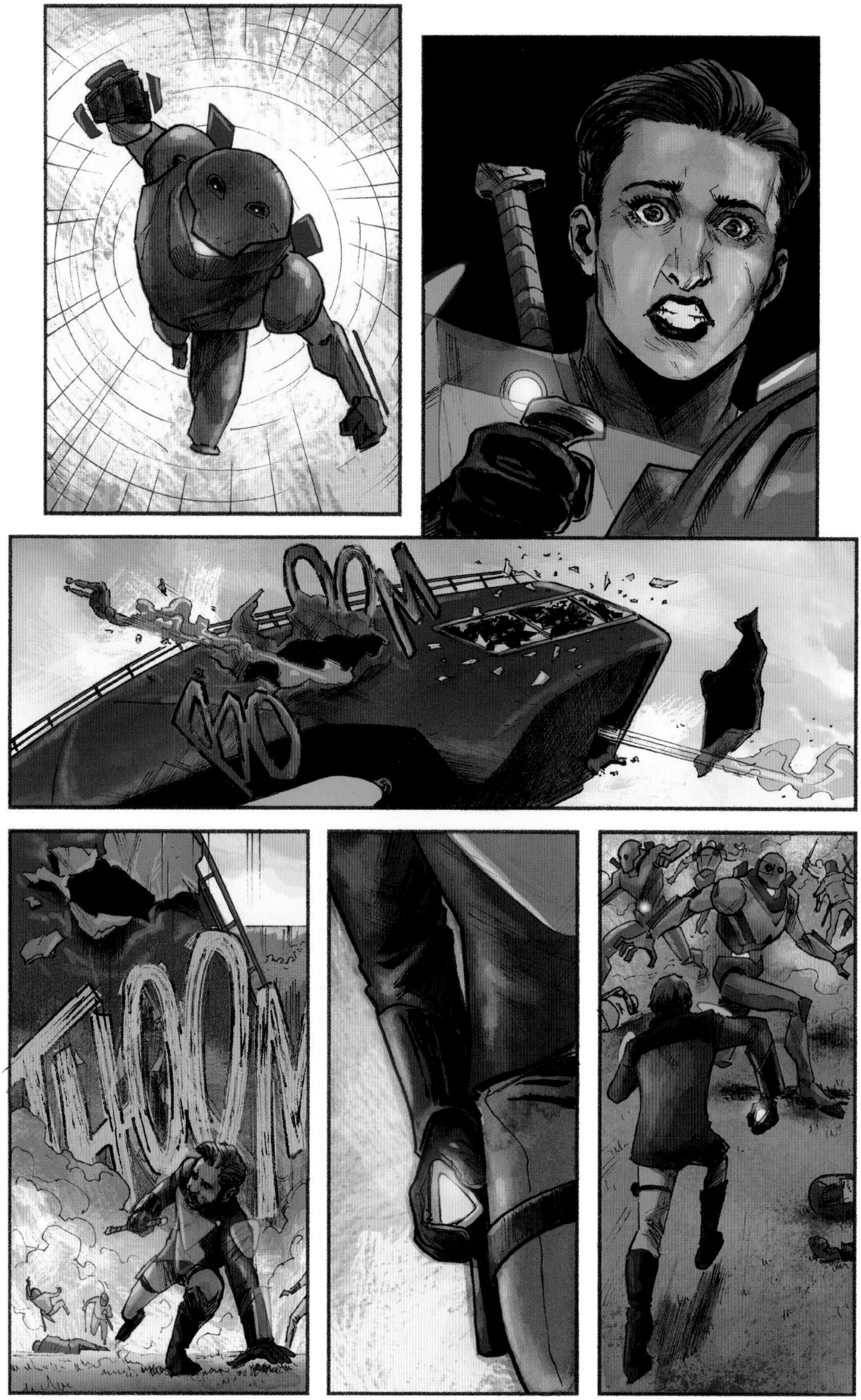
OOM
THOOM

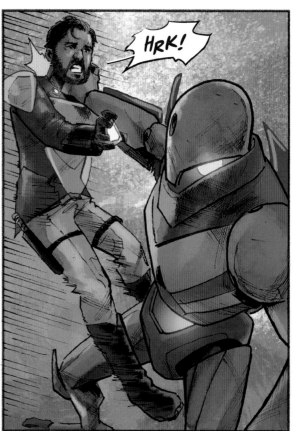

HRK!

GHKHH--
ARU...

GHKH--

RCEEEEEEEE

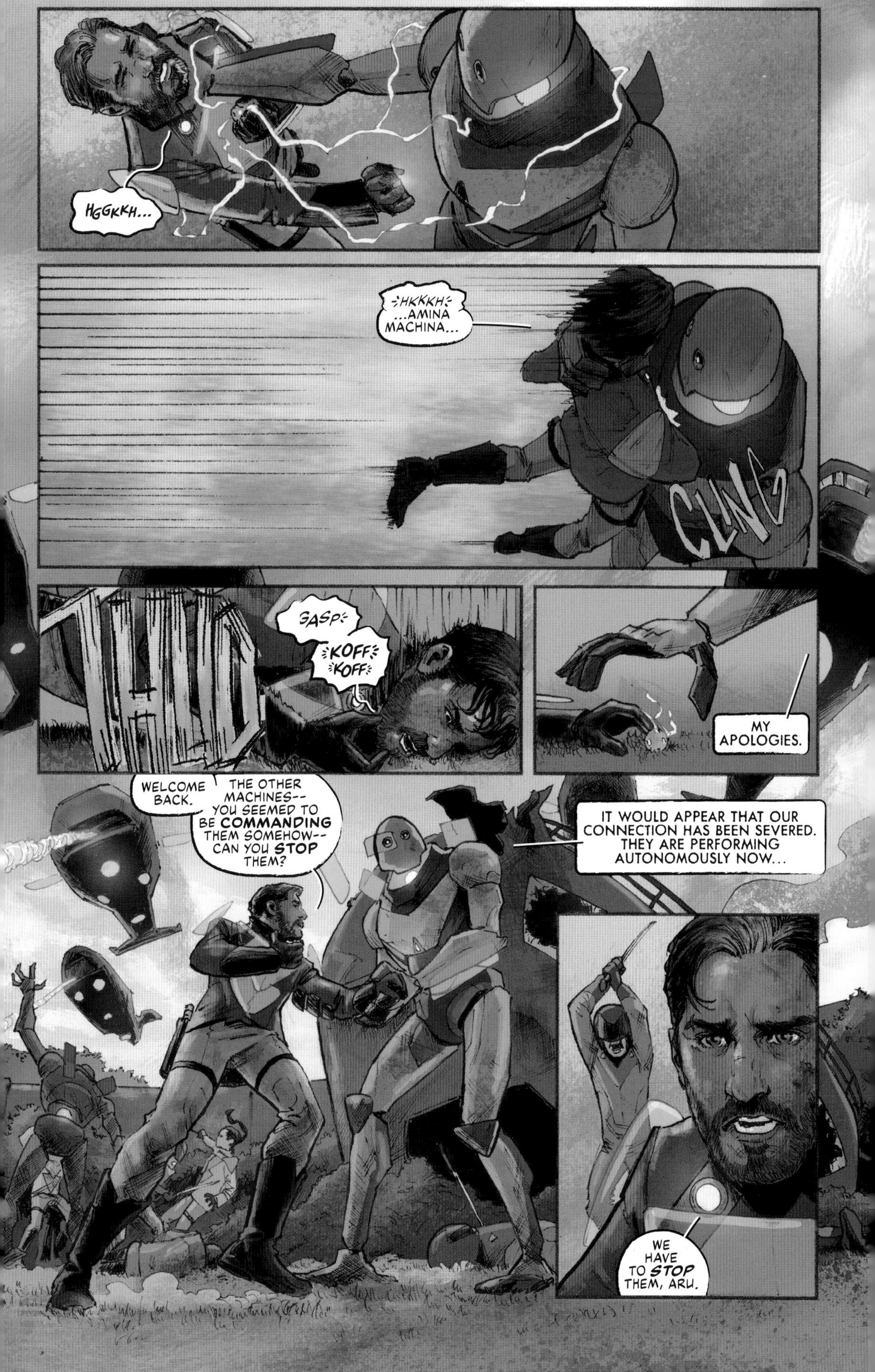
HGGKKH...
HKKKH ...AMINA MACHINA...
CLNG
GASP
KOFF KOFF
MY APOLOGIES.
WELCOME BACK.
THE OTHER MACHINES-- YOU SEEMED TO BE COMMANDING THEM SOMEHOW-- CAN YOU STOP THEM?
IT WOULD APPEAR THAT OUR CONNECTION HAS BEEN SEVERED. THEY ARE PERFORMING AUTONOMOUSLY NOW...
WE HAVE TO STOP THEM, ARU.

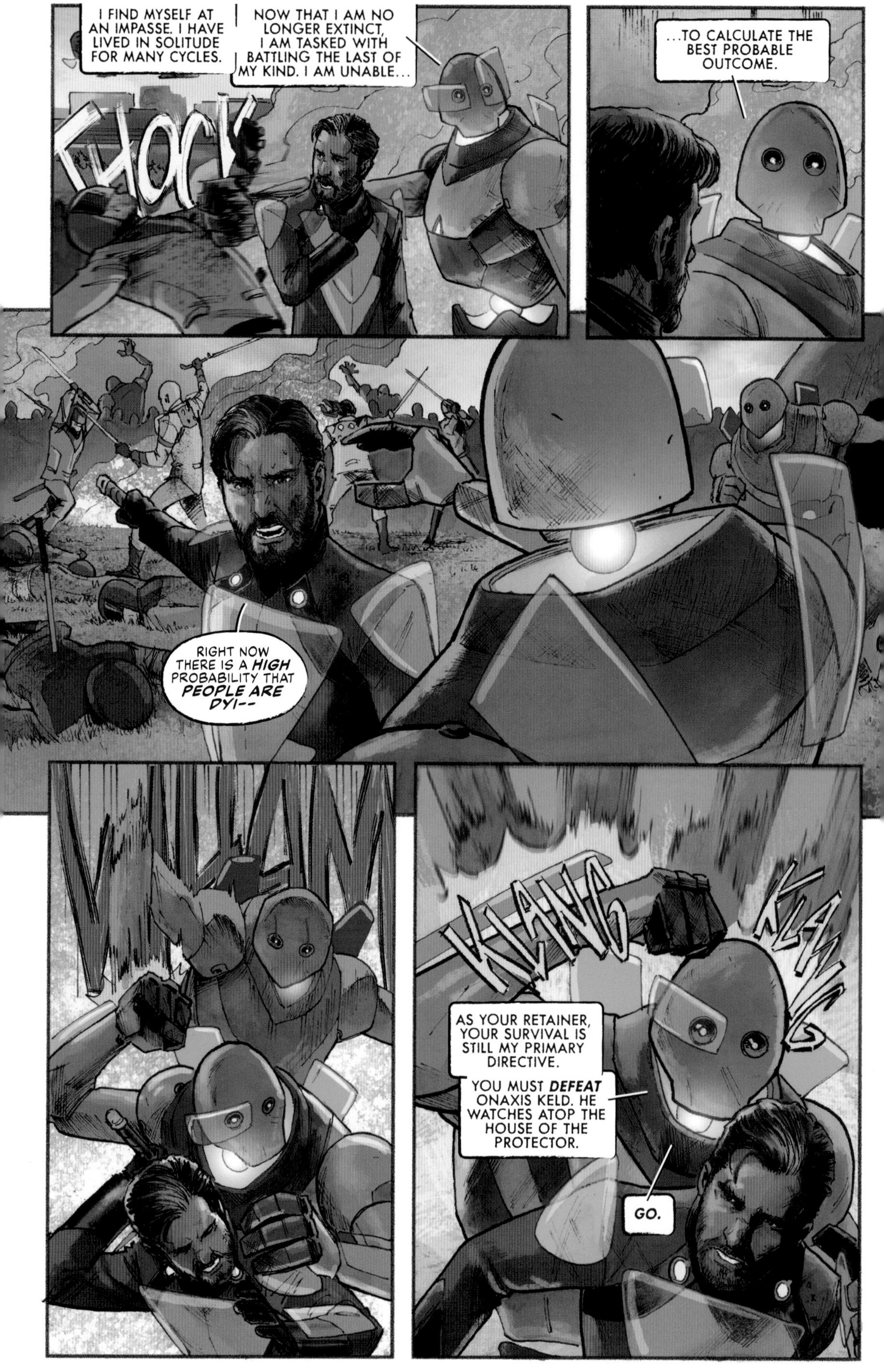
I FIND MYSELF AT AN IMPASSE. I HAVE LIVED IN SOLITUDE FOR MANY CYCLES.
NOW THAT I AM NO LONGER EXTINCT, I AM TASKED WITH BATTLING THE LAST OF MY KIND. I AM UNABLE...
THOCK
...TO CALCULATE THE BEST PROBABLE OUTCOME.
RIGHT NOW THERE IS A *HIGH* PROBABILITY THAT *PEOPLE ARE DYI--*
AS YOUR RETAINER, YOUR SURVIVAL IS STILL MY PRIMARY DIRECTIVE.
YOU MUST *DEFEAT* ONAXIS KELD. HE WATCHES ATOP THE HOUSE OF THE PROTECTOR.
GO.

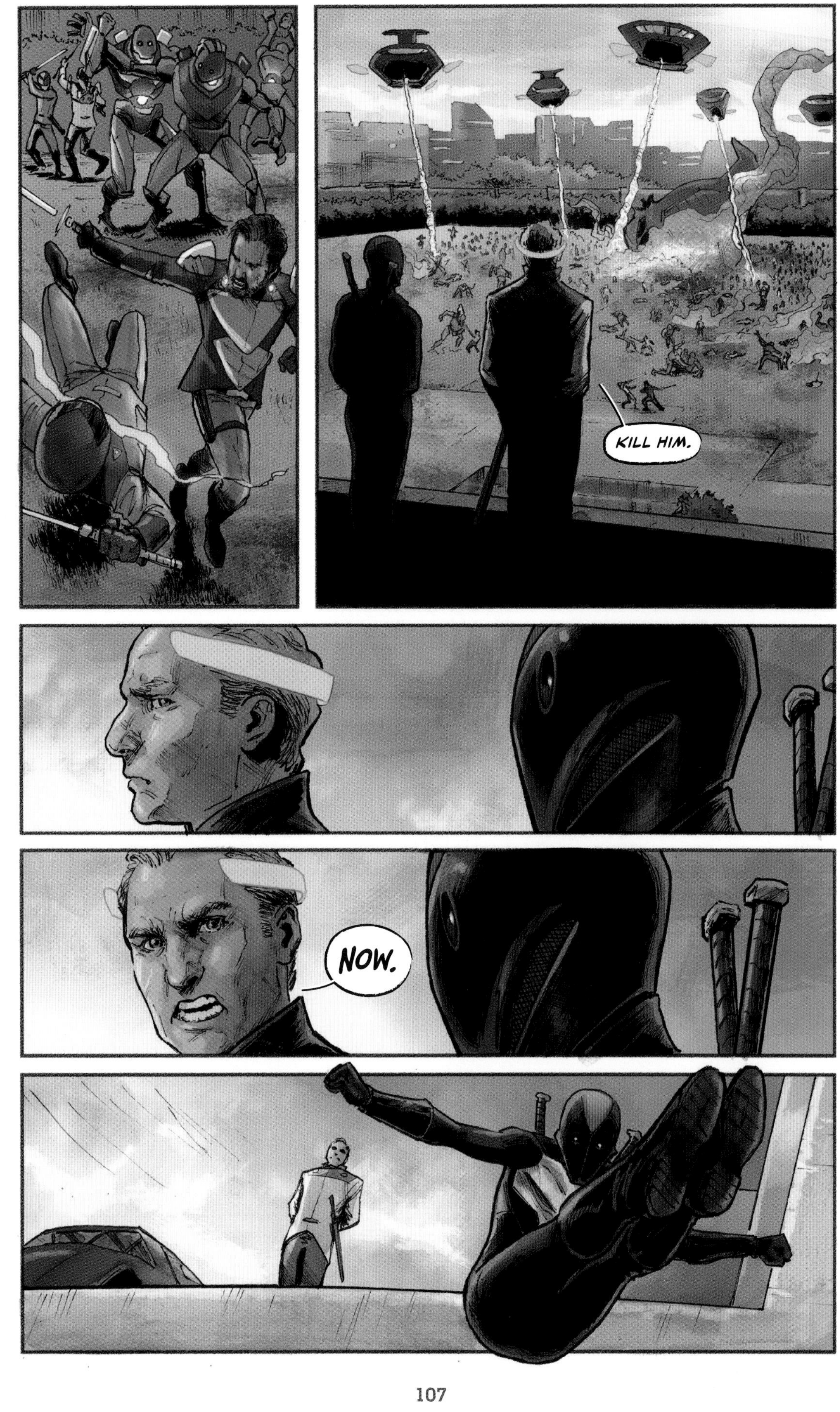
KILL HIM.
NOW.

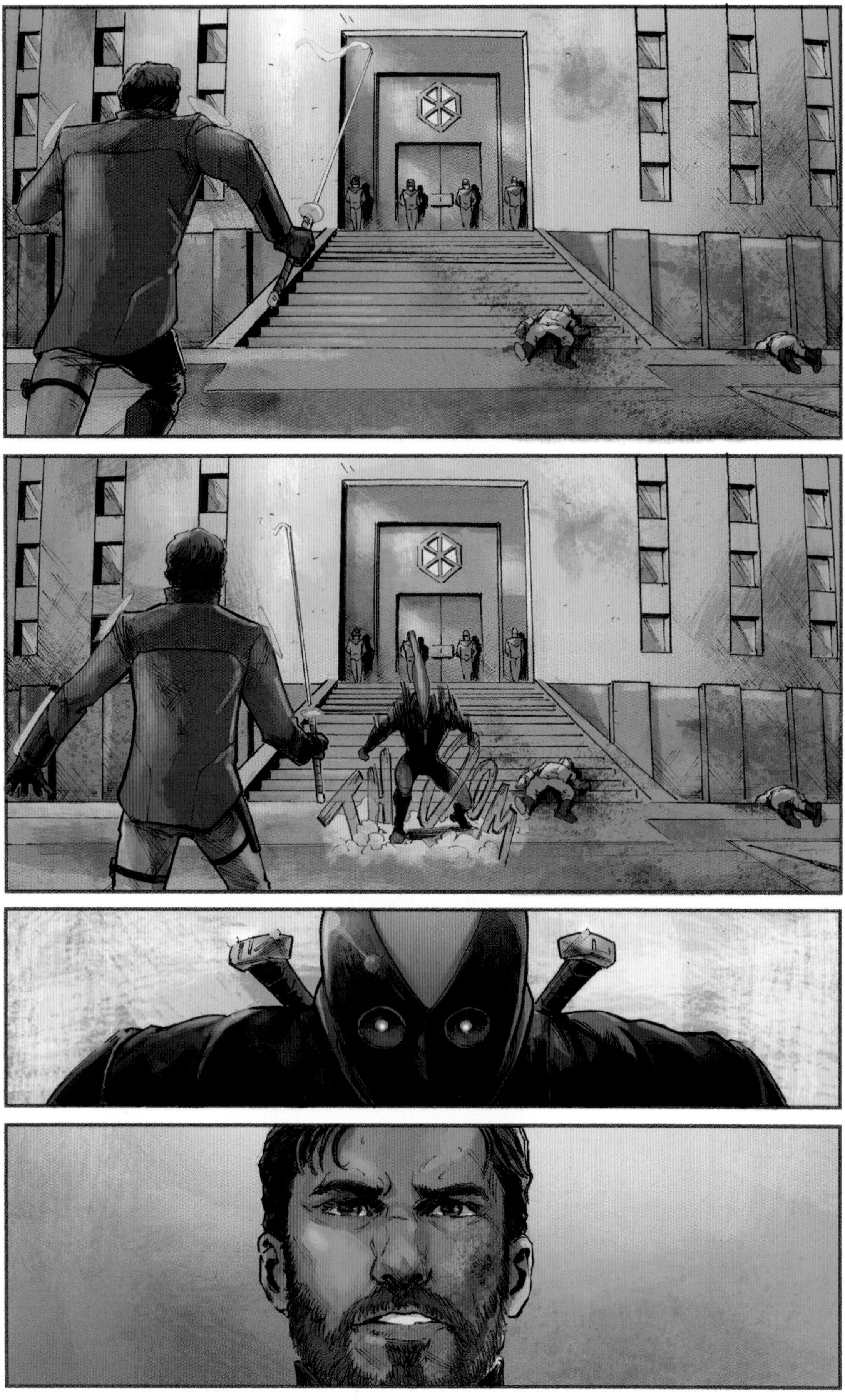
THOOM

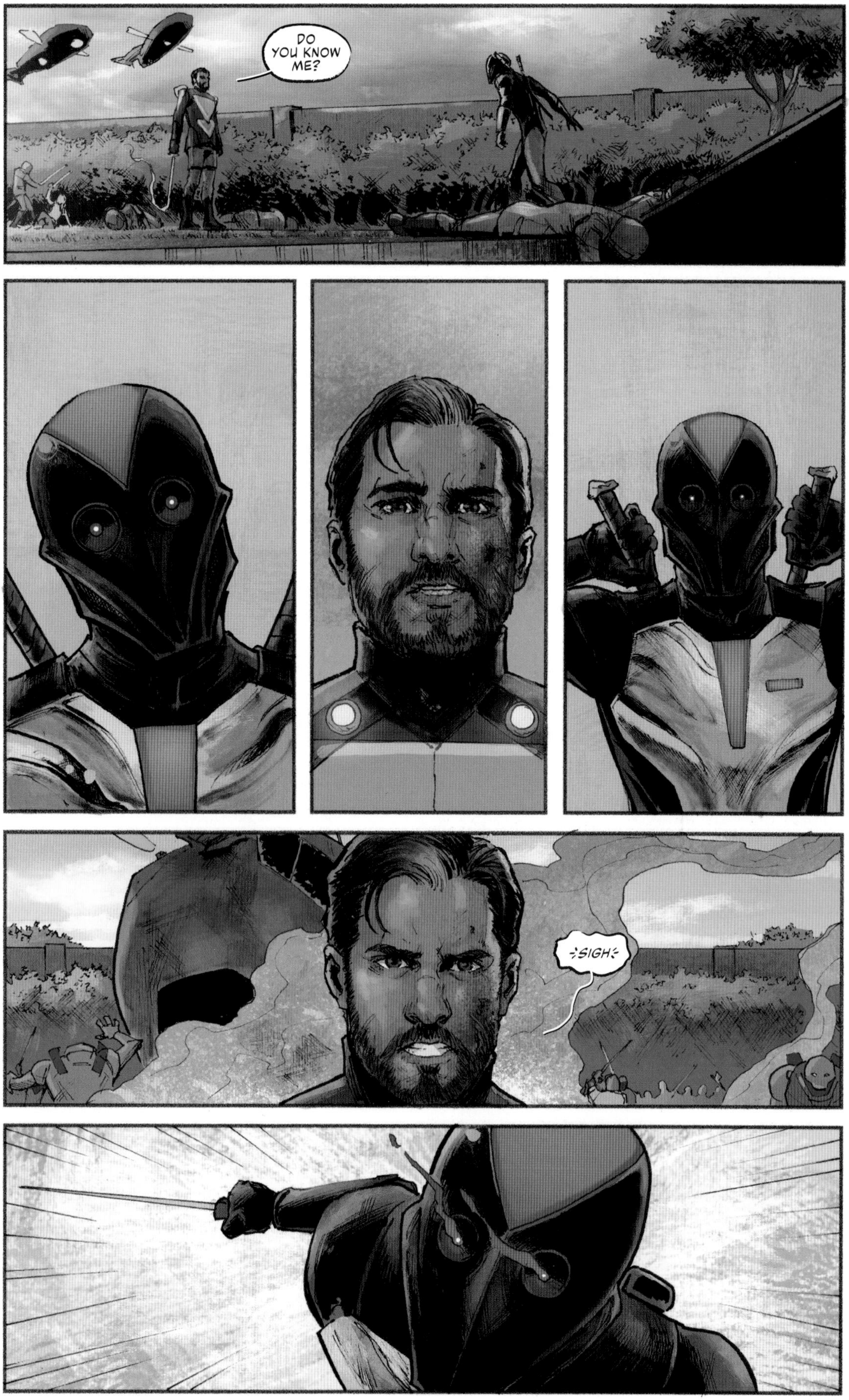
DO YOU KNOW ME?
SIGH

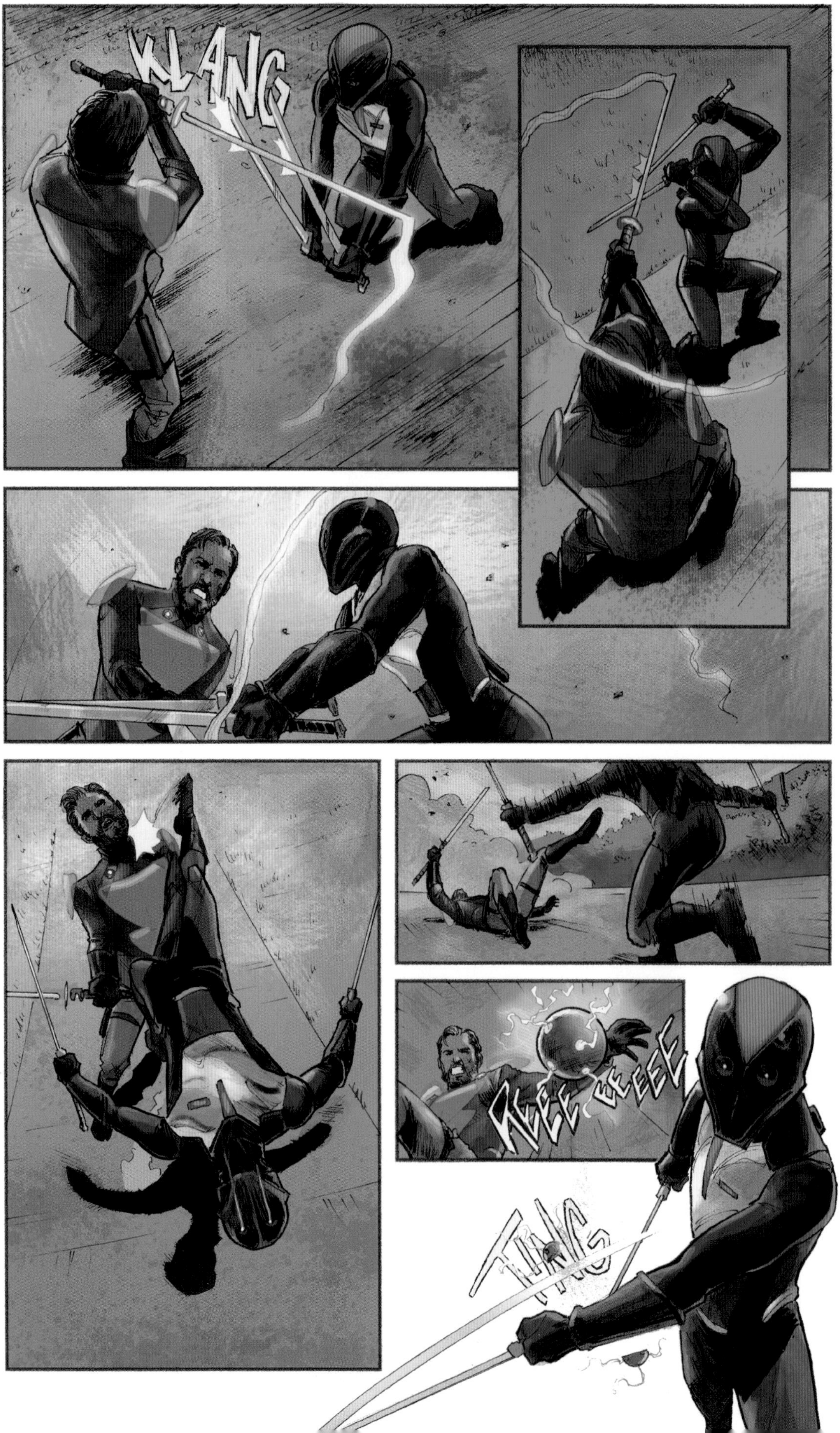
KLANG
REEE EEEE
TING

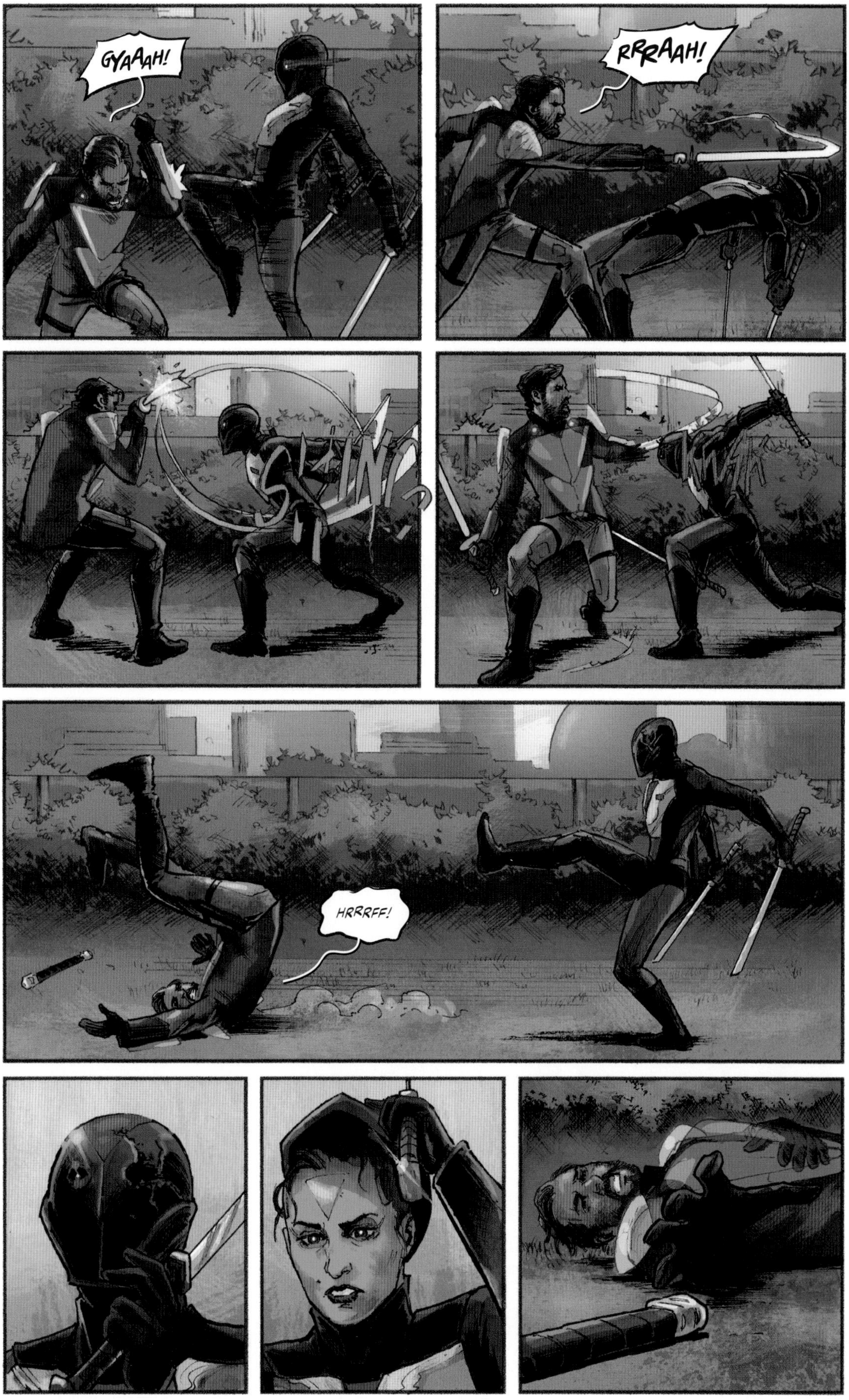
GYAAAH!
RRRAAH!
SHING
HRRRFF!

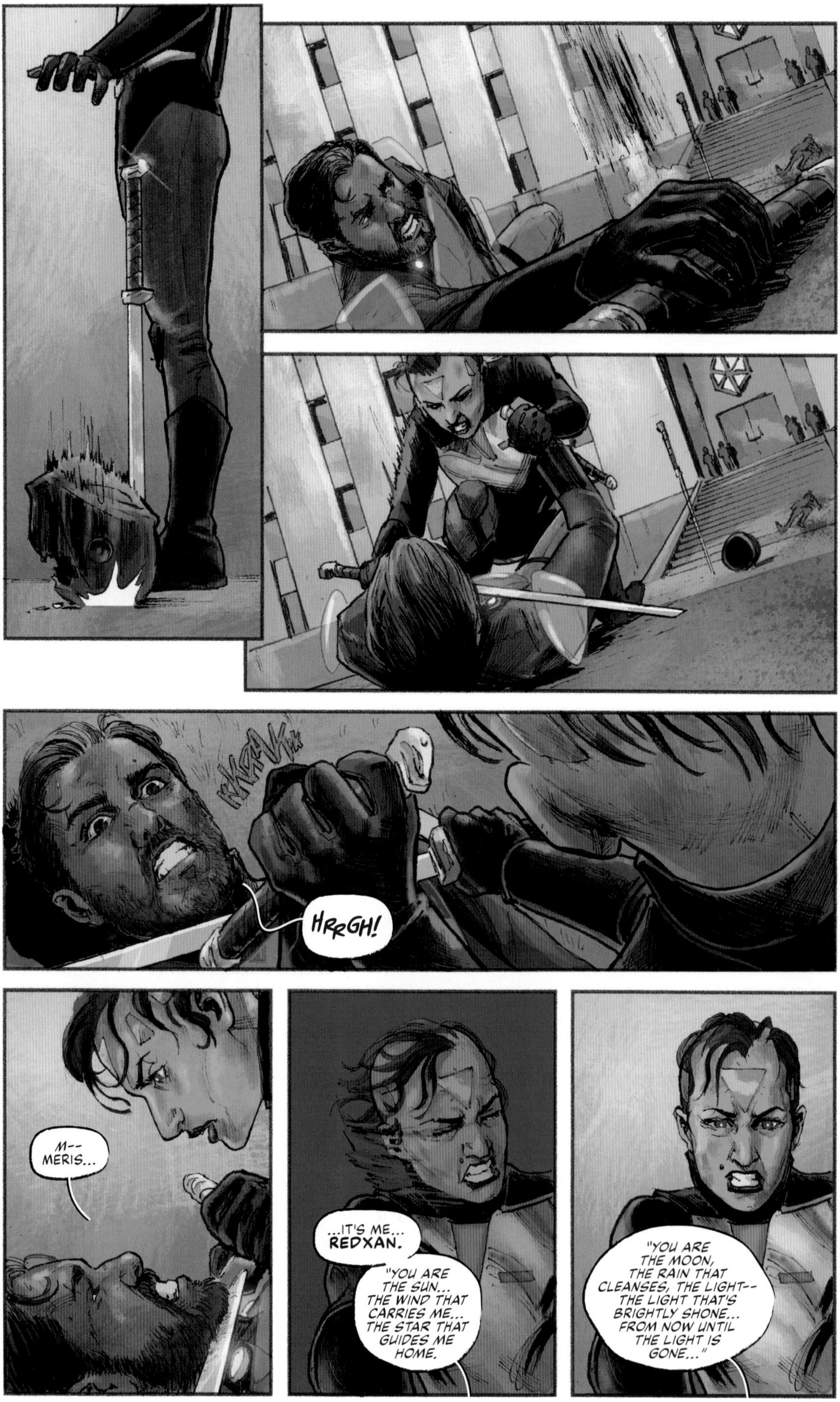
KKRAK
HRRGH!
M-- MERIS...
...IT'S ME... REDXAN.
"YOU ARE THE SUN... THE WIND THAT CARRIES ME... THE STAR THAT GUIDES ME HOME.
"YOU ARE THE MOON, THE RAIN THAT CLEANSES, THE LIGHT-- THE LIGHT THAT'S BRIGHTLY SHONE... FROM NOW UNTIL THE LIGHT IS GONE..."

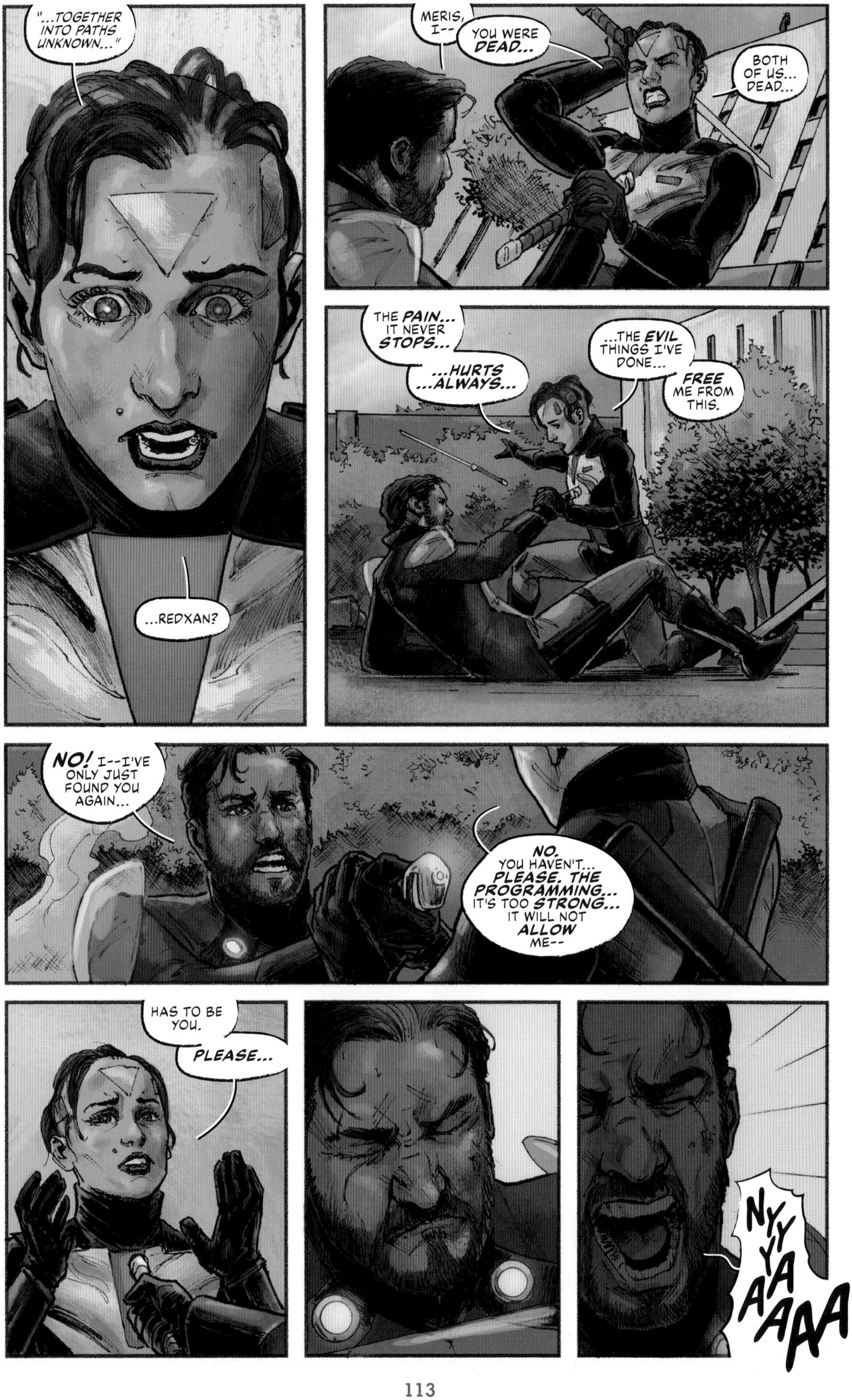
"...TOGETHER INTO PATHS UNKNOWN..."
...REDXAN?
MERIS, I--
YOU WERE DEAD...
BOTH OF US... DEAD...
THE PAIN... IT NEVER STOPS...
...HURTS ...ALWAYS...
...THE EVIL THINGS I'VE DONE...
FREE ME FROM THIS.
NO! I--I'VE ONLY JUST FOUND YOU AGAIN...
NO. YOU HAVEN'T... PLEASE. THE PROGRAMMING... IT'S TOO STRONG... IT WILL NOT ALLOW ME--
HAS TO BE YOU.
PLEASE...
NYYYAAAAA

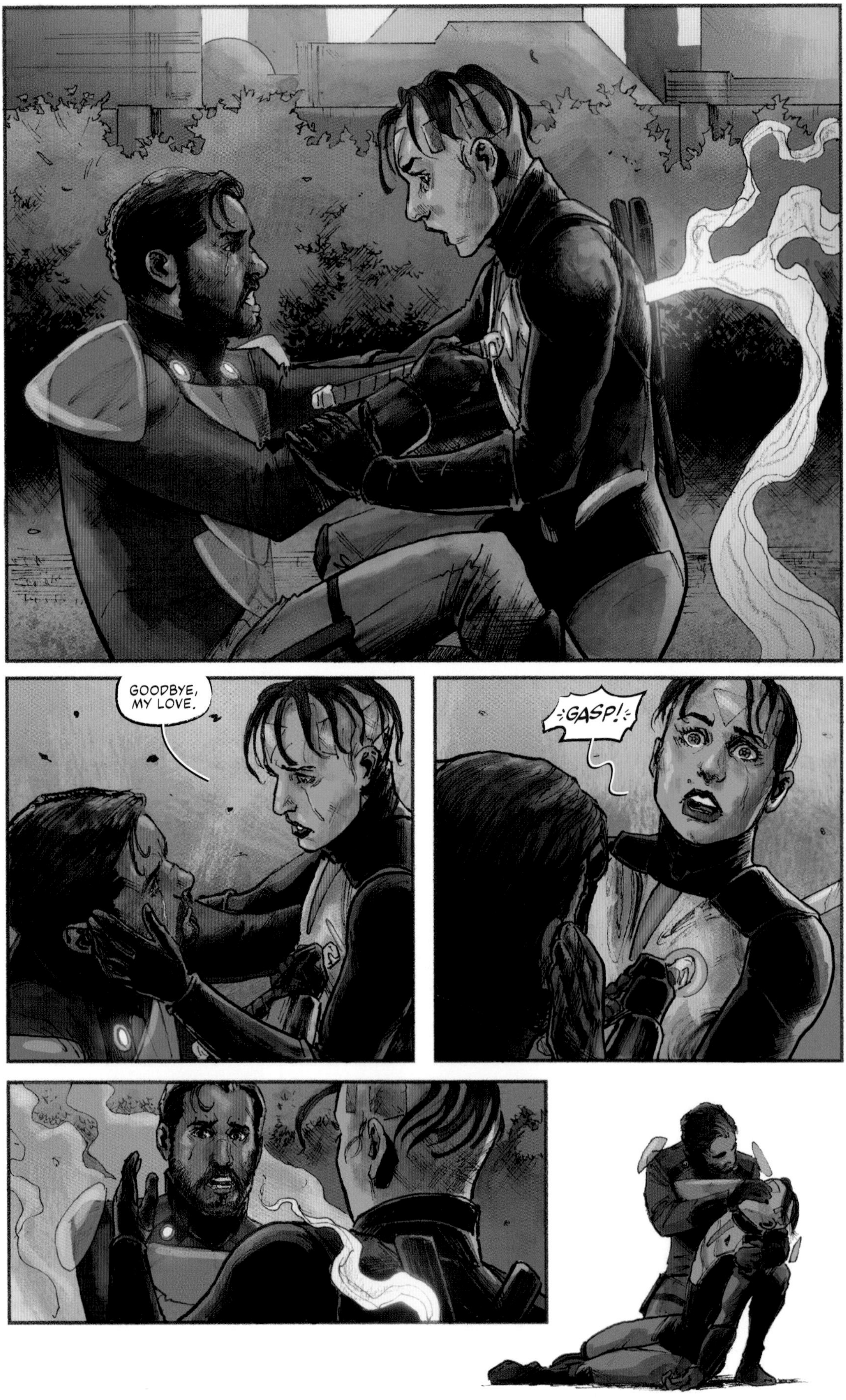
GOODBYE, MY LOVE.
GASP!

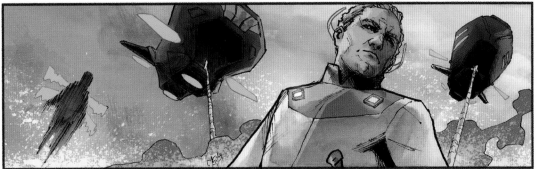

HMPH. I **SUSPECTED** YOU WERE NOT **OF BLOOD,** ASEYR. YOU'RE ONE OF **THEM.** ALL OF YOUR WEALTH CANNOT WASH THE **STINK** OF LOW-BIRTH FROM YOU.

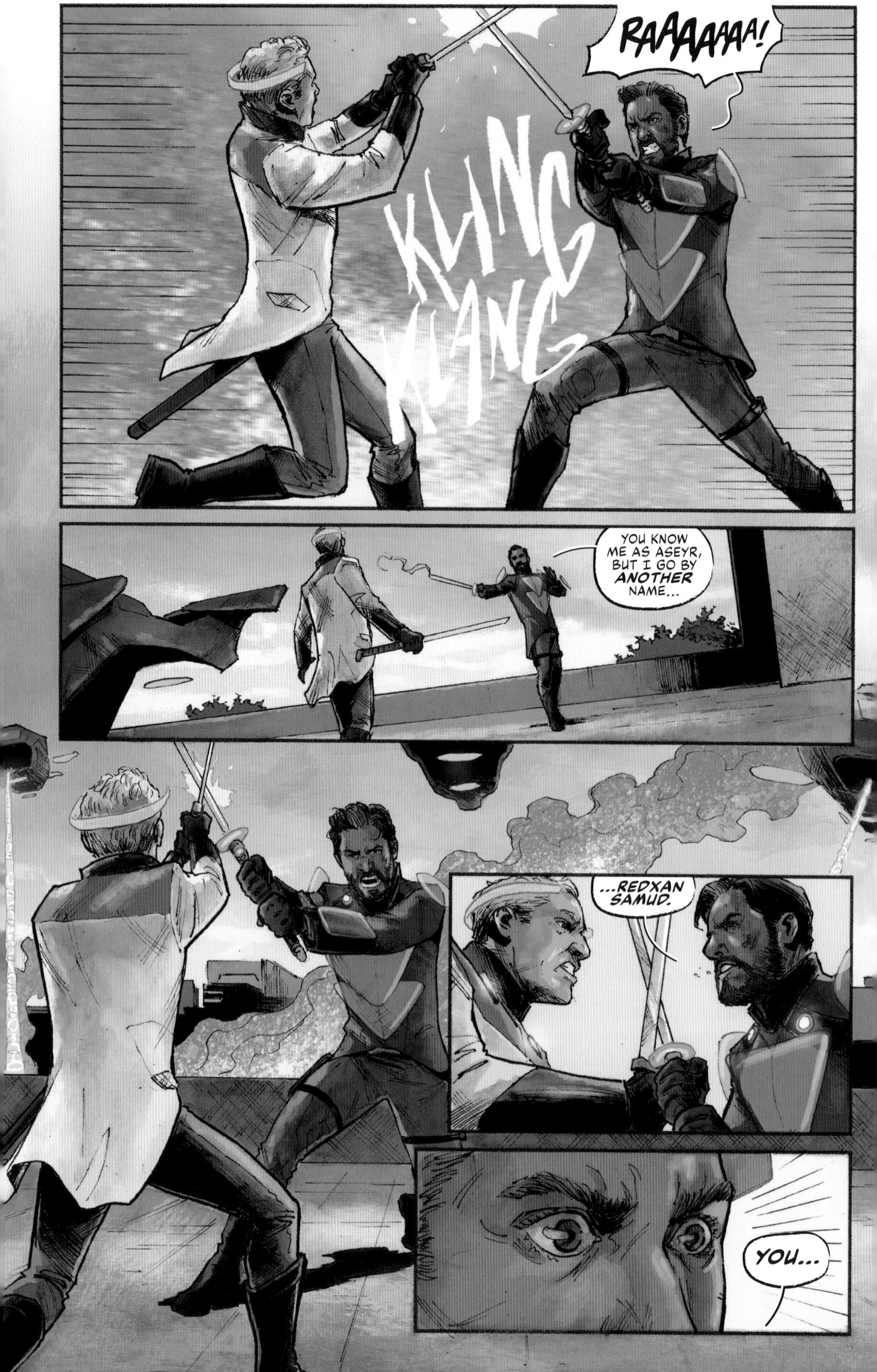
RAAAAAAA!
KLING KLANG
YOU KNOW ME AS ASEYR, BUT I GO BY ANOTHER NAME...
...REDXAN SAMUD.
YOU...

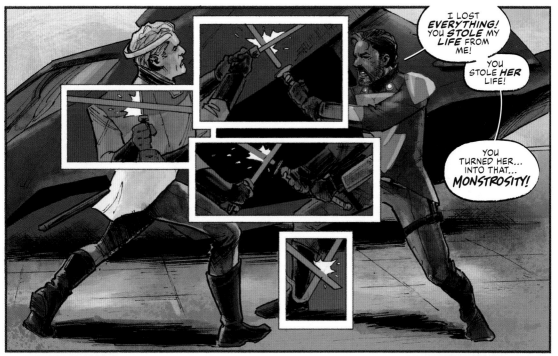

I LOST *EVERYTHING!* YOU *STOLE* MY *LIFE* FROM ME!

YOU STOLE *HER* LIFE!

YOU TURNED HER... INTO THAT... MONSTROSITY!

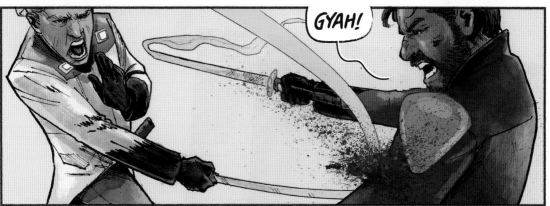

GYAH!

I SAVED HER LIFE!

IT WAS *BECAUSE* OF *ME,* MY POWER, THAT SHE *LIVED!*

SHE'D HAVE DIED SICK AND PENNILESS WITH YOU!

HRRAH!

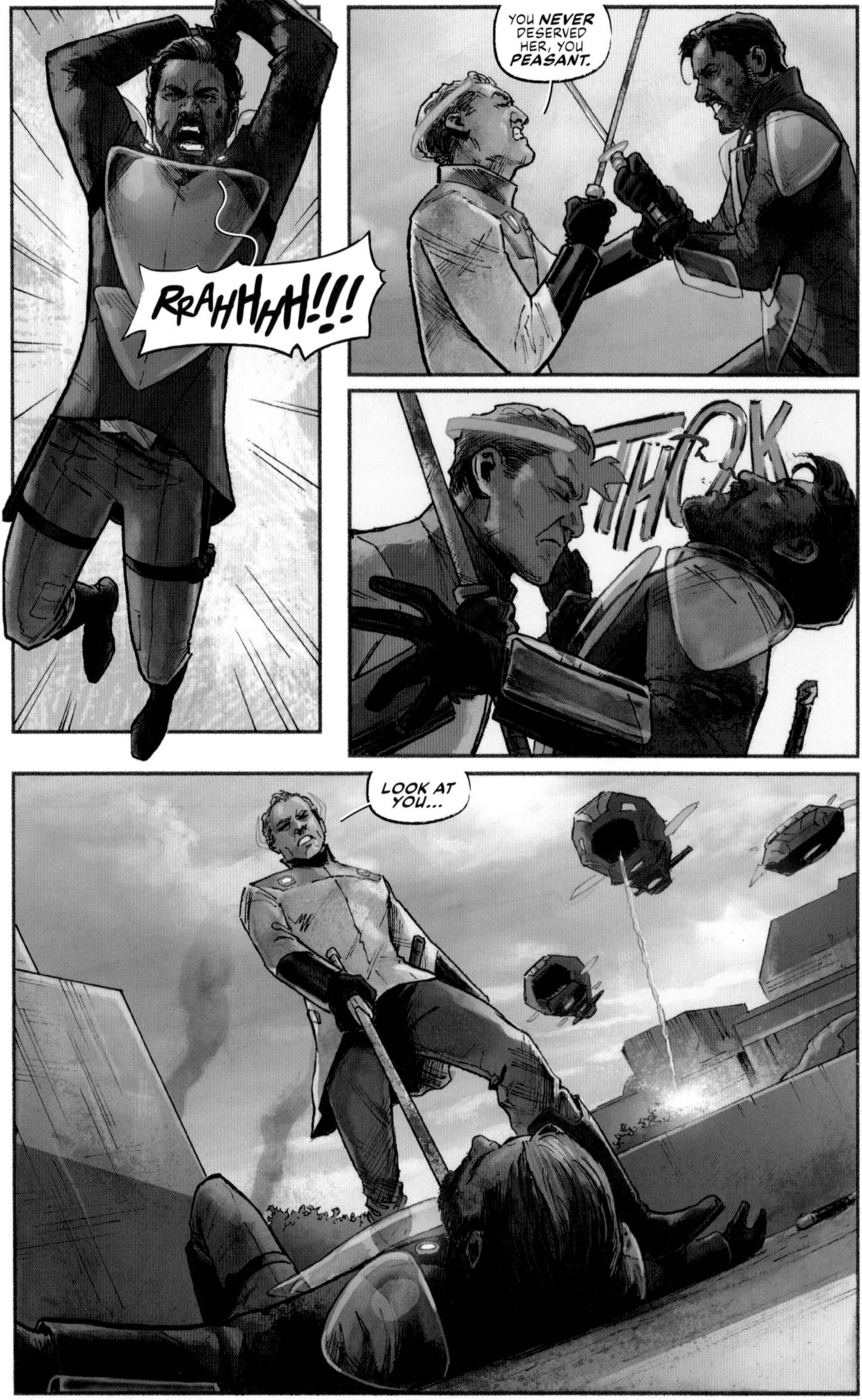

RRAHHHH!!!
YOU NEVER DESERVED HER, YOU PEASANT.
THOK
LOOK AT YOU...

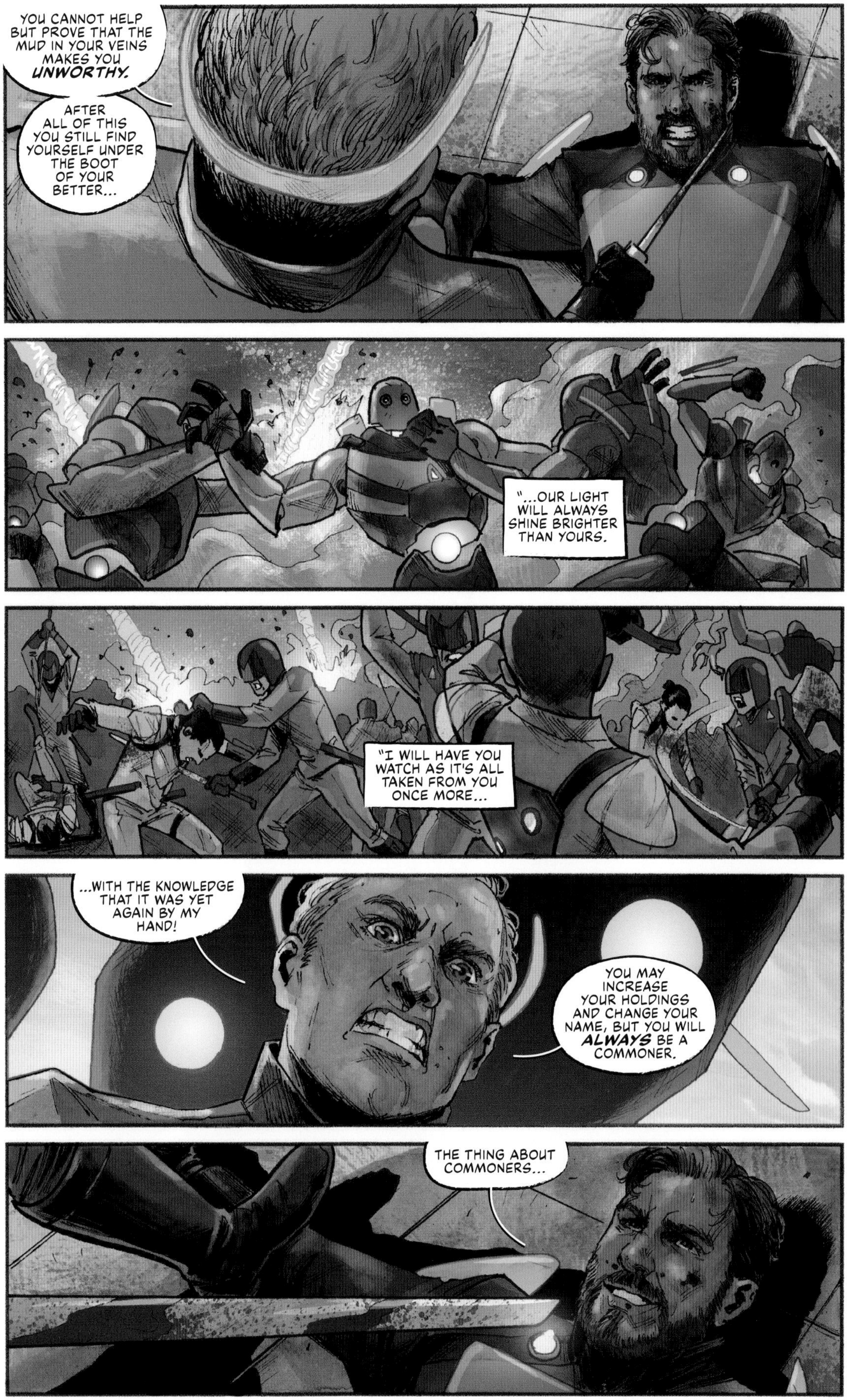

YOU CANNOT HELP BUT PROVE THAT THE MUD IN YOUR VEINS MAKES YOU *UNWORTHY.*
AFTER ALL OF THIS YOU STILL FIND YOURSELF UNDER THE BOOT OF YOUR BETTER...
"...OUR LIGHT WILL ALWAYS SHINE BRIGHTER THAN YOURS.
"I WILL HAVE YOU WATCH AS IT'S ALL TAKEN FROM YOU ONCE MORE...
...WITH THE KNOWLEDGE THAT IT WAS YET AGAIN BY MY HAND!
YOU MAY INCREASE YOUR HOLDINGS AND CHANGE YOUR NAME, BUT YOU WILL *ALWAYS* BE A COMMONER.
THE THING ABOUT COMMONERS...

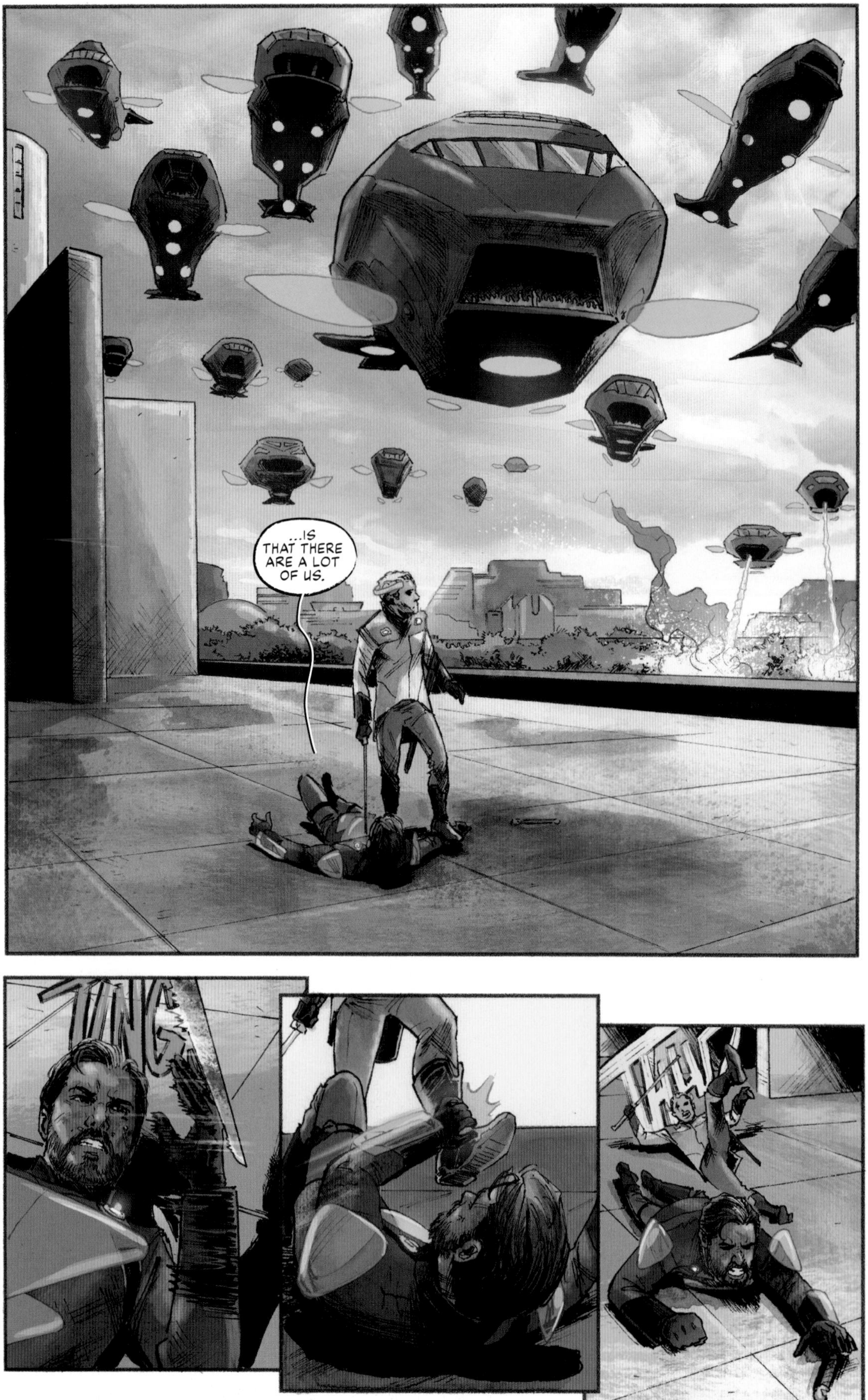
...IS THAT THERE ARE A LOT OF US.
TING

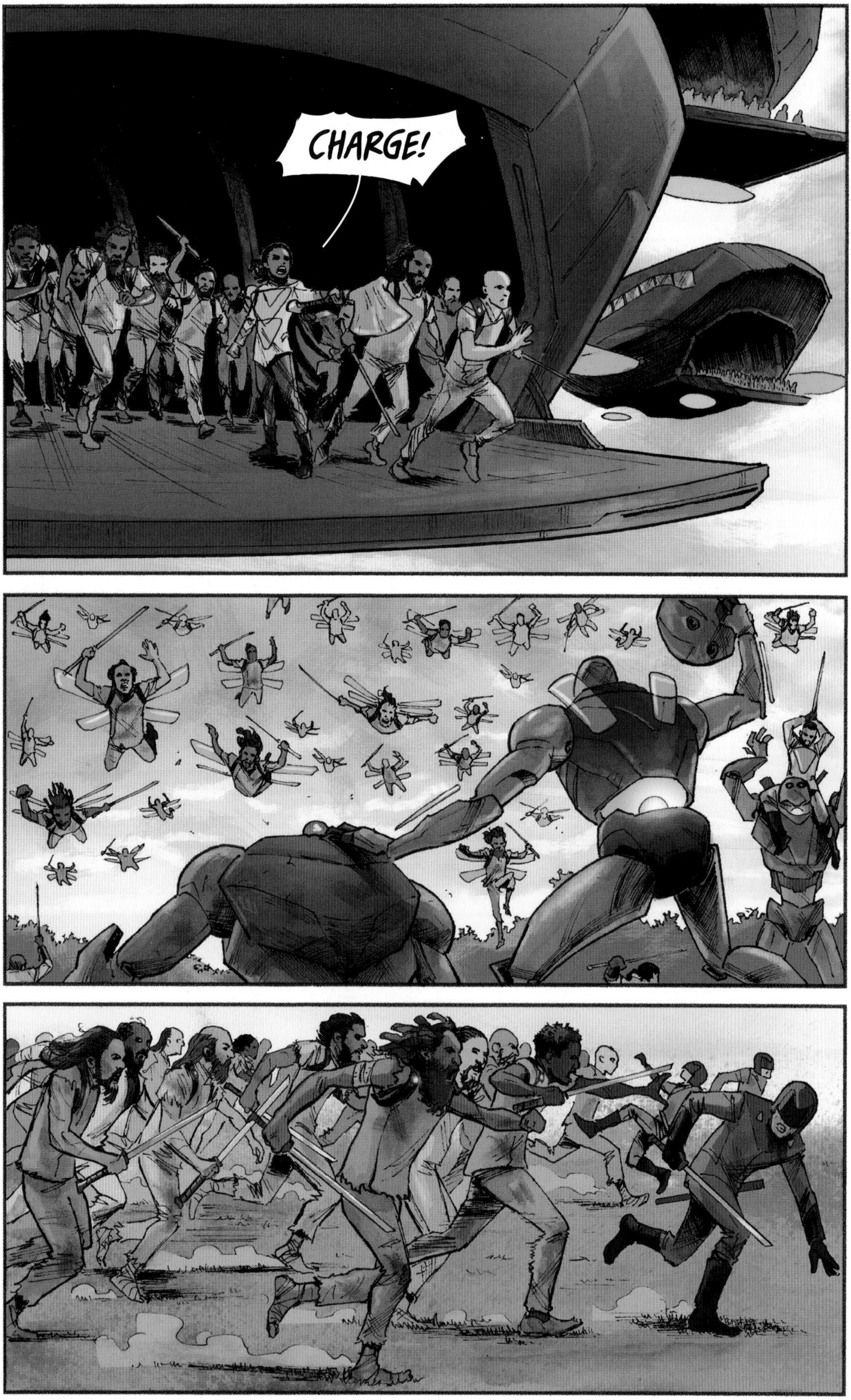
CHARGE!

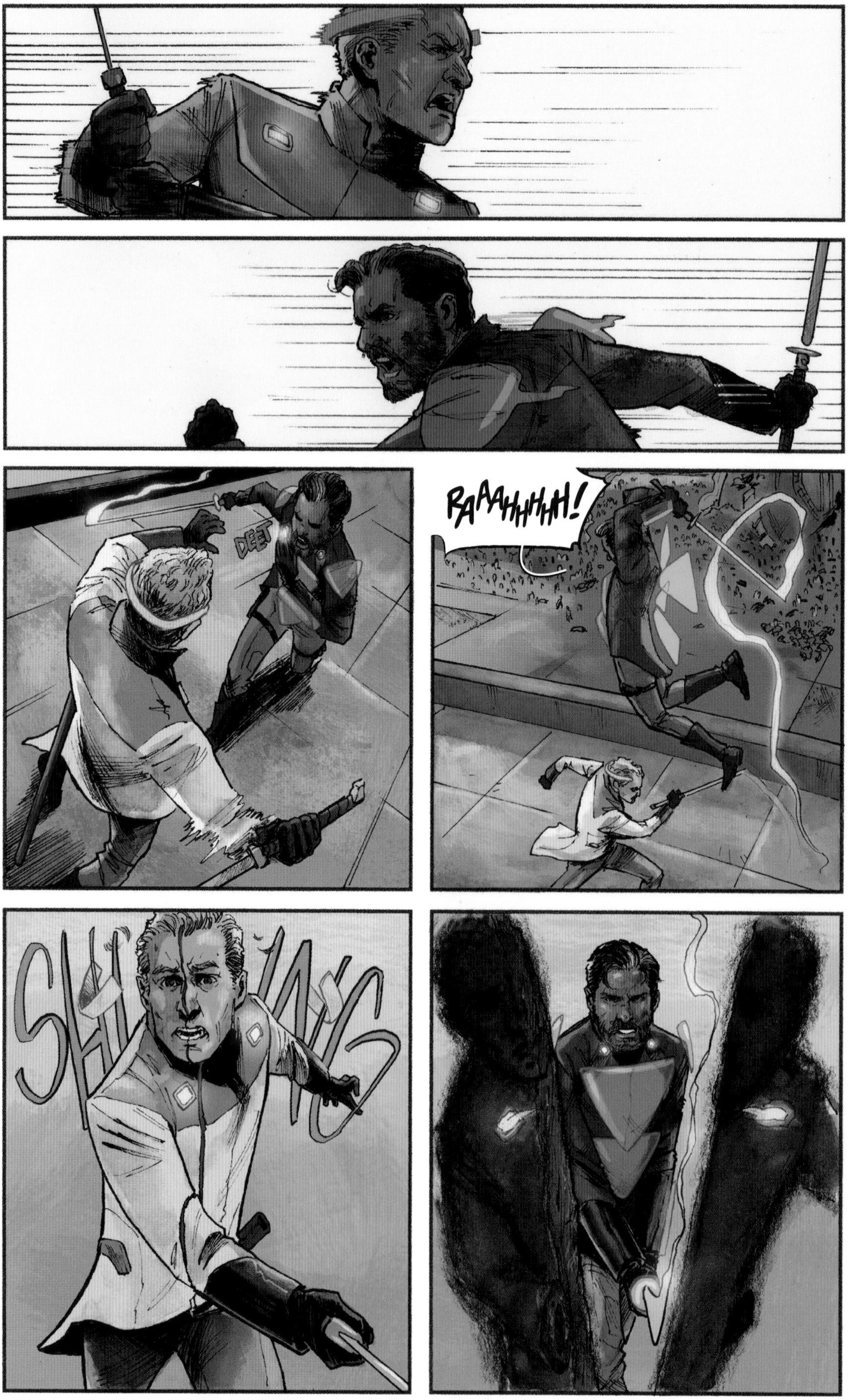
DEET
RAAAHHHHH!

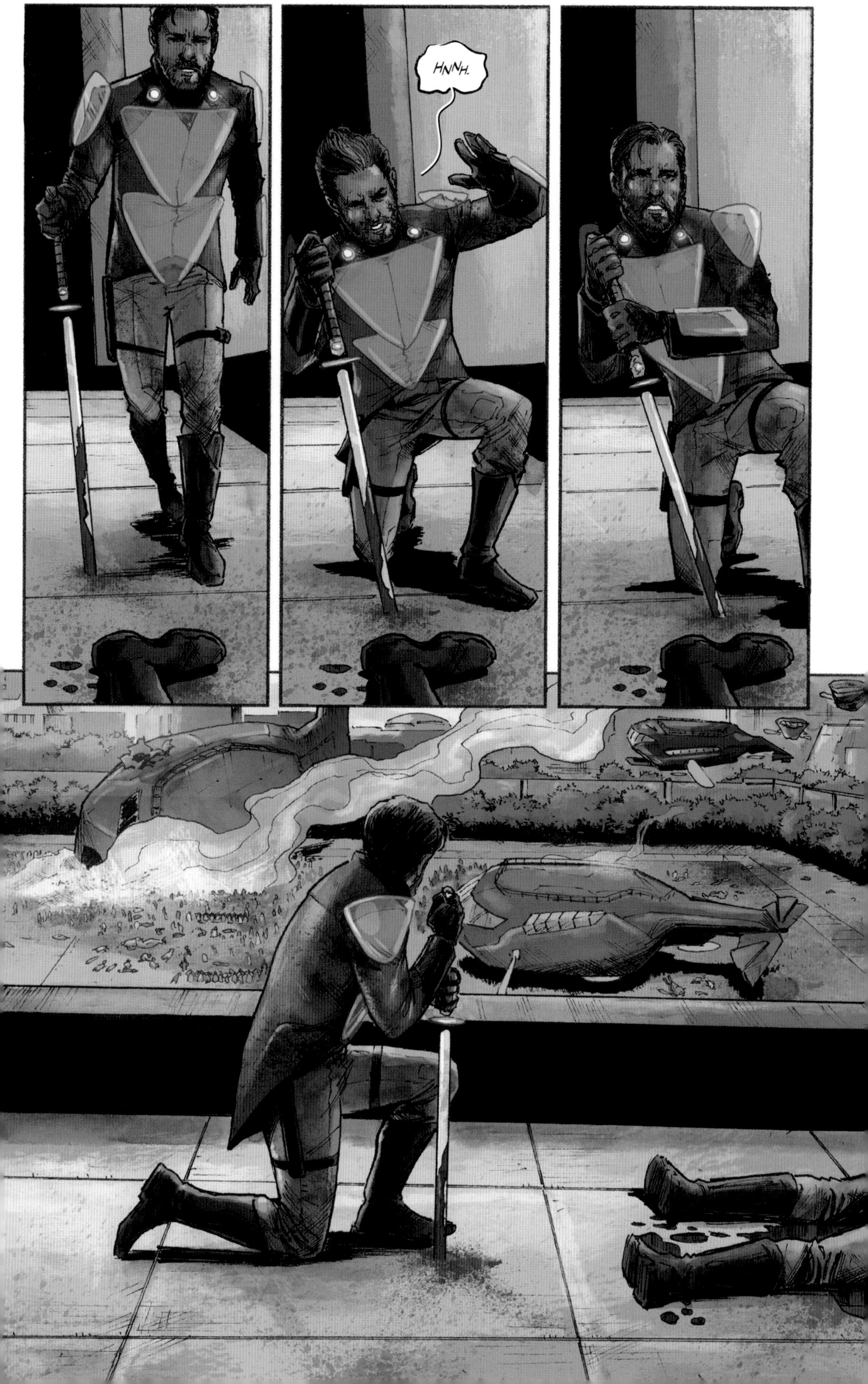
HNNH.

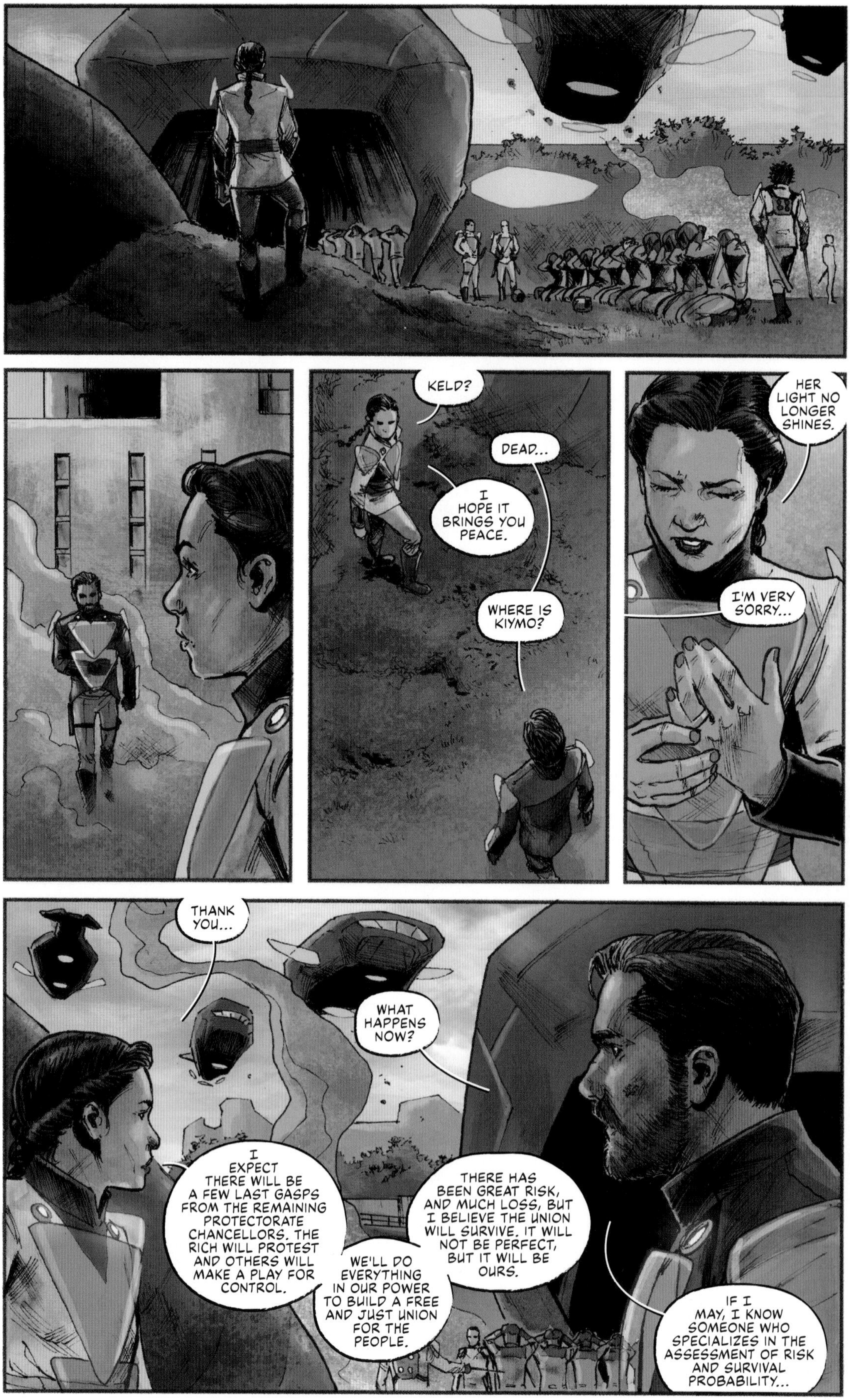
KELD?
DEAD...
I HOPE IT BRINGS YOU PEACE.
WHERE IS KIYMO?
HER LIGHT NO LONGER SHINES.
I'M VERY SORRY...
THANK YOU...
WHAT HAPPENS NOW?
I EXPECT THERE WILL BE A FEW LAST GASPS FROM THE REMAINING PROTECTORATE CHANCELLORS. THE RICH WILL PROTEST AND OTHERS WILL MAKE A PLAY FOR CONTROL.
WE'LL DO EVERYTHING IN OUR POWER TO BUILD A FREE AND JUST UNION FOR THE PEOPLE.
THERE HAS BEEN GREAT RISK, AND MUCH LOSS, BUT I BELIEVE THE UNION WILL SURVIVE. IT WILL NOT BE PERFECT, BUT IT WILL BE OURS.
IF I MAY, I KNOW SOMEONE WHO SPECIALIZES IN THE ASSESSMENT OF RISK AND SURVIVAL PROBABILITY...

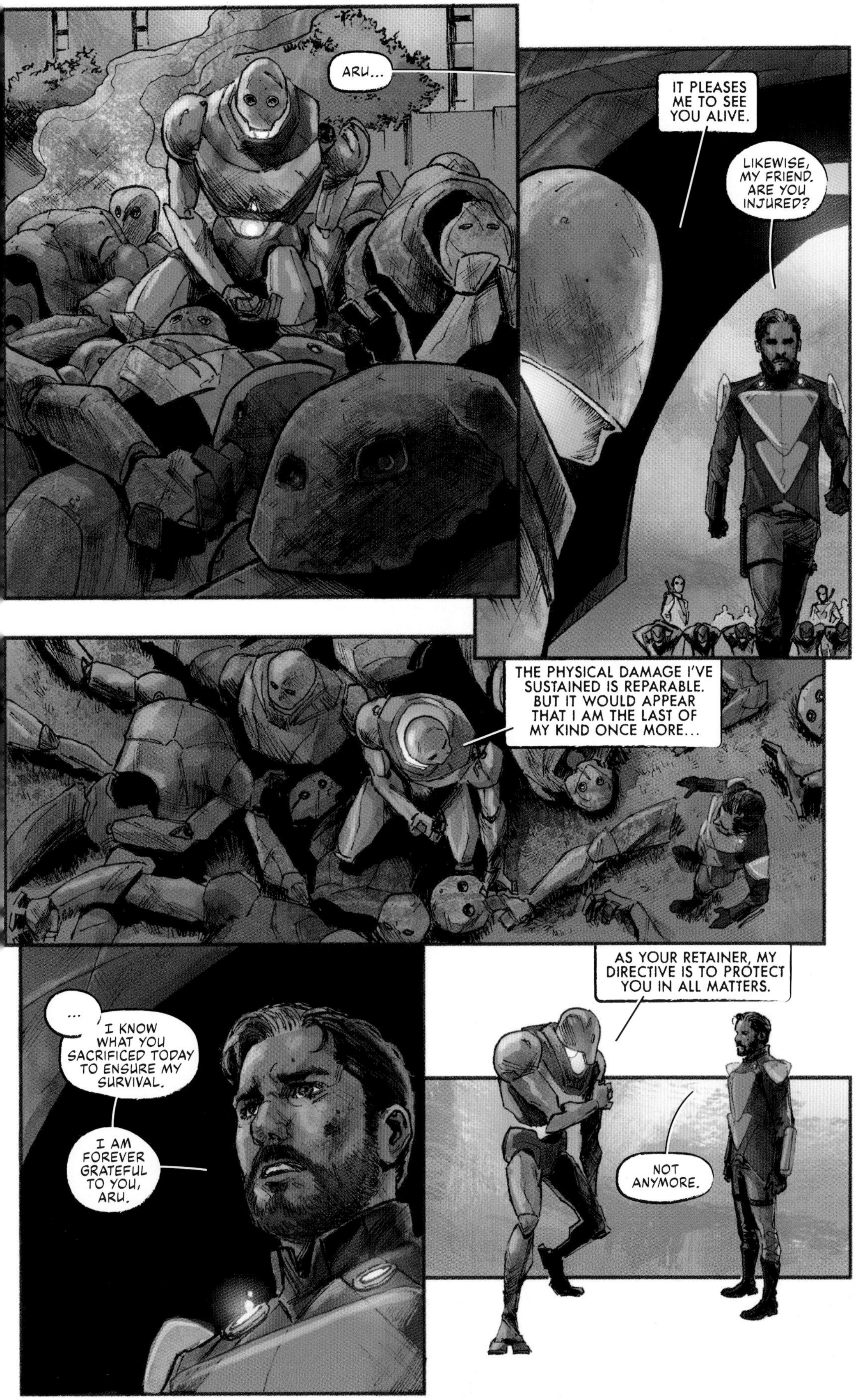
ARU...
IT PLEASES ME TO SEE YOU ALIVE.
LIKEWISE, MY FRIEND. ARE YOU INJURED?
THE PHYSICAL DAMAGE I'VE SUSTAINED IS REPARABLE. BUT IT WOULD APPEAR THAT I AM THE LAST OF MY KIND ONCE MORE...
...
I KNOW WHAT YOU SACRIFICED TODAY TO ENSURE MY SURVIVAL.
I AM FOREVER GRATEFUL TO YOU, ARU.
AS YOUR RETAINER, MY DIRECTIVE IS TO PROTECT YOU IN ALL MATTERS.
NOT ANYMORE.

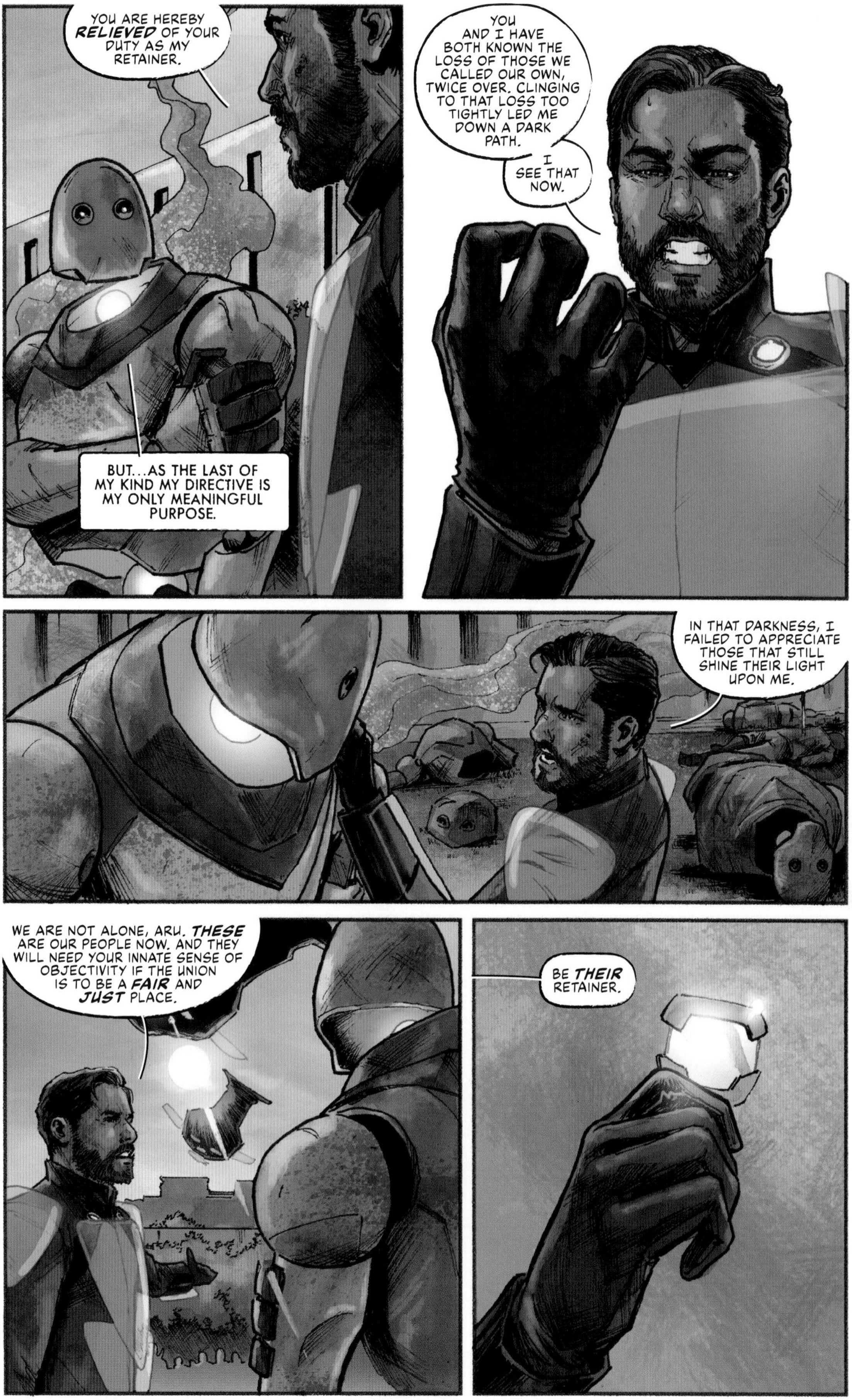

YOU ARE HEREBY RELIEVED OF YOUR DUTY AS MY RETAINER.
BUT...AS THE LAST OF MY KIND MY DIRECTIVE IS MY ONLY MEANINGFUL PURPOSE.
YOU AND I HAVE BOTH KNOWN THE LOSS OF THOSE WE CALLED OUR OWN, TWICE OVER. CLINGING TO THAT LOSS TOO TIGHTLY LED ME DOWN A DARK PATH.
I SEE THAT NOW.
IN THAT DARKNESS, I FAILED TO APPRECIATE THOSE THAT STILL SHINE THEIR LIGHT UPON ME.
WE ARE NOT ALONE, ARU. THESE ARE OUR PEOPLE NOW. AND THEY WILL NEED YOUR INNATE SENSE OF OBJECTIVITY IF THE UNION IS TO BE A FAIR AND JUST PLACE.
BE THEIR RETAINER.

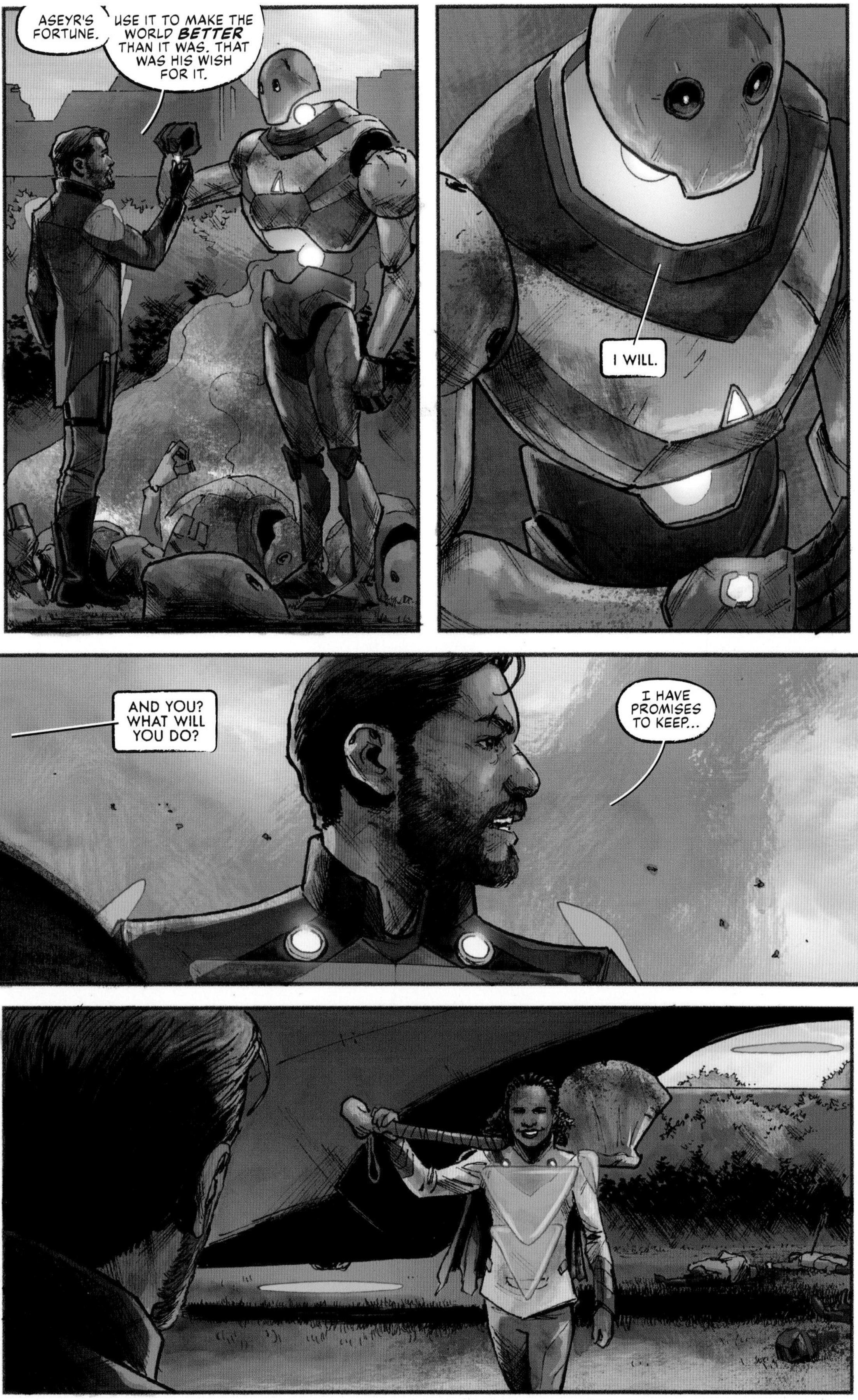
ASEYR'S FORTUNE.
USE IT TO MAKE THE WORLD BETTER THAN IT WAS. THAT WAS HIS WISH FOR IT.
I WILL.
AND YOU? WHAT WILL YOU DO?
I HAVE PROMISES TO KEEP...

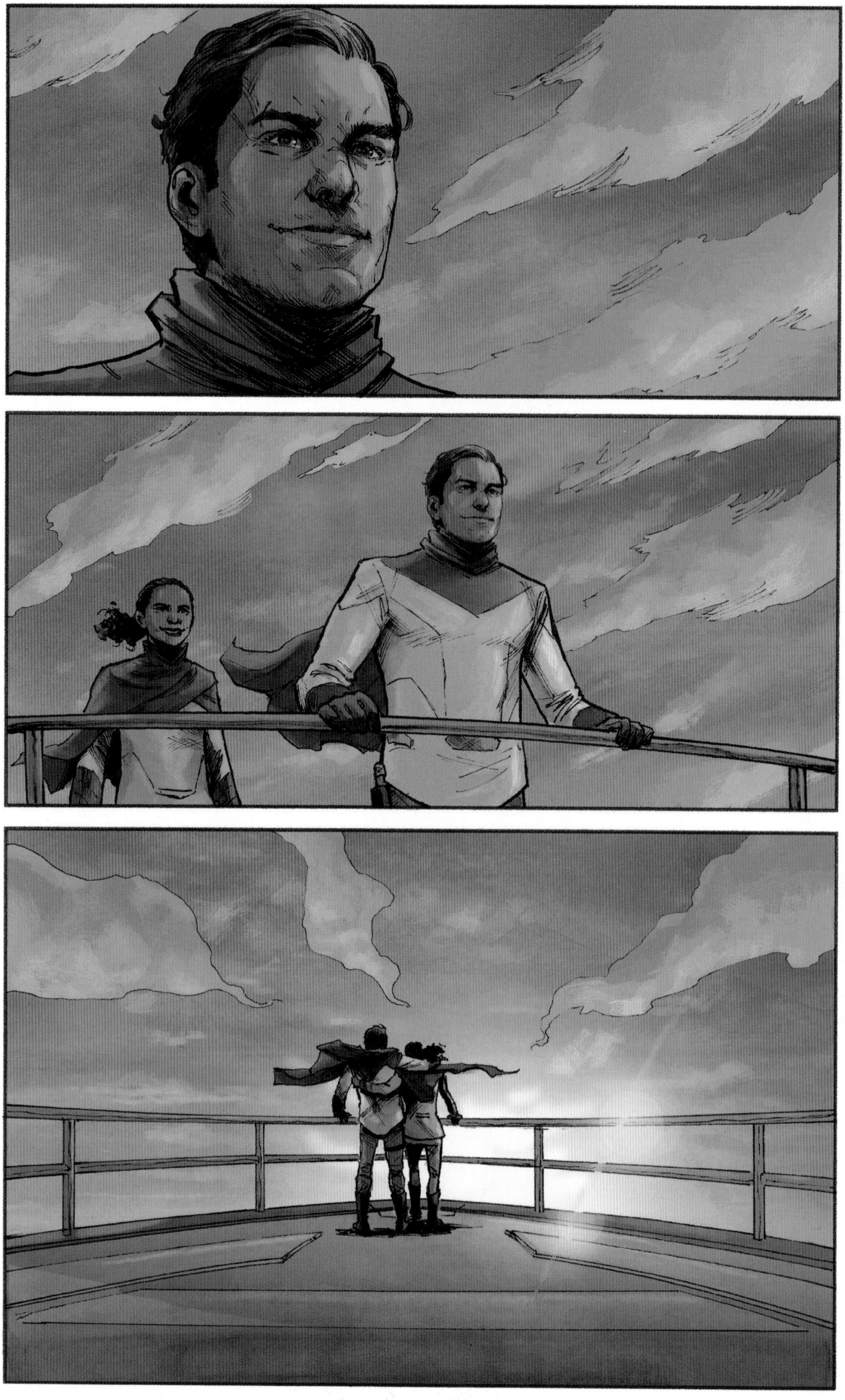

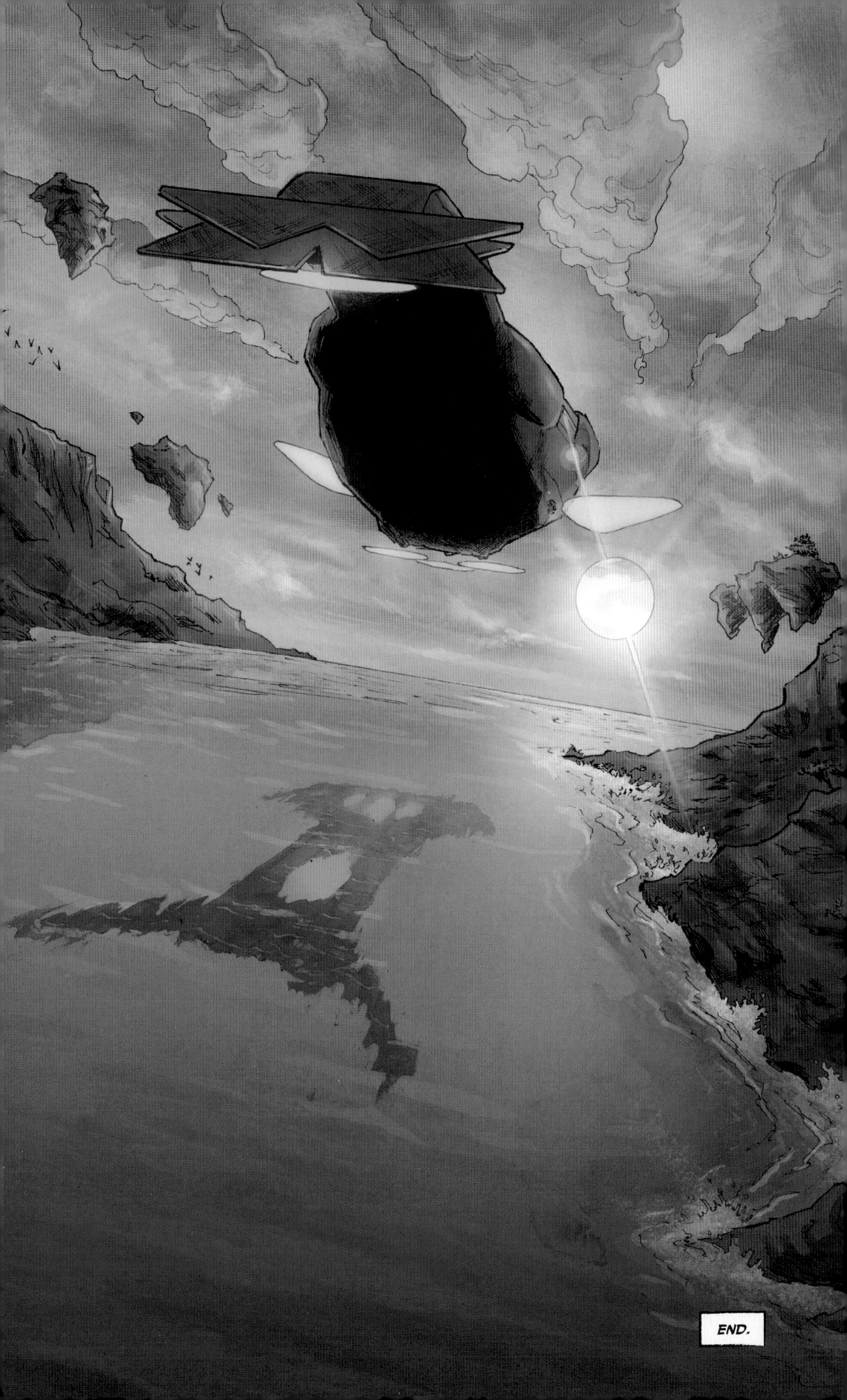
END.

MAKING IT COUNT

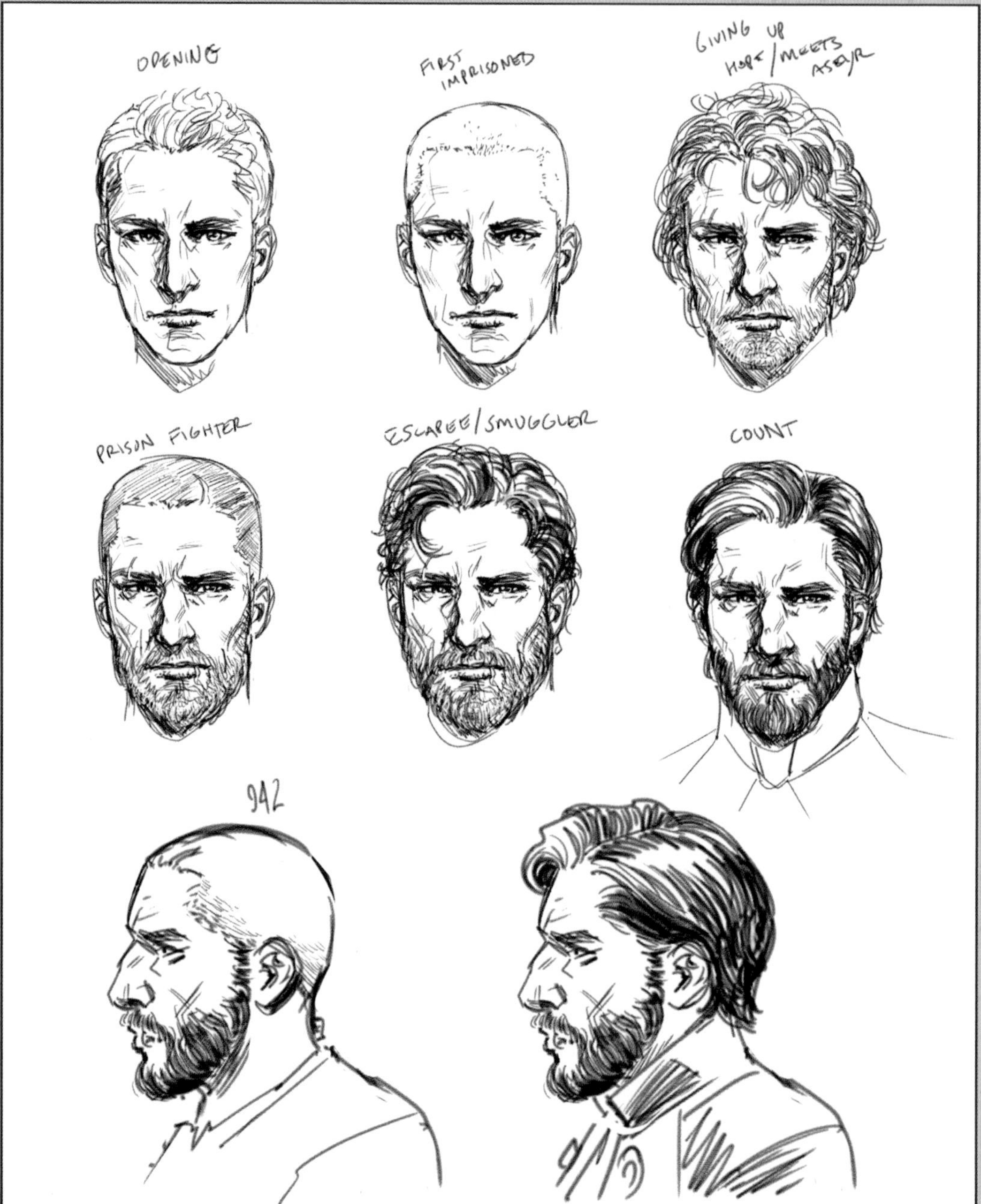
OPENING
FIRST IMPRISONED
GIVING UP HOPE / MEETS ASERIR
PRISON FIGHTER
ESCAPEE / SMUGGLER
COUNT
942

Ibrahim's initial head sketches for Redxan Samud, the protagonist of *Count*.

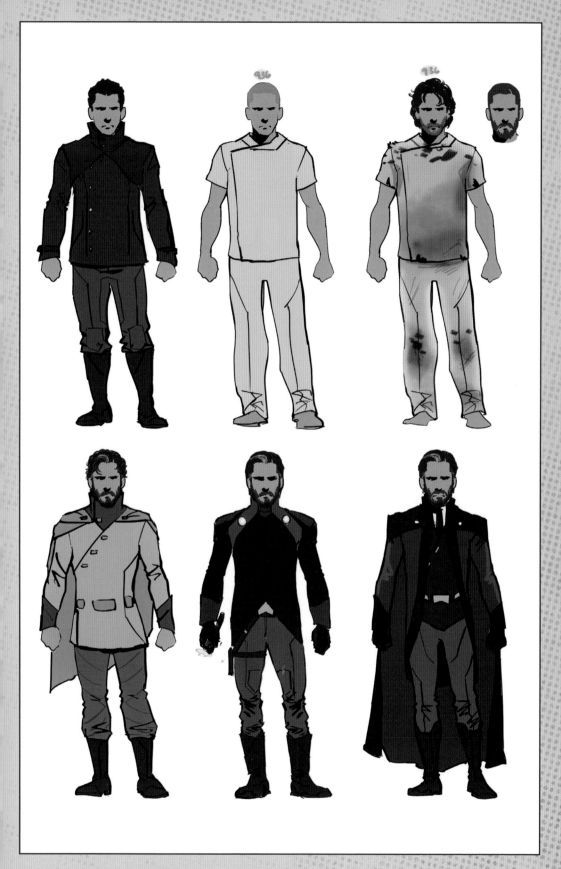

Costume designs for Redxan's various looks across the story.

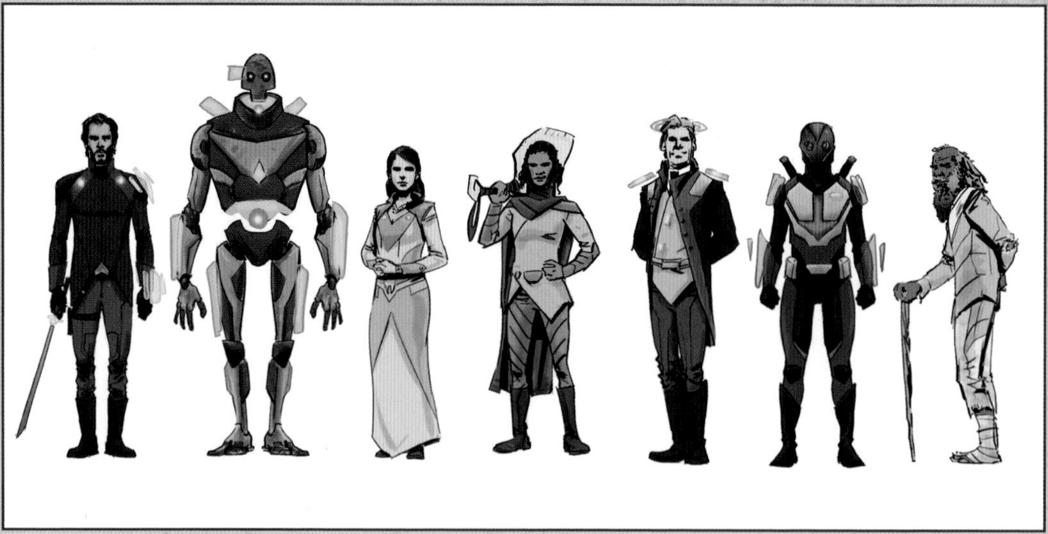

Initial designs for Redxan, ARU, Meris, Amai, Onaxis Keld, Cyn, and Aseyr.

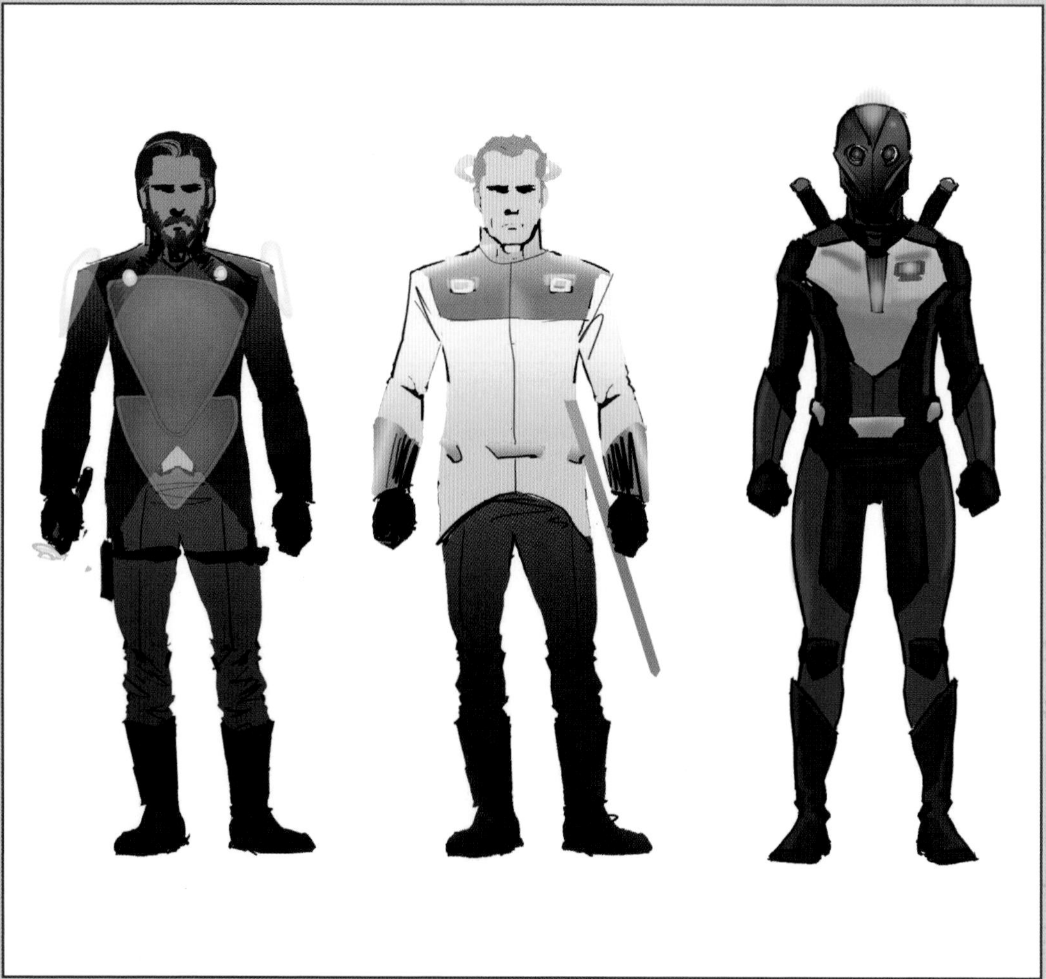

Revised costume designs for Redxan, Keld, and Cyn.

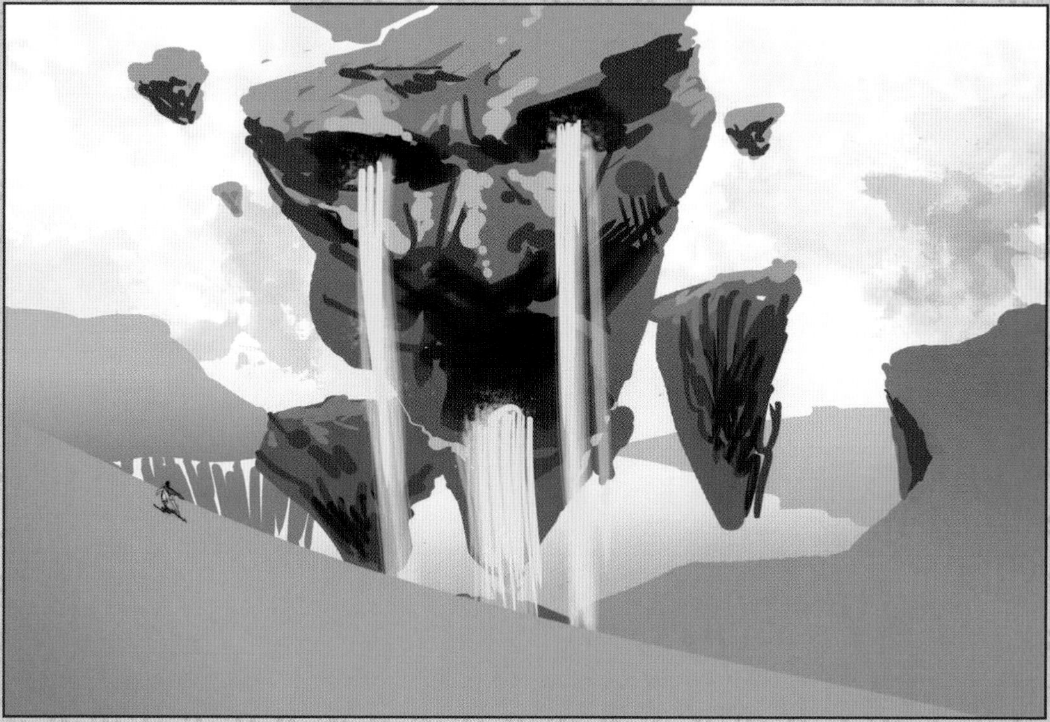

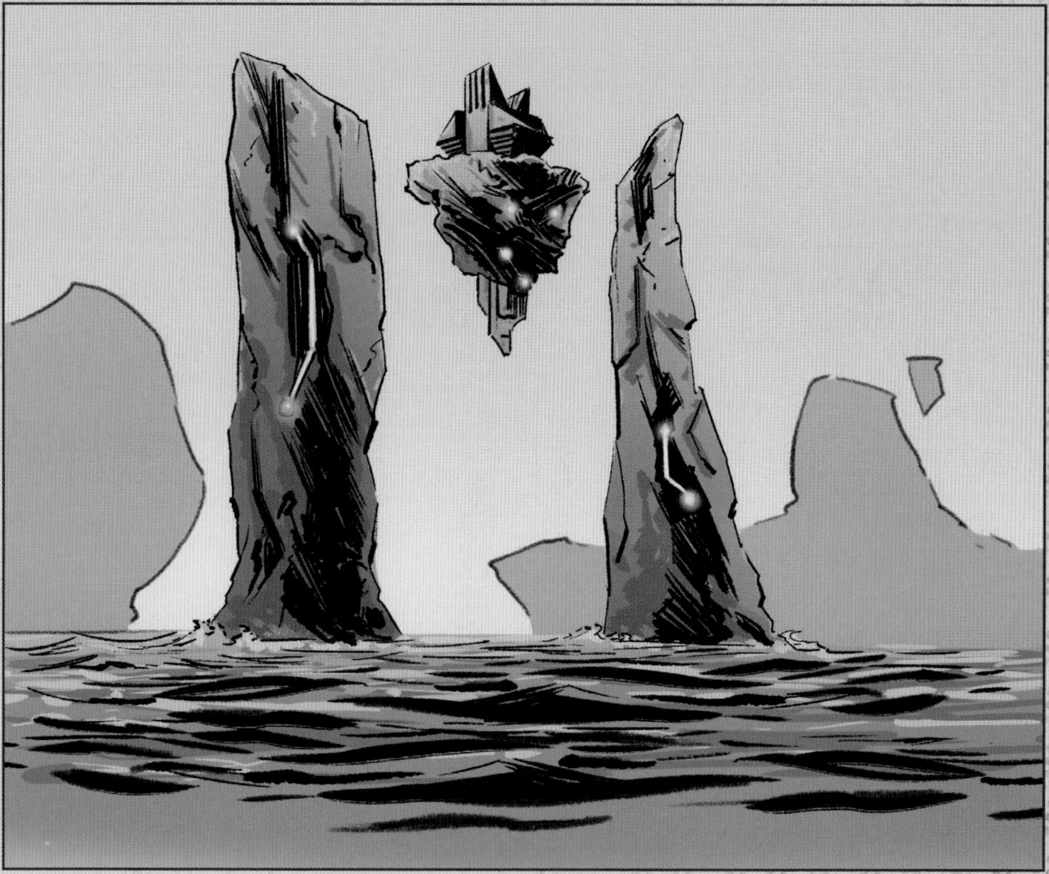

Location designs for the Isle of Sorrow (top) and the DIF (bottom).

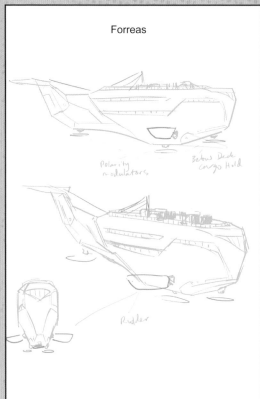

Forreas

Polarity modulators

Below Deck Cargo Hold

Rudder

(Clockwise from left) Designs for the Chariot used by "Count Aseyr," *The Forreas*, *The Buran* from Chapter 3, and the Steed Redxan commandeers in Chapter 5.

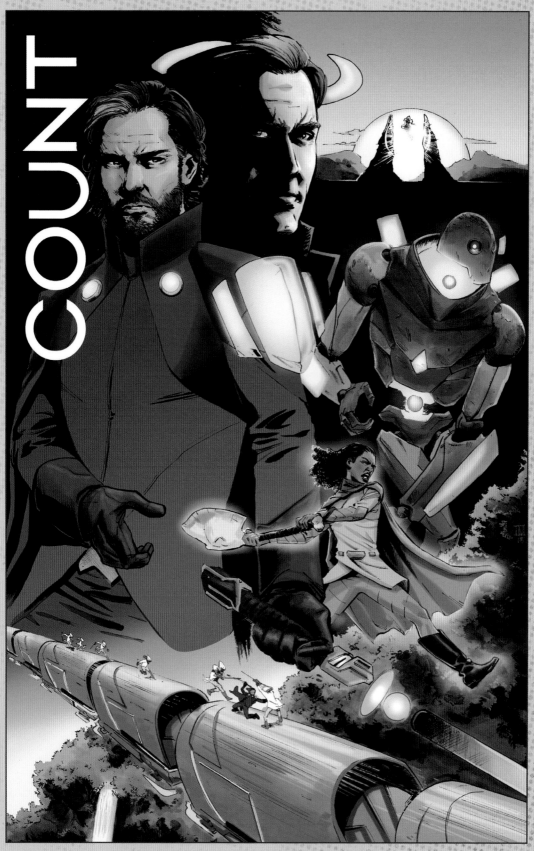

Ibrahim's initial proposal image that accompanied the pitch for *Count*.

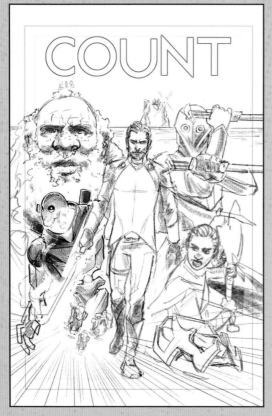
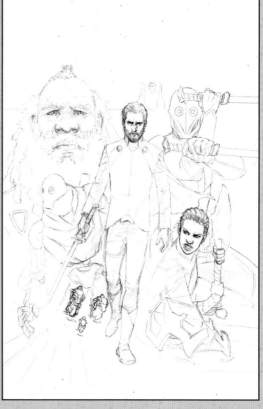

(Clockwise from left) Cover mockups, final cover pencils, and a revised sketch by Ibrahim.